ALMOST COLUMBINE

Other books by
<u>Alex Hutchinson</u>

Backyard Empire
Virgin Gloves

<u>*HAWKS Foundation novels*</u>
Before they were HAWKS
Sevlow: Mission One

All of Alex's books are available at:

Www.SuburbanFiction.com

ALMOST COLUMBINE

HAWKS Foundation Mission Two

A Novel

Alexander Hutchinson

iUniverse, Inc.

New York Lincoln Shanghai

Almost Columbine

HAWKS Foundation Mission Two

Copyright © 2006 by Alex Hutchinson

iUniverse books may be ordered through booksellers or by contacting:

iUniverse
2021 Pine Lake Road, Suite 100
Lincoln, NE 68512
www.iuniverse.com
1-800-Authors (1-800-288-4677)

This is a work of fiction. All of the characters, names, incidents, organizations, and dialogue in this novel are either the products of the author's imagination or are used fictitiously.

ISBN-13: 978-0-595-41939-5 (pbk)
ISBN-13: 978-0-595-86281-8 (ebk)
ISBN-10: 0-595-41939-9 (pbk)
ISBN-10: 0-595-86281-0 (ebk)

Printed in the United States of America

The
Malevolent Philosophy

There is no safe depository for
The ultimate powers of society

The citizens have chosen to
Passively accept the new masters
Of their governance

The remedy is to obstruct the
Discretion of the people
By forming a vigilant elite

As members of the
HAWKS FOUNDATION
We commit to participate
In stealth justice based on
Informed critical reflection

Our goal is to cleanse society
Of narcotic toxins and then
Topple the illegitimate political
Power that has forsaken us
With unholy alliances
Around the world

Acknowledgements

Special thanks to three lovely ladies who helped me remember some of the things I had been suppressing about high school, Jennifer Noble, Melissa Paulo and Jodi Brennan. I would like to thank Paul Bonney for his research and insights into the Brockton youth detention facility otherwise known as DYS. I must thank Jennifer Coll who modeled for the cover of the book brilliantly portraying the character of Becca. Lastly I must thank my girlfriend Terri Brashear whose critique of the early drafts helped me assemble a fantastic flowing storyline.

PROLOGUE

▼

Were it not for his friends, Dutch would have committed suicide by now. His was a puritanical existence absent of girlfriends or girl friends, void of physical contact or emotional understanding. It was made worse by a lethal cocktail of manic depression and the occasional trigger rage. At sixteen years old a school counselor noted that James Ballum, Dutch's real name, had the psychological profile of a serial killer. The counselor was fired soon after but Dutch became further distraught as the damage had already been done. The only time when he felt confident and in charge of himself was when he was in charge of other people. He needed to lead and it had to be for an important cause. Thus at seventeen he joined together with loyal friends and developed a maligned ideology predicated on killing drug dealers. He called it the malevolent philosophy. Its guiding principles would result in the formation of a military preparation squad known as the HAWKS Foundation. This vigilant elite endeavored to deliver stealth justice on the streets of America. As with all great things a following ensued and necessity compelled the team to recruit new members....

WHERE THE MONSTERS ARE

CHAPTER 1

▼

Norwood, Massachusetts—January 1990

"I think we killed her."

"You have no way of knowing that."

"This is what happens when a young girl puts her life into our hands," Psycho exhaled with trepidation watching his frosted breath drift away. His disillusion rested on the premise that they had not put enough calculated thought into their current endeavor and that someone else would pay the price for it. "I think we killed them both."

"Now you're being dramatic."

"We should have double checked everything."

"What for? Life is unpredictable. This will force them to make last minute adjustments. We want them to be tough, we want flexibility," Dutch pulled a stopwatch out of his coat pocket. "It's only been twenty minutes."

"I just..." Psycho had been nagging all night about the initiation of the team's two new members, Becca and Lazio. Becca was an upperclassman, or more specifically an attractive upperclasswoman, from their high school who had a crush on Dutch. Lazio was a private school educated childhood friend of Psycho's who had a crush on Becca. Psycho hated the whole situation because it could destroy team morale. He didn't have a crush on anybody. The last thing they needed was a love triangle inside their group of friends. This could ruin all of their plans.

"Calm down." Dutch scooted upwards onto the hood of a faded blue 1982 Oldsmobile cutlass. He was careful not to dent the thin metal. It was Lazio's car and he had trusted them enough to let Psycho and Dutch use it during the week after school. The two friends had a few unusual errands to attend to. One of which was the six hours of effort required to establish a challenging enough obstacle course for this night to drill the new members of their squad. Dutch was the team leader of the HAWKS Foundation while Psycho had recently been promoted to second in command. Tonight's initiation was a way to determine who had the guts, skill and sheer bravado to join their righteous military style street gang. That test was currently underway.

The other errand was a secret and would remain so until it provided them with some effect other than frustration. The HAWKS had suffered a few setbacks as of late leaving them short on men, money, and motivation. They lost their second in command to a youth detention facility after he claimed to have killed a werewolf. The actual charge was destruction of property. Shortly thereafter Gary, their demolitions expert, was dragged off to a Boston jail for having assaulted a police officer. Finally John, the smartest kid on their team, unexpectedly and most abruptly quit. He never did explain why. Unfortunately these deficits of manpower were obstructing more recent endeavors. This led Psycho to continue repeating the wrong question over and over. *What if something else goes wrong?*

"The start of the course was fine." He didn't even look at Dutch when he spoke. He never wanted Becca on the team. Lazio was fine, he appeared physically capable and psychologically tough though a little weird but Becca, she just wasn't HAWKS material. His litany continued, "Those guys playing street hockey were nice enough to chase them into woods without asking for money to do it. I give you credit for that."

Dutch smiled but hid the lower half of his face behind the high collar of his winter coat. He had surprised himself when he convinced perfect strangers that his wallet had been stolen. The perpetrators were a man and a woman both with long black hair who ran off into the alleys of Norwood. When Becca and Lazio tried to walk by the parking lot to head towards the railroad tracks they almost pissed themselves as ten full-grown men with wooden sticks chased them to the edge of the hill. Injustice is the ultimate motivator.

"But answer me this…" Psycho continued to picture the scene looking for flaws. "How did you know they wouldn't get caught?"

Dutch suppressed the smile and lifted his head like a turtle coming out of its shell. "They were all wearing roller blades. Becca and Lazio were safe the moment they left the pavement."

"But what if they took them off?"

His head sunk back into the collar, "I never said it was a perfect plan."

"See, that's what I'm saying." Psycho hoisted himself onto the hood and heard it crunch under their combined weight. "Oops."

"You think it's too tough." He was tired of hearing the same old arguments. *Becca is a girl; she shouldn't be on the team she's going to slow us down.* "Dude, when are you going to let this go?"

"I'm not. It's an unsolvable dilemma."

"All dilemmas are unsolvable, that's what dilemma means. You just have to make a decision and live with it. I made a decision to let them try, now let's just hope for the best."

"Exactly!" Psycho wasn't listening, "If we made the test easier then both of them would be undeserving of membership. However if we gave her any exceptions and dumbed down the test…"

"Because she's a girl."

"Right, if we gave her any exceptions then we are cheating her of the right to get an honest shot at succeeding."

"Tim!" It was clear that an invisible line had been crossed whenever Dutch used Psycho's real name. Being a member of a secret society like the HAWKS required a decorum that made certain issues beyond reproach. Severe and relentless questioning of the General's decisions was simply not permitted. Normally Tim insisted on such a high level of discipline, a hierarchy that needed to be adhered to but on this one issue he couldn't comply with Dutch's demands. He was terrified of having a girl on the team. Too many things could go wrong.

"But we didn't make it too easy," Dutch's voice burst forth with authority. "They escaped the hockey players and climbed the hill to the railroad tracks. Good for them! Now they will have to follow the tracks to the warehouse. Going in through a broken window they'll have to climb up several levels until they reach the top and duct tape their American flags to the radio tower on the highest ledge. Then they have to get their asses back down to the tracks and hang from the bridge while dangling over a vehicle underpass as the 12:55 Amtrak passenger train rolls over the rails three feet above them. They could be shaken off the bridge, fall to the cement and be hit by a sand truck. Tim, we couldn't have made it any harder!"

"Exactly."

"Exactly, what?"

"We made it too hard. We killed them both."

CHAPTER 2

▼

"Holy shit! Are you OK?" Lazio jumped to the edge of the shattered railroad tie and yelled down into the inky black concrete chasm to his missing friend.

"Becca!" He screamed out as panic seized his throat. There was no answer just an echo of his voice.

She was trying too hard to prove herself or so Lazio thought and this was the inevitable result. At the worst she was dead, having fallen into the crevasse between two buildings and landing on a sharp, hollow pipe that pierced through her back and out of her chest spouting blood into the air. That horrific image was all he could imagine but then again, his imagination does sometimes take too strong a hold on him. Maybe she simply fell and landed on her feet? Maybe he was deeply underestimating her capabilities?

It had been a physically easy though nerve racking task up to this point. After escaping the hockey players, they raced down the railroad tracks hopping off every other cross tie until they reached an overpass. There they stopped at the edge of the bushes, out of view from passing cars.

"We should make a break for it." She was determined to make good time. Throw caution to the wolves was her motto on this evening. Fuck everyone; forget their limited expectations and pointless chivalry. Tonight she was going to do more than succeed she was poised to excel. "Lazio, people driving underneath might see us either way but this is a timed initiation." Her argument was dismissed by his more cautious deliberations.

"No, we have to be smart about this," Lazio peered down at Nahatan Street, the often-busy road that ran under their bridge.

To the left they could see a darkened shopping plaza, now closed, and the well lit Norwood police station, always open. Across from that was the Friendlies restaurant where Becca had her first job waiting tables. She proudly repeated to every customer that this location was the oldest Friendlies in America. The job lasted only one summer. These buildings were clearly visible but that also meant their silhouettes would be highlighted to motorists if they tried to cross here.

Lazio was deep in contemplation, carefully planning his moves like a chess player. "We'll wait for the traffic to slow down a little and then…"

Becca had bolted across the bridge. She wasn't going to wait for anything. His task assessments were no longer appreciated. He had been too nice, too patient, and too appeasing over the past week. If she coupled that with his frequent pauses and time consuming deliberations it made Lazio more irritating than some of her least favorite ex-boyfriends. He was slowing them down and on this night she was *not* going to be slowed down. This was after all, an important event.

Her reservations about Lazio started with his insistence that they take the test together instead of doing it separately. In the past HAWK neophytes had always run the gamut alone and she believed that they did it for good reason. They had to know how to take care of themselves as individuals so they would be a self-sustaining asset to the team and not a crutch. Still, Psycho favored the tag team idea while Dutch had to be convinced that it was a good way for them to practice teamwork. *What bullshit!* Becca knew the truth. Lazio and Psycho both thought that she was inferior, that she was an easy bake gender warrior trying to hack her way into Dutch's heart. *They were wrong!* Becca was going to pass this test in perfect time, she was going to plant her flag first and crush any apologetic platitudes they had for her. She was sure that Dutch took her at face value. He promised to create a demanding obstacle course and in return for his trust, she was going to ace it.

Lazio lost sight of her delicate form when she reached the wrought iron connecting rods that spanned outward from the warehouse to the tracks. Becca fearlessly leapt onto the narrow metal surface, ran up towards the roof ignoring the ten-foot drop off below her and jumped onto the tarpaper. Her moves, quick and nimble, were far superior to what a heavier man could perform. Once on the roof, that was the last he saw of her.

Lazio followed fast but the unforgiving soles of his black army boots slid on the deteriorating rods. He had to grab hold of the flaking rust to steady his one hundred and seventy plus pounds. She was now taking a solid lead. He reached the roof and repeatedly skidded across the track ballast, crushed stones that sat loosely on the tar instep that rolled him like a pool of ball bearings. Blazing clumsily to the edge of the gap between this roof and the next he did not hesitate or slow down and simply dived across. Unsure footing once again brought him to his hands and knees. Still no sign of Becca, she must have accelerated even further ahead.

Lazio brushed off his black cargo pants feeling the itch of a couple small scrapes. He had never before noticed just how clumsy he could be. Maybe it's the shoes?

There was one last ledge between his slippery boots and the three story abandoned train station/warehouse where they were supposed to plant their flags.

"I'm not falling this time," Lazio snuck up to the edge and looked over. Apparently there had been a railroad tie crossing the gap between the two buildings but half of the tie was hanging from the roof and the other had fallen down into the blind alley between the concrete walls. This wasn't right, the old wooden tie was supposed to be an obstacle. Dutch mentioned it in the pre-initiation briefing. Why was it broken? Lazio stared down into the hole. Something was moving down there. "Becca?"

Lazio took a quick mental inventory of the task. As far as he could remember the railroad tie was supposed to be a bridge. He grabbed the part that was hanging from two cleats drilled tight into the tar by rail spikes and pulled the rest of it back up onto the roof. Splinters shed from the tie like dandruff on a black sweater. It was a fresh break due to untold years of rot. This had just happened.

He returned to the edge and tried to get her attention when he heard a window breaking in the alley below. "Becca?" Lazio was stunned. Had she fallen into the alley with the other half of the tie landing on top of her? If so she must have rolled it off, broke a window and entered the lowest level. How tough is this girl?

A second later her clean white face emerged from a newly opened window, "Are you just going to sit there?"

"I can't believe you're ok?" He wanted to cry or laugh or blubber something sentimental but she was having none of it, this mission was far from over. With a fierce determined voice she challenged him to a race, "I'm fine but you are *way* behind me. Meet you at the top or rather, I'll beat you to the top."

With that she was gone again.

CHAPTER 3

▼

Pinpricks of yellow from parking lot streetlights broke through the dusty warehouse gloom. For a building that was supposed to be abandon, not considered stable by building code standards, there was an awful lot of equipment. The rectangular box back of semi trucks sat in the bay just waiting for the doors to open wide so they could be connected to power wires and hauled away. Pallet jacks lined a far wall next to mechanical lifts but they were rusting in place. The depth of dust suggested they had been waiting for far too long to ever be of use again. Becca accidentally kicked the dust into the air where it was caught lingering by the yellowed light.

"The staircase," She found it while coughing away the particles. In a distant shadow wide wooden steps lead to the second level. Her goal was to ascend quickly especially as Lazio was hot on her trail. The scrapes she received on account of falling into the alley were minor. It was pure luck that she caught her balance on the way down. Becca was resilient or so she needed to believe in order to maintain this frantic pace. So far the mind tricks were working.

"Becca?" The whisper was faint and not far behind but enough so that she couldn't hear or maybe she didn't want to hear. "Becca?" Lazio stopped in a doorway and surveyed that same loading bay. Allowing a moment to peek through the room he noticed that one area was not so dirty, not so old.

"This can't be right." His curiosity was peaked by a clean office door, a shiny knob and a brand new lock just ready and waiting for...

"We have to make this quick," Three men burst through a frail outer door just to the left of a shabbily stacked pile of taped cardboard boxes.

Lazio melded back through his doorway and watched the men cross the room and open the clean office door. One man, the shortest and thinnest of the three pulled a string to illuminate the tiny room. Lazio strained to hear what they were saying.

"Three thousand…Avon…his name is…"

Only parts of the conversation echoed into the bay. The meeting lasted a quick couple of minutes before the light went out and the crisp new door lock snapped shut.

"Don't worry I grew up in that area, I can find this kid no problem," A bulky red haired brute in saggy jeans and a green Boston Celtics jacket bragged to a little man wrapped neatly in a black trench coat and tie. The Celtic tucked an envelope in his back pocket while pledging his commitment to the task at hand.

"Good," The little man said, "He's caused me too much trouble as it is," They stopped near the door just before exiting.

The third man, taller than the others, stopped them from turning the knob. He held his ear cocked upwards.

"What is it?" The little man asked.

"I thought I heard something."

"It's squirrels, who cares, let's go." He prompted towards the door.

"Squirrels don't come out at night."

"Maybe they're nocturnal squirrels?" The Celtic said stupidly.

"There's no such thing as nocturnal squirrels." The tall man stated knowingly.

"Will you two shut up!"

"But Joey, I think someone's been in here."

"It doesn't matter," He raised his hand lightly to the man's cheek as if he was imitating an Italian gangster from a mob movie. "There is nothing here worth stealing." He lowered his hand.

"But what about…"

"Forget it, no one would find anything."

"Joey," The Celtic stepped past both of them to the middle of the room. He was looking up at the ceiling and listening intently. "I heard something too."

"I said it doesn't matter. Enough of this!" He opened the door and waved them out. "Vinny," He stopped the red haired man who was resisting his insistence, "This job," He gestured at the room, "has nothing to do with you. Just stick to what I need you for."

"But Joey, I…"

"Look, we're not kids anymore. This isn't some alley in Southie where we could call all the shots ourselves." He got close to Vinny's chest, placing one hand on his shiny green coat, "It can't be like it was, as much as I wish we could run things."

"But you inherited everything."

"No, I'm responsible for everything and I can't afford to lose any more ground. You're going to help make sure that we keep our lock on..." He tightened his grip on the jacket, "Vinn, just do your fuckin job, no excuses, none at all."

Vinny nodded and wanted to reply but held his tongue. He had to learn a newfound respect for his childhood friend. They were now employee and employer, it was a tough dynamic to get used to but if he didn't reach a new level of complicity then things would surely get ugly.

Lazio let go of his breath as the door shut behind them. What the hell had he just witnessed? Was that the mob? Was it really the Boston mafia or a traveling theatre troupe? They seemed too dumb to be real gangsters. Perplexed he walked out into the empty bay staring at the door fearing that they might change their minds and burst back into the room.

"Those guys almost went after Becca. That was a lucky break." He let out another deep breath. "Oh shit! Becca is kicking my ass." Lazio ran to the stairs and bound up them in a race to the third floor. Now he really was *way* behind.

CHAPTER 4

▼

"It's locked!" Becca had been kicking at the hardwood door but it wouldn't give way, not even an inch. The stairway had narrowed by the time it reached the third floor. She was standing in murky darkness working with a hand held flashlight small enough to hold between two fingers. She had come prepared for the dark but not for the deadbolt.

"Becca?" Lazio was lumbering up the stairs. His stride said a lot about him. It was confident and eager yet clumsy. His footfalls were heavy and desperate. One thing was sure; he was gaining on her.

"Damn it!" Becca kicked the door again but fell off balance and banged her shoulder into the wall to her right. The wall moved. "What the...oh yes." She pushed the wall with both hands and it swung open. Hearing Lazio closing in she ducked inside the room and shut the wall behind her.

"Becca?" His voice was drowned out as he reached the top of the stairs. He would have to contend with the deadbolt using his own talents; she had found a way around.

Holding her arm out to guard against the cramped ceiling Becca aimed the small light out into what had to be the top level of the warehouse. Cluttered with old wooden chairs stacked haphazardly on top of desks and a tipped over metal shelf, she stepped carefully through the jagged junk towards the room's only window. There was a pungent smell of animal feces in the air that became more apparent as she lifted the old rotten casing to let in the crisp winter air.

A large hook unlatched a broken wooden brace and pushed the two weather beaten shutters outward revealing a twinkling Norwood skyline.

A sprinkling of gifted skylight dazed her senses. The view was vast and beautiful. From this height she could see every business on Washington Street from the Caritas Norwood hospital on her left to a huge brick spire of what looked like a catholic church on her right. Broadway, Central, Park and Vernon streets were surprisingly peaceful at this time of night. Becca breathed in the nippy air ventilating her nose and then stepped out onto the roof carrying inside her heart a welling of victory.

The radio tower was bolted to an extra padding of shingles on her right. It sat alone in the center of the roof reflecting moonlight. Becca stood next to it and marveled at its height. The round metal base started at seven feet wide and got smaller as it went up.

"Thank god I don't have to climb anything else." She pulled the small American flag out of her pocket, its quaint wooden handle was broken, probably from her earlier fall. She unfolded a four-inch piece of duct tape and climbed up two steps. Stretching high she stuck the flag to the tower and climbed back down. There was no point in taking any further risks. They said it had to be on the tower, they didn't indicate how high. She stepped back and smiled at her achievement.

The door inside the small cluttered room burst open by the power of a heavy boot. Lazio tore his way through the chairs and desks scattering them in every direction. He jumped through the open window and shrunk with disbelief as he saw Becca standing calm, elegantly embraced by a picturesque skyline wearing a winning grin.

"What took you so long?"

"I got hung up." He pulled out his flag, climbed the tower and stuck it a full ten inches above hers. "You beat me, big deal."

"Don't be a sore sport." She teased as they walked to the edge of the roof. Becca studied the back building for a way down while Lazio dazed off into the distance.

"Are you looking at the church?" She raised her head again; a faint breeze blew her wavy hair to one side as its icy chill sent goose pimples up her spine. "This city is beautiful. I never really noticed it before." She had grown up mostly in the town of Avon and only came to Norwood on occasion when her parents were fighting. After Avon became too dangerous it was decided that she was to live here permanently.

"What church?" He held his palms up.

"That one; the tall brick thing."

"Oh, that's the town hall."

"It looks like a church."

"No, but it is one of the oldest buildings in town." He pointed to its peak, "It's a neo-gothic structure, 170 feet tall, made of Weymouth seamed-face granite." He tried not to grin; she might not believe him. "It's a 51 bell carillon tower with stained glass windows depicting pictures of Captain Aaron Guild. He helped fight off the British at Lexington."

"Oh, ok…how the hell do you know all that?"

"Book report, sixth grade."

She shrugged timidly, somewhat impressed, "You've got a good memory."

"No, not really, I used that same book report in the eighth grade and the tenth grade. It was the same subject but different teachers; got an A all three times. I think I still have it."

"Are you saving it for college?"

"Perhaps."

For the first time she found herself amused. Lazio caught a glimpse of her changed mood and took it for admiration. Maybe he did have a chance with her?

"Ready to finish this?"

"Let's go." Her smile erased all doubts.

CHAPTER 5

▼

"There they are," Psycho pointed to two silhouettes racing across the railroad tracks towards the bridge. They were nothing more than faint shadows flickering through a backdrop of scattered nighttime glow.

"Told you we didn't kill them."

"And neither did anybody else thank-god." He let out a snort watching the two dark bodies sprint to the top of the bridge and duck down against it as a car passed beneath them on Guild Street.

"Honestly," Dutch asked with a deliberate air, "What do you think of Lazio?"

"I told you he's a good guy. We went to middle school together, he scared the other kids a little with his dark eyes and long fingernails but I've never seen him be mean to anyone."

"So what is his kink? Does he think he's a vampire or something? We're supposed to have military standards and his long hair doesn't fit the bill. Besides after what we went through with Damian I don't want another potentially dangerous person on the team, someone whose imagination runs away with them."

"No it's nothing weird, it's well…Ok, it's a little weird…he's a witch."

"A witch."

"Yes, a witch."

"But he's a guy. Wouldn't that make him a warlock?"

"I haven't a clue."

"Ok, and that's not weird because?"

"Because he's really a witch. He grew up pagan. His parents are pagan and even his sister is a priestess. He's a real, practicing witch. They have ancient books and incense and I guess pagan holidays. It's a family thing."

"Does he go to a witch church?"

"No, they go to a grove."

"What's that?"

"A grassy field."

"Does he think he can cast spells and shit like that?"

"Yeah I guess," Psycho scratched his chin with the scarred knuckles of his left hand. "But he doesn't actually use magic. He's got some quirk about how using it can come back at you three fold. On top of that he does brag a lot about how pagans have been prosecuted over the years…

"You mean persecuted?"

"I don't know; you'll have to ask him."

"Do you think he'll make a good HAWK?" Dutch had been unsure of Lazio since they met. Those dark eyes of his were intimidating and inquisitive but that only added weight to his already formidable appearance. The only edge that Dutch had over Lazio was that his new junior member of the HAWKS didn't know anything about the military, gangs, street life or the mob. Lazio was a civilian, an academic while Dutch was the leader of a suburban gang determined to kill drug dealers. Well, someday that's what they would do. In the meantime they had to survive a different kind of war zone—public high school.

Lazio, on the other hand, went to a posh private school. He was a creepy bookworm with a shifty attitude that was often lost in his love for all things renaissance. King Richard's fair was to Lazio what Christmas is to everyone else. He practically worships the month of October. He and his family dressed in their practical magic robes and drove up to Salem where they would spend Halloween doing god knows what with a few thousand other modern day witches. Perhaps it was just a cultural difference and if so they will adapt to it but if not…

"Dude," Psycho nudged Dutch's arm with his watch. "We're looking at 12:49am. That train should be in sight soon."

"It's ok, they're in position."

Becca and Lazio had knelt down in the two-foot gap between the crossties. They were standing on the solid structure of the bridge where three large beams passed above the expanse of the two-lane road. The shiny rails lay perpendicular on both sides of them.

"Did you know that the MBTA reaches seventy miles an hour on this route?" Lazio stared off into the darkness from which the speeding passenger train was soon to emerge.

"That's pretty fast," She looked over her left shoulder to catch a glimpse of Dutch and Psycho as they slipped down the hood of the Olds. Becca didn't have a watch but being in between the tracks she was sure that she'd know when the train was near.

"In fact," Lazio continued, "it goes so fast that if we didn't duck down in time it wouldn't be able to slow itself." His body seemed to lock in place as if he was waiting for impact but the only thing churning was his imagination. "The engine car has a snow plow on its lower front. Out west they call it a cow plow. It could chop our bodies in half. The top of our bodies would probably go flying into the air and our legs would separate and dangle from the bridge dripping blood on passing cars. That would be a sight huh? Just imagine you're driving home from work and instead of taking the normal route you decide to sneak a shortcut through the warehouse district but as you drive under the train bridge someone's severed legs falls from the rafters and splatters on the hood of your car. What would you do?" He didn't leave her any room to answer. "I'd probably freak, I'd probably swerve wildly because I'd be afraid that I hit a homeless person. I'd slam on my brakes and lose control careening into the rock wall."

"That's a nice image," She snuck a word in but he was only listening to his own vivid descriptions. *Where is all of this coming from?* She wondered.

"I bet that by hitting a solid wall at that speed my car would just explode. They'd be scraping brains off the rocks for weeks. They'd have to use a power washer to clean the blood away so that it doesn't attract rats and you know what else..."

"Lazio!" She blurted out, "That's enough, I can picture it and I don't want to picture anymore, it's not going to happen."

"Sorry," He leaned back against the rail and laid his outstretched palms on the cold metal. "Hey,"

"What? Do you have another nightmare dreamscape for me to listen to?" Becca snapped at him. She didn't mean to do it but his obsession with all things morbid was getting to be, well, morbid.

"Put your hand on the rail."

She hesitated expecting this to be the beginning of a practical joke but as soon as her fingers touched she could feel it too. A steady but slowly increasing vibration shimmied up into her arm. That was her confirmation. It was certain, the initiation stunt that was meant to test their guts, meant to prove their willingness to put themselves in harms way, meant to make them into HAWKS, was about to happen. The train was on its way.

CHAPTER 6

▼

The headlight started out as a distant pinch of illumination hiding amongst a hundred reflected streetlamps. Like starlight penetrating the vacuum of space it grew both in intensity and velocity. Becca removed her hands from the rails, she remembered that one of the beams had power in it, electricity, or was that only with trolleys? Lazio removed his hands as well; the shaking was unnerving them both. If it was vibrating this hard now, how bad would it be when the train was riding inches from their heads?

"I'm not so sure…" Lazio's eyes became transfixed on the oncoming beam.

"We're not going anywhere!" She slapped his arm, "Look at me!"

"What?" He said out of the side of his mouth. His eyes were locked on the speeding train.

"Lazio! Look at me right now!"

"I…I um," He was freezing up. This was what the test was all about and Becca knew it. If they were to be street soldiers facing the barrel of a gun they first had to be sure they could react with confidence. This death plow racing their way at seventy miles an hour was producing an anxiety equal to that found on any battlefield. Dutch told them of his father's experiences in Vietnam where teenagers quickly learned how to face sudden horrifying situations else they die within a week. This was true danger, a moment when they must keep their cool, a moment when their lives depended on tapping the instinct to survive.

"They're stuck." Psycho took two steps away from the car. He was preparing to run towards the bridge and help out if need be. Though it's unlikely he would make it in time.

"They have to do this on their own," Dutch didn't budge. If Becca and Lazio wanted to be HAWKS they would have to earn it. Everyone had to risk their lives for this team, everyone read the *Malevolent Philosophy*, the team's guiding bond, and thus knew what they were getting themselves into. Every soul pledged their loyalty and from time to time that loyalty had to be tested, bested and earned.

"Lazio!" Becca was screaming at him but he was lost in a hopeless state of mind. Perhaps Lazio did not want to live? For whatever reason and there could be many that his new friends didn't know about, this could be his chance to leave this earth. Perhaps he wanted to be cut in half and thrown in the air, killed by an oncoming train. Was he trying to die right here in front of her? They didn't have time to discuss it. She had to make a decision; no way was this going to happen on her watch!

"Ouch!"

Becca slapped him across the face as the train came into plain view. They had to duck down and hang from the bridge; no more time could be wasted.

"C'mon," She grabbed him by the front of his black sweater and pulled him forward but he wouldn't budge. "Put your hands on the beam, when I say go, we both let our feet dangle until we are hanging from the bridge."

He looked at her with empty eyes. What had come over him? Why was he acting this way? All he could picture was the speeding snowplow aimed right at him. "I won't ever have to go back." He said cryptically making no sense at all.

Becca kept a firm hold on his shirt. She had no idea what he was talking about, had he lost it completely? She kicked his left shin and forced him to go down between the rails.

"Lazio, let's count down from ten, Ok?" She started the count but he was still dazed, he picked it up at six.

"Five," They both said at once, "Four, three, two…"

The sound of the heavy passenger cars roared overhead and squealed in deafening waves of pain. The vibrating bridge structure became impossible to hold onto.

"One!" They're bodies dangled uneasily over the street. Both were hanging on with every ounce of strength but the quake above was weakening them by the millisecond.

"I told you they could do it," Dutch said with a smug grin.

"Yep, you were right and hopefully they'll see that truck going under the bridge."

"Truck? Oh shit! Fuck, let's go!" Dutch and Psycho broke into a sprint as an eighteen wheel Peterbuilt Semi with an extended blue cab turned underneath the train bridge. There was only a foot and a half of clearance between the roof of the cab and the bottom of the bridge. Becca and Lazio were no longer visible as the Peterbuilt's bright headlights temporarily blinded Dutch and Psycho.

"Where are they?" Psycho darted to the left of the truck and into the tunnel. The Peterbuilt drove past as if nothing had happened.

"I don't see them," Dutch stopped and let his eyes run back and forth along the metal girders looking for a leg, a foot, a hand, anything. Hopefully the body part would still be attached to its owner.

The train passed by leaving the night to its normal quiet, like a sudden thunderous storm it faded slowly into the distance. Now they had to find out if it left the shredded remains of their two new members.

"Do you see…?"

"Looking for us?" Becca poked her head through a hole in the dark metal. Then she let her body hang from the girder and let go landing roughly on the concrete.

"Whoa," Dutch ran over to steady her. "Warn a guy before you do that."

"I'll warn you both," Lazio said as he let his legs hang down before releasing his grip. Psycho ran up and gave Lazio some help; being heavier he hit the Guild Street sidewalk a lot harder.

"It's good to see you two are alright but how did you do it? How did you see the truck in time?" Dutch asked as he brushed flakes of brown metal off of Becca's uniform.

"First," Lazio said with a hint of shame, "Becca saved me from the train. I…um…got stuck." His head sagged a little.

"But then," Becca continued graciously, "Lazio pulled me out of the way of the truck."

"Did we do it?" Lazio peeked at Dutch, "Did we complete the course correctly?" He felt like a coward for freezing up. Becca had covered for him so that it sounded like they saved each other's lives. Maybe that would be enough to redeem his performance. Lazio desperately needed friends. He'd do anything to be a part of the team.

Dutch reluctantly nodded his head in the affirmative. "You guys are in."

"But it didn't go perfectly…" Lazio checked.

"Nothing is ever perfect," Psycho explained. "We set the obstacles but you two had to find your own way to survive them and you did just that. You survived certain death."

"Twice," Dutch added. "You did what you were asked despite the danger and you saved each other in the process so I'm proud to say…that you are both officially members of the HAWKS Foundation."

CHAPTER 7

▼

"These guys were dressed like gangsters, I don't know what they were hiding but..."

"Lazio, knock it off. Psycho and I were across the street and no one went into that building." Dutch's voice carried with it a firm reprimand.

"They were right in front of me..."

Psycho shook his head, "That parking lot was empty the whole time you were gone."

Becca swallowed her pride, she didn't know what to think of this new story but she did know that Lazio's imagination is out of control. She told them that he pulled her up out of the truck's way but that fabrication was meant to help him save face. She lied by extolling the virtue of a selfless act that never happened. This mysterious male Witch made it onto the team by accepted her charity but was it the right thing to do? Here he was telling a tall tale that sounded ludicrous to all of them and he wouldn't give up on it.

"Not another word!" Dutch shut him up with sheer intimidation.

"Wait, wait, I got something to show you guys." They had barely walked out from under the tunnel when Lazio pulled them back towards it.

"What, where are we going?" Psycho pulled his arm free as the four of them reached an open alleyway between the bridge and the warehouse wall.

"What is this? Lazio?" Psycho stopped cold. "Where does this lead? Are you going to tell us that the gangsters are hiding in there?" A shadowy crack in the concrete of the city hinted at a dangerous understructure behind the bridge and below the tracks. Psycho had faced the unknown before so he wasn't spooked by ghostly noises but he was spooked by Lazio's insistence that they venture into this unstable location.

"It's a secret, I can't tell you. You won't believe me. I…I have to show you." He turned slowly into the alley and disappeared behind a gray wall. If they wouldn't listen, maybe they would follow.

Psycho and Dutch looked at each other baffled by these dramatic pronouncements. Lazio's creepy, pagan, horror movie personality was kicking in again. It made them all feel uneasy. Becca said they were being prejudice because of his religion but then she didn't want to explain why it bothered her as well. Maybe she should tell them what really happened?

"Let's just see what it is." Psycho said simply as he walked around the wall. Becca and Dutch followed behind.

Lazio hadn't stopped to wait for his friends; he kept right on to the next room while they lagged behind. The first room had a dirt floor and three gray concrete walls but one wall had a rectangular man size opening in it. This led to the second room; here the walls were covered in black graffiti, spray paint, chalk and marker. They all took a moment to stop and read them, or at least they tried to. The writing was archaic, twisted, like graffiti written by a blind man. It was deliberate in technique but eerily confusing.

"An upside down pentacle I could understand, an anarchy symbol would be obvious or maybe a goat head but…" Using her index finger Becca traced what looked like a broken capital letter F in the air, "I don't know what any of this is."

"It's just the scribbling of a couple black magic wannabe's." Dutch was using his snide criticism to stave off the twinge of nervousness that this odd place demanded of its inhabitants. Only this time his chides were not working.

"There is no black magic," Lazio said in a deep, throaty response. "Magic doesn't adhere to Judeo-Christian color codes."

"Christian color codes? Yeah but he meant…" Psycho was cut off by Lazio's sudden serious embrace of the argument.

"Intentions decide the morality of an action, magic is relativistic not absolute. These are symbols of protection meant to stave off bad intentions. There are here to save you." He had stunned them into silence with his sternness but what the hell was he talking about? No one wanted to sound dumb so they let the remarks slide as he turned his back again leading them into the third and final room.

"Is this it?" Psycho asked as the room came into clear view. "This isn't so scary. It's dark and some weird noises are echoing off the warehouse but…"

"This isn't what I wanted you to see." Lazio stood tall on a concrete block in the center of the room. All along the edges of the block was a pool of water and while two of the walls were clearly solid the third was obscured by a deep shadow. All four of them balanced on the wide, flat block suddenly feeling trapped.

"Becca, do you still have that flashlight?" His long bony finger pointed to the darkened wall. His continued theatrics were not appreciated. This room didn't need any help.

She aimed the small beam into the enveloping shadow as Psycho and Dutch cautiously stepped forward towards what they thought was a solid wall. Within the shadow was an enormous crack in the concrete over four feet tall and three feet wide but that was only the first layer. Beyond the rim of concrete, inches inside the hole hid a tunnel. Her arm snaked forward so the light ran along the edges of the inner opening. A burnt red brick tunnel fell away from the beam to such depth that the light could not penetrate far enough to see the bottom.

"It bends to the left," Psycho edged a little closer to the opening, his boots coming to the edge of the block. "They must have used this to build the rail system, it goes right underneath it."

They all raised their eyes to see that secondary rails crossed five feet over their heads.

"It goes deeper than that," Lazio whispered.

"So what's in there?" Dutch asked straightforward as he was getting a little fed up. "You seem to know this place pretty well Lazio, let's hear it."

The HAWKS had seen false terrors before and proved them all to be figments of their imaginations masking a real life danger as something more than it was. People simply have the ability to scare themselves into delusion. The HAWKS named such an experience 'The Jigsaw Effect,' and had seen one of their own succumb to its lure. The team had been shaken to its core by such revelations in the past but they always broke through to reason, to pragmatism. Cold, simple logic was the honest to goodness cure. Watching their new teammate Dutch and Psycho feared that Lazio might be a vessel for a whole new wave of hysterical imaginings.

If this cave was a sign of things to come Dutch wanted to head it off at the pass, "Well? Explain?"

"We found Mideon. Of all the hiding places in all the towns in this world, we found it." He stoically pointed again to the hole. "It's down there."

"What's Mideon?" Becca hid herself partially behind Psycho.

Lazio glared eagerly at her, "That's where the monsters are."

"Meaning?" Psycho had to clear his throat as the closeness of the room was starting to feel claustrophobic.

"As a kid my friend Dennis and I were exploring these rooms when we found this cave. Dennis made the trip down and told me all about it. It opened up into another world, an underworld of...well, monsters. In complete blackness he was attacked by...I don't know what but he escaped. He showed me the scars and told me all about it."

"What did it look like?" Dutch demanded.

"I said complete blackness. He could only hear grunts and growls. He escaped its grasp and we both ran all the way home. While we were getting cleaned up he found cuts and bruises all over his arms and legs. Plus, he found the bite." Lazio hunched down towards Dutch getting within inches of his face, "A second longer and he would have been torn apart." His arm reached over Dutch pointing to the second room. "Those symbols are the only thing keeping the creatures down there. That room is like an electric fence of spiritual energy shocking any bad intentions from breaking through." He pointed again to the brick hallway down into the darkness. "They are being contained in Mideon so long as the protection is maintained. Dennis is..." He stopped and thought about whether he wanted to share the next part of the story. "He's..."

"He's what? He's undead? A werewolf? A Zombie? What?" Psycho yelled at him.

Lazio hunched down a little, as he understood that he was not being taken seriously, "He's no longer a friend."

Dutch felt a chill race through his body. He was waiting to hear a more outlandish outcome but the fact that Lazio backed off his story was even more bothersome. The tale was obviously an elaborate children's fantasy but Lazio believed so strongly in it that he had to withhold the rest of the details from them. Just then a wind blown sound whistled its way up out of the cave. Psycho, Dutch and Becca felt an aura of derangement surrounding them but it wasn't coming from the sounds or the black pictograms or from the story, it was coming from their new teammate. Lazio was staring down into the darkness with dead eyes like a trauma victim suffering the shock of a previous frightening memory. If only for an instant he was clearly out of his mind. Instead of testing a new teammate they may have inherited an unforeseen liability.

PENNY
BITCHES

CHAPTER 8

▼

"It's not what you do, it's what you get caught doing," Peter pulled the car door handle slowly and quietly so that it opened without a sound.

"So just don't get caught that's what you mean?" Paul sat impatiently in the driver's seat of his silver 1985 Chevy Camaro. He had only just bought this car and now feared that he was going to get nabbed. Paul's eight-cylinder hot rod was sitting with two wheels on the curb one street away from the house Peter was about to rob. The get away man can race off if he has to but the Brockton police have a negligible reputation for deadly car pursuits. Granted Paul had carefully fine-tuned his fiberglass sled for speed, its small block 305 had a feedback fuel system and brand new racing tires but it would still be little match for a super-charged police car. The few criminal's who escaped the tenacious Brockton PD, did so only after climbing out of the smashed remains of their overturned vehicles. That was a risk he was not willing to take.

"I won't be long, just chill. I'll be right back." Peter nudged the door closed and slipped through a hole between a chain link fence and a street side wooden wall.

Paul looked in the rear view mirror at the empty road behind him. Jodi, their plump blonde tag along girl friend, was getting bored in the backseat. She yawned at him and moved her head. The pot marked cement between where his car was parked and the quarter mile behind them faded away into a long curve. He had the window half open and the radio volume turned as low as possible while still being able to hear it. Paul hummed chords from his *Ride the Lightning* tape by *Metallica*. He had to stay distracted. His hope was that on this one night, for these few minutes that nobody drove down this exact road, especially no police cars. Their plan could be foiled in the worst way if bad luck interfered but Peter, his best friend since middle school, had insisted that this would be a chance worth taking.

Paul hummed himself into calmness, "For whom the bell tolls."

"Don't sing." Jodi punched the back of his seat. She may be stuck in his car until they took her home but the torture would be limited to weak sex and cheap alcohol. Jodi could see Peter's form through the chain links as he advanced on the house. He never did tell her exactly what he was after but she was often kept out of the loop. "You boys and your games. This is so stupid."

The yard behind the fence was typical of Peter's drunken, white trash father. Mr. Aubrey Truelson was a New England redneck. He spoke with a normal Massachusetts drawl, dropping his R's and blurring his words together like Elmer Fudd but that was not why his son despised him. The hate came from a feeling of insignificance. Peter was only one of an unknown number of kids Aubrey had conceived in his travels. These carnal journeys never took him farther than Fall River or New Bedford but the women were countless. The encounters were often paid, always inebriated and sometimes forced. Aubrey had been arrested four times for abusing his first two wives, and once for stabbing his seventh child in the face. The mangled eight-year old boy suffered through reconstructive surgery while Aubrey spent only nine months in Bridgewater State Prison. This man had a miraculous talent for drumming up favors from high-powered local defense attorneys when he got in particularly bad trouble. He didn't, however, use this talent to help his son Peter when he too got into trouble for committing similar acts on a lesser scale.

Peter stepped over a fallen black charred grill, past a row of twenty half empty paint cans and walked lightly on the sidewalls of three truck tires in order to reach the back porch. Climbing over a wobbly railing he stopped to make sure that all of the windows, top and bottom floor, were absent of light. He had already seen the front of the house when he and Paul drove by it earlier. There was no car or at least not one with any semblance of mechanical ability. While all of these signs of silence should assure that no one was home, Peter knew his dad. Aubrey didn't have a normal existence. He worked only when he wanted to and the jobs always changed. If he had taught his son anything, it was that you had to have a real job once in a while in order to justify the few things you own. Otherwise people will get curious; neighbors, social workers, police, the IRS and then they'll start asking questions. An occasional legitimate job halted all such inquiries. So in reality Aubrey could be home right now, sitting in the dark all alone, just waiting for someone to arrive.

Peter stopped at the back door and stared at the handle. His father never locked the door, relying only on his reputation in the neighborhood to stop anyone from even considering entering his home. It was a metal door with two broken triangle windows covered over from the inside with cardboard and duct tape. Peter played with the handle using only the tips of his fingers.

"Gently…" He whispered as he pushed the handle down. *Click.* It opened and a faint creak escaped from the hinges as he eased his way into the kitchen. The first step was complete; a deadly step to say the least but he had a strong motivation. Peter decided that this was the only way they were going to get their hands on another gun without having to pay for it. Aubrey had a closet full of weapons in a house full of secrets but Peter only needed to find one.

He crept slowly into the rank, smelly kitchen and closed the door behind him. *Click.*

CHAPTER 9

▼

"Quit your whining," Paul wanted to backhand Jodi. She was just going along for the ride, she should be happy they wanted to hang out with her at all.

Jodi grew up in the quaint but forgettable Massachusetts suburb of Avon alongside Peter and Paul. She also went to school with Dutch, Tommy and Gary of the HAWKS. Since the latter three didn't party and Jodi didn't want to go home where she'd be stuck sitting alone, she accepted Peter's offer to go for a ride to Brockton. They had yet to find a liquor store who would sell to them, as they were all underage, and now they were parked on a street corner waiting for Peter to do god knows what. Her patience was wearing thin.

"I'm giving him five minutes and then I'm gone," She blurted loudly not far from Paul's right ear.

"Where are you going to do?"

"I'll walk you asshole."

"At night in Brockton?" The city was predominately black, encased in old shoe factories, ghettos and low-income housing. For a blonde haired white girl, even a slightly overweight one, to walk these streets near midnight was about as safe as wearing a Yankees hat while sitting amongst the committed Red Sox fans at Fenway park. Either act could get someone killed.

"Yes, I'll...hitchhike." She was bluffing.

"Good, I'll get to read all about your mutilated remains in the newspaper tomorrow." Paul turned up the radio.

She was pissed that he called her bluff so easily. "Yeah, well, you probably can't read anyway." She had nothing. It was better simply to wait.

Just beyond the kitchen inside the house, Peter was edging his way down the hallway. His footfalls were born of a stealth practiced during countless nights of sneaking down to the kitchen to eat more than he had been allowed. Peter had loved this house on weekends from time to time but mostly during summer vacation when his Mom didn't want to put up with him anymore. Maybe love was too strong a word. He was fond of it not because his Dad was around to show him how to shoot squirrels with a slingshot, even though that was fun, but because his Dad would leave him alone. These patches of privilege lasted for hours, days, once for a whole week with no parental supervision. It was a different kind of freedom but he came to appreciate it.

"No, no…"

Peter stopped at the bottom of the stairs. He heard a faint female voice protesting from the second floor bedroom but couldn't imagine who it could be? His Dad wasn't dating anybody. He never brought his 'Penny Bitches', that's what he liked to call prostitutes, home with him. He said they were all crooks that stole wallets and jewelry in the middle of the night as they tugged up their wet panties while running out the door. No Penny Bitch was stealing from this house and to ensure that, none ever seemed to enter it.

"Who?" Peter's eyes targeted the top of the stairs and the open bedroom door. Then he looked to his right at the standing gun safe in the living room. A battle of conscience ensued. His Dad was clearly distracted so he could easily unlock the safe, grab a gun and run out of the house before Aubrey would get a chance to put his pants back on. This was a risk he could avoid but an insatiable curiosity was compelling him to climb those stairs. Aubrey *never* brought anyone home with him. It went against everything he believed in so this was highly unusual.

"Fuck it, I'll do both." Peter took two wide steps into the living room and quickly unlocked the safe. To his surprise there was only one gun left. Aubrey must have started hiding them again. He did that from time to time; perhaps for fear that they might get stolen. *Too smart for his own good.* However, the one weapon that was left was a beauty.

"It's my lucky day." Peter's mouth fell open at the sight of a brand new Remington 11-87 twelve-gauge Police entry shotgun. His father used to brag about how he could get his hands on weapons that only the authorities used. This was one of his prized possessions. The 11-87 was a little different from the twenty-two gauge that Pete had stolen before. This had a short 14-inch barrel with black parkerized finish and a polymer stock making it small and light. He let his fingers run along the barrel. This semi-automatic, gas operated shotgun was designed for close quarters use and now it was in his hands. *Oh the damage he could do with this glorious creation.* Granted it didn't look or handle anything like his old one but he was sure that Schmel and the other gang members would be impressed. They wanted to see a gun and he was going to show them one. It wasn't the same one he used to shoot Dutch a few years ago, he told his new friends that he still had that weapon but they wouldn't be able to tell the difference. Only Tyrone had seen the original so he could get away with this. There is a certain power to being armed and that alone should earn him some respect in the Spring Street Posse. As it stands with them or any street gang, respect is all that matters.

Peter laid the gun across the corner of the table bumping aside a small stack of Guns & Ammo magazines. Peter grabbed one before it fell to the floor. As he placed it back on the table he saw a handle sticking out from under a pile of yellow and brown stained Chinese food boxes. He carefully pulled out a pistol from the pile. It had no clip and looked to be in rough shape but he may be able to use it anyway. Peter placed it next to the shotgun in a position that would make them both easy to grab. Unfortunately neither would do him any good tonight because the safe was absent of ammo and it was unlikely that this weapon was loaded. Aubrey only left one gun loaded and that was the one he had tucked in between the mattresses of his bed.

As Peter recalled the size of this father's hidden arsenal he paused on the bottom step. Aubrey was a dangerous man who should never be underestimated but Peter just *had* to know who was up there with him. *Why would he bring someone home?* Was there a slight flicker of naïve hope sewn into his curiosity? The mildest belief that his Dad, the great criminal, might be settling down a little, accepting the graces of middle age with some amount of serenity? If Peter were able to say it out loud he'd probably laugh the idea away but so long as he was forced to be quiet, so long as the possibility remained trapped in silent speculation, it would knaw at him. He had to find out the truth.

The old wooden steps were very tricky. If not for his previous years of sneaking up and down them he never would have made it halfway. The third step has a loose nail on the front hangover so he leaned towards the back. The fifth step is warped on the left side so he toed the right. The sixth step was practically a booby trap. He lost count of how many friends and relatives fell down the stairs after that sixth step gave way beneath them. Peter extended over it and with two more swift leaps made it to the top of the staircase.

The bedroom was the first door on the left but almost as suddenly as it had started the faint feminine whimpering was gone. Did Aubrey hear his approach? Was the big man sitting on the bed with a large bore handgun ready and aimed as he waited for his victim to turn the corner? Peter didn't make a sound as he braced himself against the wall and inched up to the frame.

There were only creaks coming from within.

Peter took three short breaths to prepare for a likely confrontation and then with his mind and body revved for battle he swung around into the open doorway.

CHAPTER 10

▼

Kaitlin Mason never had to walk home before. This would have been her first time. Her grandmother usually picked her up in front of the school all the while complaining about how her irresponsible child, Kaitlin's Mom Michelle, should be doing this herself. Michelle hadn't been around much lately, ever since she moved out of Grandma's house and in with her boyfriend leaving Kaitlin behind. The little girl wasn't allowed to move since the boyfriend's apartment was a weekly rented closet and not a stable leased residence. Grandma Mason wasn't even sure if the guy had a job. He was secretive, clearly ashamed of himself and probably a drug dealer. Michelle called grandma racist after she had spent half an afternoon convincing her daughter not to give him her food stamps even though he claimed he could sell them for twice their worth. These scams were rampant in Brockton's social welfare system. Girls got pregnant time and again; leaving their children with various family members while the girl ran off with the monthly welfare check and food stamps. Having babies provided free money. For some it had become a way of life. Grandma Mason blamed herself. Her job at the shoe factory was now obsolete but it was all she had ever known. Now they didn't make shoes the way they used to. New high tech machines were the norm and there were even rumors that the businesses who housed those machines might be moving to Mexico or even Taiwan. She had no job skills to teach her daughter and this debauchery was the inevitable result. Michelle was now on a dismal, lethargic, dead-end path to nowhere and Grandma felt helpless to stop her.

The boyfriend's closet was in a building known as the Renaissance, a crumbling downtown apartment structure that sheltered many of the city's most criminal elements. It had a long history of housing gang members, crack addicts, gun dealers and even a few innocent minorities who couldn't afford to live anywhere else. Grandma Mason had lived in Brockton her whole life and knew that trouble is like piled garbage in an alleyway, you can walk through as carefully as possible but the stench follows you.

"He does not have a suitable place to raise a child," Grandma was fond of saying. In fact, she said it so often that Kaitlin memorized the statement and repeated it to her Mom whenever she was angry.

"That's not a suitable..." Kaitlin would start in her little girl voice before her Mom cut her off.

"You're Grandma doesn't understand shit! I'm trying to find a place for us to live."

"Grandma says you should...need a job...for money." Her innocence went for naught against the strained hunger of her mother's desperate state of mind.

"Grandma won't baby sit you while I'm working. She's sabotaging me. How am I gonna keep a job if I have to watch you at the same time?" Michelle was stuffing another garbage bag full of clothes to bring to her boyfriend's rented room.

"I can baby-sit me." Kaitlin's eyes filled with sadness. She didn't want her Mommy to leave, not again.

"Oh, no honey. No," She knelt next to this beautiful sobbing doll decked out in an orange one piece dress, her face squared by long brown pigtails but she could only feel regret. "You need to take care of Grandma at night, besides I'll be there to pick you up from school in the afternoon."

"You'll tell Grandma," She knew that if her Mom only said she would be there then there was no guarantee but if she told Grandma NOT to be there then she would have to show up.

"Yes honey, I'll tell Grandma. I'll be there when you get out of school tomorrow, I promise."

"Will you tell her now?" Kaitlin asked using her only skill, innocent persuasion.

"Ok god damn it!" Michelle stomped on the floor as she got to her feet and stormed out of the room. Kaitlin might have been scared of the tantrum if not for the rising hope that this time her Mom was actually coming to get her. She imagined what she would tell her friends. She wanted her Mom to meet her teacher. It was going to be great! A delicate smile curled up the sides of her pink cheeks as her Mom rounded the corner and said,

"It's final, I'll be coming to get you, not Grandma."

Kaitlin was as excited as a child could be. This was like having Christmas all over again. That night she was so ecstatic that she dreamt of how it would happen. For the very first time her Mom would drive up in a big car, climb out to meet her daughter in front of a crowd of her classmates and impress her teacher with her beauty and her smile.

The next day Kaitlin bragged to all her friends that this was the day her Mom was coming to get her. As the bell rang and kids poured out to the waiting cars she also ran in search of the fantasy.

Since she didn't know what Michelle would be driving Kaitlin carefully looked into the windows of each car as she walked by. Most people waved or smiled at her but none of them was her Mom. As she reached the end of the driveway she still hadn't seen her.

There was one car left. Just beyond the driveway, on the side of the road was a bronze mid eighties Cadillac. It looked a little like the one her Mom's boyfriend drove or at least it was almost the same color. That had to be her, she promised to come and that was the only car left.

Kaitlin left the school grounds, far out of sight of the teachers and walked up to the door of the Cadillac. The window wound down slowly. It wasn't her Mom; it was a strange but friendly man. Kaitlin wanted to cry. The man tried to cheer her up and within seconds she had been promised a ride home.

CHAPTER 11

▼

Peter turned the corner to view a ghastly scene inside Aubrey's bedroom. A large soiled double mattress lay in the middle of the room surrounded by a whirlpool of discarded clothes. Its formerly white sheets stank with a wave of sex, blood and urine combined into a yellowish roving stain. More frightening were the specks of red dried to the wooden headboard. These dots were especially numerous at its far sides where duct tape remained tangled in knots as if the last person who had been restrained by them twisted their bodies over and over trying to make the tape brake free leaving behind layers of skin.

"Mommy..." Peter heard a mumble from the far side of the room. In a tan chair beyond the bed, a pile of blankets moved.

"Who's there?" Peter whispered back. He knew his father had to be up here somewhere but the person hiding in that pile was definitely not his father.

"Mommy..." The weak mumble responded.

Peter carefully walked around the end of the bed and leaned towards the chair. Taking a deep breath he reached one arm out towards the pile of blankets and pinched a green comforter between his thumb and forefinger. In one quick jerk he yanked the blanket away and let it fall on the floor at his feet.

"Holy shit..." The little girl was about six years old or maybe seven. She was naked, wrapped loosely in old blankets and clutching a dirty towel. Tears had left wide swaths down her face but it was apparent that she couldn't cry anymore. Her brown eyes were dilated, her face expressionless, shock had overcome her normal senses and all she could do was beg for her mother.

"Mommy…" The words dribbled out of her mouth. She was looking directly at Peter but unable to focus on his face. She knew someone was there in front of her but she couldn't see him, not really.

"What's your name honey?" Peter knelt down by the chair and peeled away one of the blankets. "Are you Ok? Are you hurt?" *Of course she's hurt.* It was a stupid question but what else was there to ask? Maybe he could snap her out of it with the sound of his voice? Maybe this wasn't as bad as it looked? Maybe this little girl was the daughter of whomever his father was now dating and he was merely watching her for a night? It was possible, wasn't it?

She tilted her head to the right where his voice was coming from but her answer was always the same, "Mommy…" It wasn't really a question anymore, merely a long embraced hope that her Mommy had finally come for her. Her fragile mind was on autopilot and her mother was the only idea of safety that her consciousness could cling to.

"No, I'm not your Mommy but I'm…I'm gonna…" Peter didn't know what to do. If she didn't belong to Aubrey's new woman then he must have kidnapped this child. Judging by the blood on her body, especially down around her legs, he may have raped her. That would explain the shock; it would explain everything.

"I don't know what the hell I'm going to do," He wiped away some crud from the corner of her right eye. "Honey…"

"Kaitlin," She mumbled making an acknowledgement that she knew what he was saying. She was at least partly lucid so she could hear him or at least she could try.

"That's your name? Ok, Kaitlin I need to ask you a question and please do your best to answer."

"Kaitlin," She said again but it sounded like a yes to him.

"Where is the big man who brought you here? Where is Aubrey? Did he leave?" Peter begged the question hoping she could give an answer. "Where…"

Kaitlin replied by allowing her eyes to point towards the bathroom doorway. She was looking at the big man right now.

"You motherfucker!" Aubrey was only wearing shorts; his thick orange body hair did little to hide a wide, powerful chest over a bulging belly. The resemblance with Peter was uncanny; he was a larger, meaner version, the original Brockton pit bull. Aubrey would do anything to protect his secrets even if that meant killing his own son.

"Come here you little bastard!" Forgetting the bed and his own inebriation Aubrey charged forward and fell over the soiled mattresses.

Peter dodged the dive by throwing himself into the far wall and then running out of the room and stumbling down the stairs. He jumped the trick step and made it to the bottom. Stepping into the dining room he grabbed the twelve gauge with his right hand and the empty pistol with his left.

Aubrey saw his son reach for the weapons from the top of the stairs. "That's my gun you…" The words slurred out of recognition. Aubrey reeled back into his room finding his own loaded weapon and then set off down the stairs. Aubrey's foot hit the sixth step sending him crashing head over heels down towards the first floor.

For Peter there was no time to think. He couldn't run through the kitchen so he grabbed the handle to the front door, hit it with his shoulder and exploded out into the frosty night air.

Peter banked a hard right outside the front gate and escaped from view as Aubrey re-opened the door, pistol in hand.

"You better keep your trap shut Peter! I know where your mother lives!" The threat echoed off the houses in this tight cul-de-sac, he was sure that Peter heard him and was doubly sure that he understood. Aubrey could have chased him down and emptied the chamber into his back but an unplanned murder was strikingly hard to cover up. If his son knew what was best for him, he'd stay silent and keep his distance.

"Open the door Paul," Peter rounded the corner and dove into the car, "GO, go, go!" The tires ripped out beneath them scorching the air with a smell of burnt rubber.

"What happened? Did he catch you?" Paul saw that he had two guns but couldn't imagine that Aubrey would ever let someone escape his home especially after having stolen such important items.

"I out ran him, that's all, I…" Peter was tempted to tell them about the little girl. He should, it was the right thing to do but…

"Peter what happened?" Jodi asked from the back seat. She read the perplexed expression on his face to mean that all did not go as planned. Peter appeared spooked from something stronger than a fear of his father. "Peter?"

He pictured Kaitlin in his mind. That little girl was going to die in there. This was worse than all that he already knew of his Dad. His own flesh and blood had kidnapped and raped a child. Peter had to say something; he had to, didn't he? Then again, he heard Aubrey's last scream as he was running away 'I know where your mother lives!' The threat was an effective one. Even if he turned his father in to the police, the man would call his lawyer buddies and be out of jail a hour later with every intention of acting out his homicidal tendencies. Aubrey would kill his mother, his friends and save Peter for last. Whose life was more important? That little girl would be dead soon and Peter was still alive, he had to make a choice.

"Nothing happened, I got away. That's all."

Paul raced down Brockton's east side back roads heading for home, speeding towards the safety of Avon.

TRANSIENT
NIGHTMARES

CHAPTER 12

▼

"Maybe we can sneak you up to my room?" Becca placed the extra blanket on the neat pile of bedding Dutch had accumulated in the empty first floor apartment of her father's building. It sat in a neat line next to his pile of folded army fatigues, a backpack full of weapons and a copy of *Andrew Jackson* by *Robert Remini*. Lazio heard that Dutch was fond of former President Reagan but thought that with his trigger temper he might be more interested in reading about President Jackson. He had yet to open the book.

"No, I'll be fine." He assured her while sitting on the floor putting on an extra pair of socks.

"But with the wind-chill it's going to be in the teens tonight and there's no way to heat up this room."

"There is one way," He smiled shyly. Flirting was still a foreign tongue to him but maybe he could get used to it, with practice.

Dutch and Becca curled up together on the bedding and attempted to kiss. Their noses bumped head on.

"Ouch."

"Sorry."

"It's ok, really."

While she had a litany of boyfriends before him; Dutch never had a single girl-friend. Becca was the first girl he had ever kissed, the first girl he had ever hugged at any length and the first girl, hopefully, who might sleep with him though that was still hard to imagine. It had been an embarrassing start to their relationship with Psycho in full opposition to her acceptance as a team member. Dutch was torn between his desire to have a girlfriend and his responsibility to lead his team. They couldn't afford to have wedge issues between them, the team that is.

"They'll go after her when they want to hurt us." Psycho kept repeating the mantra to Dutch that "You can't have loved ones if we are going to be killing drug dealers for a living. The mafia, the gang bangers, they always go after your family." Maybe it was a Hollywood cliché but that was the only image they could picture clearly and then, if it were true, he would be putting her in danger. The future he had planned for the team almost guaranteed that trouble would always be a few steps behind.

The HAWKS Foundation was his creation. He intended to train a squad of suburban teenagers to fulfill the mandate by Ronald Reagan who proclaimed that illicit drugs must be removed from American society. They were soldiers in the war on drugs, well, they were going to be soldiers soon enough. They wouldn't be teenagers forever. Dutch started his own propaganda by reminding his friends every day that illegal drugs are chemical poisons that eat away at not only the bodies and minds of American citizens but also at their souls. "These narcotics are destroying the moral fabric of the greatest nation on earth, dissolving old glory like an acid." His eyes would glaze over with a hysterical euphoria and the team would wait until his sanity returned. John used to try to point out that Reagan had been out of office for a while now and that the war on drugs was metaphorical not literal but Dutch could not let go of that mandate. He came from a long line of soldiers who all went off to war but this time the war was here at home. He was committing his life to this purpose and he had plenty of good reasons that were a lot closer to his heart, reasons that were growing stronger with each school day.

Thus far in his short seventeen years on this planet Dutch had suffered the wrath of countless druggies. That's what he called them—Druggies, people who used and sold habit-forming chemicals at the expense of law and order. Some of these druggies had stomped on Dutch for *not* using, for *not* being a part of the crowd. He was an innocent victim, a person who stayed clean and always did the right thing. For this he suffered greatly. It started with his schoolyard brawl against Peter Truelson in Middle school all the way up to weekly fistfights with Joe, Matt and Rodger in High school. Dutch endured endless abuse against overwhelming odds all because he didn't use drugs. They had beat him, locked him in a bathroom, threw food at him, taunted him at every turn causing repeated humiliations, shot him and finally drove him to the brink of suicide.

It was then, hanging from the I-beam high above the high school gymnasium when he decided that it was time to fight back. What changed his mind was a comforting face in the crowd below that seemed to know his pain. It was a girl with brown hair and soft brown eyes who understood what he was feeling. The rest of the gym class thought he was pulling a stunt for their amusement but she knew his real intentions. He could never get her eyes out of his mind and yet he never found out who she was…

"It was you," He pulled his lips away and stared into those same soft brown eyes as if it was the first time he had ever really seen her.

"What? What's wrong?" She tried to lean in but he held the sleeves of her sweater tight and looked at her face trying to connect the fleeting spots in his memory. Back in school Becca had approached him about the team, she used to sit at the lunch table next to his and overhear his conversations. She had been in a couple of his classes and one of them was definitely gym.

"Two years ago I tried to commit suicide in the high-school gymnasium, I hung from the ceiling…"

She was nodding her head in recognition as if knowing what was going to come next. She remembered it clearly.

"But then I saw a face in the crowd," Now all the pieces were coming together. How could he never have figured this out before? It was her all along. "So that's how you knew so much about me."

Becca giggled but stopped herself as Dutch was having an epiphany and it needed to be respected.

"You understood what I was doing that day. But why?" He never got a chance to finish his sentence.

"They say that girls attempt suicide more often than guys but that guys are often more successful at it." She reached down to grip her covered forearms. Becca always wore long sleeves, even at school, even in the summer. He had never seen her dressed otherwise. Now she gripped her arms tight but he couldn't figure what she was doing. "My teenage depression earned me the attention of my father and a therapist but I think I always knew that I wasn't going to do it. You on the other hand," she tried to kiss his cheek but he stayed back. "When I saw you climb the wall. I knew you were going to do it but I'm so glad that you didn't."

Dutch's eyes felt heavy; he started to blink as the tears filled up from below his lids. "I think we should…" He didn't want her to see him cry. He wasn't sure what he was feeling? Gratitude? Shame? He had been known for his heroics, his talent for saving other people but no one had ever saved him before. How was he supposed to feel?

"It's ok I understand," Becca climbed to her feet. It was better to let him grasp this in his own the way like she had to when she was younger. "I should probably go to sleep anyway. I'll be back down at six thirty to wake you up."

"Ok," He held back the tears, he felt so stupid for letting his emotions get out of control. "I'll see you in a little bit."

"Goodnight James," She used his real name to separate this moment from the times when he was her superior officer. Right now they were just a couple kids dealing with life as best they could and hopefully, falling in love.

"Becca one last thing," He stood slowly and walked to her, his eyes never leaving hers. His hand reached out to gently grasp hers. He leaned forward and kissed her one more time with the most genuine sincerity that she had ever felt from him. His heart was racing out of rhythm; its beat took a steady thump, thump, thump like a person about to dive off a cliff into icy waters. It took all of his self-discipline to maintain his composure. The cold layers that hid away Dutch's emotional world flash melted for one brief moment of vulnerability.

"Um," Now it was Becca's turn to blush. She felt the fullest expression of his gratitude and perhaps just a little hint of admiration. "You're welcome...and...goodnight."

CHAPTER 13

▼

Dutch curled up under two layers of blankets often tucking his head underneath for long breaths of time to warm his face and ears. Eventually he'd run out of oxygen and have to pop back out into the stale cold of the unheated apartment. Massachusetts could be painfully frigid in January. This cold, when attacking an unprotected human body, would come in two waves. The first makes a person want to fall asleep, to hibernate away. The second wave causes unstoppable shaking, this is the nervous system's internal alarm used to force movement in the muscles so that they will warm just enough to keep the body alive. On this unforgivable night the blankets were not enough.

Dutch was freezing and could not keep his eyes closed. Born with a persistent sleeping disorder he thought he would never fall asleep under these conditions but what choice did he have? Three hours after Becca left for her warm upstairs apartment he curled up in enough comfort to let the first wave roll him into a strange semi-dream state fraught with constant jerks that forced his eyes open. He would pinch the tips of his ears to warm them and make sure he wasn't succumbing to frostbite while knowing that if he did fall asleep he may be severely damaged by the air around him. Luckily he knew a few tricks, as this was not the first time he had been forced out into the cold.

Being in such a strange location, so far from home and in bleak nearly inhuman conditions was making him constantly aware, vigilant of every second and perhaps more paranoid than usual. From where he lay there was only one window visible and twice on this night he could swear that he saw a figure pass by it. Was he dreaming or losing his mind? It could easily go either way. It seemed like the longer he stayed away from home; the more he was losing touch with reality.

But really, what was home? Ever since his parents lost their only house by falling behind on the mortgage, his roots left with them. What is home to a person without a place to come home to? Would he find solace on a couch in the living room of his parent's Middleboro apartment? Was it his Grandfather's spare cellar room that he missed so much? Was Avon, the town he had grown up in, his only true home?

Dutch had been away from his Grandfather's house for two months and away from Avon, for one very rough week. After sneaking out of Grandpa's back window in the middle of the night, clothes and equipment in hand, he traveled by foot to his best friend's house. Using a natural ladder built into a tree behind the old brown two level he snuck into the second floor bedroom of Thomas Charles Robbins, known by his friends as TC. Dutch continued attending high school classes in the daytime as if nothing had happened and TC brought up extra portions of food so he could scavenge his way through the nights. He didn't mind having Dutch as a temporary refugee. It gave them both someone to talk to, as their parents were not socially available. As much as it deepened their bond it was not enough to make up for their differences in personality.

Fed up with the atrocious condition of TC's messy bedroom Dutch couldn't help but to clean the pigsty from top to bottom. Big green lawn bags full of clothes, spare sneakers and old toys were sealed tight and stacked in the closet from floor to ceiling. He even had to expel three full bags of garbage, real waste, food, old drinks that had dried up and started to grow mold. These were nothing compared to the innumerable cardboard boxes from Jimmy's pizza shop and Styrofoam containers that once held greasy Chinese food. TC was a great and loyal friend but god was he a slob.

Dutch was uncomfortably cramped living in this bedroom but at least it was warm and he could ration himself from day to day. It worked until the first day of TC's new job at the Avon pizza parlor downtown. After becoming his very best customer Jimmy felt it was only right that he hire TC to make the food he so often consumed. On that first day of work Martha, TC's Mom, was in a very bad mood as her newest pair of Reeboks was mysteriously missing. While searching through the house, from room to room, she stopped at TC's bedroom door and heard noises coming from within.

Tommy was supposed to be at work, it was his first day. *Did he skip it? Did he quit already? Or, did he lie about having a job?* It was this last question that motivated her to throw the door open and scold her son.

"Thomas Charles Robbins you better...?"

There on TC's bed lay Dutch completely naked with his right hand pumping away as a 1970's porno played on an old Philco television atop the bureau. "Oh my god!" Dutch leaped to his feet as Martha slammed the door shut.

He slapped the TV button off and jumped to the other bed grabbing his clothes and sneakers up in his arms. Without even getting dressed Dutch tucked the clothes under one arm, opened the window and climbed down the tree to the backyard. He ran naked and freezing out into the woods.

When Martha caught her breath enough to calmly knock on the door a few minutes later there was no answer. She slowly opened the door hearing no noise at all.

"James? Are you in here?" Martha knew James very well but she didn't know he had been staying at the house. She was a little angry that he did so without her permission but then she took a good look at the bedroom. It was clean. From wall to wall desks were dusted, the rug was clear of obstacles, the trash was gone. It was startling. She couldn't remember the last time she had seen the floor.

"James?" She looked under the beds and at a pile of pillows in the corner but he was hiding very well. She then shut the open window. Martha didn't know about the ladder that circled down the tree outside so the idea that Dutch left via the window was possible but not a real consideration. He had to be here.

"James?" She circled the bureau and stood in front of the closet. "You can come out." Martha opened the bulging doors and a pile of garbage bags poured down on top of her like a tidal wave. "You damn kids!"

Meanwhile James made his way to the HAWKS summer headquarters, a well designed fort out in the woods. The fort was elaborately built up in a tree with latch doors, a fire pit and hinged windows but it was not suitable for a winter stay. He climbed to the roof and entered through a hatch putting on his clothes as quickly as possible. The plywood walls were a half-inch thick with no insulation. Dutch rolled himself up in a ball shocked and depressed. Here he pondered his existence.

This was the very bottom of his life, the lowest he could go or so he thought at the time. James Ballum spent one freezing night in the tree fort where he finally decided that it was time to take up Becca on her offer for him to sleep in an empty downstairs apartment in her father's building in Norwood. He had run out of options. No one wanted him here so he was off to another town. Norwood was a long trip from Avon for a person with no car but once again he was taking whatever opportunities he could to get out of the cold but the offer had its limitations. This brutal winter was not going to let him off easy.

"Thiiis was not such a goooood iiiideaa." His lips were shivering and he couldn't feel his nose. The blankets were not helping and he had run out of tricks. If Dutch stayed on the floor all night he feared he might not awake at all. He had to get warm no matter what. It was time to climb the stairs and spend the night in Becca's bedroom. She had already done so much for him and she just kept offering more. What was he afraid of? Her generosity was such a foreign concept. He was tempted to contest her sincerity, to be untrusting of benevolence but why continue on that path? She had no reason to hurt him and every reason to want to help. He could only conclude that Becca cared; she really cared, maybe she even loved him. It was about time he accepted her kindness and more importantly, her warmth.

CHAPTER 14

▼

"Can I come in?" Dutch was dangling from the outside of Becca's third floor window.

"Yes, are you crazy?" She reached down to grab the jacket near his elbows and pulled him up.

"I got it," He said stubbornly as he pressed his arm against the windowsill and pulled his bodyweight up so he could roll into the warm bedroom. He was elated to feel the thick heat pressing down on him. "That's so much better."

After climbing the stairs from the vacant first floor and failing to pick the lock of the main door he climbed out onto the roof and tapped at Becca's window. The small angled roof was covered in a thin layer of frost and Becca was fast asleep. Dutch leaned closer to the glass and tapped while poking his head into view. She rolled over and opened her eyes.

"Dutch?"

"Yes," Then he heard movement from the ground below; someone had run through the backyard beneath him. "Who the...?" He slipped on the roof and grabbed the windowsill hanging by his fingers before she opened it and helped him in. He told her that he thought some creep was peeking into the windows around the first floor apartment but he definitely saw someone run through the backyard.

"That's why you came up here?"

"An ex-boyfriend might be stalking you or us."

"The doors are all locked." She said while shutting and locking the window for good measure. "And I don't have any ex-boyfriends who live around here."

She waved off his paranoia and started peeling off the stiff fabrics that were clinging to his skin from six hours without any heat except the fading radiance of his own muscles. Dutch continued to shake uncontrollably as Becca stripped him to his underwear and tucked his body under the heavy blankets of her bed. As he tried to settle down she reached blindly under the covers for...

"What are you doing?" He asked as his eyes went wide. She was taking off his underclothes.

"I'm going to warm you up."

His heart thumped like a rabbit on speed as Becca peeled off his underwear and socks. She occasionally caressed his side or his head allowing his comfort level to rise. He was further embarrassed by the way his body was responding to her touch but at least the warm layers of blanket were hiding his astute attention.

Becca stood at the edge of the bed and watched him adjust himself before she removed her pajama bottoms. Her lower womanly form unraveled its silk skin revealing the slight of her hips and well...what was odd was that she would not discard her sweater but at this point he was not going to argue. It was the first time he had ever seen a girl mostly naked. Granted he'd previously looked at girly magazines and X-rated videotapes but this was different, she was real and now she was curling up her warm soft body into his embrace.

"You're still shaking?" They were spooning under the covers. Dutch's nerves were at their peak now that his patriotism was pressing against her curves.

"It's not from the cold."

"You'll be fine, I promise." Becca gently eased his hand up into her sweater and rested it on her breast.

"I'm feeling a lot warmer." He said trusting her acceptance.

"So am I." Her body urged back against him.

CHAPTER 15

▼

"Becca? Why is your door locked?" Becca's father banged away as the two threw off their blankets and stood on the mattress. Dutch was naked, Becca was half-naked and there was nowhere to hide.

"I'll be right there Dad," She grabbed her robe and wrapped it around her sweater while pushing Dutch into her closet under a thick wall of hanging clothes.

"Just stay quiet," She whispered through the crack of the door. Dutch curled up into a ball in its deep reaches and held his breath.

"Morning Dad," Becca swung the bedroom door wide open so he could see that her room was empty of occupants. "Sorry about the door, I must have locked it by mistake."

Dutch listened from within the interminable darkness. He was deliriously tired. They had only cuddled up an hour ago and suddenly it was time to get ready for school. His speeding adolescent clock never allowed a moment of real rest. Even now, in her closet, it was hard to keep his stinging eyes open or closed despite listening to fragments of the odd conversation between Becca and her Father.

"Did that little bastard Jeffrey ever call you back?"

"He wasn't a bastard Dad."

"He wasn't good enough for you," Mr. Loans was sitting on the bed next to his daughter but Dutch could only see her robe through the centimeter of space between the sliding doors. Was his hand on her lower back?

"Rebecca, now I know you'd tell me if one of these boys from school..."

"Dad! We are *not* having this talk right now!" She leapt off the bed and stood by the door. "If you'll excuse me I have to get dressed, I have to catch the bus."

Mr. Loans stood slowly leaning to one side; Dutch moved his eye to another crack in the door. Did her Dad just wobble? His body language was unsteady as he leaned against the doorway.

"Rebecca, you let me know if that Jeffrey comes back here and I'll give him so many lefts that he'll beg for a right," His hands punched at the air lacking any semblance of grace or practice. Clearly Mr. Loans was a big mouth, not a big fighter but he seemed to love his daughter, perhaps a little too much.

She closed the door behind him, waited with her ear against the wood for him to walk away and then silently locked it again.

Dutch climbed out of the clothing, knocking much of it off the hangers and sat on the bed next to her.

"Your Dad, is he a little…"

"Drunk. He might be."

Rubbing his pained, red eyes he considered if he should probe further. "Does he…I mean…he seemed a little frisky."

"I don't want to talk about it." She stared at the floor and then changed the subject. "Are you going to school today?"

"No, I'm pretty tired besides I have some HAWKS work to do."

"Like what?"

"Top secret."

"But I'm a member now. I completed the initiation. I even beat Lazio to the top of the warehouse. I should be included in what goes on."

"Becca, you're a junior member. Psycho, TC and I have been at this for two years, we have some long standing enemies to deal with and sensitive goals to work on. You'll be included to the degree that you prove yourself useful."

"But I know all about the gang wars."

He looked at her skeptically, "What do you know?"

"I know that the Boston Mafia is being investigated by the Feds because of something to do with corruption in the teamsters union. The mafia is losing control of certain neighborhoods so they are targeting gang leaders. Because of the killings the gangs are fighting over turf and we're in the middle of their territory."

"No, I'm in the middle of it." He corrected trying to keep the responsibility on his own shoulders but she did have her part to play. "I'm the leader of this team so they're going to target me."

She turned away. "I just want to help."

"I know you do. Look, you seem to understand this stuff well enough so...I do need you to help me with an important part."

"Like what?" Her eyes opened a little wider.

"Intelligence work."

"Meaning?" Now she absolutely sparkled with anticipation. *Intelligence work, that sounds dangerous.* Was she going to sneak into the police headquarters or act as a double agent? She grabbed his hand excitedly as he spoke.

"This gang war produces casualties, police reports, the kind of stuff that is printed for public record. I need you to read as many newspapers a day as you can, collect any pertinent information that might be gang related, especially if happens in Brockton or Avon."

"You want me to read the newspaper?" Her hand slackened along with her mood.

"It's important."

"Dutch we're all on this team, they might kill us just to get to you and the only useful thing I can do is to read the newspaper?" She crossed her arms feeling left out. "I thought I was going to be treated fair in this group?"

"You are being treated fair. It always sucks to start at the bottom and have to earn you're stripes but that's how it works. We run this team like the military, with discipline, loyalty and rules that *everyone* has to follow."

"Everyone?" She asked referring to Lazio.

"Lazio don't know shit," He assured her as his hand slid around her back to comfort her closer. "I promise..."

"Ok but I have to get going." She pulled away. "Some of us are still going to graduate."

"Fine."

"I hate to ask you this but I always keep my door unlocked so until he goes to work...could you..."

"I know, I know...back into the closet."

CHAPTER 16

▼

"Mom, I know, I don't care if he's mad. I'm still going to school so what does it matter where I live?" Dutch yelled into the red, plastic phone as he stood near its wall attachment in the kitchen.

Becca caught the bus hours ago but her Dad left for work only thirty minutes after Dutch woke up. He had dozed off in the closet and the confined space brought on a volley of nightmares. He sprung out of the hangers in a shutter forgetting where he was at first and then carefully checking to make sure the apartment was safe before he got comfortable.

After a bite of cereal, a quick shower and a few push-ups to get his heart pumping he picked up the phone to check in with his mother. She was living in her new apartment forty miles away in the town of Middleboro.

"I just want to make sure everything is ok with you that's all," His Mom's mannerism was of constant appeasement. She had an alcoholic husband so her daily job consisted of breaking up fights when he got sloshed. Often he picked a child or a neighbor as a target and Mom had to settle the peace. Oddly enough when he was sober he was the symbol of a decent, tax-paying citizen. He voted in every election, participated in Dutch's childhood events like soccer & basketball and made an effort to give his kids enough space to live their own lives. Only when he was liquored up did the demons from his past dominate his psyche. Dutch's Dad was only eighteen when his boots hit the jungle mud in Vietnam. He simply wasn't mature enough to contemplate the horrors of war so he never forgot them and every time he got blitzed, he would relive them in spades.

Upon further consideration maybe that's why Dutch held so much empathy with Becca? They were both the children of alcoholic fathers. The slight emotional similarities could very well have been the start of their bond. He shook out the thought and tried to concentrate on whatever his mother was babbling about.

"Your father wants you to come home."

"Home? You guys lost our house! I don't have a home anymore."

"James you know what I mean."

Dutch was resentful of their thoughtlessness. "No Mom, Middleboro is too far away."

"But James...hang on...what?" She was trying to cover the phone with her palm while Dutch's father said something in the background.

"James, your Dad says that you can finish school here at Middleboro High."

Dutch fell silent. Everything his parents did had a certain approach avoidance clause to it. They want him to move out there and yet he'd end up sleeping on the couch in the living room because they never planned for him to live with them at all. His exclusion from the family was understated. His parents wanted him to go out into the world on his own but they had never taught him any of the social or career skills that are necessary for such a difficult transition. At almost eighteen years old he knew that he wasn't yet ready to assume that responsibility. Maybe staying away for long stretches of time was an appropriate step towards independence.

"Ok, don't worry about it right now. Just as long as you stay in school then we're not going to argue."

"Good," He ran his index finger along his eyebrow smoothing out the little hairs as he thought of what to say next. "I'm staying with friends."

"We figured you were at Tommy's house."

"No, I'm staying at Becca's Dad's place in Norwood."

"And her Father is ok with that?" She asked skeptically.

"No but he's playing along."

"Ok, well...oh, I did have one thing I wanted to ask you."

"What?"

"Did you break into Grandpa's house last night? Someone broke in and we thought it might have been you, we thought you might have forgotten to take something with you."

"No it wasn't me Mom."

"You're sure?"

"Yeah, if I wanted to go back I'd knock on the door or I'd sneak in, I wouldn't break in. Why? Was anything stolen?"

"No, someone broke the lock to the back door and then went into your old room downstairs but that was it."

"Ok," He was stunned by the news but he didn't want her to catch wind of it. His Grandpa has guns in that house so if a burglar wanted to steal anything, then maybe that's what they were looking for? Then again, there was nothing of value in his old bedroom, nothing at all. "I'm gonna get going Mom. I'll talk to you later."

"Ok, we love you."

A silence followed.

"Um…Ok, bye." He hung up the phone and slumped into a chair. Someone had broken into his old bedroom at Grandpa's house. This confirmed his worst fear, the very thing that Damian had warned him about. In a letter sent from his youth detention facility it was Damian who explained in detail that Boston's La Cosa Nostra mafia was facing the strain of a teamster's related federal investigation. While the Feds were rounding up mob members, all the local street gangs had begun a turf war. In response to increasing threats from the lowest level, the mafia set out to eliminate the heads of each town's gang. Dutch was the leader of the HAWKS Foundation and that put him on their list. It didn't matter that the HAWKS weren't really a gang or that they didn't care about turf, all that mattered to the mafia was that the HAWKS were becoming well known in the media. They were visible and thus appeared to be larger and more influential than they really were.

His first reaction to such hyperbole was to scoff at the notion but why was it so unrealistic? Boston had a history of mob rule going back to the days of prohibition. From the Gustin gang in the 1920's to the North End mob of the 40's to the Winter Hill—Charlestown street wars of the 1960's, there has always been a seething underground in Massachusetts. Men like James 'Whitey' Bulger and Stephen 'the Rifleman' Flemmi were infamous household names. Every other family living here has a story about how the mob had once threatened a relative or muscled their way into a contract. Their very influence scared away the motion picture industry from filming in the area despite its rich history and natural beauty. The Mob was very real and no matter how insignificant Dutch felt he had to assume the worst.

This break-in confirmed Damian's hypotheses. A very careful and calculating individual was hunting him down. They left no note behind, no clues to follow or a reason to investigate as nothing had been stolen. This wasn't the work of a gang. Whoever broke into that house was looking specifically for him. It was one person, a quiet, cunning professional who didn't find what he was looking for. The timing was too distinct to be a coincidence.

Dutch bit down on his lower lip and let the pain fill him up with energy. The mafia threats were legit. They really wanted him dead. "I've got to hit them first!"

CHAPTER 17

▼

"There it is, a broken railroad tie in an alleyway, just like she described it." Dutch followed the path that Becca told him about and found the easy access window on the first floor.

He easily climbed down the wall and landed gracefully in the alley. "Time to find out for sure." Even the break in the window fit the image he had in mind. He squeezed through the hole, careful not crack any more glass and then snuck into the dusty warehouse.

Unbeknownst to them Becca and Lazio had risked their lives for two reasons. On the surface they were out to prove that they deserved to be called HAWKS but underneath the initiation Dutch and Psycho had sent them on a mission that might have proven fatal.

The warehouse was once a central shipping location for merchandise being sent out of Boston and heading towards locales in southeastern Massachusetts and Rhode Island. Dutch knew this because his uncle was a truck driver who stopped here several times a week to load up. His uncle was a kind, talkative and somewhat naïve member of Avon's large Ballum family. He did his job and never asked questions but he was righteous enough to refuse loose money when the mob started to float it around. However he was dense enough not to realize when they were lining his shipments with illegal products. As a kid Dutch often traveled with his uncle in the cab of the truck and heard the whispers of trafficking that leaked about in every truck stop and highway café. Dutch would sit there quietly, just a little kid sipping a cup of hot chocolate, listening while truckers would complain to his uncle about how they would like to push off the extra money but they needed it to pay the bills at home. They didn't want to drive truck forever; they hardly ever saw their families. During those countless trips a seed had been planted.

When Becca offered to let Dutch stay at her Dad's apartment building he first consulted with Psycho about the idea. Psycho had an elementary school friend, Lazio, who lived only a block away from there. Both of them lived a mere six blocks away from the old warehouse that had been condemned due to years of neglect. It was a perfect fit.

Dutch and Psycho set up an initiation intent on finding out if the warehouse really was empty or if the mafia was still using it as a storage space. Becca and Lazio would quickly discover if it had alarms or perhaps a couple of guard dogs. Apparently she came through with flying colors proving that there wasn't anything guarding the building, no sounds or colors so to speak, where as Lazio actually saw men enter the building talking about money and shipping products. That confirmed what Dutch believed all along, the warehouse was not abandoned, it was a black market storehouse, an illegal shipping locale for the Boston chapter of La Cosa Nostra. The very men who sent someone to Grandpa's house in order kill Dutch were right here in Norwood making the plans to do it. Well, that might be stretching it or maybe Lazio was exaggerating but that's why Dutch made a visit. It was time to find out.

Sneaking through a short hallway he carefully checked each empty room as he moved from one side of the bay to the other. He peeked inside the trucks, opened a number of cardboard boxes and noticed the tidy office door. This part of Lazio's story rang true. The door had several new locking devices and on the desk was a red blinking light. He couldn't break in and risk a silent alarm; it was possible that someone who lived by was responsible for killing rats, so to speak. Besides, they couldn't hide stolen merchandise in the office, it was too simply too small. Giving up on it he headed upstairs. The second floor was just as empty as the first. It was stacked with wooden pallets, broken machinery that hadn't been used in ages and piles of flattened cardboard boxes.

"It's a fuckin ghost town," He returned to the first level. The only room he couldn't get in was that damn office. He could see through the chicken wire lined glass but there was nothing incriminating. It held a metal desk, a table calendar from 1985, probably the last year that the warehouse was legally used, there were several pressed wood shelves stacked with old papers and one black safe on the floor.

"Too bad there's no way in." Dutch studied the door and all the surrounding edges trying to determine if the office had a weakness. Unfortunately it was the best built room in the entire building. "Figures," He kicked the bottom of the door and left back through the broken window.

On top of the railroad tracks Dutch walked along the rails until he was in sight of the train bridge where Becca and Lazio almost bit the dust. "I wonder," He stopped and looked down and to his left. "That hole in the wall must be right...under...here."

"He said the 23rd and no sooner." A deep voice rung out from underneath him in the empty concrete rooms that Lazio called Mideon. Dutch laid flat on the rails, certainly out of sight, as he listened to the argument below him.

"We don't have that kind of time, this is a fragile environment and it can't be used non-stop like this." The second man's voice was lighter, more articulate.

"What could happen?" The deep voice asked.

"It could collapse, all at once and then where will we be? Shit out of luck, that's where."

"It's not my decision so quit bitching at me about it, K? There's nowhere else right now."

Dutch crawled forward by inches until he could see down into the cavern but by then the two men had already left the rooms and took a right turn under the bridge heading towards Broadway Street. He was losing them.

He jumped to his feet and ran across the tracks. Through a few empty branches hampering his view he watched as the two figures exited the tunnel on the other side, climbed into a silver gray Lincoln continental and drove way.

"Can't see the license plate," He gave up on chasing it and turned back to the caves. They must have come out of the hole, could this be where the mafia was hiding...well...he didn't know what they were hiding but it had to be illegal. Why would anyone go through so much trouble to conceal it?

Dutch hung from a railroad tie and fell down onto the concrete block that was surrounded by a small pool of water. The dark crack in the wall had the same chilling effect on him this time that it had the first time he saw it.

"I won't be happy if I run into Baphomet," The chill burrowed itself into his clothes as he remembered Lazio's long story about how Mideon was based on a movie, and the movie on a book and the book on a myth that many people in the Witch community believe to be true. Baphomet was supposed to be the human-ish life form that the hidden freaks of the world consider to be god or rather a pagan deity older than God. Mideon was created by Baphomet as a place where the freaks could live in peace but the peace was always broken up by humans or naturals as they are called. Dutch didn't really believe the story but that didn't mean it made this any easier. He could be spooked just like anyone else and right now he was seriously debating about leaving the monsters alone. In his personal battle between fear and curiosity…

"I have to find out what's down there." Curiosity always won. He reached into the hole and felt the brick walls; they were wet and cold. Using his hands as guides Dutch crept into the darkness and felt his way down. The tunnel angled slightly but the angle got steeper the further he went. Then it suddenly leveled out and stopped hard. On the plus side he no longer felt the wind chill from up above but the chill in his bones was amplified by the hollow echoes that bounced like a ping-pong ball down this brick shaft.

"One dead end after another." He felt the solid wall in front of him but with no light and an odd smell forcing him to block his nose every few seconds. He was forced to give up his search.

"Fucking urban legends, they always end up being frauds." He crept back out into the gloomy light above. There were no monsters, no shipments, only a dead end cave, a locked office door and two suspicious men having a smoke. It wasn't what he hoped for but the day hadn't entirely been a waste. He had learned that Lazio is out of his mind but at least he's not a liar because Mideon was definitely a well of secrets.

Avon House
of
Gossip

CHAPTER 18

$$\blacktriangledown$$

"So I heard that Damian killed the family dog and his Dad tried to stab him with a broken bottle."

"Jimmy where do you get this crap?" TC chuckled as he set the last stack of pizza boxes on the edge of the metal sink.

"I have my sources."

"Whatever."

"Did you finish making those?"

"Yep," TC grabbed the cardboard pile so it wouldn't tip over and slid it carefully against the wall.

Jimmy stood in front of the counter with a smirk on his face and took one last look at the inside of his quaint but clean pizza parlor which was settled comfortably at the busy crossroads of downtown Avon. He was still not sure about TC's competence and started to wonder if it was smart to leave his new employee alone. "I'm going down to Big Jim's Liquors, can you hold the fort for a while?"

"What do you need at Big Jim's? I thought you stopped drinking?" Tommy stood up from behind the counter. While the smooth surface reached most people's chest, it only barely hid Tommy's waist. With scrubby short brown hair and a constant five o'clock shadow it was hard to tell that he was only nineteen years old. One thing was for sure as long as Tommy stood behind the counter the pizza parlor was safe from intruders but it may not be safe from TC. As the clumsy but gentle pagan dimwit of the HAWKS his kind nature was counter to his appearance. With tattered hand me down clothes that barely fit his bony frame he looked like an angry mountain giant who was having a bad hair day.

"I'm just meeting someone and if I choose to drink anything it's none of your business." Jimmy directed him with a calm smile. He knew that behind Tommy's lanky yet menacing exterior was one of the noblest people he had met in this town. TC always meant well and most importantly he could be trusted provided his magnetism for trouble remained deactivated. Luckily the catalyst for most of his trouble, his best friend Dutch, was nowhere to be found so in theory the pizza parlor should remain intact for at least a couple hours.

"Whatever dummy," Tommy swept a clean rag over the counter in a circular motion. "Go ahead, go get you're drink on, I won't tell anyone."

Jimmy scuttled out the door as a police car pulled up in front of the store. Being that the police station was across the street, this was a common occurrence.

"Oh great my first customer." Tommy leaned on his elbows resting his face in his hands.

The bell dinged as officer Gillman flung open the door, took one wide step, stopped just short of the counter and stared slightly down at the HAWKS tallest member.

"It's about time you got a job but Jimmy is a fool to leave you alone. Did he lock the register?" Officer Gillman's eyes ran over the whole store as he spoke. His deep voice was as insulting as it was intimidating.

Tommy gave a compliant smile. "Can I get you anything? Some cheese perhaps?" To ease the effect TC stood to his full height and looked Gillman eye to eye.

"It's been a few months since you and you're buddies broke into that house up on Crown Street."

Tommy made no movement to acknowledge guilt or innocence. His was a calm plain stare born of hundreds of hours relaxing in inspired meditations that taught him to ease his soul in times of stress or in front of cops. He could feel his spiritual power welling up within him preparing for a grilling. "Is this official business?"

"TC, that's what they call you right?" Gillman asked with derision as Tommy's confidence started to melt away. "TC and Dutch and Psycho, that's what's left of your gang isn't it?"

"We're not a gang," TC bit his lip. He didn't want to say anything but Gillman drew him in. How did he know so much? How did he know their nicknames? The HAWKS did break into that house but Damian took the fall for the team and no one knew that the rest of them were involved. It hadn't been planned that way but it worked out so that only one of them went to juvie.

"Do you realize how much trouble Dutch is in? James Ballum's fingerprints were all over a shotgun we found in the woods. Possession of any illegal firearm will earn you one year in prison. That may also have been the weapon used at the Crown Street murders. More over, that was a stolen weapon registered to Aubrey Truelson of Brockton. Our detective talked to Mr. Truelson who said he would be happy to press charges when we find young James." Gillman let his threat hang in the air as the bell dinged behind him.

"Hey Lucy," Tommy waved to Dutch's younger sister.

"Hi Tommy."

Gillman turned his head and watched her walk around the corner with her new boyfriend towards the Ninja Gaiden video game at the back of the room. He didn't seem to know who she was or at least he didn't seem intent on questioning her the way he was Tommy. Lucy was a Ballum and being such she was part of a family that had a lot of pull in town so unless Gillman could justify his actions it was better to investigate the HAWKS and especially James Ballum under the radar.

"Those fingerprints may implicate him for murder." Gillman lowered his voice a little. He was especially menacing when he knew he had someone on the ropes.

"Are you sure I can't get you anything?" Repeated TC with no emotion. "A large mushroom perhaps? A small dead fish?"

Gillman ignored his passive clowning; he knew TC was bothered by the news. He leaned in so that Lucy couldn't hear, "Your buddy Gary is in a Boston jail, your pal Damian still has five months in the Brockton youth correctional facility and your best friend James may be implicated in a murder. As soon as he comes back to this town, I'll have him and then you'll be next."

Gillman had always suspected that TC was the leader of the HAWKS despite evidence to the contrary. It had a certain logic to it. TC was older, he was larger than the other kids, he looked over twenty one and that alone gave him access to guns or alcohol or whatever it is the HAWKS were into. Gillman based his negative gang model on his own adolescent experiences never contemplating that the HAWKS could be anything other than mindless criminals.

Tommy swallowed hard and spit out the only refrain he could think of, "What makes you think he'll ever come back?"

Gillman opened the door and stood against it before answering, "James Ballum has lived his whole life in this town. His parents grew up here, his grandparents own several houses. He is as much a part of Avon as it is a part of him. He won't be able to stay away. In fact, I *guarantee* he'll come back."

CHAPTER 19

▼

Lucy playfully bumped her hip against her new guy friend as they played Ninja Gaiden at the back of the pizza parlor.

"You're no match for my skills…I'm Ryu," His voice fell off into a mumble as his ninja engaged in combat.

"Right," Lucy lightly elbowed him forcing his hand off the joystick long enough for him to take one too many blows. "I'll kick your ass with girl power and steal the dragon sword," Lucy chuckled as the enemy killed his ninja.

"No you didn't just do that," Stepping back he stood directly behind her and waited for the right time to trip her up.

"Don't you touch me. Hey, I'm busy here, I have to become the ninja dragon and avenge my father's death. This is serious business." Lucy tucked her elbows tight against her sides and tried to concentrate on keeping her ninja alive.

He ran his dark hands down her thin pale white shoulders, along her arms and onto the small of her back. At first he ran his fingers through her straight brown hair giving her a sense of ease as he planned his next move.

"Don't do it," She warned bracing for the tickle.

"I ain't done nothing," he waited for her to get near two enemy ninja's that were particularly lethal.

"No!!!" Lucy squirmed as he slipped his fingers up under her arms and then down along her sides. No matter which way she twisted Lucy couldn't stop the tickle. "My guy's going to die. Oh no!!!"

It was over as soon as it had begun. Lucy's mighty ninja had fallen at the sword of his enemies. Lucy spun around looped her arms around his neck, pulled him close and then licked his cheek.

"Yuck," he pulled away wiping his face with the sleeve of his shirt. "That was nasty, you ain't no ninja dragon, you're just a weird chick that lives in a town with only three roads."

"Avon has more than three roads." She tried to tickle him back but he was holding his breath and tightening all of his muscles.

"No, North main, East main and West Main, Avon has three roads."

"Whatever," She gently punched his gut, "you can't count anyway."

"Oh yeah, I know how many nipples you have and I'm going to twist them off."

"No!" Lucy squirmed out of his reach and they wrestled up against a table until a glass saltshaker rolled off and fell on the floor with a clink.

"Are you guys going to order anything?" TC yelled from the front of the store. He had watched the tickling and the licking in the large corner mirror before deciding to veer them away from anything more carnal or potentially messy. He did not want to watch his best friend's little sister make out with some strange guy while busting up the pizza shop.

Lucy and her friend sauntered up to the counter. As they faced TC he suddenly recognized who her friend was. Tall, dark skin, a friend of Peter Truelson, it had to be…He was about to say his name out loud but wanted to make sure he was right. Does Lucy know who he is?

"Tommy I'm so proud of you." She taunted him.

"Why?"

"You got a job."

"Very funny."

"So…" She paused for a second, "Have you heard from my brother? He's been gone a while. My Mom's worried."

"I…" TC looked at her friend and decided that Dutch's whereabouts would have to wait. "I don't know. I mean, I haven't heard from him. Have you?"

"No, Grandpa was upset that he left like that. My whole family thinks he's running from the mob or something ridiculous but then someone broke in Grandpa's house last night so…" Her sentence faded away. She thought it was all ridiculous. Why would her brother be running from the mob? He liked to talk tough but that was giving him way too much credit.

TC decided that it was a good thing she wasn't willing to believe the truth. Again he looked back at her friend, "He's running from a lot of people."

The guy gave TC a curious glance. Good, thought TC, this kid doesn't know anything.

"So where are you guys off to now?" He hinted that he didn't want people hanging around if they weren't going to buy any food. The pizza parlor had a bad reputation for attracting crowds of teenagers who could get a little rowdy after too many of them accumulated. One kid got stabbed right in front of the store. It was a huge gossip story for months. The wound was minor but if you asked any-one around town they'd describe a gory scene with bodies all over the street. That was how the grape vine worked around here and it usually started at the pizza shop.

Tyrone stepped to the door and TC nodded. He wanted to show Jimmy that he could be trusted if left alone at the shop. A shortage of penniless teens would prove that he could take charge when needed. A safe empty shop was better than a packed powder keg.

"Um," Lucy shrugged her shoulders and looked to her friend. "We're gonna meet some friends for drinks." She told TC.

"She's like fourteen dude," TC warned him.

"Fifteen," Lucy corrected.

"Whatever," The guy turned around and opened the door. He was tired of being dissed by this Ichabod Crane looking, pizza making fool. Lucy followed but before the door shut TC said a bold farewell.

"See you later Lucy and you watch yourself…Tyrone."

CHAPTER 20

▼

"So you're actually going to do this?" Bill Griffin was beside himself as he sat in a rusted folding chair in the third floor of a pale green house on East Main Street in Avon. Peter and Paul sat across the kitchen table wearing matching black trench coats. They were intent on recruiting for a revival of their small town gang, Peter said it was time that they expanded their operations and he had a plan on how they were going to do it.

"We need to know that you'll have our backs when we pull this off." Peter's voice was always intimidating but now he spoke with a sense of purpose. It helped that his new 11-87 shotgun was leaning against the wall next to him, a symbol of his courage. This plan of theirs was enormous, intricate, so much bigger than anything these friends had ever done before. Most importantly, it was so much more dangerous.

Bill shifted his overweight form in the chair looking down at a cockroach scuttling into a slit behind the stove. Peter was worrying him but he knew why, "Pete, I've only ever seen one other person talk the way you are right now. I've only seen one kid who thinks like this, like he can control people and warp the world to his sense of justice."

Peter knew who Bill was talking about, "Don't you dare say his name!"

"Fine but let me tell you this Pete, you are just as fucking crazy as he is! Messing with a Brockton gang? Stealing their members and…"

"Are you ditching us?" Paul asked with his eyes locked on Bill who was shifting uneasily in the creaking chair. The truth is that Bill never had the same twisted aspirations as his friends. He didn't mind getting high or drinking once in a while and maybe they would shoot aluminum cans in the woods or hang out watching gangster videos but these guys took it too far. Sure Scarface is a good film but you don't try to emulate it! The Godfather is entertainment for the masses not scripture for the criminally insane. These are movies not recruitment tools, why couldn't they tell the difference?

Two years ago when Peter shot James Ballum in the chest with a shotgun at point blank range and then tried to bury him, that was when Bill started to grow weary of his friends. Suddenly the on-screen characters came to life right in front of him. Peter and Paul wanted to run with the gangs or worse yet, join the mafia itself. This was all crazy talk and yet here he was trying to escape from their hooks. Granted Bill didn't know what he wanted to do with his life but he was sure that this was not it.

"I don't think I'll be of any use. I don't have…"

"You don't have the fucking balls, that's what you don't have! You have sympathy for the enemy!" Paul stood and leaned towards Bill who leaped to his feet and backed away towards the door.

"Yeah, well you sound like the enemy." Bill shot back as he stepped further away.

"Come here you fuck!" Paul showed the pistol tucked in his pants.

"Paul, that's enough!" Peter stopped his best friend and stared at Bill for moment before letting him off. "Bill, we've all had some fun together. I know this sounds intense but it's been in the works a long time. You can't say you didn't see it coming?"

Bill nodded and shrugged. He was softening to the rhetoric but could he actually do this? He had never wanted to be a gangster. They were becoming adults, wasn't it time for the games to end?

"I want to give you one last chance to join us. This is our big move and we want you to be a part of it. What do you say?"

Bill's eyes flickered back and forth from Peter to Paul trying to gauge their level of restraint, "I'm sorry."

"You fucker!" Paul spat at him.

"No, it's ok." Peter held the table steady. "We don't have any grudge against you just so long as you don't mention our plans to anyone."

"No problem Pete, I don't want any part of it."

"Good, Paul let him out…oh, and Bill if you happen to see Chris…"

"I won't see Chris. He moved last month to Randolph to be closer to Regina and he's leaving for the Navy two weeks after graduation. He's long gone."

Peter nodded to the news as Paul begrudgingly opened the door. Bill was walking away from a group that had been together since they had graduated from

Crowley Middle School. He never imagined it would come to this. At some point in high school, everything changed. Peter and Paul dropped out in the ninth grade, Bill in the tenth and only Chris was going to graduate. Amongst the rubble of family hardships, street fights and drug use, the friendships had passed away. Peter and Paul were moving downward, focusing their aggressive tendencies in ways that might make some fast money or earn a little respect but it would probably get them killed. Worse yet, they were certain to kill others.

There was a knock at the door only minutes after Bill exited.

"I've got it," Jodi darted out from her bedroom and grabbed the knob. "Hey guys come on in." Jodi wrapped a big hug around Lucy and moved a chair aside for Tyrone.

"Well, well, well," Peter eyed his dark skinned former party pal and offered him a seat. "Tyrone it's funny that you stopped by, we just happen to have a proposition for you."

Tyrone knew this crew, he had hung out with them before but much like Bill he was scared away the night that Peter shot James. Tyrone was a fringe member of Brockton's Spring Street Posse, the city's largest gang, so he wasn't afraid of Peter and Paul but he certainly knew what they were capable of.

Lucy and Jodi scampered off into the other room to finish off a calzone and sip a mixed drink. Tyrone sat at the table crossed his arms and gave Peter and Paul a look of deep skepticism. "This better be good."

CHAPTER 21

▼

"You've got to be kidding me." TC only had two orders the whole night and they were both take out so the store was empty. Jimmy had yet to return from his journey to Big Jim's, which coincidentally was less than two miles away. Then again this is Avon, at only four square miles everything in town is less than two miles away.

Throughout the night fascinated gossipers who had set off that cowbell felt compelled by curiosity to ask about James Ballum. The HAWKS had been the subject of a second Avon Messenger front-page story concerning a rash of break-ins around town. In the article TC had been asked if the HAWKS had anything to do with the recent crime spree but he stumped the reporter with his own question, "What was stolen from these houses?"

The answer was that nothing had been stolen. Regardless, there was little else to talk about worthy of a headline. The rest of TC's questions had to do with the October investigation of an abandoned town kennel on Crown Street. It was now known as the 'Avon Wolfhouse' and was fast becoming a suburban legend complete with werewolf tales and rumors of HAWKS participation in the murders. Officer Gillman might have had a hand in spinning some of these stories but TC denied knowing anything about it. He repeated over and over that he didn't know where James Ballum could be.

Standing bored at the counter TC just once wanted a customer to come in who was absent of knowledge about the lurid tales. Alas, he would have no such luck.

Two black trench coats flashed by the front plate glass just a second before Peter and Paul burst into the shop.

TC stood calm before them giving the same emotionless expression he afforded Officer Gillman and all the other gossips. "Can I help you?"

"You're going to answer some questions for us," Paul said with his finger pointed at TC's face.

TC let out a shallow sigh. "Ok," he said with no emotion. He might as well play along. After fighting off reporters, the police and all his neighbors, he was simply too tired to keep it up.

"Yeah and you're *gonna* answer our questions," Peter threatened patting the side of his trench coat.

"I already agreed to answer your questions."

"Right, cause you're *gonna!*" Paul snarled at him.

"Right I already said I would." TC's eyebrows tightened over his eyes. "Are we doing a comedy routine? Ask away retards, what the hell do you want to know?"

Peter and Paul glanced at each other. They hadn't expected him to be so accommodating; it took all the steam out of their tactical bullying.

"Tell us where James Ballum is!" Peter demanded.

"He's in Westwood."

"What?" They glanced at each other again. TC gave them an answer. Again, they hadn't planned for that.

"Where is Westwood?" Paul barked back at him.

"It's northwest of here I think. It's closer to Boston somewhere."

Again they looked at each other. What the hell should they do now? TC told them what he had been keeping from everyone else. He let the cat out of the trap and handed it to two of Avon's most notorious idiots.

"Where in…Westwood…is he staying?"

"Key Street."

"What number house?"

"2132."

Paul was getting frustrated with all these straightforward answers. TC had to be lying. He turned towards Peter and whispered, "Why would he tell us all of this?"

"I don't know, how can we confirm it?"

"Let's ask for a phone number?"

"He doesn't have one," TC said over their whispers. He was standing at a high angle and the store was very quiet so he could hear everything they said. "James is squatting in an empty apartment. He has no phone, no heat, no food and no money. You might as well just wait for him to come back because I don't think he's going to last all that long."

"Sure," Peter felt like he was catching on, "Why are you telling us all of this?"

"Why?" TC smirked and stared down heavily at them, "Because I don't think you dimwits can read a map."

"Oh yeah," Peter shot back, "But we can definitely pull a trigger." He opened one side of his trench coat to reveal that he was holding a shotgun next to his leg.

"Nice," TC complimented. "It would be even better if you had some ammo huh?"

"What?" Paul was dumbstruck. "How the hell did you know...?" He stopped himself but Peter had taken up the same shock.

"Well maybe you'll listen to this." Paul pulled out the pistol but kept it low.

"Needs a clip right?" TC asked.

"Who told you that?"

"Jodi was in here earlier getting a calzone. You forget Peter this is the Avon pizza parlor; no rumor is too small. Jimmy hears about everything that happens in this town and now so do I."

"You son of a..." Paul never got to break into his expletives as Jimmy opened the door behind them. They stuffed the guns back into their trench coats.

"Hey Peter, Paul you guys here for dinner?" Jimmy asked them both with a wink and a knowing grin.

"No thanks Jimmy, not as long he's making the food," Peter responded as he grabbed the door.

"Yeah Jimmy, as long as Tommy's smelling up the pizza's you can count me out." Paul said as both of them slid back out into the night.

"Tommy," Jimmy walked around the counter and stood in behind the register, "If I'm going to lose Peter and Paul as customers then I may have to keep you working here for a long time." He laughed as he counted the drawer. "So what did they want?"

"They wanted to know where James is?"

"Did you tell them?"

"I gave them the wrong address." TC handed him the balance sheet.

Jimmy started counting the change as he shifted to his favorite subject. "So I heard a rumor over at Chapman's warehouse."

"I thought you went to Big Jim's?"

"I went a few places. Do you want to hear this?"

"Yes, what?"

"Those break-ins around town. My friend Mario says he saw the person who is doing them."

"So who is it?"

"He said it was dark out but he spotted orange hair and a green Boston Celtics jacket. The vagrant was under six feet and knew his way through the backyards." Jimmy stopped counting and looked up at TC, "He was 80% sure that it was Gary Collins."

For the first time that night TC's face showed real surprise, it was that jaw opened dumbstruck expression he was so famous for but this was truly the right moment for it. The Boston police department had arrested Gary Collins, one of the original HAWKS, for his part in an assault on one of their patrolmen. He got little leniency for being under the age of eighteen and that meant two years in jail. So far he had only served a few months. TC burst through the bubble of his previous silence, "But that's impossible."

Jimmy shrugged, "From what I hear, he's already the prime suspect."

The Worst Day
Of his
Life

CHAPTER 22

▼

"Hey watch it fucker!" Dutch yelled at Rodger as they bumped into each other in the doorway of Mr. Cudmore's second period social studies class.

"Why, you got a weapon on you Dutch?" Rodger teased him knowing that several people were looking on. "Dutchy-poo, what are you going to do?"

Dutch had made the mistake of having his code name etched in the back of his black jacket. Now everyone knew what he was calling himself and how seriously he was taking his gang. His black jacket read Dutch in Orange letters arcing across the back while his left shoulder had the HAWKS trademark letters HKS. Thank-god he left off his rank of 'General.' That would have been a hazing nightmare as if high school wasn't bad enough already.

"I'll throw you out another window asshole." Dutch reminded him of a previous struggle they had in the windowsill of a third floor math room.

"I never did repay you for that," Rodger, who stood a full four inches taller than Dutch, dropped his bag and grabbed Dutch by his jacket. Dutch struggled back against the bigger kid but his own knapsack went flying and something inside smashed as it hit the floor.

"Feel the love you two," Mr. Cudmore slid in between the students and calmly broke them apart. A short, deeply peaceful man with a bushy white mustache he had the innate ability to sooth high spirits when needed. "Rodger, off to your next class. James, please get your bag and take a seat."

Dutch could feel the rage building up inside him. He knew he shouldn't have come to school today. It had started off bad and just kept getting worse. First he fell asleep on the bus and Becca had trouble waking him when the bus broke down. His eyes were stinging red, his mouth felt like cotton. After the transfer to a new bus they weren't allowed to sit together so he sat alone swatting away spit-balls that were coming from some jerk in the back seat. He knew who was shoot-ing them but Dutch just slid under the height of the seat seething and plotting. It was always the same group of miscreants who pulled this kind of shit. He knew them well. There was Joe, the football player on steroids, Matt the white trash former hockey player and Rodger an oversized stoner who followed the others. In the same way that Peter and Paul were his street enemies, Joe, Matt and Rodger were his in school tormentors. One day he would get his revenge and judging by his growing temper and inevitable decline in inhibitions that day was coming soon.

Rodger and Dutch broke off and did as they were told. Rodger disappeared into the flow of the hallway as James sat in the third row, middle aisle right behind Angela Virtue. She knew what it was like to get hacked on because of her name. She's been rebelling against it for as long as he knew her. As soon as he sat down she turned to face him. Angela had soft brown eyes and a constant smile though she couldn't seem to make up her mind what color her hair was supposed to be. Right now it was ash brown on top with sandy blonde underneath.

"You shouldn't let him get under your skin." She offered up a kind nudge with her elbow.

"Right now I'd rather nobody tells me what I should or shouldn't be doing." He snapped back but she wasn't offended instead she frowned. These electrical shop kids were torturing Dutch one day at a time and it had been nearly three years. Angela had seen some of it first hand and would always defend him but if there was any true deterrent to their behavior it was not apparent. He always fought for himself but they seemed to enjoy it. The other option was to give in but if he ever did such a cowardly thing he had a feeling they'd make him regret it. He's their toy, the sole source of their demented power trip and he had no right to stop their fun. Angela tried to comfort him.

"I think that you are better than they are."

"I know I'm better than they are. Once a druggie always a druggie." He snapped self-righteously.

"That's not true. Experimenting is a phase, it's harmless…"

"Bullshit. You guys are never going to stop. After you've left high school and moved on to the real world you won't know how to deal with anything because all you ever did was hide from your problems. As adults you'll probably take even more pills than you do now. Except maybe…" He struggled for clarity, "Maybe a doctor will prescribe them but it will still be drugs."

Angela was undisturbed by his rancor, "Do you feel better now?"

"A little."

"Good but now you need to rise above this hatred, it's only going to tear you apart from the inside. How other people conduct their lives shouldn't bother you so much." Her pep talk fell on deaf ears.

"Whatever," Dutch opened his social studies textbook, linked his fingers together across the page and rested his head on his hands. "This is never going to end." He mumbled.

She heard him and was trying to think of some way to get through to him when Mr. Cudmore gathered the class's attention.

"Good morning young grasshoppers," He gleefully swooned. "Now if you'll open your books to…"

Dutch's attention remained internal. He wasn't intentionally trying to be mean to Angela but he knew all about her illicit after school activities. She partied with his tormentors on occasion so he couldn't help but to think that she was protecting them as much as she was helping him. Angela is a druggie and even though she was cute and kind and reasonable, it didn't matter. All druggies are evil! They all hide some type of depravity behind their outward social mask so she was no different. She simply had a prettier mask than most. In his reasoning druggies hid their secrets and she was a druggie so she couldn't be trusted. Since so many people used drugs in high school this greatly limited his array of possible friends. Then again that's why he had the HAWKS. They were clean, drug-free and honest. They alone would have to be enough, a community unto themselves.

Under the weight of his own exhaustion he drifted off to sleep, his head on the open book. Every couple minutes he'd flash awake but keep his head low. In these flashes Dutch started scribbling in the back of his notebook. Three years of torture, that was his motivation. Starting today he decided that revenge on the largest possible scale had to happen before he graduated. With only a year and a half left his time was falling away fast. Atop the page he scribbled 'Master Plan' and proceeded to list his targets. This would take ingenuity, assistance and money. He would have to use the HAWKS to their fullest potential in amassing the weapons, training and execution of this plan. The sudden, brutal death of several of his druggie classmates could very well be his greatest accomplishment, now all he needed was…

"Mr. Ballum?" Mr. Cudmore addressed Dutch as the bell rang.

Dutch covered the paper with his hand, "Yes?"

"You're leaking."

"I'm what?" Dutch went to stand but as he did he noticed the orange pool of liquid that enveloped the dirty white floor beneath his desk. It was orange juice.

The small bottle he had stored in his bag for lunch had smashed when Rodger grabbed him. The entire class stood to see what the teacher was talking about. The pool of orange directly under his chair made it look like he had pissed his pants. A couple people snickered but most brushed him off and left the room at the bell.

Dutch had the humiliating job of cleaning it up as another class slowly filed in with a whole new wave of stares and snickers.

Why? Why was it never one small problem but rather a litany of compounding irritations? Why can't it be simple, or just? Why can't the punishment for sins committed equal the sins themselves? Dutch felt his face well up with color as the stinging of his tired eyes begged for tears to fall. The paper towels from the teacher's desk were running out and not getting the job done.

"You might want to get a mop from the janitor." Mr. Cudmore pointed to the doorway. "Make it quick son."

CHAPTER 23

▼

"I'm not going to talk to him, not even for a moment," John was showing a much higher level of personal worth than Psycho was used to seeing. "Dutch is psychotic, he's thinks he has me caught in his net of fallacies but I'm my own man. I'm not a HAWK anymore and nothing you say can get me back on that team."

"We have two new members," Psycho assured him. "We have a girl on the team." He watched John's reaction of disappointment. Psycho was hoping he might see something else. "We're not desperate for muscle John, we need your mind. You're smart, you're honest. You keep us on track…"

"On track?" John's thick glasses slid down his nose as he yelled at Psycho hell bent on proving his independence. "You're going to get her killed. Two of your members are in jail. Dutch is wanted by the Avon police. He's being hunted by the Spring Street Posse and is probably on the hit list of the Boston mafia. If you consider this to be 'on track' then I don't want any credit for it."

The two friends were standing outside the door to the graphic arts department in the acoustical hallway of the bottom level of Blue Hills high school. John had been actively avoiding Psycho and Dutch for the past couple months but Psycho had finally caught up with him. Now anyone walking within fifty feet could hear his displeasure.

"John how did you know that?" Psycho whispered him down. John was a new member when the dead body was found and yet still a neophyte when they exposed the murders at the wolfhouse. He was never let in on current information and yet he seemed to know more than Psycho did. "Where did you hear all of this?"

"The newspapers. You guys are the most misinformed," John wanted to swear at him but he wasn't mad at Psycho he was mad at himself for looking up to these guys in the first place. "The Brockton Enterprise wrote all about the wolfhouse and then mentioned the HAWKS in an article on local gangs. No doubt they snagged that info from the Avon Messenger. Oh and by the way you might want to tell Dutch that the Soviet empire has fallen so his dream of being a part of World War three is gone, it's over. It's time for you guys to come back to reality."

Psycho was quiet throughout the whole spasm of angry news. He didn't know what to say, John was right about everything. "He gave up on that. Dutch knows that we're not going to be invaded by the Russians."

"It took him an awful long time to figure it out."

"Look, Dutch is focused on the druggies, especially the ones in this school. He realizes that innocent students won't be safe until some of these dealers are nabbed but you're right he is out of touch and he does go too far. John, this is why we need you on the team. If anyone can ever talk Dutch down from the tower, it's you. He listens to you, just give him a chance and…"

"No, absolutely not, no fucking way! I'm out and if you're smart you will leave too. The HAWKS are as much a danger to themselves as they are to everybody else."

"But we're the good guys." Psycho said as if it should be obvious.

"Tim, you've labeled half the school as being druggies. It's easy to be the good guy if you get to decide who's right and who's wrong. You're *not* the good guys and I'm not one of you." John opened the door to the Graphic arts department and stopped. "Look…I don't have anything against you."

"I know."

"Just do one thing for me."

"What? Name it, anything."

"I'm guessing Becca is the new female member?"

Psycho hesitated to respond so John knew he guessed right.

"Tim, get her off the team in any way that you can, no matter what it takes."

That was what Psycho wanted to hear. "Because she's a girl, she shouldn't be a warrior?"

"No you dolt. There have been women warriors since the beginning of recorded history. The Japanese had female ninjas, the Russians in World War two had female snipers, that's not the issue."

"Then why do you want her off the team?"

"Because she's in love with Dutch."

Psycho cringed but tried not to show it.

"Tim, she's going to overcompensate for her lack of skills by trying to be more daring than any of you. She's going to kill herself trying to impress Dutch. You don't want her death on your hands. Get her off the team."

John left him standing in the hallway. Maybe he had said just enough to cast a doubt in Psycho's mind. Maybe the unfortunate future of the HAWKS could be averted if John kept plugging away at its false premises. Maybe he could stop them from ending up like Gary and Damian or worse. To save the HAWKS from themselves would be the ultimate heroic act and no one would ever need to know that he did it. Now that's stealth justice.

Psycho lowered his head in frustration and walked away feeling defeated.

CHAPTER 24

▼

Dutch raced to his next class, Science, where once again he slept but this time much more deeply at the back of the room. He had performed well during the first semester in this class so the teacher cut him some slack and let him rest. It was a useful trick to know that teachers with large classes often judge a student more by their first impression than their continued achievements. This allowed a lot of people to coast.

Forty-five minutes passed in a flash and the bell rang like a gun shot jolting Dutch to his feet. Strangled by clouded urgency he darted out of the room racing to his locker. Rodger had felt the knife under his jacket during the earlier altercation in the doorway so Dutch had to hide it. During the three minutes between classes when everyone is hustling through the hallways he unclipped the military belt that held his survival knife firmly underneath his armpit, tucked it behind a pile of books and locked the door with his alternate padlock. He bought this lock at the Avon hardware store in case the janitor got any bright ideas. It looked like the normal assigned combination lock except it had a keyhole in back that required a small key to be inserted or it wouldn't work at all. Dutch had rid himself of the knife to keep himself safe from teachers but this left him completely unarmed while still deep within hostile territory.

Dutch next had a technical drawing class held at the Graphic arts department. He was walking across the bridge and soon would be climbing down the staircase where his three biggest enemies were plotting.

"I think he's carrying," Rodger told Joe and Matt at the bottom of the staircase.

"He doesn't have the balls," Joe assured him while craning his neck. His bulging trapezious nearly reached his ears if he flexed hard enough. Joe was feeling antsy. He just had a special 'meeting' in the bathroom of the electrical shop with a senior friend. After these meetings he was always ready for a good fight. He told people that it kept him feeling aggressive, like a wild animal, an attitude that was encouraged by his coach.

As far as the football coach was concerned, beating on a kid like Dutch was simply survival of the fittest. This lame misuse of Social Darwinism was a cliché repeated often amongst bullies in the school but it was doubtful that anyone realized it had been indirectly taught to them. The misguided adaptation of natural selection to social criticism has fueled the stupidity of masochists since Herbert Spencer and Bill Sumner devised the retarded theory. Now a misunderstood hundred-year old philosophical inclination fueled the self-righteous justification of Dutch's tormentors.

"It might be a blade," Matt was the former hockey player from Randolph. He was short but still taller than Dutch by half an inch, he had slick black hair that was balding in the front over a fishy face. Unlike Rodger who was almost thrown out of a third story window by Dutch or Joe who let Dutch fight back, Matt was without Mercy. His beatings were delivered with bad intentions, allowing no room for self-defense. He wanted to inflict as much pain as possible without leaving a mark and he never, ever allowed his victims to strike back.

"I don't care what he has," Rodger pleaded with them. "We need to send him a message. If he starts pushing us and people hear about it..."

"Rodger this is really your problem, not ours. You let him push you back. You let him dangle you from that window." Matt scolded him.

"He didn't dangle me..." Rodger felt the shame of being unable to control their victim but as time wore on, Dutch became angrier and thus more dangerous while the three of them seemed to be losing control.

"Look I don't care about all that. If James Ballum brought a gun to school he did it for one reason, he's planning to use it and who's he going shoot? One of us!" Joe craned his neck again as his eyes rolled back in his head. "Let's just get this over with." He was ready for a fight, he didn't care who the target was; Dutch was merely a convenience.

Light footfalls tapped their way down the steps above. Someone was coming.

"I'll hide on the other side of the door." Rodger went for the handle when Matt grabbed his arm.

"You wanted to disarm him so you are going to stay right here." Matt pulled Rodger away from the door and told him to hide next to the railing. Matt and Joe both went through the door to listen from the other side.

Dutch stopped on the stairs. It had been such a shitty day maybe he could skip class and take a break? No one would notice. There were so many kids in the school with rotating schedules that the teachers stopped taking attendance after the first month. He sat down on the stairs and took a deep breath. God how he hated high school! With his grades declining it wasn't like he was going to graduate. Of course they did advance him from tenth to eleventh grade even though he failed three courses. They might be pushing him through the system to get rid of him. He'd heard stories of students graduating that couldn't even read the diploma. Well, he could read so maybe all he had to do was show up once in a while and they'd hand him one just to get it over with?

Dutch leaned back on the steps and rested his head. If not for Psycho & Becca he would have no one to talk to at lunch. If not for classes and teachers, where his participation was at least partially required, he'd have no social life at all, no connection to other people. Still the sadness lingered, it was easier to be lonely amongst people, surrounded by them, than to be completely alone. Left by himself, his anger would fester into a personality destroying rage. Left alone, without the occasional mental stimulation of school, his ideas might invert into self-destructive extremes. Maybe it was better to keep everything as normal as possible? That may be his only key towards staying sane.

"Fine, fine I'm going." He convinced himself to get to class after all. He clung to the hope that he had reached rock bottom already and the rest of the day had to get better. What else could possibly go wrong? Dutch walked down the steps blindly advancing towards his mortal enemies.

CHAPTER 25

▼

John was only visiting the Graphic arts department to update his teacher about a class change that he had made. The change allowed him to start taking a college level course while still a junior. He might as well get a jump on credits if he was to start at Bridgewater State College when he graduated. As he got to the double doors an explosion of violent ruckus burst out from the stairwell.

"James Ball..." Mr. Collum, the word processing instructor, was about to open the door when Dutch burst out of the Stairwell and slammed into him. Mr. Collum recognized James a split second before he was shoved to the floor bouncing his head off the hard concrete that knocked him out cold.

"Oh shit!" John's reaction to the accident was too slow. Before he was able to reach Mr. Collum three more kids ran out of the stairwell and chased Dutch down the hallway at full speed.

"No, hey!" John tried to yell from behind but nothing was stopping them. Dutch had broken free and they were determined to make him pay.

"Fuck," John knelt down next to Mr. Collum. He was still moving but unconscious. John opened the door to the shop and yelled to the closest student, "Hey, hey you, get a teacher over here Mr. Collum is hurt."

The kid pointed to himself.

"Yes you, go get a teacher right now!"

The kid ran off to find someone while John pursued the three students. He had to help Dutch; three on one was not going to fall in his favor. Granted the General was a tough kid and even though he had a knack for escaping dangerous situations John also knew a lot about those brutes from the electrical shop. Those kids were athletes, often hopped up on cocaine or steroids, some of them carried weapons and none of them played fair. These particular teenagers were extraordinarily violent and completely absent of conscience. What made it even worse was their talent for committing hazing crimes and never being punished for it.

"Not this time!" John huffed his way down the hall, his extra bodyweight slowing him down. He couldn't see any of the perpetrators but he knew exactly where they were heading.

Up ahead Dutch spun around the corner only to find that classes were letting out and he was now in front of the electrical department's shop rooms. One senior recognized him and then gave a hand signal to Joe who was running up from behind. Dutch was trapped. He darted into the closest open door and sprinted through an empty shop, maybe he could make it out one of the windows.

"Oh no you don't," The three teens and the senior ran in after him. Joe jumped onto one of the long worktables and raced across it grabbing Dutch around the waist as he tried to shimmy out the ground level window.

"Get him back here, put him in a booth." Matt helped Joe carry Dutch back into the shop. He kicked and clawed, tried to get loose but they were too strong.

"I'll turn on the power." Rodger ran to a switch on the master control box. This box turned the voltage on for all of the electrical booths each one with metal boxes screwed to their wooden walls and each box had several ungrounded wires sticking out. Under normal circumstances these wires were used by students to construct electrical systems but with the power on they were deadly to anyone who touched them.

"Where are you going to run now Dutch?" Joe taunted the smaller teen who was trapped inside a wooden booth only four feet deep.

"Don't wait just hit him!" Matt dived at Dutch and using all the weight of his body thrust a solid punch into his chest. Dutch was driven back into the boxes.

"Aaarghh," He let out a scream as three wires stuck through his brand new jacket and into the skin of his back giving his whole body an electrical jolt. As soon as he pulled away Matt let loose with a front kick that sent Dutch back into the wires again.

"Aaarghh you fuckin!" Pushing off the wall Dutch dived back at Matt but Joe was there to meet the charge. Dutch threw punches with all of his might only to be met by much harder, heavier blows from his football player antagonist. No matter how hard Dutch hit him, Joe was not feeling any pain. Dutch, on the other hand, was losing energy fast. The blows he was taking to his arms and chest hurt so bad he could barely lift them to block the oncoming flurries. Punches and kicks from all three assailants were akin to receiving a hundred Charlie horses on every soft inch of his body. While these blows were painful they rarely left a mark.

Rodger grabbed a long metal rod and waited for an opening. As soon as Joe stepped back Rodger stabbed Dutch in the gut with the pole and shoved him back into the wires. Dutch shifted the pole off to his right and pulled Rodger into the booth. With the big kids body weight stumbling towards him Dutch let loose with his best weapon, a solid front thrust kick to the groin.

"Oww fuck!" Rodger fell to his knees but Joe jumped right over him and elbowed Dutch in the face. This time he fell backwards and his unprotected head hit the live wires.

"Aaarghh," He crumbled to the floor of the booth holding the burnt skin on his scalp. Matt took the opportunity to start kicking him in the ribs.

"Hey leave him alone!" A voice came from the doorway of the shop. All four students turned to look but John had bolted back out the door. He knew they would follow. Instead of running down the hall he crossed the hallway and hid in the opposite shop.

"Where did he go?" They all ran after him. Matt made it to the hallway first. "You guys go that way." The senior student and Rodger ran off to the right while Matt and Joe ran to the left.

Inside the opposite electrical shop John watched them run off. Then he grabbed a pair of pliers from a worktable and smashed the small vial of glass on a red wall-mounted fire alarm. The alarm blared loud causing further confusion. Students drudged out into the hallways starting towards the fire exits. Joe, Matt, Rodger and the senior were caught in the crowds and ended up out on the lawn where teachers were parading students away from the building.

John quickly crossed the hallway and jogged up to the booth where Dutch was curled up on the floor still shivering from the last electrical shock that burnt a patch of hair off the side of his head.

"You're going to be Ok, just relax."

Dutch twitched his eyes upwards. One of his eyes was completely bloodshot; the rest of his face was hot pink. "John?" He whispered.

"Yeah it's me. You're going to be alright."

"John?" He begged.

"What is it?" John leaned his head down to look Dutch in his one clear eye.

"I need you back on the team."

Fate of
the Father

CHAPTER 26

▼

"Follow me, we gotta be there on time or we'll miss the window." Schmel led Peter, Paul, Tyrone and Raphael up a back alleyway behind the City Center flea market. The flea market was a beige metal building like an airplane hangar sitting one block away from the renaissance apartment building that the Spring Street Posse called home. The flea market also sat diagonally across the street from an independently owned Exxon gas station. The large yellow tractor-trailer truck parked next to the station was their immediate goal.

"There it is," Schmel held up his hand pointing to truck they were about to rob. Peter noted that the palm of his hand was much lighter than the rest of his body. Schmel was second generation African American or to be accurate a Jamaican American. His parents moved here just before he was born twenty years ago. Raised on the streets of Brockton Schmel was taught how to survive through physical strength, intimidation and the black marketplace. His father had been arrested on several occasions for selling drugs downtown; that was until his Dad found a way to protect himself. He united with other dealers, local shops, street vendors, family and friends in a pledge to defend their businesses from the Brockton police department. The police was their main competitor in the narcotics trade. Under these conditions they had to look out for their own. Schmel's Dad always justified his vigilance by saying, 'When everyone is guilty, then no one is guilty.' Schmel repeated his story to tonight's newest members.

"That's how it is," He stopped at the edge of the building. Rafael nodded behind him but Peter and Paul made no recognition of the story, they had heard it before.

"So let's get on with this. Peter you are going to be the lead man, get up there." Schmel pointed to an empty booth next to the truck by the gas station.

"What am I supposed to do?" Peter walked out into the parking lot but then turned back for instructions. He was wearing the SSP's simple colors of blue jeans and a gray hooded sweatshirt. This uniformity allowed them all to look alike so that if they were caught, no one could be distinguished in a line up. Schmel called it urban camouflage.

"Go to the back of that truck, grab a box of food and drop it in the window of the empty photo booth."

"Then what? Grab another?"

"No." Schmel stepped right up to Peter's face. "You take one box, hide it and walk away."

"But what if I have time to grab more?"

"Don't do it. We've been pulling this off for three years without anyone getting caught. We don't get greedy, we keep it real, we keep it smooth." Schmel wanted to see if Peter could listen to orders. That was the real test. On an average route they would steal a single box of food or cigarettes and then move on to another station.

"I know. I hear ya. I'm keeping it real."

"Don't give me that shit!" Schmel wanted to slap him. "White boy you've been begging for brownie points all night and the shit's got to end. Knock it off, I'm in charge and we do things my way, got it Avon?"

Peter could feel a charge of anger rise in his chest whenever Schmel disrespected him in front of the others. He wished that he had brought his shotgun to display a little authority but Schmel said that these scams were done without weapons because of the mandatory charges that came with them. Besides, calling him white boy didn't hurt because it's true, he's Caucasian but calling him Avon was a much deeper insult. It was Schmel's way of saying that Peter was just a small town suburban poser who wanted to front as a gang-banger to prove his manhood. He was not used to this kind of abuse. He wanted to be on the other side of giving orders. He had been trying to play it their way for weeks completing one task after another to prove that he deserved the right to stand in the SSP's inner circle. He did everything they wanted, stealing a gun, threatening an enemy and kicking out his former friends who didn't want to join the gang. Peter was scoring street credit any way they dictated but the prize of inclusion was not being rewarded for all of his hard work. So tonight, Peter, Paul and Tyrone came not to impress, not to beg but to enact a plan of their own. This plan would dramatically change the dynamic of the SSP. It could make anything possible. But for it to work, someone would have to die.

"Ok Schmel, I got it. Be right back."

Schmel watched with doubt as Peter crossed the street heading towards the back of the truck. He had agreed too easily, Schmel's instincts told him that Peter was up to something foul.

He faced Paul, "If you're friend pulls a fast one out there, you are going to pay for it." His eyes allowed no leeway for mistakes, no gray areas given to interpretation or creative changes in the plan. Paul simply nodded not knowing how to react. He didn't want to give away their real intentions.

Schmel was the man who called the shots and he had earned it the hard way. Ever since two Brockton cops gunned down his father, the son has become a brilliant marketer on the city streets, a kind of back alley prodigy for the drug trade. He even went so far as to plant a pound of cocaine in one officer's house and then have his girlfriend tip off the narcotic's division. Without checking to see who lived at the address six officers broke into the residence and seized the drugs. Having ignored the need for a warrant the evidence against the officer was inadmissible in court but by then it didn't matter. The scandal prompted a media storm that descended on city hall forcing the Chief of Police to ask the officer in question to resign. They were sure he had been set up but politically they couldn't do anything about it. Schmel was cheered as a hero by his friends for raining a measure of justice upon one of the cops responsible for his father's death and for bringing a single beam of light exposing some of the department's darker tendencies. He was Robin Hood with a Mac-10, the Jamaican prince of Spring Street and that was why his boyz would follow him into hell. That was the legacy Peter, Paul and Tyrone were here to shatter.

Schmel watched carefully as Peter reached into the back of the truck, grabbed a box of food and dumped it into the empty photo mat booth just as he had been told to do but Peter didn't stop there.

"What the fuck is he doing?" Schmel stepped out into the parking lot. He was preparing to run across the street and beat him down for altering the plan. If Peter took too much the truck driver would notice. As it was the driver usually didn't figure out that there was missing inventory until the truck returned back at the distribution point in New Bedford. By then it's impossible for him to know where the goods were stolen. It was a conservative and foolproof plan. The only thing that could screw it up was greed.

Peter returned to the truck and climbed up into the cab frantically searching the seat area.

"What is he looking for?" Raphael, Schmel's cousin, walked up next to his man and waited to see what Peter produced. The Avon wannabe had already taken too long.

Schmel whispered to his cousin. "When I give the word we are gonna punk this traitor."

"Word," Raphael agreed as he watched and waited. It had been a few weeks since the two of them got to beat on a transgressor. Peter was already a fraud in their eyes. A sad white trash limp dick that wished he had grown up righteously black and city bound. It was such a stupid thing for anyone to want. A man would have to be a fool to choose to live on the streets, growing up surrounded by violence, attending schools that had more guns than a police academy. Who would want to see their friends dying off before they even graduate that is if they graduated at all. Schmel and Raphael only allowed Peter along because he appeared to be easy to manipulate but as it was, he was turning out to be more trouble than he was worth. His eagerness had morphed into malice, his malice a thin paranoid shade of ambition. He wanted too much, he was trying to ruin their scam. This could not stand.

"That's it, let's get him!" Schmel and Raphael sprinted across the pavement. Peter saw them coming and jumped out of the rig holding a pistol in his right hand.

CHAPTER 27

▼

"Back off!" Peter roared at them but Schmel was already on top of him. The leader of the SSP wrestled the gun out of Peter's hand and shouldered him into the open door of the truck.

"Oww, what did you…?" Peter never got a chance to finish his complaint as the driver's work boots could be heard thunking from the store towards the cab.

"Who's over there, get away from my truck!" The man growled as he rounded the hood.

Peter, Schmel and Rafael ran down the side street.

"You fuckin kids!" The man stopped to check his cab to see what was stolen.

The three of them took a hard right behind an auto shop across the street.

"Quick in here!" Schmel hauled them both inside an unlocked window into the shop's main bay.

Peter stumbled on a fiberglass fender falling onto his hands and knees, his left hand landing in a pool of oil.

Rafael hopped over Peter but still managed to crash sideways into a stack of rims that rung out like gong when they collided with the tire-mounting machine.

"Quiet Raf," Schmel yelled at him before returning his attention to the window to see if the truck driver was following them. "I swear to God Avon if that redneck calls five-o it's gonna be your ass."

Peter moved as cautiously as he could into a more comfortable position, sitting lightly on the in-ground lift.

"Schmel?" He whispered back.

"Shut up."

"But Schmel?" Peter wanted to move closer to the window but Schmel pulled out the pistol and aimed it at Peter's head.

"I said shut-up." The unfeeling defiance in Schmel's eyes was born of man who grew up too fast. When it came to dealing with people he threw away all the cautions of patience, he asserted his authority quickly and painfully. He lived practicality in fast-forward and right now it urged him to pull that trigger. Bringing some nagging white brat along was the biggest mistake he could have made. The SSP was for brothers who had no other choice than to live united under a code of trust or die trying. Peter could not be trusted. He was too ambitious. His motivation was built off a craving for power, not a need for survival. Clearly this arrangement was not going to work out.

"Schmel, what if this shop has a silent alarm system or something?" Peter could see a blinking red light on the far wall. "Isn't that a motion detector?"

Schmel didn't look at the light, his eyes stayed locked on Peter. "It's a fake, now shut up."

"But how do you know?"

That was it! He couldn't take anymore of this uppity fraud. His brothers knew how to listen to orders, his brothers knew when a situation was truly dangerous, and Peter was not one of his brothers. Schmel stretched out his arm, aimed the gun at Peter's forehead and pulled the trigger. *Click, click, click.*

Peter finally shut up. Forget the inner circle, forget any circle, his inclusion into the SSP was over. Schmel hated him so much that he wanted him dead and this was his confirmation. Good thing Peter's back up plan was already in play.

The fearless leader of the SSP calmly looked at the weapon, saw that it was missing a clip and then slid it into the backside of his pants.

"Schmel?" Rafael carefully addressed his cousin.

"What Raf?"

"What about the blinking light?"

"It's a fake. This is my uncle Leroy's garage."

Rafael took a seat on the floor and let his eyes fall wearily on Peter. This was all his...

"Fuck." Schmel poked his head out the window where flashing lights reflected off the glass. "That fucking truck driver called the cops...he's pointing over here...they're coming this way!"

CHAPTER 28

$\blacktriangledown$

"Across the street!" Schmel was yelling to Rafael as they exited the body shop through another window and tried to slip off into the night. He was so reeling with anger at Peter for all his presumptions and incompetence that he offered no instructions and gave no help when Peter got stuck in the window. He stopped for one moment of consideration but then continued running.

"Wait up, I'm coming," Peter was either undeterred or unaware that they were trying to leave him behind as he freed his foot. Either way, he was slowing them down.

The patrol car was on a routine pass of Spring Street when the truck driver insisted that the store clerk call the police. After several attempts at stalling, the clerk finally gave in and dialed 911. The black and white cruiser pulled up onto the lot in less than a minute. This gas station had been robbed too many times and the thieves always got away. There had been five shootings at this same spot in the last year, two of which were fatal. One of those murders was of a newly wed woman named Danielle Malone. No amount of surveillance ever ended in an arrest for her murderer. Sure they could snag several five foot seven inch tall black kids off the street and bring them in but they were all wearing the exact same clothes, blue jeans and a gray hooded sweatshirt. No one could possibly make a positive identification so all of the cases went unsolved. Danielle's killer was never found but now her husband, a Brockton cop, was on the beat and he was not going to let another thug escape his grasp.

"Let's go!" Officer Degan Malone blew off protocol and would not pause for investigators to tell him what he already knew; the SSP had struck again.

"What about the clerk?" The other officer stood one foot outside the car with his hands in the air wondering what to do.

"You handle it!" Degan saw two black kids both dressed in standard gang threads running across the street on the other side of an auto shop. He pulled his gun and ran down the side street. They were in reach and tonight, for once, he was going to nail the right people.

"Just call the dispatcher and send them my way!"

"But Degan," The officer jogged around the car and stopped. This was not proper procedure. He opened the driver's side door, sat in the seat and called in for back up. "Gonna get us both fired…"

"What's he doing?" The truck driver came out to talk to them and saw Degan sprinting down the road with his weapon raised.

"He's going overboard…again." The officer looked at the open door of the rig. "What did they steal?"

"Nothing so far as I can tell."

Schmel and Rafael had a head start on Peter as they crossed into a brick alley between large sections of an old shoe factory. The alley turned out to be a dead-end only forty feet in. On the left was a white wooden door bordered by a hundred five inch glass blocks that took the form of a frame. On the right of the alley sat the aged remains of a tow truck, its wheels replaced by cinder blocks with half it's mechanical guts rusting on the broken earth.

"How are we getting over?" Rafael watched his cousin try to kick in the white door. "Schmel, that thing's been painted shut since they closed the place."

"Well it needs to open," Schmel continued to kick the door ever harder with his ninety dollar Nike blacktops.

"Schmel the cop is coming!" Rafael was panicking. They were trapped with a twenty-five foot wall and a hundred year old door as their only means of escape.

When Peter caught up he ignored both of them. He ran directly to the tow truck frame almost as if he had been there before. Scraping his knee on the hood he took a big step over the cracked windshield and up to the base of the winch. The wall suddenly didn't seem so high. If he ran up the eight-foot arm and jumped he might reach the top and be able to escape.

"Schmel?" Rafael was almost in tears, his voice screeching as he tried to persuade his stubborn cousin to try another way. Raf turned his head just in time to see Peter make a successful leap off the truck. He pulled his legs over the top of the wall and out of view.

"The cop is coming!" Peter yelled down to them as he waited for Rafael to catch up.

"I heard it move!" Schmel screamed at them referring to the door but Raf wasn't waiting around. He climbed the truck just as Degan turned the corner. Rafael ran up the winch and reached the wall. Peter grabbed his arm and pulled him over the ledge onto the other side where he rolled on the small pebbles of a flat roof.

"Fuck, we gotta help Schmel!" Raf jumped to his feet and looked over the ledge at the same moment that Schmel pulled the empty pistol out of his pants.

"NOOOOO!" Rafael screamed as the Officer opened fire. Peter quickly pulled Raf away from the ledge as bullets ricocheted off the bricks below.

"Let go of me," He struggled against Peter's strength while several shots were fired in rapid succession.

"If we don't get out of here we'll be next!" Peter wasn't letting go.

"No Schmel, Schmel!" The gunfire had stopped. Rafael broke away and grabbed onto the wall just as the blinding glare of a flashlight blocked his view.

"Come on let's go!" Peter pulled him away as they both ran along the vast expanse of roofs far from the alleyway.

It only took three minutes to find the back wall and hunt down a fire escape. When they reached the bottom Raf grabbed Peter by the throat and slammed him against the metal ladder holding him in place until Peter's superior strength shoved the smaller teen off.

"This is all your fault!" Raf cried at him through a bluster of sobs. "You had to blow the plan didn't you? You had to get greedy! You fucked everything up! You probably got Schmel killed!" Tears poured down his face. He started to stumble away when Peter echoed in a cold, chilling voice.

"If everyone is guilty then no one is guilty."

"What the fuck is that supposed to mean?" Raf faced him but this time he saw Peter in a different light. The orange haired kid was calm, despite being so close to the gunshots, despite being so close to getting caught. For a brief moment Peter was composed as if he wanted all of this to happen or rather, as if he planned it all along. Did this teenager, this suburban white kid from Avon just manufacture the death of Schmel Hastings, the leader of the SSP?

Peter let his frosty breath hide an icy glare until Raf had figured it out.

"You didn't find that gun, did you?" He couldn't believe it. No way did this white trash wannabe outsmart the leader of a citywide gang. There's no way he could have known that a trigger happy cop was going to show up, was there? Peter was a kid not a criminal genius; he was a fucking kid! Rafael grabbed his own head overwhelmed with emotional pain.

"It's funny huh?" Peter was mocking him. "That's the same way his father died. He faced off with a couple cops and pulled out a weapon that wasn't loaded. They turned him into a fucking fountain there were so many holes. God I got tired of hearing that story."

"Fuck you man. Fuck you for this."

"Don't be such a baby Raf especially when addressing your new leader."

"What are you talking about?"

"If I understand the rules correctly, by killing the leader, you become the leader. This little adventure tonight puts me in that position. The SSP is mine."

"What? Motherfucker there is no way..." He was so overcome with confusion and rage that he couldn't fix his sentences so they made sense. "There is no fucking way you will ever run the SSP...they'll kill you first...I'll kill you first...Over my dead body Avon!"

"So be it." Peter grinned, this time with the complete confidence that he could back up his words. The Spring Street Posse was as good as his. "So tell me Raf, how did your daddy die?"

BAPHOMET
TOLD ME

CHAPTER 29

▼

Lazio's family lived in a timber frame home only a block away from Becca's building. That day John drove Becca, Psycho and Dutch from school to Lazio's for what would be the most important meeting the HAWKS ever have. The beating suffered by Dutch along with the subsequent rescue, fire alarm and gathering of friends started a hurricane of speculation about what would happen next. Two years ago Peter tried to murder Dutch. Such an atrocity forced him to create the HAWKS team for the sake of self-defense. Now that a similar attack had happened they possess the ability to respond with deadly force.

"This is what we train for." Psycho agreed enthusiastically.

"Right, we will buys guns and kill these fuckers once and for all!" Dutch was frantic as he wobbled on a stool by the oak bar holding an ice filled cloth to the side of his head. "This should have been done a long time ago. We should have struck them first. I told you Psycho, I told you they'd do this."

"Yeah you did." He wasn't going to argue.

"But we can't..." Becca started but Dutch ignored her completely. The emotional atmosphere was too intense, no one was in the mood for dissent. She quickly shut her mouth.

"You only have to be sixteen to have a firearms identification card." He didn't need anyone's approval this was going to happen. "That'll get us some guns right? They can't deny us if we have the card right?"

"An FID card won't get you a concealed weapon, not here in Massachusetts." John wanted to dissuade him but dared not speak directly in the line of fire. Dutch had every reason to be angry and the kids who attacked him were all drugs users so shooting them fell easily within the parameters of the malevolent philosophy. Whether or not John believed in the team credo, others might and he didn't want to step on anyone's shoes.

"Shouldn't we get some training first?" Lazio asked out of sorts. He was all for going after these punks but…"It has to be organized, right? That's our modus operandi, we're tactical, like Special Forces."

Dutch nodded. "But if John's correct an FID card won't allow us to buy pistols." He drummed his knuckles against the hard countertop as his rapidly scheming mind was having trouble pulling a plan together. "It hurts when I think. My head…"

Becca rested her hand on his side trying to comfort him but he brushed her away.

"I can ask around town," Psycho sat back on the couch. "Maybe we can find some black market weapons."

Becca felt dejected, useless to console her boyfriend. She sat on the couch next to Psycho who moved aside to give her room. She grabbed a newspaper from the stack they'd been accumulating. If she couldn't help ease the pain, maybe she could lose herself in one of the local news stories she had been following. Dutch assigned her to do intelligence work and at the moment it was a good place to hide.

Psycho racked his brain, "There's got to be a gun dealer in Norwood, someone who would break the rules for us. Maybe we can bribe a shop owner?"

"Doubtful," said Lazio.

"But we should ask around," replied a determined Dutch as a sharp pain sent a white flash of light across his eyes. "Oww," He held the ice to his forehead and the pain subsided.

"Maybe we should take you to the hospital? Your injuries are…" Becca's soft voice was shouted down.

"I'm fine!" Hadn't he suffered enough for one day? Sympathy was the last thing he needed, this was about justice! This was about long over due problems that required violent retribution.

"Sorry," She whispered pulling the newspaper up to hide her embarrassment. Surprisingly enough Psycho patted her arm to let her know that she was appreciated despite the General's outbursts.

Dutch picked up where he left off, "John, for the sake of having a plan B, I'll still need you to get an FID card. If Psycho can't find us a dealer we'll have to settle for rifles and shotguns. They'll be harder to sneak into the school but we can pull it off."

John had been staring at the odd pagan artwork on the living room walls but he heard what Dutch instructed.

"We're going to shoot them inside the school?"

"Yes, do you have a problem with that?"

John swallowed his pride, "No. But where do I get one? The FID card."

"Go to your town hall in Holbrook, bring your license." The drumming of his knuckles was getting harder.

"Will it cost anything?" John asked.

"Jesus you do ever stop bitching about money?"

"Sorry." John felt like such a wimp. He had spent all these weeks building up to the moment when he would tell Dutch off and now he was once again bowing down to him.

"Maybe ten bucks, no more than that. They'll run a back ground check on you but we already know your record is clean so it won't take a minute."

"What should I do?" Lazio asked feeling out of place. As a pagan he had never been around guns before, he considered guns, bombs, shooting and murders to be Christian hobbies. Even so, Lazio was more violent than most witches. He had no problem causing pain to someone who had bad intentions.

"Lazio, can you think of anyone who might be connected to the gun trade? Anyone at all?"

"I've heard rumors. There was this one kid who I was friends with, I told you about him, he found Mideon. They accepted him as NightBreed and he hasn't been the same since."

Dutch finally looked up. "What are the rumors?"

"That he got into drugs, lots of fights, I heard about guns but...I can't be sure."

"Can you contact him?" Dutch asked curious of the prospect. Maybe this kid was saner than Lazio. It was a long shot but it was better than nothing.

"Yeah, I think I still have his phone number but I doubt he'll talk to me."

Psycho smiled. "I'll call him. This is so cool, buying guns on the streets. Damian won't believe how far we've come without him."

Becca shifted disapprovingly on the couch. She had been uneasy ever since they left the school. At first she was worried about Dutch and felt really bad about the damage that had been done to him but by the time they got to Lazio's house her sympathies were deflected by his attitude. He was excitedly serious about killing the teenagers who had done this. There was something sinister in his eyes. He wanted to kill them publicly, inside her high school. Before today it seemed like bravado, a fantasy about vigilante team members who would scare drug dealers, but to actually kill them? Wasn't this going too far, too fast? As she understood it the HAWKS plan was first to graduate high school, then join the military to get training and then create a street team to take down drug traffickers. There was a mature logic and simplicity to the plan but now it was being fast-forwarded.

A strange thought crossed her mind, what if Dutch didn't care about his injuries or how they happened? What if he was using this beating as an ignition to do what he always wanted to do? No one was going to question his motives now, so why not start the killing early? He once told the team that he was predestined to become a serial killer, what if he still believes it? Is that what he's all about? Becca had to be a voice of reason; god knows John wasn't saying anything and he was supposed to be the sane one.

"Fuck it," She had to stand up to Dutch and bring this to an end before he gets what he wants. "Dutch," She left the couch and got intimately close to him. "Can we go outside and talk?"

"No, we're having a meeting."

"But this is really important."

Dutch saw Psycho roll his eyes with indignation while Lazio was watching him with intense concentration, or was he watching her? Never the less, these were his men and they wanted leadership, they wanted to get this started. They wanted action.

"Dutch I really need to talk to you." She whispered under the gaze of all the men's eyes. "Please."

"Is it team business?" He gave her an easy out.

"Yes, it's about the mission, there's something you need to know."

"Then tell us all." He said in a very loud and embarrassing manner.

"But it's also about me and I won't tell anyone but you." Becca was folding under the scrutiny of the stares.

"Then whisper it to me," Dutch was not giving in. This moment was too important. He had learned two years ago when Peter shot him that survival begets credibility. Right now Dutch had credibility, he had justification for revenge but he had to use it while it lasted. If he stalled too long the pain would ease and his followers would lose faith in him. He couldn't fall prey to Becca's weakening sympathy or petty hesitations.

"Tell me now!" He said starkly forcing the truth out of her with his eyes.

Becca folded, "I'll tell you but it's very private."

Dutch's eyes softened a little. *What fact could be so confidential? What story did she want to share?* The anger was replaced by curiosity. He decided to recognize her need for privacy.

"Ok, let's go outside."

CHAPTER 30

▼

"You can't do this in a fit of rage." Becca barely waited for the front door to close before she started her moral protest. There were no facts, no secret stories, only her indignation. "This is going to fail if it's done too hastily and for the wrong reasons…in the wrong way…"

"Wrong reasons? How many more times do I have to take a beating or be chased down a hallway or be humiliated before I finally fight back? How many more times should they be allowed to get away with this?" He was livid, screaming at the top of his lungs in Lazio's front yard. His voice was so loud that the other HAWKS could hear him from inside the house.

"But you do fight back."

"So I should let them get away with it?"

"No, I'm not saying that we…" Becca couldn't penetrate the veil of outrage that flooded his mind. She just had to let him pour it out. Dutch was overflowing with emotion, it choked his thoughts, stunted his ability to reason. She couldn't see any sense of lucidity in his eyes.

"So what did you have to tell me?"

"I…ah. Look these guys can't be all bad, maybe they have had tough lives and…"

"Are you joking? They are druggies!"

"But you're labeling them without knowing…"

"Becca? Do you have any idea what it's like to go to school each day knowing that at some point someone is going to stab you with a live wire or grab you in a headlock? I couldn't walk down the hallway without one of these fucking electrical shop assholes coming out of nowhere just to punch me in the shoulder and slap me in the face. It was a game for them! They didn't care what kind of damage they did! I'd have a bruise for weeks and then they'd hit it again! Small daily tortures each and every time I turned around. Jesus how can you…" Dutch had to walk away from her as he caught his breath. He wanted to explode and was afraid he might strike out at her.

"Dutch I know what you think but I…"

"Is it sympathy, for them? Is that what you have? Do you feel sorry for them or is it something else? What aren't you telling me? Why do you pity them, I'm the victim!"

"I don't pity them but I know how you can get out of control and I…"

"No, you don't know! You don't understand, you couldn't possibly understand unless you've been there! I wanted to call in sick every single day so I wouldn't have to face them! I've wanted to buy a gun for so long and now after they pulled this shit I have no more excuses to stop myself. This is it! I'm going to get a pistol, walk into that electrical shop and kill every last one of them!"

Becca reached out her hand to his shoulder but he forcefully shoved her away. Becca's shoes slipped on the sidewalk ice and she fell to the ground. Dutch didn't even try to catch her. A split second later he crumpled into a sobbing pile in the snow next to her. Unhurt she climbed up to her knees and reluctantly wrapped her arms around him. She knew that he didn't mean to do it.

"I'm sorry, I…"

"It's ok, it's ok. We'll get through this…"

Soon enough his tears were buried in her sweater.

Psycho, John and Lazio had crowded up to the window when they saw her fall. They were afraid he was going to lose control and hit her by accident but instead their General was weeping uncontrollably on the ground as she curled up to him.

John commented to the HAWKS inside the house, "I don't think any of us can talk him out of this. It's not a group of friends anymore; we're a gang. We have to be. The werewolf games are over, the war is about to begin."

"You're not leaving?" Psycho said lightly testing John's temerity.

"No, you're going to need me. This is too serious to walk away from."

Psycho thought hard about John's fears. It was bound to happen one day, Dutch always had a short wick and his tormentors were throwing matches every day. You can only push a person so far. Even the kindest soul will eventually turn to violence when inflicted by overwhelming injustice.

"Maybe we shouldn't try to calm him down. We have agreed to everything he ever proposed and yet we signed up for this thinking that Dutch might not be completely serious," A daunting silence lingered in the room before Psycho finished his sentence. "It looks like we were wrong."

CHAPTER 31

▼

"His name is Darren Walker but he calls himself D-Rod. Lazio said he was selected by Baphomet to..." Psycho could not believe what he was saying and instead shrugged his shoulders as Dutch looked disinterested at the empty and lifeless neighborhood in the distance. Night had fallen around 5pm and the frost-covered grass in the field glistened reflecting the streetlights on the far side of the baseball field. The grass had frozen white, as if scared by the sneaky Nor'easter that caught it by surprise. In places it crunched under their feet, each blade breaking into a thousand crystal shards. They couldn't move an inch without making noise.

"D-Rod? He's nightbreed? Do you realize how ridiculous that sounds? Can we take him seriously?" Dutch leaned back against the car. He was way past doubt when it came to Lazio's membership. Now he was facing regret.

After Lazio gave a fuller explanation about Baphomet and the NightBreed he then pulled out the movie of the same name by horror director Clive Barker. They all watched it with an air of boredom and turned to Lazio afterward as they now understood even less than they did before. He excitedly tried to illuminate them by citing passages from Cabal, the book by Clive Barker that predated the movie, but again none of it made sense. Dutch proclaimed that it was fantasy, "pure and simple." Psycho thought it was fun to watch but utterly absurd to infer that there could be any real world correlations. Becca fell asleep against Psycho's shoulder, that's what she thought of it. John left early after laughing heartily about the whole idea of an underground civilization in Norwood. Despite all of these misgivings they still agreed to meet a kid who was supposed to be one of the sacred and hidden freaks of the Breed. Why? They had no other leads.

"Lazio knew him when they were kids." Psycho was plodding slowly beside Dutch as they walked out onto the grass crunching in unison.

"Did you know him?"

"No but I've met him. He showed me his own 25-caliber pistol; it was silver with a white handle. He had it in his pocket. I guess he's always armed."

"That's good to remember." Dutch unconsciously reached in his pocket to feel the cold metal of a single hatchet held in place by a utility belt beneath his overcoat. Psycho held his own short-handled sledgehammer under his second layer of clothes. They were willing to meet with the guy on this night, even though they had no money, but he didn't know that. All D-Rod knew was that Dutch and Psycho were the leaders of a gang that was wanted by the Avon police and now they were hiding out in Norwood. Being wanted gave them gravitas. Their guilt was an easy fact that could be confirmed with a simple phone call and if D-Rod was the pro he claimed to be, they expected to be checked on.

"What did he say he could get us?" Dutch had no idea how they were going to get the cash to pay for the weapons but it made sense to scope out the dealer first.

"A Glock 9 millimeter and a 38 special revolver, for now."

"The Glock is a good gun."

"It's German right?"

"Yeah, which one did he mention?"

"The G-22." Psycho knew a little about the weapon because he had read an advertisement in a recent gun magazine. He repeated the pitch to Dutch, "They claim you can drop it from an airplane and then run it over with a truck but it still won't fire until you turn off the safety."

"That's what I hear."

Psycho was testing him. Dutch was well groomed in his knowledge of weapons but he didn't give up the info easily. He decided to taunt it out of him. "So I guess you don't know much about it?"

"The 22? It's a polymer-framed pistol, less torque than a 45, lower perceived recoil, smooth trigger pull and even though it's inexpensive I seriously doubt D-Rod has one."

"Why?" Psycho hid his smile under his coat collar. He loved it when Dutch showed off.

"Because it just came out on the market last month and they mostly sell them to cops."

"Oh." That's not what he wanted to hear.

"Will we see both guns tonight?"

"Don't know. I figured that's what we're here to find out." Psycho was also stressing over the money but at the very least they could connive John out of a few hundred dollars. He was the only HAWK who had a job, well, not counting TC but considering his track record they didn't expect him stay employed for very long.

On a distant street the headlights of a small gray foreign made car came over the hill. The car slowly edged its way alongside the field and came to a complete stop near home base of the diamond. It was partly obscured by the solid wooden wall of the caged dugout but they heard a door open and shut.

"Is that him?" Dutch asked standing straight up and squinting into a brisk breeze.

"I don't..." The car suddenly sped away tearing out, as it's front tires left a small splattering of slush behind. In seconds it disappeared out of view.

"Fuck, do you think he made us?" Dutch asked.

"How could he? That had to be someone else."

"Maybe not," Dutch pointed back to the field itself. A small figure dressed in layers of black was walking across the field. The dark hood of his winter overcoat was blocking the light from reaching his face. His hands were deep in his pockets. The frightened field made little noise from underneath his untied army boots. His gait was confident but ominous; he was unafraid.

"Psycho?" Dutch moved forward looking for assurance that this was the guy.

"From this distance it could be anybody."

Psycho saw the kid flex and twist his hand inside the winter coat. The reason a person might adjust their hand so awkwardly is if they are holding an item too big for the inside of his pocket. "Dude, watch his right hand."

"I got it," Dutch said just as the kid stopped in the exact middle of the field and waited.

"It's him," Psycho gestured to Dutch as they both advanced farther out on the glittering white grass.

The walk towards this dark figure felt endless. Every step was akin to a gamble. If D-Rod thought they were coming to meet him tonight with hundreds of dollars to buy black market guns then all he would have to do is pull out a loaded weapon and rob them. When they claim to be broke he could flip out and shoot them both for lying. On the other hand Dutch and Psycho had a plan of their own that involved apprehending D-Rod and torturing information out of him. Maybe, if they were quick enough, they could steal his silver 25. Either way this covert confrontation could very easily end in violence. Worse case scenario, someone gets shot.

Dutch gripped the hatchet's handle in his pocket as they approached. Psycho held firm to his hammer. They stopped five feet away from the kid and said nothing.

After an awkward twenty seconds Psycho spoke up, "Did you bring the items?"

The kid lifted his head and they could see the faintest white skin under a shadow. "No. Did you bring the money?"

Psycho turned to Dutch who answered decisively, "No."

"Why not?" The kid asked them both.

"We had to make sure you could be trusted. We wanted to see the items before we buy them. Surely you understand?" Dutch was trying to act like a businessman and treat D-Rod the same way. Nothing was promised ahead of time so no promises had been broken.

"I'm with that," The kid threw back his hood. He had scruffy brown hair that covered part of his face. His dark eyes gave him a haunting presence but it was blurred by an ignoble easiness. "Before I came here I asked my god if the HAWKS were trying to hurt the breed."

Dutch and Psycho considered him carefully but made no move to reply. They didn't want him to know that they thought he was crazy.

"You might say I wanted to see if I could trust you as well." Again his cryptic words betrayed even his sincere countenance. There needn't really be a god of dark wanderers for him to believe firmly in such a delusion.

"And..." Psycho asked about his god's conclusion.

"Meet me tomorrow outside the high school. You give me the money and I'll give you a set of keys. The guns are in the trunk of a Nissan that will be parked near the center of town. You take the car, drive it back here to the diamond and take the guns out but leave the car with the keys in the glove box."

"Why all this cloak and dagger shit?" Dutch asked.

"Precautions my man. You naturals always have a sniff of fear on you so I need to know when a trap is being set. More importantly, I must know if the trap is to be feared and avoided. We all go to great lengths to protect ourselves, don't we?" D-Rod turned his head towards the dug out box and then over at the bushes in a front yard to his right and then back to Dutch. "Well, you are certainly not dangerous."

They had been made. D-Rod knew that Lazio was hiding in the dug out and Becca was behind the bushes. This kid was good, he was being stalked, watched by an armed gang and yet he showed up anyway. In a street sense he had to be legitimate. Who else would go through so much trouble? Only the very best would take the time to be so precise, so patient.

Dutch accepted their inferior position, "Fine, we'll see you tomorrow in the front of the high school."

"Hey," Psycho tried to break the mystery with an ill timed question, "How did you know?"

D-Rod spun on one heel joyfully crushing the dead blades into the frozen ground and walked back the way he came. Without turning one iota he spoke into the air and let his words drift beyond him.

"Baphomet told me." With that he started to laugh underneath his black coats. The headlights of the foreign car were coming over the hill.

CHAPTER 32

▼

"Do you think we look suspicious?" Psycho sat in the passenger seat of Lazio's car tapping his metal rings against the window.

"Those are new." Dutch said of the oversized finger jewelry adorned with spikes and sharp edges. "They're not very pretty."

"Lazio gave them to me. I guarantee they can break the skin if I punch someone."

"Did he curse them?"

"Probably."

"Maybe you'll get a chance to use them today." Dutch hadn't gone back to school since the fight. He didn't want to return until he had the hardware he needed to exact his revenge. His notebook was starting to fill up with plans; it had everything from locker-bombs to classroom ambushes. He had been digging through weapons catalogs dreaming about all sorts of deadly toys that could easily be smuggled into a school but he was keeping the details to himself.

While Lazio, John and Becca were attending class, Dutch and Psycho were waiting for D-Rod in front of the Norwood high school as was specified. They brought the cash and awaited the keys to the Nissan so they could get their new weapons.

"John wasn't happy about giving us the money." Psycho didn't want to mention it but even he was afraid that Dutch might take too much advantage of his plump friend's charity. John had given them two hundred dollars for two guns, the only two guns that D-Rod trusted them enough to tell them about though he hinted that he could get more. Lazio was clueless as to how his ex-friend obtained such a mighty arsenal but he assumed that they had to be armed in Mideon. He had even heard crazy rumors about D-Rod involving automatic weapons and shootouts in Boston's Chinatown. Dutch and Psycho were all the more willing to believe in his supposed shootouts than the endless tales of comic book bullshit Lazio continued to spew at them.

"We'll give John the 38 and teach him how to shoot, that will shut him up for a while." Dutch finished his thought just before he spotted D-Rod crossing the dead grass towards them. He wore the same dark winter cloaks and untied army boots.

"I'm fine with that. I trust John, he'll be responsible with a weapon and I'll be happy to teach him, but answer me this...who's going to teach us?" Psycho opened his door climbed out to greet their new gun dealer. The handshake was hearty, allowing money and keys to be exchanged underneath the cover of coat sleeves and smiles. D-Rod whispered the location of the Nissan and then he slipped away just as fast as he had arrived.

"What street?" Dutch asked Psycho as he shut the car door.

"Turn it around. We're going to Vernon Street, downtown."

"Downtown? Fuck."

Dutch drove back the way they came and passed a rusty brown two door Nissan of indistinguishable model. He turned the corner passing the car and parked against the curb.

"Did you see any cops?" He asked as he looked out the back window at the four cylinder rust box. It was an older vehicle, a survivor of too many winters and no doubt abused by enthusiastic teenagers.

"Something doesn't smell right." Psycho paused as he looked for anything that might be out of place. A hundred questions ran through his mind. Were they being watched? Was this a sting operation by the Norwood police? Did they have a 21 Jump Street group like on television? Who owns the Nissan and why..."Hey, why don't we just open the trunk here and take out the..." Psycho stopped himself.

"You know why." Dutch said.

Psycho let the idea play out in his mind. They couldn't simply walk up to a car on a busy street, open the hatchback and pull out two guns in front of a hundred people. They had to move the car to a safe place and D-Rod told them where to park it.

"We can't just sit here." Dutch unlocked his door and told Psycho to hop into the driver's seat. "Gimme the keys. I'm going to jog up there and snag it. If you see anything out of the ordinary...just bolt."

"But I can help if..."

"No, bolt, get away, don't get caught. I'll need you on the outside to save my ass later on. If we get separated we'll meet up at Lazio's house."

"And if it goes normal I'll just drive to the field?"

Dutch nodded holding the keys tight in his left hand. "Ok, lets do this." He jogged up the street. Psycho watched as Dutch rounded the car, opened the door and revved it to life.

It took only ten minutes for both cars to make it to the baseball diamond where they parked by the dugout. No one had followed them, so far as they could tell. Psycho stayed in Lazio's car while Dutch shut off the Nissan, ran around to the hatchback and opened it.

The decrepit hatchback slowly climbed upwards but the hydraulic arms stopped before he could see what was under the panel.

"Fuckin thing," He lifted it fully open. His eyes went wide as he stared down into the trunk space. "Oh fuck!" Dropping the keys on the ground he ran to the passenger door of Lazio's car and jumped in.

"GO, GO, GO…"

"What? Why? Where are the guns?"

"Drive! Now!" Dutch screamed looking out the rear window at the car behind him and at the area surrounding them. This had gone entirely wrong. He knew he couldn't trust that psychotic Baphomet worshipping nut bag!

"WHY?" Psycho demanded as they tore away.

"We've been set up!"

Department of Youth Services

CHAPTER 33

▼

"Damian Burke?" The guard called out as he stood in the doorway of the plain white walled room.

"Here." Damian said not lifting his head so that loose blonde hair hung over his blue eyes. He had grown so accustomed to the three times daily check-in that he hardly noticed when Al, a 6'5" guard with a nearly inaudible rumble of a voice, was there or when he left. He only knew that when the rumble called his name, he would respond.

"Darius Waters?"

"Here." An extremely dark skinned teen sat next to Damian on the bed. They were both paying attention to a newspaper article in the Brockton Enterprise. This block of residents had been given certain privileges due to good behavior. The guard had no idea that low volume conversations were not the same as gentle intentions. This brood was organized, they had in fact been scheming for days on end that was until this article appeared in today's paper and sent them into a state of shock.

"I can't believe he's dead." Darius was visibly distraught and Damian was sympathetic. The other four teens sat somber on their beds, the words of rebellion and rage stolen from their mouths as Damian read on,

Schmel, Rafael and an unknown Caucasian perpetrator had been fleeing police when Schmel pulled the pistol from his pocket and aimed it at Officer Degan Malone. Seven shots were fired. Schmel was struck in the right arm twice, in the left side of his hip, one cracking his collarbone and the fatal bullet that passed through his throat severing his spinal column. The other two bullets were found in the wall behind him. It was later discovered that Schmel's weapon was unloaded despite Officer Malone's claim that he had been fired at. It's no coincidence that Officer Malone had lost his wife in this very neighborhood only a year earlier...

Damian swallowed hard. He had learned that Schmel was the infamous leader of the Spring Street Posse. While staying here in DYS, Damian had befriended the gang in order make his time a little more hospitable. DYS was the nickname for a rehabilitation program run by the state's Department of Youth Services. It was a holding tank for underage offenders based at the YMCA on Main Street and sometimes it could be a little rough for first timers.

The gang wasn't too thrilled about having a white skinned, blond haired, blue-eyed friend but Damian's slick talking quickly put an end to that. He told them that he had once been a member of a rival gang from Avon known as the HAWKS Foundation. Luckily one of the kids had heard of the HAWKS after the Wolfhouse incident made it to the newspapers. Who knew these kids could read? Damian went on to explain that the HAWKS were gunning to wipe out the SSP over the next few years as a part of their overall strategy to kill local drug dealers. All of which was basically true so they bought it without question. Damian fig-ured that anyone desperate enough to join a gang must already believe that the whole world is out to get them so the story held water. Damian also promised that he would use his knowledge of the HAWKS to help the SSP take them down. He convinced Darius that he'd been set-up by Dutch and wanted a little revenge of his own. Again they bought it rather easily but today the focus was not on Damian, it was on the death of their beloved leader.

"That's the same way they did his Dad." Darius covered his forehead with the palm of his hand and squeezed. "He was fuckin set-up. Those fuckin Brockton cops."

Damian nodded. No surprise there, everyone in DYS believed that they were the victims of some kind of police conspiracy. "Who's Rafael?" He asked trying to put together the big picture of what this meant for the SSP.

"Raf is Schmel's cousin from Taunton."

"Will he run the operations now?" Damian asked cautiously.

"I don't know...I don't...fuckin cops!" Darius couldn't think straight. The despondence was fading as a confused and aimless rage slowly filled its place. "Fuckin cops need to die!"

"Yeah."

"Word up Darius."

"They did him just like his Dad."

Darius was getting the room riled up. As each member raised his voice about what had happened to their leader, it echoed off the sentiments of the others.

Each pithy crack of the tongue bounced around the room fueling the next and the next until…

"Quiet down in here!" The rumble returned from his counts and stood in the doorway. It was a huge mistake. Al was dressed in his uniform, dark slacks with a tan shirt. He had an ID card on his pocket, along with a badge around his neck and a pair of handcuffs in his right hand. He stared down at the angry youths and ratcheted the cuffs back and forth. The jarring noise was meant to intimidate. On rare occasions an out of control teen would be cuffed to a chair and bounced around a little by the staff. It was their way of applying discipline but Al was the best at administering it. He would take a single kid onto the Al-evator and ride up and down with him until the kid knew how to keep his mouth shut.

Normally they would all hush up when the rumble came around but not today. A cop had killed Schmel but it felt like a blow to them all. Al stood in the doorway alone, unaware of their rage but worst of all, he wasn't armed. If ever there was a wrong moment to look like a cop, this was it.

Damian braced for the rush as Darius blew his top and gave the order to attack. That meant Damian would have to attack as well, there was no getting out of it. He dived to the front of the rush, if nothing else he would be the first to fall.

CHAPTER 34

▼

Damian slouched at the table with his head hanging down over clasped fingers. The youth detention board members sat before him at another pressed wood table behind stacks of forms spilling over from their own weight. A brown haired lady with thin silver glasses anchored the far right end waiting for Damian to make his decision,

"I can't turn anyone in." He whispered.

"You can't because you don't know who started it or you won't because you want to protect your friends?" Her stare was penetrating his conscience. Damian knew he was in the wrong but this was a no win decision. If he gave up anyone for starting the riot and attacking the guard then Damian would be next on the hit list but then again if he didn't give up anyone he was likely to get a longer sentence. Maybe if he reasoned with the board, maybe he could get them to understand his situation?

"Can I have a few minutes to explain myself?" Damian had lifted his head for the first time, his naturally tanned cheeks wet with tears half wiped away by the back of his hand. The puffy pink around his eyes gave the sincere appearance of suffering.

The board members looked around at each other but there was little hesitation. This was an in-house hearing concerning a teenager who was holding in a lot of grief. It was common for the residents to denounce the criminal justice system or claim to be victims of police brutality but they did it during fits of anger using incoherent arguments. In contrast Damian was calm, almost grieving his decision. He was on the verge of giving in, clearly torn between opposing psychological forces. The board was not interested in passionate lies but they were always hoping against hope. They joined this institution to resurrect young lives, not simply to detain them. At the heart of their convictions was a desire for reform, an inclination towards reducing recidivism. This may be one of those rare chances, so if he walked to talk then they were ready to listen.

"You've got two minutes."

Damian cleared his throat, "Before I came here I thought I was a pretty messed up person. I had problems at home and I guess I'm rebelling but I'm nothing like the kids in here. Some of them enjoy hurting people, some enjoy hurting themselves and they have no sense of right or wrong, none at all."

"Listen, I'm a straight A student at Avon High School. I've been a boy scout for seven years. I play the drums, I read comic books and I love my country." Damian tilted his head and swallowed hard letting the remaining tear slide down his cheek. He was hamming it up but so long as they were buying the product then he was going to sell it strong.

"I'm here because I made a mistake. I fell in with the wrong crowd. Now that I'm on the inside, I have fallen in with another group that is far worse than anything I ever imagined. I wish I could get out, out of the group, out of this facility, out of my old life. The longer I stay here the worse it is going to get for me. The more these guys will ask of me, their demands for proof of loyalty will end in failure and I'll suffer the price. What I'm saying is that, there was no way to avoid the attack on Al. When the others ran him down I was at the head of the crowd to prove myself. When his forearm hit the side of my head I fell to the floor in pain but made believe I had been knocked out."

"You were conscious through the whole incident?" The lady chided him, "And you let it happen anyway? Mr. Burke that makes you even more guilty than if you *had* been unconscious."

"Mrs. Blanche let him finish," The white haired man in the middle gave Damian his time back.

"Thank-you. Um, I regret not knowing what to do in that circumstance. I regret what happened to Al, and I hope he recovers quickly. I would apologize in person if I could but I don't know what else to do. If I tried to stop them then I'd be the one in the hospital. I'm in over my head. Some of these kids are so…they are crazy…they are without conscience or remorse…some of them will justify anything. I'm not trying to say that I'm innocent but every single day I'm making moves to protect myself. Day by day, hour-by-hour I try to find ways to stay safe. If you want to punish me for that then I'm screwed from both sides."

"I don't know if anyone could walk out of this place without being beaten for their lack of loyalties. These teens act like wild dogs, one sniff of weakness or a hint of doubt and they will rip me apart. I'm saying; it was either me or Al." The tears were again crowding his vision into a gray haze but he had their full attention.

"If I told you who gave the order there is no way I would walk out of this building alive. Even if I did escape they know my name, they know where I come from. They will call other people outside on the streets to hunt me down." As if on cue the tears fell freely down Damian's face this time on both sides.

Two of the board members were getting choked up. One wiped his eyes repeatedly embarrassed by his own inability to stop such an unfortunate dynamic. Before them was a smart, decent young man who had made a common mistake and was about to be dragged down into a system that trapped so many people. This young man appeared to be an upstanding student and citizen. Maybe he was a little rambunctious but what kid isn't? Should he be grouped in with those who were bound to be lifelong criminals? Shouldn't he be saved from such a fate? Or, maybe he was faking it? But even so, he was smart enough to know all the right words to say and any person that clever is often smart enough to fix themselves in the long run. Provided they get another chance to do so.

Damian finished his argument red faced. "You are asking me to kill myself and I can't do it. I don't imagine that anyone in my position would."

"My silence here today is based on self-preservation. If there is any other way I can help you without slitting my own throat please let me know and I'll do it, I promise. I just want to get out of here in one piece." Damian's fingers came back together as his head lowered in sobbing spasms. All he could do was cry until the guards took him away. It was an Oscar worthy performance and though it flew a little over the top, that might have been just the effect he needed.

CHAPTER 35

▼

"The board is considering shortening or rescinding your sentence." Emily Burke, Damian's Mother, was an intrepid newspaper reporter with an irrepressible nose for justice. She had always believed that her son was innocent of the charges. If not completely innocent then at least he shared the blame with the rest of the HAWKS gang and yet they were running free.

"Can they do that?" Damian was on the edge of his seat in the cafeteria. This was where parents, friends and loved ones could talk to the residents during mid afternoon hours. Damian's Mom had not been around for a whole month but she had been working hard on the outside to change her son's status.

"Yes and no. They can make recommendations to the judge, and so can your caseworker. I'll be filing a 51A form through the Department of Social Services alleging that they did not adequately protect you while being held here but you have to be ready to give them what they want." Her piecing eyes were magnified through a large set of thick black-rimmed glasses. "Can you please tell them what they want to hear?"

Damian sagged a little on the bench and rubbed his face. "Yeah, I need to get out of here. I'll tell them whatever."

"No Damian. Whatever is not going to do it. You have to turn in your buddies from Avon, tell them what really happened at that house on Crown Street. Leave out any mention of your mythical Sevlow creature or you will lose all credibility. Just give them the names and affiliations of the gang members you met here in DYS and in Avon. You will give them details, dates, locations and then maybe, maybe you can be screened out of the program."

"I can't do that Mom, you don't understand."

"You can and you will." Emily pulled a file of papers out of her briefcase and opened it in front of Damian. "These are copies of your police files. You've been picked up by the Avon police five times, you've been questioned for suspicion twelve times…"

"They pick on me, you know that."

"…you have been chased six times without capture but they had a positive identification…"

"I was jogging, swiftly."

"…stealing from April's market, breaking into the Library…"

"I was returning a book."

"…running around on the roof of the high school?"

"A tennis ball got hit up there."

"This is not a joke, none of it!" Emily shuffled the papers and shut the file. "These types of accusations will haunt you later in life. Anything you do can be compromised if the wrong people get a hold of these files. You could lose jobs. You could be accused of crimes you didn't commit. Someone could use you as a scapegoat all because these charges suggest that you are already a career criminal. Damian, public image is important. This has to stop!"

"They throw those out when I turn 18."

"No, they're supposed to throw them out but they may not. You're in here for a level 1 infraction, that's the lowest level but let me tell you, from here on in the charges only get worse, the time only gets longer and harder. Deal with this now!"

He was rapidly tapping his foot under the table. She was looking out for him and the board was right, he was going to have to turn all of these people in. Emily fervently believed that Damian had taken a fall for the HAWKS and now he was becoming a pawn for the SSP. Maybe he was starting to recognize it as well. If ever there was a time to prove himself, a least partly innocent, this was his chance. If he didn't speak up while those in charge are willing to hear him out, they may never listen to him again.

"Call the board, I'll do it." He rubbed his face furiously as if punishing himself for agreeing to this betrayal. "I'll talk, I'll tell them everything. Let's get it over with." His sneaky smiles were gone, his Oscar imaginings defeated. This was one fiasco he couldn't act his way out of. Damian had to become a rat.

CHAPTER 36

▼

"You one sly mother fucker." Darius walked up behind Damian who was packing his clothes for the trip home.

"I'm redeemed, sort of," Damian said without emotion but did not elaborate.

"No conditions of liberty?"

"None."

"You're smart. You convinced the board to unlock the chains. I've..." Darius walked over the closest cot and sat on the end. "I've been going in and out of juvie a long time, I'm about done serving a level 5 infraction but I've never seen anyone jump the fence the way you did."

Damian wanted to assure Darius that he did not give up any information about the SSP but his desire to placate the gang member might be seen as a pre-emptive attempt to cover his own ass. It might be easier to guide his assumptions than confirm any facts.

"But how did you do it." Darius wasn't asking; his tone had changed to that of a soft command.

"I did what you said," He faced the king thug keeping hold of his greatest weapon, a brilliant poker face that told no lies. "You said that if I want to be in the inner circle then I'd have to give up the HAWKS. Well, I turned in enough info so that the police can get a warrant to arrest Dutch. Without Dutch, the HAWKS are as good as done."

Darius's eyes floated away from Damian as he considered what this meant. Damian may have turned against the HAWKS but it was probably more to save his own ass than to show loyalty to the Posse. Or was it?

"I've got someone on the outside I want you to stay in touch with. He'll be your contact; he'll be your guide to our people on the streets. If you prove yourself, he'll bring you into the circle."

"Prove myself?" He had already done that hadn't he? "I took the first shot at Al. I charged the rumble."

"And you got leveled."

"But…"

"Listen Sly," Darius walked up to him putting only inches between them. "Ratting on your friends isn't usually a good way to show your teeth so even though I'm cool with it, others may not be. Let's keep that in our pocket, k? Besides, we all fought the rumble so if the other boyz are to approve of you it has to be for something else, some other feat."

Damian nodded and was about to ask again.

"To prove that you are no longer a HAWK and to prove that you are loyal to us, you're gonna have to face down the leader of your old team. I think that should clear things up, settle all doubts."

"Dutch? You want me to…fight Dutch? Um, they're probably going to arrest him so…" He had been careful only to use James's code name so that the SSP would know very little about him but to fight him? Damian was tough but he was also two years Dutch's junior and more importantly they had been good friends since forth grade. He couldn't fight Dutch. There was no way…

Darius expected hesitance. To take down the leader of your old gang was no easy task but that's why it would work. "Can you take him? Is he so tough that the Sly one is gonna have problems?"

"No, no problem. If he's not caught that is. I mean…if you think it'll work then I'll do it. When I get out of here I'll meet up with your man, take him to find Dutch and I'll…I'll kick his ass in front of everyone. That should put the last nail in his coffin."

"I thought you'd want revenge as it is?" Darius spoke through side of his mouth.

"I do, I just figured he'd end up in here."

"Good, SSP for life." Darius held his fist sideways to his chest. "Schmel knew that, he died for us. His dad knew that and now you're gonna learn."

"For life," Damian whispered. "So who will I be meeting on the outside?"

Darius was walking towards the doorway, the same spot where they had attacked the giant guard only a week before. He looked at the remainder of the bloodstain on the rug before aiming his eyes at Damian.

"You might know him, he hangs out in Avon. He's my brother, my younger brother. His name is Tyrone."

DUTCH'S BLOODY DEFEAT

CHAPTER 37

▼

"He called me last night," John placed his jacket on the back of a handmade wooden chair in Lazio's kitchen. The table was covered with trade paperback and hardcover books, so many that they threatened to spill onto his feet. Stunned by the dark covers he stopped mid-sentence to read the titles. *Mastering Witchcraft* by Paul Huson, *History of Witchcraft* by Jeffrey Russell, *Witchcraft theory and practice* by Ly de Angeles and then he had to turn the next book to catch a long title in it's entirety—*The Cult of Kinship in Anglo-Saxon England: The transition from Paganism to Christianity* by William A. Chaney. Lazio must have been deep in study before this special meeting was called.

"What is this one about?" He asked totally sidetracked.

"Oh," Lazio tapped the cover with his long bony finger, "That tells the story of how Christianity began by stealing pagan symbols, rites and rituals and then calling them their own."

"Guys?" Psycho called them back to the stunned face of Dutch who had been waiting to hear John's important news.

"Damian called you last night?" Dutch repeated the statement in disbelief. "Why didn't he call me?" He was questioning himself more than John but his friend had an immediate answer.

"He's being watched."

"By who?" Psycho bit off half a salted cracker and set it next to his hot chocolate. The days had grown darker and colder since Dutch and Psycho foolishly stole a car just after giving away two hundred dollars of John's money to a local gun dealer who believed himself an earth worthy disciple of Baphomet. John had grown colder as well.

"What difference does it make?" He swept snow off the shoulders of his coat and sniffed the air just to see if his frostbitten nose was still working. "You have to get my money back and tell me what the fuck happened."

Psycho explained the exchange and how it turned out to be a set-up. He told him that when Dutch opened the hatchback of the car there were no guns, only a piece of paper that read, "This is a stolen car," and "You are being videotaped."

John put his face in hands but then pulled them away because they were so cold. "So is this a blackmail attempt? Does he want more money? Fuck him! I'm not giving you guys a dime until this gets settled."

"We haven't heard from him," Psycho mumbled, "But I think he did all this so that he could sell us the guns without reprisals."

Again John's look of bewilderment might have been amusing if not for the situation.

"No really, follow me on this. I think he wanted some insurance to make sure he could control the transactions from here on in."

"From here on in?" John's frozen lips slurred the words a little but he got them out with enough derision to end the debate.

"No, John's right, we can't trust D-Rod." Dutch said firmly. "So let's move on, now, John, if Damian is being tailed then it must be important, we need to…" He knew that John was pissed but his portly friend only cared about his monetary loss due to their incompetence.

"We need to get my money back, that's my priority. We need," John walked into the living room and stood looking at Psycho, Dutch and Becca on the couch. She was again enfolded into the latest newspaper as he spoke down to them. "We need to get the guns we were promised so I can shoot D-Rod in the fuckin temple!"

The three of them sat silent. John has always been the complacent member of the team, the brains, the calm innocent follower but that all changed when his hard earned money got involved in team business.

Psycho finished his cracker, Dutch stared at the floor and Becca hid behind the local section. She involved herself in the continuing saga about the search for a little girl named Kaitlin. This was the fifth story that followed the details of her disappearance. She was still missing and no body had been found but the grandmother of the six year old had not given up hope.

Luckily Lazio broke the silence. "John do you want some hot chocolate? It has no cellulose, diglycerides or artificial colors."

John stopped brooding and tilted his head to one side. "Lazio, does it have any taste left in it?"

"Yeah it's good." Psycho assured him while holding up the warm cup.

"Is there some witchcraft potion in here?" John sniffed it carefully. "I'm not going to turn into a hedgehog or anything?" He finally tasted it. "Ok, I'll have some." His train of thought broken by the promise of food he found the closest chair and sat down heavily. The chair creaked from his weight.

"Careful that's made of Teak."

His brow furrowed, "Teak? Ok, I'll bite, why is it made of Teak?"

"In case of Vampires." Assured that the chair was not going to break; Lazio returned to the kitchen.

"So if a Vampire breaks into your house, are you going to beat him to death with it?" John smirked.

Lazio answered him with a serious tone, "Only if I have to."

He wanted to harp on this illogical possibility but Dutch was persisting with his questions.

"John, what did Damian say?" He asked with more respect than he was used to giving.

"Oh, he ah, he said he joined a gang while he was in juvie and now they are tailing him around Avon hoping that he'll bump into you."

"Why me?" Dutch was calming down a little, after all he had been through recently he was hardly afraid of another gang but his nerves remained on edge.

"He's supposed to fight you in order to prove to the gang that he's one of them. Plus he said something about Peter trying to be the new head of the gang too or whatever."

"Or whatever?" Dutch jumped to his feet and walked up to John. "Or whatever? My best friend is supposed to fight me, engage in hand to hand combat with me and you say Or whatever?"

"It's not his fault," Psycho lowered his cocoa back onto the table just in case Dutch lost his temper, well, more than he normally does.

"So you'll fight him and get it over with." Lazio was comfortable with the idea. He circled the counter and handed the warm cup to John. "You can take him right?"

Dutch shivered with anger.

"Dutch..." Becca spoke calmly but he shot her a warning stare and she stopped in her tracks.

"I don't believe you." Dutch growled down at John, "Damian wouldn't leave the HAWKS and if he did he wouldn't call you." Or rather Dutch didn't want to believe that Damian wouldn't call him first. They were friends weren't they? They had a warrior's bond. It had to stand for something.

"He probably couldn't find you." Lazio said unafraid using simple common sense.

Dutch's intensity faded a little. He was a hard man to find and everyone was trying.

"Are you going to stand there all day?" John asked while lifting the white porcelain glass to his lips.

Dutch drifted over to the frosted glass windows and watched a department of public works dump truck with a large yellow snowplow push aside mounds of white dirt as it passed Lazio's house. "What did he want?"

John didn't hear him as Becca had turned on the television.

"What did he want?" Dutch said loud enough so everyone could hear him.

"He wants a meeting." John answered.

"With all of us?" Psycho asked.

"No, with me." John kept his eyes on Dutch.

Dutch took a deep breath in through his nose. He was trying so hard to keep his cool. "Ok, we can do that."

"We?" John wondered aloud.

"We need to be there." Psycho amended.

"We're *going* to be there." Dutch said without allowing for any dissention. "I have one question though."

John couldn't believe they were doing this. When was this James Bond mentality going to end? What were they going to do, bug John? Give him a tape recorder and cover the meeting like a sting operation? This was ridiculous; they are teenagers. How bad could it be?

"John," Dutch continued. "Who is the gang that he supposedly belongs to?"

"They're from Brockton. It's the Spring Street Posse."

Dutch and Psycho locked eyes.

"This shit just got way worse." Psycho put down his cup and broke eye contact.

"Fuck!" Dutch clenched his teeth. "This would be so much easier if we had those guns."

"And my money." John interjected.

"Guns are not our best weapon," said Lazio who finally decided to add his two cents. "We are organized. We are smart, certainly smarter than a Brockton street gang. We can design a way to beat them at their own game and get back at this Damian at the same time."

"We're listening." Becca chimed in happy to see that she wasn't the only one who didn't like the idea of gunfire being the solution to everything.

"I've got a gizmo that will help us out nicely." Lazio dug through his workta-ble, reached under a pile of loose parchment, pushed aside a book of shadows and pulled out a small black box with four buttons and a microphone. "I've got a mini-cassette recorder."

John rolled his eyes. "I fucking knew it."

CHAPTER 38

▼

"He's not late, we're early." Psycho looked at his black waterproof watch and recalculated military time just to make sure his assessment was right.

"Dude you don't have to add hours just minus twelve from whatever the number is." Dutch pointed to the wall clock.

"Oh yeah, that's easier." Psycho again played out the mental math and this time came up with 2:16 in the afternoon.

"Table for two?" A flighty waitress picked up two plastic coated menus and started walking to her left.

"No, we'll take the smoking section." Dutch corrected.

"Oh, ok." She reversed and headed for the right side of the restaurant.

"That would have been dumb," He whispered to Psycho whose eyes were locked on the dainty waist of the 108pound waitress who promptly set their table. Dutch was a little embarrassed by his friend's ogling when he got the idea that she knew she was being watched.

"Someone will be right here to get your orders," The speed with which she walked away made Dutch feel like she was suspicious of them.

"C'mon," Psycho played with Dutch's attitude of moral superiority, "She was cute."

"I'm not disputing it." He picked up the menu and scanned the chicken dishes. "I thought she knew…"

"What?"

"Forget it."

Psycho dismissed Dutch's paranoia as a byproduct of his continued lack of sleep. "Can we see from here?" He looked over the waist high wall into the bar and then over the bar into the non-smoking section.

"Well?"

"It matters where they sit." He slumped back down but then turned to look at the entrance. "At least they won't see us when they come in." Their view of the entrance was blocked by painted glass and a chest high cash register.

"Are you going to order something?" Psycho asked of Dutch who was eyeing a picture of chicken cordon bleu like a cat ready to pounce on the table.

"I can't...no money."

"Yeah me neither."

"But we can't just sit here."

"We'll order drinks..."

"And then what?" Dutch was being very naïve for someone who wanted to live the life of a rogue spy.

"I don't know. Don't worry about it until the time comes." Psycho found thirty-seven cents of loose change in his pockets and set it on the table.

When the waiter arrived they ordered drinks and briefly explained that they were waiting for a friend. Psycho did a good job making sure the conversation was short and not very memorable, if things went bad they didn't want the waiter or anyone else to have a good make on them.

"They're early too." Dutch stood the menu up on the table and peered over it with his eyes.

"That doesn't look suspicious," Psycho shook his head but didn't turn back to the door just in case they could see his way.

"There's three of them," Dutch gave a running commentary, "There wasn't supposed to be three...oh good they're going to non-smoking."

The waiter placed the drinks on the table and Psycho waved him away suggesting that they were not ready yet.

"They're sitting almost exactly across from us," Dutch turned the menu to keep his face hidden.

"Can they see us?"

"No, they're in a booth."

"Will you put that down," Psycho pulled at the top of the menu but Dutch snatched it away from him. "I'm being careful."

"You're being ridiculous, just trust in the plan."

"It's my plan."

"Yeah but it's a good plan so leave it alone."

Dutch lowered the menu and watched as the three engaged in subdued conversation. The spying thing bored Psycho. He decided to reach for the dessert menu when the hammer in his pocket banged loud against the pressed wood bench he was sitting on.

"What are you doing?" Dutch shushed him. Still in the absence of guns they had both brought along the usual weapons in the pockets of their coats. The idea being that if John was attacked or Damian brought one too many people then at least they had something that could do a little damage in a fight.

"Sorry," Psycho sat up straight and adjusted his coat so that the handle was sitting flat within the pocket next to his right hip.

"There he goes," Dutch watched John head to the bathroom. That was where he would turn on the mini-cassette recorder and then return to the table to talk business. Meanwhile Dutch tried to make out who the third person was but the guy's head was half blocked between bottles of Pinot and Chardonnay. "I think…he looks familiar but…"

"Are they talking? Where's John, he's taking too long. And he's back," Dutch smiled at how well it was all progressing.

"Oops he rubbed his nose, no, wait, he's got the sniffles," Psycho was mocking him under his breath. "How does it go, if he wipes his forehead with his left hand then we firebomb the bar but if he picks his nose with his right finger then we jump the waitress?" Psycho smiled.

"You just want to jump the waitress."

"Don't you?" Psycho looked for her again but his beloved eye candy had retreated to the safety of the closed off kitchen.

"No."

"Speaking of which, did you and Becca?"

"That's none of your business."

"So that would be a no. Why hasn't it happened, I thought that's what you wanted? A HAWKS groupie."

"That's not what I want, now knock it off or you'll get no dessert." Dutch tried to playfully jibe away the questions but underneath it really bothered him. *Why hadn't he had sex with Becca? What was wrong with him? She said he wasn't ready yet but ready in what way?* As always he shook away the discontent by returning to the task at hand.

On the other side of the restaurant John was trying hard to keep his cool. There were so many things that could go wrong. The tape player could make an odd noise or the tape could run out and click in his pocket. The conversation was nerve racking enough without having to worry about being found out as a double agent. He listened intently to every word they said and tried not to react at all.

"We've got Rafael right now and he's for real but Peter is making his move." Tyrone's gibberish of names and places meant nothing to John.

"But your brother Darius will be out soon, how is he gonna take it that you're with Peter?"

"I'm not with Peter."

John thought this meeting was going to be about him but Damian and Tyrone mostly just argued with each other. He decided to play cool, like he didn't care and for twelve excruciating minutes that's exactly what he did. In the end they gave John the info he needed and the meeting was abruptly over.

"They're getting up." Dutch almost stood himself but then remembered his cover.

"That was fast."

The three young men hadn't ordered anything. John broke away again visiting the bathroom to turn off his microphone and within seconds they were walking out the door.

"It was also uneventful." Psycho really wanted to fight someone but unfortunately the plan went as planned.

"Now what?" Dutch wanted to get up and go but they still had to deal with the check.

"Relax, I'll walk all the way to the other side and use the bathroom, there's another exit over there." Psycho steadied the hammer in his pocket. "Meanwhile you get up and walk out the front door. No one's watching us. We'll meet at the car, just be smooth about it."

Dutch gulped hard and took the last swig of his Pepsi, well; the ice had melted so it was more like ice water with a dash of Pepsi. "Ok, I'm fine."

Psycho stood and walked off. Shortly after, Dutch slid out of his seat and sauntered out the front like nothing had happened.

CHAPTER 39

▼

"I can't hear anything." Lazio turned up the volume and put his ear against the machine. "O wait it's there, it's faint but I can hear a little." He stopped the recorder and rewound it for the third time.

"Lazio it's not a message from space, they're voices, either you can understand them or you can't." Dutch sat at the study table with Psycho. They were playing poker with tarot cards. It was amusing only so long as Lazio was insulted by the game.

"I made us some hot tea if anyone is interested?" Becca was still wearing her HAWKS uniform. Dutch & Psycho returned from Brockton and met up with Becca who had been exercising the day away while waiting for them. She wanted to go on the mission, insisted in fact, that she could be valuable but they denied her.

After picking her up, their first order of business was to take a drive past an apartment complex on the other side of town to find out if Lazio had completed his mission. In a light blue house across the street from a convenience store Lazio had been knocking on doors and asking questions about D-Rod. He used what little he could remember of the kid from a few years earlier and it turned out that his memory was remarkably accurate. D-Rod lived with his mother in a third floor apartment visible from the parking lot across the street. They had the address, the floor, and precisely when his Mom went to work, 10pm. He had found D-Rod so that when the time comes, when they have an arsenal, they can nail him to the wall as he had done to them, twice.

After picking up Lazio they all returned to Becca's apartment. Her father had gone away for a short weekend vacation so the HAWKS had a warm home for a couple more days. Lazio brought along his tarot cards to help determine their immediate future but almost immediately Dutch and Psycho were trying to fling them into a black beret on the coffee table ten feet away. When their aim proved weak, they changed the game to poker.

"I'll have some." John was laid out on the couch with his feet up on a table. "Since hell is freezing over we might as well enjoy a little tea." He had been snide since feeling that he was taking more chances than anyone else and well, he was right.

"John c'mon, let's hear it." Dutch nudged his feet off the table and sat precariously close. Psycho lost interest in the cards and slumped on the floor going through the ten channels on the television looking for appropriate programming, something with guns and bombs would be nice.

"Damian was acting way more macho than I've ever seen before." John said with great relish.

"You think he was putting on a show?" Dutch asked.

"When is he not putting on a show?" Psycho added.

"Is he an actor?" Lazio, who had never met Damian, didn't realize he was part of a stream of interruptions.

"Let him finish," Becca carried three steaming mugs into the room and set them on the table.

"I just assume he's always lying." John shrugged, "All I know is what he said. He joined the SSP in juvie his inside contact is a guy named Darius who gets out next month. Darius wants to lead the SSP now that a guy named Schmel is dead. Killed by a cop."

"So that wasn't Darius who came into the restaurant?" Since it was void of any manly action movies Psycho shut off the TV to follow their own drama.

"No, that was Tyrone, he's Darius's younger brother and he's Damian's outside contact. Tyrone is supposed to be there when Damian fights Dutch, as a witness. He'll report back to his brother to get accepted or whatever, I think it's their version of the flag tower run."

"So the fight," Lazio stopped the recorder and joined the conversation, "is an initiation?"

"It makes sense," Psycho chimed in, "it kills two birds with one stone. Damian takes out the leader of the HAWKS and proves his loyalty to the SSP. He destroys one gang and joins another."

"But is he serious?" Dutch asked no one in particular.

"I don't know." John replied in frustration. He couldn't read Damian's mind, no one could. Damian lived in the moment; he existed only to influence his audience. It was possible that no one really knew what he was like except for Dutch, or so he claims. "Besides there is something else going on. Damian and Tyrone disagreed over who actually leads the SSP. Like it was up for debate."

"They said that to you?" Psycho edged a little closer and reached for the last mug on table.

"No, not directly. They argued over it. Tyrone said Darius was going to take over for Rafael who was temporarily running things. Damian asked how Rafael could be in charge if Peter was running a crew out of Avon. It was very confusing."

"Peter has SSP guys in Avon?" Dutch almost fell over at the news. "What the hell does he have to do with all this?"

John glanced around the room as all eyes locked on him. Dutch knew that Peter was a gangster wannabe but how far had he gone in these last months to make it happen?

"When are you ever going to read a newspaper?" John asked Dutch directly.

"That's Becca's job."

"Well then she should know that the kid who used to run the gang, Schmel, was killed by a Brockton cop last week. Peter and Rafael were identified but escaped from the scene. It made the front page cause this vigilante cop put five bullets in Schmel only to find out that the kid was carrying an empty pistol."

"He was running the gang?" Lazio asked.

"Yes, the newspaper said he inherited the role from his father who was also killed by Brockton cops."

"So with Schmel dead the leadership goes to...?" Psycho asked as if John knew more than the paper explained. Oddly enough John put together the pieces from Damian and Tyrone's spat.

"They said Rafael is Schmel's cousin so I don't think he wants to give up the family business to either Darius or Peter."

Dutch turned to Becca, "Did you know any of this?"

"Aah, I read about Schmel," Becca was struggling to follow all the facts, as she had not put together these pieces in any order. The family heritage was John's theory but it didn't hold water with her. "Why would the bloodline matter?"

"I don't know, maybe they see drug dealing as if it were a business. When the person who owns a business dies, the company gets passed down to the heir. This is a big deal to them, they seem to think that whoever runs the Posse is the king of Brockton."

"What I want to know is, whose side is Damian on?" Lazio asked probably more concerned about his own seat at the table than Damian's allegiance.

"To be honest I think he's on his own side. I don't think he cares who wins; he seems...stuck in the middle. For that matter so does Tyrone." John was ambivalent as well. Why should they care who is running things?

"So when do we have this fight?" Dutch asked in submission to the fact that it needed to happen. Win or lose it would settle things between Dutch and Damian and it just might get Damian off the hook with the SSP. Dutch owed him one, he couldn't back down from this, he had to fight. Besides, this could lead to bigger things.

"You can't fight him, are you crazy? He's your friend." Becca sideswiped Dutch but only received docile looks from the room. They agreed with his decision, either that or they just wanted to see a good fight.

"I have to. He went to jail for me. Damian wants to do this for reasons that I don't yet understand but I do know that it has to happen." He lifted his eyes to John for an answer.

"He wants to meet tomorrow by the town hall...in Avon. He said to bring whomever you want."

CHAPTER 40

▼

"When is he going to show up?" Dutch was sitting on the back of Lazio's car as it rested in the shadow of the twisted tree behind TC's house in Avon. They were angled across the street from the town hall and would see if a car drove up or if anyone arrived by foot. There was a juvenile tension in the air, a schoolyard yearning for the tussle that was soon to come.

"He said to be here or he'd find us..." John shrugged at the verbal threat but caught Dutch's sharp look over his shoulder.

He'd find us? Just how serious is Damian taking all of this? Was his old friend that far gone so as to believe in his own hype? If so, Damian knew he was at a disadvantage in age, in size and skill to guy who had faced far more treacherous threats. What if Damian was desperate to win? What if they threatened his life or his family to ensure a victory? *What if*, and Dutch got chills about this one, *what if Damian brought a hidden weapon to make sure there was a conclusive ending?* He didn't have to express any of these fears with his brood; they had the same nervous reaction as if they were going to be fighting themselves. Then again, anything could happen.

Damian suddenly appeared.

"Took long enough." Dutch jumped to the ground and instinctively tightened a fist inside his fingerless gloves.

Psycho jogged up to Dutch's side and whispered low, "You ready for this?"

"Don't have much of a choice do I?"

"Maybe they'll start a brawl and we can all jump in?"

Dutch looked him in the eyes, "Be ready for it."

Damian had rounded the corner of the small yellow store one house away. On his right was Paul, on his left Tyrone, Peter was nowhere in sight. Damian held the lead until he reached the dirt clearing. He held out both arms to stop his comrades, "I said I would handle this," He reminded them.

"We got your back." Paul promised with a sneer. Tyrone said nothing. He was here as a witness and didn't act like he trusted Damian or Paul. He appeared ready to run if this whole thing turned out to be a fraud but the HAWKS couldn't read him so long as he stayed cool and distant.

Damian stepped far ahead of his new crew and stood in the middle of the dirt clearing waiting for Dutch to meet him half way.

"What's this all about?" Dutch asked with Psycho following him right up to the line of battle. Dutch could feel his knees weaken as the igniting sensation of fight or flight started to take hold. He measured self-control as best he could. This was one fight he could not walk away from. Damian had his reasons for being here so they had to see it through. Besides, he owed him one, that's what he kept reminding himself, he owed him one.

"You know what it's about," Damian said in theatrical tones so everyone could hear. "I went to jail for you mother fucker! I had to sit in a plain white room in Brockton for the last three months because you ran away from the police. What's up with that? I thought you were my friend? Why didn't you tell the cops the truth? You wanted to raid that kennel, you wanted to attack that Randolph guy. It was all about the money that was supposed to be stashed in the house. It was your plan Dutch; now face up to it! Or are you a coward?"

"The money?" Dutch caught a wink from Damian or at least he thought he did. Was that a wink or was his former friend trying to talk his way out of this?

"You planned the break-in, admit it. You thought it would be an easy payday. You said that guy had stereo equipment and a safe full of cash."

Psycho was perplexed as to what the hell Damian was talking about but he didn't want to interrupt. There may be some lying going on but judging from Damian's body language he was clearly ready to fight and Dutch was not backing down. Lying or not, scam or front, it didn't matter, this was going to happen.

Dutch stepped up, "You made your own choices! Now you have to live with them! Traitor!" He moved closer and strained his voice with anger. His left foot steadied slightly ahead of his right, it was the making of a fighting stance. Their bodies were positioning to attack. These two had been on a competitive collision course ever since the day that Dutch aced Damian's record during the flag tower run. They have always been trying to one up each other. On that day Dutch became the leader of their circle of friends and Damian fell to the level of subordinate. He never truly got over it.

Dutch's imagination was consumed by his current hostility. Maybe this was Damian's chance to reorder their world, as he believed it should be? Forget Darius, Rafael and Peter, maybe it was Damian who wanted to run the SSP? If that were so then Dutch would have to stop him!

"Face it Jamie Ballum you don't have the balls to..." Damian ate the wind of his next words as Dutch's left knee slammed up into his sternum. It was followed by an overhand right that carried all of Dutch's weight and power behind it. Damian saw the huge punch coming and pulled his head back. A fingerless glove tore across the skin of Damian's throat slicing open a clean gash.

"Get him Sly!" Paul yelled from only five feet away as he had closed the gap closer to the action. On the other side Psycho also moved up just in case Paul tried to jump in. John and Lazio remained frozen at the back of the car disbelieving the show in front of them. Dutch and Damian, fast friends since forth grade were engaged in a bloody fistfight. For some reason they never believed that it would happen but this was as real as it gets.

John could feel a twisting in his stomach and started to wonder what would happen to the HAWKS if Dutch lost? They would be done, over, disbanded, that was exactly what John wanted but he didn't want it to happen like this. Things would be even worse if Damian won. Dutch was mental in his own way but Damian was certifiable. No, John decided as he watched the two spin around in what had become a standing wrestling match, Dutch needed to win. "Kick his ass Dutch!" John yelled at the top of his wind finally getting behind his General.

"Where's your karate kick now mother fucker!" Damian chided him while grabbing Dutch in a side headlock as they wrestled closer to John's car. Everyone cleared out of the way.

"Fuck you traitor!" Dutch blasted back just before his face was slammed into the car's grill with a crunch. Damian rammed his friend's head into the molded plastic again and again until Dutch slipped out of the lock. His face trickled with crisscrossing imprints but there was no time to stop, he had to even the score.

"I'm going to fuck up that pretty face of yours!" Dutch grabbed Damian's blond lochs and pulled his head down into an up rising knee. Damian half blocked the blow so Dutch pulled back to knee him again and again slamming them into his arms and elbows. The moves looked to be happening in slow motion. Each thrust was off balance, each block ready for the next blow.

"What are they doing?" Psycho couldn't help but notice that it didn't look quite right. *Are they whispering to each other?*

Damian grabbed one of Dutch's legs to stop his momentum and they rolled against the front of the car falling to the ground. Dutch, slightly the stronger of the two, managed to push Damian's face down in the dirt and raised his right arm for another huge right hand. Damian was clinging with all his might so that Dutch would not be free enough to throw the punch but his fingers were slipping away. Dutch was simply too strong, he pulled back his right arm for the final blow...

"Guys, the cops are here! Someone told them about Dutch! I heard it on the police radio!" TC screamed down from his bedroom window to the mass of friends that had circled around the fight.

Dutch and Damian looked at TC and almost immediately heard the siren's coming down West Main Street. They were pulling up in front of the house.

"Fuck," Dutch whispered in the lowest possible breath so only Damian could hear him, "What do you want to do?"

Damian tilted his head a little, "Wait for the sirens to get closer and then *you* run away."

They held their position for a few seconds more but it was starting to look suspicious.

"What the hell are they doing?" Tyrone asked. He was not happy about hearing that the police were coming. He started to back away.

A police cruiser reared so close to the front of the TC's house that it's squealing tires made everyone jump in fright. It was that one moment of trigger fear that did the trick. Chaos erupted.

"Fuck they're here!" Tyrone, ever-afraid Avon's cops because of all the rumors of racism, was the first to turn tail and run off but he stopped just long enough to watch from behind the adjacent houses.

Damian and Dutch pulled free from their struggle at the same moment that everyone scattered. Dutch stared back at him for one brief instant but then turned and disappeared into a field of rhubarbs.

"Come back you coward!" Damian screamed at him as Dutch bolted into the woods. He had run away from the fight. Damian won and Tyrone watched it happen.

The only people who stayed behind were TC and Damian. It was TC's house and he was adept at stalling the police while Dutch disappeared. Damian, for some odd reason, waited for the police. He was not going to run, be identified, caught and arrested all over again. This time he had a whole new tactic for staying out of jail.

FREE THE CHILD

CHAPTER 41

▼

"Now what the fuck is this?" Aubrey had just pulled off Warren Avenue when he saw the flashing lights streaking out from the side street on which he lived. Granted it was a bad neighborhood so maybe the disturbance had nothing to do with him but that was never his first instinct. He turned slowly into the curve to see that his porch was being raided by a significant number of Brockton police. As he got a better look he realized it was the BRATS, the Brockton elite SWAT team led by Lieutenant Baravella, the most feared cop in the city.

The SWAT team must have broke their way in through the front door, the back, and several side windows simultaneously as the house was swarming with guns and uniforms. While he watched the circular rhythmic movements of flashlights held perpendicular to gun barrels he was just in time to see Baravella himself burst back out the door cradling a thick white comforter.

"They found her." The barely breathing body of Kaitlin was wrapped in that blanket and being rushed to a still running cruiser.

"Fuck this!" Slamming his car in reverse Aubrey backed into a police car that had quietly pulled up behind him. "Fuck!" He was trapped but he was not going to let them take him. They already found Kaitlin and after a rough search they were going to find everything. His guns, his drugs and the pictures he kept of other children he had abducted would be used against him. *I knew I should've stuck with niggers.* Kaitlin was the first white girl he had ever coerced to come home with him. The rest of the little kids had been black and hardly anyone looked for them. With that little girl alive there wasn't a legal loophole big enough to help him escape the noose they'd have waiting. For the very first time there was no easy way out. Aubrey Truelson had to run for his life!

Swinging open his driver's side door he dived out of the car and sprinted across the pavement. He could have grabbed the pistol that was hidden underneath his driver's side seat but if he was armed they wouldn't hesitate to shoot. Aubrey knew the law. Right now he was simply a suspicious figure fleeing on foot. They had no idea that he was owner of the house being raided. It would take them another hour before they would find out. Information of this type travels slow and that always gave him an advantage.

"That's him, he's getting away!" One officer yelled as he pried himself out of the damaged cruiser. Luckily another uniformed officer had seen the incident from the front yard and began pursuit on foot. He barked out requests for assistance into the CB attached to his uniform. "I've got Aubrey Truelson heading down Nilsson Street towards Montello. Assistance on...I need a car at the Nilsson Street Bridge to cut him off..."

Aubrey could hear parts of the request. "How the fuck do they know me?" He mumbled in a breathless rage while jumping a wooden fence and racing through a backyard. *How do they know who I am? How did they recognize me so fast? What the fuck is going on?* Aubrey had to head for the hill that led down to the railroad tracks. He couldn't outrun them on the street so there was no other way to go. An officer yelled for the Nilsson Street Bridge so instead he switched directions and stumbled down the hill towards his left. When his feet splashed into a puddle next to the rails he felt his ankles twinge with pain. He had landed the wrong way but it was not going to stop him.

"He's on the tracks...make that the Grove Street Bridge and he's slowing down..." The officer climbed carefully down the hill. The fading light made Aubrey's form into little more than a shadow within a shadow. The officer raised his gun and moved in a slow jog towards the Grove Street underpass as he had already lost immediate sight of the perpetrator.

Red and blue flashing lights illuminated the night sky over the bridge. A large round spotlight beamed down to the officer jogging along the tracks. "Get it off me, check the other side." He commanded as the beam sliced through the darkness.

The high angled light cut into the woods, along the edges of each side of the tracks and then out into the distance. Aubrey was nowhere to be found.

"He didn't pass by the bridge..." The beam man yelled down to his cohort. "He must still be under there."

The slow-moving officer on the tracks was holding his revolver ahead of him as he wondered if Aubrey was armed as well. In that moment he decided that he'd fire at any movement just in case. This was not a game. He had a wife of four years and a child of two months to take care of. He had a brand new Ford Bronco and a two story Duplex on Hillcrest Ave to pay for. He didn't want to get even a little hurt. There was no reason not to kill this guy so why take chances? Slowly he reached around his waist for a small flashlight clipped to the back of his belt. He unsnapped the button to turn it on as a shadow raced at him. He lost the split second he would have needed but in the rush he pulled the trigger anyway. The shot hit the bridge causing the officers up top to pull out their own weapons and aim down at the tracks. The stunned officer felt a hand knock his gun upward while he could only brace for the impact of a blade that found its way angled sideways under his left armpit.

"There he is!" The beam found the struggle and one reflexive shot was fired but two intertwined bodies crashed to the ground. The light jerked aside leaving the bodies in darkness again.

"What are you doing?" The second beat cop was too late. The spotlight widened its beam to identify who had fallen. A uniformed body was stretched out on the tracks his empty left hand shaking uncontrollably, his wide open eyes straining at the sky as he gasped for air. The shadow of Aubrey had bolted into the trees and ran alongside the hill under the cover of heavy, snow-laden branches. He had dodged the beam, stole the revolver and they never saw what direction he sprinted off to but it was clear who got shot.

"You hit the wrong guy. God damn it!"

Up went the radio may day, "We have an officer down...get an ambulance to the Grove Street bridge...Aubrey Truelson is still on the run and now he's armed with a police issued revolver."

CHAPTER 42

▼

"Dude I don't want to rent that." Paul took the empty brown VHS box out of Peter's hand and placed it on the wrong shelf. "It's my Mom's video card so we're not watching the Godfather again."

"Fine then you pick." Peter's mind wasn't into it anyway. He was innately worried about the phone call he had placed five hours earlier. It took real effort to keep his hands busy lest he continuously made fists in which his fingernails would dig nervously into the skin of his palms. The pain was a welcome distraction, keeping his mind far away from the consequences of that phone call. It would all be a little easy to handle if he had something strong to drink.

"Good, I'll get the movie and you can...*wander a little*." Paul's eyes shifted from Peter to the liquor section and back. They were of the same mind.

Peter wandered past the wines and scanned the store for attentive clerks. So far as he knew Big Jim's liquors was still a little slow on technology. They didn't have surveillance cameras or electronic tags on their products so if a bottle fell gently into his pocket then it was hardly his fault. They should have done a better job.

"Yeah gimme the Marlboro's on top. No the box on top, yeah that one." A familiar south Boston accent cut through the air reaching Peter's ears.

He could see a figure beyond the potato chip isle; the guy was wearing a blue wool winter cap and hid his features within a shiny green Boston Celtics jacket.

"Yeah thanks man, have a good one." The Celtics fan took his smokes and stepped hard towards the door. Just before reaching the handle his eyes flashed back at Peter who shuddered from the recognition.

"You done yet?" Paul arrived with three videos in his right hand. "Pete? You Ok?"

"Huh?" He snapped out of it. He knew that guy, well maybe, but it had been so long. "Hey didn't we hear that Gary Collins went in for like two years?"

"Yep, he decked a cop I think. Why?"

"I swear I just saw him. The same face, the same freckled skin, might have gained some weight though."

"You want to go check it out? The HAWKS might be around if he's here. Maybe we should follow him?"

"Yeah lets do that," He followed Paul for three steps, took a quick look around and slipped a large bottle of Jack Daniels inside the coat that was underneath his oversized silver and black hockey jersey.

"You coming?" Paul waved him on. He had already checked out the videos and had no intention of paying for the liquor.

"Yeah, just wandering a little."

Outside the frigid night air sent a reminder to their bodies that any operations would have to be limited in time. It was too cold to fuck around. They were not going to engage in combat with the wind chill in the teens. Besides, the figure Peter had seen was already out of view.

"Which way?" Paul held out his hands one pointing towards Gill Street and the other at East Main.

"I'll check the corner, you go up the hill." They split off. Paul jogged carefully on the snow-padded cement up the slight incline of Gill Street. He should be able to see most of the way up it from the top of the snow bank. Peter half jogged, half slid down the parking lot to the corner of Big Jim's building. He peeked around the white painted concrete and gazed up East Main Street. There were very few cars on the road and the sidewalk was empty all the way to April's market. Gary's bright green jacket would stand out in the blinding white background. Spinning in the slush he jogged fast to the bottom of Gill Street and walked around an overgrown hedge at the edge of the next yard over. Nothing, the sidewalk was...

"Keep it quiet Pete I don't want to litter the snow with your guts." The accent bit at his left ear as Peter was grabbed from within the hedge and pulled into its depths. "Now I don't have a lot of time for stupid so fess up fast. Where is he?"

"Who? Paul? He went up the street to..." Peter was nearly pissing his pants as the gun barrel dug its way deeper between two ribs in his back creating an unbearable pressure.

"No, James Ballum, you're best buddy. Where is he?" The man's voice gave away nothing. If this was Gary then Peter was totally fooled. He sounded like an older person, more rugged, grizzled.

"I don't know. He's not my friend."

"Not the answer I want to hear." The barrel bit deeper and twisted for effect. Tears welled up in Peter's eyes, he wanted to wipe them away fast as he was afraid they might freeze in the corners of his eyes but he couldn't move. The pain was stifling.

"James Ballum is not my friend, we're enemies. I swear. I fuckin hate the kid. If I knew where he was I'd tell you."

"You're fucking lying!" The man jabbed the barrel into Peter's right kidney and then stuck back between his ribs.

"No, I'm telling the truth, I promise, I hate him."

"So he's your enemy? And you don't know where your enemy is?" Now the man was making fun of him. "Then you got bigger problems to worry about, don't you? Well listen up Pete if you do happen to see your enemy before I find him you tell him he's fucking with the wrong people. Tell him he can't hide forever."

"Um, yeah Ok. Look mister I..." Peter had gathered all the strength he could by positioning his right heal against the base of the cement wall under the branches of the bush. He could care less what the guy was saying, for right now he just wanted to escape.

"What do you got in your coat?" His hand reached under the hockey jersey and pulled out the bottle of JD.

"Keep it!" Peter took his chance and broke out of the bush running and sliding out to the parking lot towards the building. Paul saw him coming and ran up to aid his approach.

"What are you doing? Why are you running?"

Peter slid in the snow nearly falling to ground; Paul grabbed his jersey and helped him stand steady.

"What, what is it?" His friend was shaking and red in the face, frozen tears glistened on his cheeks.

"I just got robbed by the guy. He was in the bushes, I knew we should have brought the guns."

"Was it Gary Collins? Should we go after him?"

"No, no it wasn't Gary, I think he was a..." He didn't believe what he was about to say, how did Dutch garner so much attention? Peter wanted to kill him for long standing reasons but why did this guy want him so bad?

"I think he was a professional."

"A hitman?" Paul scoffed but the stunned contortion of Peter's body language spoke volumes about what he had heard and felt.

"A *real* hitman." He let out a long cold breath.

"What did he want?"

"He wants Dutch. I think he wants him dead."

CHAPTER 43

▼

"C'mon you little punk, take out your keys..." Aubrey followed a kid out of the Westgate mall and towards the parking lot.

"There you go..." Aubrey was mumbling under his breath as the young man, who seemed barely old enough to drive, took out his car keys and moved towards the center isle.

"Which one is yours?" The predator eyed all the remaining cars. This kid probably still lived at home so if he had a car it was either a shit-box that he bought with money shoveling snow or it was a reliable Mommy car that he had borrowed for the evening.

"It's not the Bronco...nope...it's not the Van...It's..." A rush of kids ran past Aubrey nearly knocking him over in a tidal wave of teenage adrenaline.

"Hey dude you're giving us a ride right?" One of the kids said as he walked backwards in front of the driver as they leaned towards a light blue station wagon.

"Fuck..." Aubrey lowered his head and walked to his left. He couldn't steal the car with all those damn kids around, too many witnesses.

Fighting off the cold he wrapped his arms tight inside his coat and felt the reassuring grip of the cop's revolver in one pocket and his own blood-covered knife in the other. It was almost 9pm, the mall was about to close and he was running out of targets. Having traveled all this way he couldn't wait any longer to get his hands on a car. It had been a difficult trip and his patience was fleeting.

After escaping the cops on the train tracks by passing on the Grove Street Bridge he clumsily survived an obstacle course of icy, swing-set infested back-yards. A long tenuous walk through block after city block of back alleys and side streets brought him to the BAT bus station downtown.

The BAT or Brockton Area Transit authority is the city's commuter bus system. Its headquarters, a brick parking lot off Centre St, is inconveniently located across from the police station and is always under the surveillance of a couple patrolmen. They watch the busses load and unload passengers who frequently transfer to other routes. Aubrey knew that half the city must be looking for him so he stayed close to the largest crowd of riders and followed them onto whatever bus they happened to be boarding. Seventy-five cents got him onto the route 4A bus that ended at the Westgate mall. It wasn't where he wanted to be but he made the best of it. He grabbed something to eat at Woolworth's sit down counter and gave himself a little time to think of how to get out of the city.

The questions were like a whirlwind, a vortex of hate windsurfing through his rampaging mind. *Why were the cops at his house?* They needed a warrant to enter and they needed provocation to get a warrant, all of these things take time. *How long did they know? And what did they know? How did they know what he looked like?* Even his past mug shots were misleading and he never let anyone take his picture. *How did they know what he was driving?* He had borrowed the Lincoln from his friend Pat. Someone must have turned him in but who could possibly have all of that information and be able to turn it over without him ever knowing? After finally asking the right question, the obvious answer came to mind. Only one person has that kind of access to his life, only one person has a recent motive to do this.

"Peter, my own flesh." It was time to kill that kid. Now he knew where he needed to go. Aubrey had to get to Avon. That's when he started following people out of the mall in order to steal their keys and jack a car. The kid hadn't worked out because of his friends but young kids are never easy targets. They possess too many variables. He needed someone softer, someone he could overpower and outrun if need be. He needed an elderly person and five minutes later, he found one.

"C'mon lady, take em out." Swearing under his breath he spotted and followed a single, late sixties grandma with bluish hair. Mrs. Mason was wrapped in multiple layers to keep out the cold; she was walking in a pink cocoon of helplessness. The layers may be keeping her warm but they were inhibiting her already limited movements. It had been a long day as she was nearly ready to give up hope concerning her granddaughter Kaitlin. The child had been missing for weeks and to make matters worse, Kaitlin's Mom had not returned in days. She could only guess that Michele was now living with her boyfriend in the Renaissance. Stricken with a heavy heart Mrs. Mason felt older and slower than ever before.

She was pulling out her keys only ten feet from a white Crown Victoria. That was certainly her car.

"There it is you old bitch." Aubrey broke into a run, reached low and grabbed the keys out of her hand. A firm shoulder block sent Mrs. Mason slipping onto the slushy cement. She fell hard landing on her fragile left hip. He cornered the car and used the key marked *Ford* to open the door.

In a glorified instant, he revved the engine, spiked the heat, and caught a glimpse of movement in the side view mirror. Mrs. Mason had climbed to her feet. She was shaking, struggling to balance herself and reached for the car handle. He was not taking her car!

"Fuck off Grandma, I've got a kid to kill." The tires spun a shower of slush into her face as the car pulled away from her gloved hand. Having gripped the handle just before he sped away the car jolted her forward and her temple hit the rear bumper on her fall to the ground. Mrs. Mason saw her car race away through a blurry gray fog. A final prayer for Kaitlin was her last thought as the white sky descended.

It would be twenty-five minutes before anyone would find her half frozen and unconscious body lying in a mound of slush in the parking lot. By then her heart had given up. She would never see her granddaughter again.

CHAPTER 44

▼

"What if it goes wrong?" Peter couldn't get into the movie. He sat in a wooden chair searching through the frosted window convinced that his father was on his way.

"Dude after what you told the cops they will send a fucking Army to that house. I bet he's already sitting in a cell." Paul lit a cigarette, his eyes never leaving the dusty twelve-inch screen.

"What if they don't catch him?" Peter had asked the question a hundred times in his head but this was first time he said it aloud. "Maybe we should check the news?"

"We already missed the eleven o'clock news. Look, Pete, they'll do an all points bulletin. They know what he looks like, what he's driving, who his friends are…where he hides his guns. Pete, he's nailed."

Peter cast a doubtful glance but then returned to his post. From this elevated view he watched a light accumulation of snow pile up on the driveway. Beyond the slope was a barren sidewalk and a blinking yellow light at the corner of Spring Street and East Main. It was late and there were very few cars on the road. The inactivity was creepy, almost isolating. There would be comfort in traffic, the more people the safer but as it was he suspected every passing car as potentially being driven by his enraged father. The Brockton pit bull knew no fear, no guilt, and no remorse.

Peter mumbled under his breath, drifting off into paranoia, "He always gets away."

Paul heard the mumble but he wasn't sure if Pete was still talking about his Dad or if he was talking about Dutch. "You told the cops that you were…"

"I know," He snapped. "I told the dispatcher that I was James Ballum but that doesn't mean they are going to tell him who called. Especially if…"

"If he got away." Paul finished his sentence. Maybe his paranoia wasn't so far fetched. It was a clever idea to pretend to be someone else when reporting the crime but not if the message didn't get through.

Peter raised his eyes to the black sky. It was the bleakest winter he could ever remember. Changes happened so fast since Schmel died in a rain of gunfire leaving a gaping hole in the SSP's leadership. That was the greatest plan he had ever devised and yet the outcome was not what he expected. Afterwards he had tried twice unsuccessfully to rally some of the Posse members at the Renaissance. He had so many ideas about how he would run Brockton drug routes out of his Mom's apartment only one town away but no one was biting. They didn't want to make the change; they didn't want to follow a white guy.

Rafael was better known in Brockton and so in the backrooms and alleyways of the city new alliances were formed. Some of them put Rafael in power but others splintered off seeking new leadership. The real fireworks would start when Darius got out of DYS. They would flock to him and no doubt, he would take members left and right from Raf who was considered more of a supplier than a leader. There would not only be battles between gangs but also a war within the largest one. It was a mess to be sure but it was also an opportunity. If only he could figure out how to capitalize on it, how to force them to destroy each other leaving the posse with nowhere else to turn.

It was so frustrating to dwell on. His only consolation was the hope that his rival, Dutch, was facing a far harsher life on the streets of some other city. Peter almost fell into despair when he learned that Damian wasn't able to take him down. He was happy that the fight happened but the outcome was disappointing. Furthermore the police were unable to arrest him and then once again, he disappeared. The Avon police can't catch him, even a Boston hitman can't track him, "Why does he get off so easy?"

"Who?" Paul said with his eyes half shut. He was falling asleep in his chair a lit cigarette dangling from his right hand.

"No one."

All he could do was hope. If they raided Aubrey's house and found all the guns, narcotics and that little girl, Kaitlin, they would plunge him into the deepest cell in Massachusetts. Hell they'd probably tell all the inmates that he was a baby raper so he'd get his just deserts. Inmates have an honor code of their own. If word got out about what he did they'd kill him inside a week. Peter was sure that he made the right decision if only to save that little girl's life. He hadn't told anyone about Kaitlin, well, except for the police who had been looking for her. In part he was hoping there might be some reward money but he couldn't claim it as he had called using Dutch's name. Despite it all there was one solid benefit that would come from his father's absence, it would open up his Dad's house for business. It was only blocks away from the center of the city, a perfect location. If he had a whole house to work out of the other Posse members were sure to align themselves with the new king on the block—Peter Truelson, leader of the Shotgun crew.

It was a bold dream that allowed for the smallest hint of a smile on the corner of his mouth. Now he just had to keep an eye out through the night until he knew for sure that his Dad had been arrested and locked away.

SCARS
OF A FRAUD

CHAPTER 45

▼

Dutch's face was spectacled with dark red dried blood. Marks a quarter inch wide splayed across his pink skin, his lips rough, his cheeks jagged. Much like the star chart of rock salt that had once mapped his chest with pain, his face once soft, now bore the brunt of further proof that his years were being earned too quickly. Again he pulled his head up to the level of the mirror in Becca's bathroom and winced at the image of his disgrace.

"What they must think..." Maybe an altered explanation could permeate his subconscious forcing him to recollect a whole different reality but he doubted it. If he didn't lose why did it feel like he lost? Why couldn't he shake the memory of his face hitting the grill of that car or his side as it landed ungracefully on the ground? Worse yet, how were they going to handle this? His teammates had to stand by as their leader exchanged blows with a traitor two years his junior. His opponent was a smaller, weaker fighter who fought Dutch to a stand still. In the game of expectations, he had lost before the fight even began. Anything short of a one-punch knockout was a loss and he missed that one punch by a split hair.

"Dutch, there's a phone call for you." Becca banged on the door but his eyes were locked on the travesty that had become of his complexion. He looked like he had been in a car accident and hit the windshield face first. Could they ever respect him after witnessing such a lame expression of violence? Dutch was supposed to be the ultimate warrior, the grand leader of a tough and unforgiving force and yet, in the mirror, he saw only the scars of an egotistical fraud. If this loss of confidence was visible to everyone then where did that leave the team? The air of mystery he once projected, the earned bravado now exposed. He didn't want to answer the door or ever leave that bathroom because he knew that the

HAWKS were out there waiting and he would have to face them without being able to explain anything. Not yet anyway.

"Dutch? It's TC on the phone." She twisted the knob but he had locked it so that no one would witness his inconstant shallow sobs.

"Ok, ok…" He splashed cold water on his face, ignored the towel and opened the door long enough to snatch the phone from her hand pulling it into the bathroom.

"No, you'll cut the cord." She pleaded but the door clicked shut. The cord had just enough room to stay clenched without being broken.

"TC, what's up?" A natural recall of strength came back to his voice. He may not look like someone who would be in charge but he still sounded like the General.

"You doing ok?" TC sounded morose.

"I'm fine, my face has a little more character that's all."

"Good, now you'll look more like a soldier."

"Thanks but um, what happened after we left?"

"You are in big trouble my friend, the Avon cops are going apeshit. Plus, that black kid who showed up at the fight with Damian, that's who you're sister is going out with. I meant to tell you earlier but it slipped my mind…"

"Tyrone? Lucy is dating Tyrone, a member of the Shotgun Crew, an accomplice of the Spring Street Posse?"

"Your Mom might not like the extended title."

"Whatever," The joke went right over his head. *How stupid can she be? She is always mad at me, is this revenge?* He didn't have time for this right now. "Forget Lucy. TC, tell me, what did Damian say to the cops?"

"It's not good. They don't like him in the first place but at least they can catch him. You they hate and Damian made it even worse. He said that he came to talk to you and you attacked him, he said you tried to kill him. He said he'd be willing to press charges if they ever find you."

"I what? Is he serious?"

"Well, you did throw the first punch."

"Tommy!"

"I know; I'm not helping." He wanted to be comforting but the wave of misfortune was reaching epic proportions. How does anyone smile during a social disaster?

"No, you did fine. Listen, I might have to take some time off, you know, to heal but I want you to know that not everything is what it seems right now. I've got another plan brewing underneath all of this but I can't tell you just yet. I can't tell anyone."

"Is it about your high school?"

"No, that's separate. That's a much bigger plan."

"But you can trust me."

"I know, you've have been more faithful than anyone else but this is very big, very, very secret and right now I need a little time off to um," He struggled with his wording suddenly fearful that he might give something away. "Time to think, to readjust."

"It's ok with me. You know that I'm by your side no matter what." TC had no idea what he was talking about. With all the gossip that was circulating about the fight and with the cops he had little time to put any pieces together. In the end he just wanted to stay on the inside and help anyway that he could. If Dutch had a plan to double cross some gang-bangers, then Tommy was in. If Dutch wanted to shoot down his old high school classmates, Tommy would load the gun. "Whatever it is, I'll be ready when you are."

"I know, and...thanks buddy."

CHAPTER 46

▼

"Where did Lazio go? And where's John?" Dutch came out of the bathroom to a gloomy duo that lacked any semblance of spirit. Lazio and John had retreated away. Psycho and Becca were both wearing their civilian clothing and had packed away all of their HAWKS gear.

"They went to Lazio's." Psycho murmured while shuffling tarot cards. A phone rang in the background.

"What for?"

"Um, food or to talk about..." He missed his hand as the cards scattered across the coffee table. "Fuck."

"There's another call for you." Becca held the plastic phone out in front of his face.

"Does everyone know where I am?" He snatched it away from her. "So much for my undisclosed location."

"It's your Mom." She snapped before storming into her bedroom and slamming the door.

"What's her problem? And what are they talking about?" He asked Psycho who only shrugged as he laid out the cards to play a newly invented version of solitaire. His eyes never left the cards but his mind was elsewhere.

"Mom? How did you find me?" His tone had not abated. Had he already been betrayed by his fellow HAWKS? Were they giving up so easily? And what the hell did his Mom want?

"TC gave me your number but I have to talk to you it's very serious." Her gentle voice was more rigid than usual.

"What could be so...?"

"Your school called." She stopped his rant before it could begin. Had the school learned of the beating that he suffered? Were they going to press charges against Joe, Matt and Rodger? Perhaps he'd be vindicated after all. The glory of justice was at hand.

"And?" He asked excitedly.

"You've been expelled. They want you out of the school—permanently."

"What!" Dutch yelled so loud that Psycho lifted his head to listen. "They what! Why?"

"They said that you assaulted a teacher in the hallway. They said you pushed him down and he hit his head on the floor. It caused a concussion."

"Are you...I was being chased by three people did he see them?"

"Who was chasing you?"

"Did anyone else get expelled?"

"Not that I know of."

"I can't believe this! They attack me and I get thrown out of school?"

"Who attacked you, what happened?" She asked deeply concerned.

"Some fucking kids."

"Are you Ok? I heard that you got into a fight but TC said it was with Damian in Avon."

"Yeah I fought him too."

"Why are you fighting everyone? Are you all right? Do you need to go to a hospital?" She asked very gently knowing that he often overreacted to what he called 'injustice.'

"I'm fine, I...I got a couple scratches and maybe a burn or two."

"A burn?"

"At the school they burned me with electrical wires."

"Oh my god, please come home."

"Forget it! Listen, can I get back into the school?"

"No, they want you out. They found a knife in your locker. I don't think they'd even be willing to listen, they were very angry."

"This is so unfair. Why don't the guilty people ever get caught?" His voice echoed through the apartment. Becca could hear him in her bedroom with the door closed and Psycho sat silent feeling like the world had come crashing down around them.

"They think you pushed that teacher, did you? If not then maybe..."

"I'm not guilty!"

"James, they told me that you had a number of suspensions that you didn't serve. They said you climbed to the roof of the gym and scared the hell out of a class of students. Plus the knife in your locker, they had lot's of reason for wanting you to leave."

"I scared them? They clapped for me when I came down the rope and I don't give a shit about their reasons."

"The guidance counselor, Mr. Landon, said you get in a lot of fights, that you yelled at people in the cafeteria and..."

"They threw meatballs at me." This was going nowhere. "Mom, I've got to go..."

"No don't hang up. Your father and I have been talking and we want to make a deal with you."

Dutch was caught off guard. His parents had always followed a philosophy of non-interference when it came to his life. They let him have free reign, not that they could stop him but still, they never seemed to want to be a part of anything that he did. The fact that they would come up with a bargain of any kind was at least worth listening to. "What kind of deal?"

"Your father bought an old Dodge van and we figured that if you come out to Middleboro to fix it up then you can drive it to see your friends."

"I can't afford to fix anything, I don't even know how."

"We'll pay for the parts and well, we can figure it out when you get here."

Dutch considered the offer for a moment before he realized that it was one sided. "Wait a minute, what do you want from me? You're not going to give me a van for nothing."

"We thought that maybe you could start evening school at Middleboro High in September."

Dutch pulled the phone away from his ear while he weighed his options. The truth is that he needed a deal like this. An Army recruiter would never let him join the service without a high school diploma so for once his parents had a reasonable option. As it was the HAWKS were going through a tough period, he was already thinking about taking some time off in order to refuel. He had so many kinks to work out if he was going to stage his huge attack at Blue Hills. After hearing that his tormentors had gotten away he was double sure that this event had to be enormous. Maybe this was the break he needed? If it all worked out then the HAWKS Foundation would have a van, their very own war vehicle, a way to transport guns and...Hmmm.... "Ok, I'll pack my stuff and I'll see you tonight."

"You will?"

"Yep, thanks Mom."

"You're welcome." Filled with suspicion she hung up the phone. That was way too easy.

CHAPTER 47

▼ ———————————

"What the hell is she pissed about?" Sitting uncomfortably in the back seat of John's Cougar, Dutch turned to glare at Becca through the back window as they drove away. Her once deep brown eyes were circled red, he didn't look into them anymore; he didn't kiss her anymore. Recent events had hardened his heart.

"You didn't hug her." Psycho turned his head just enough to watch Becca cross her arms as the car turned out of view.

"Are you shitting me? We're supposed to be a suburban hit squad and she's angry that I didn't hug her?" He knew what he did wrong; he was pushing her away. What was more disturbing to Dutch was Psycho's awareness of Becca's emotional world. Those two had been spending an inordinate amount of time together for two people who supposedly didn't like each other. He was beginning to get suspicious. "So aren't you going to say I told you so? Aren't you going to remind me that we never should have had a girl on the team?"

"Well…it's not so bad." Psycho conceded with pause.

"Not so bad? Are you kidding? You were ready to throw her into the jaws of the Sevlow back in Avon, what happened?"

"She's done everything we asked of her. She passed the initiation…"

"You thought she was going to die during the initiation."

"But she didn't." He corrected admitting that he had overreacted a little. "Then she followed orders when we met with D-Rod…"

"He knew that they were there."

"Yes but that was our fault. Becca and Lazio did as they were told. They did what soldiers do; they followed orders without question. We didn't plan it well enough. We underestimated D-Rod, twice."

"Fine, but what about all this emotional shit?"

"She's in love with you!" He couldn't believe that Dutch could be so blind. "That girl worships you. She would do anything for you and for that matter, forgive anything that you do."

Dutch sank a little in his seat. He didn't want to fall in love with anyone, what did *he* have to offer a girl? All he could envision in his future was a life on the run, a life of danger and endless escapes. A girlfriend doesn't fit into a world like that. Shaking out his head like an etch-a-sketch he moved on to another pressing subject.

"So what's Lazio's problem? He's been acting funny since the fight."

"He lost a little confidence that's all."

"In me? He lost confidence in me?" Dutch ran his hand over his face feeling the dried bumps of blood from all the little gashes.

"It's not really you. Lazio has always been weird. You know how he is. Don't let it bother you."

"A member of my team thinks I'm a pussy and I'm supposed to get over it?" He wasn't angry so much as hurt. The street credit he had gained by surviving a beating by high school attackers had all been lost with a reckless wrestling match against one friend. If only he could tell them the underlying part of his plans, the part that would vindicate all that they were building towards. But no, they wouldn't understand, they might not even believe him. If he couldn't tell TC then he couldn't tell anyone, not yet.

John was sitting quietly in the driver's seat contemplating his level of involvement. Dutch sat in back but John appreciated the distance. Every failure of this militant rat pack was a victory for sensibility, an argument for reason and sanity. In a way John was routing against the team from succeeding and yet he still didn't want them to fail, either outcome could be disastrous. He stayed quiet knowing that one day the answers he knew to be true would eventually be obvious to the rest of them. In the meantime he would sit back, watch and listen. It was better to be on the inside when the team finally crashed than to derail them from the outside where his suggestions would be less desirable. When it was all over maybe he could offer a new direction, all in due time.

"We just need to get you back into training that's all." Psycho pepped up unexpectedly. "You've been stuck in that apartment or hiding in Becca's closet so much that we don't get a chance to practice our tactics or our fighting methods."

"I'll have some time to re-coup while I'm stuck in Middleboro. It might take a while to get the van up and running."

"That's cool, take all the time you need. Our enemies aren't going anywhere." Psycho was referring to the SSP whom he felt was the biggest threat. He was not talking about the kids at Blue Hills but much like John he was reluctant to voice opposition. The hope was that Dutch would forget about the bullies, as the gang war grew more prominent in their lives.

"I know they'll still be around."

"Right and this way you can go out to Middleboro where no one knows who you are. The police won't bother you; the gangs won't be looking and, well, the mafia…"

"Can't find me." That solidified it; a tactical retreat was not only helpful to his health, it also took the pressure off his friends. It was possible that one of them could take a stray bullet that was meant for Dutch. Their lives were at risk by simply being near him. Besides, when he returned the rest of his grand plans would be unveiled allowing him to regain the respect of his men. Dutch settled into the seat and closed his eyes; it was a forty-minute ride to Middleboro and so far as he was concerned, there was nothing left to discuss.

CHAPTER 48

— ▼ —

The knock at the door brought Becca to her feet in an instant. Had he come back? Was Dutch's cold attitude merely a front that he used to hide his true emotions? Had he commanded John to turn the car around telling them that he forgot something important using it as an excuse to return and reassure her of his affections, the love he was afraid to show in front of his friends?

"Dutch...I..." Becca opened the door with her heart full of hope.

"I need to talk to you." Lazio barged into the apartment uninvited. His demeanor was intense; his eyes searched the kitchen and scanned her open bedroom door.

Becca was surprised and a little creeped out so she shut her bedroom door and, while keeping the front door wide open, asked him what he wanted.

"We need to talk about Dutch. Where is he?"

"He left, he's going to Middleboro to stay with his parents for a while."

He must have thought Dutch was hiding in the bedroom because Lazio couldn't get his eyes off the door.

"He's gone?"

"What about him?"

"Our fearless leader is full of shit." Lazio wouldn't look at her directly. He stared at the wall and bit every word as it left his lips. "I don't know what they told you about the fight but he got his ass kicked. He's not the black belt fighting machine he claims to be. All his karate shit was worthless, all his lies about fighting off four kids at his school, all of his posturing."

"He never said he was a black belt."

"Well he acts like it." His harsh tones tore her confidence down in the same way her father did. Becca got the sense that for once she was seeing Lazio's true colors. This supposed Witch was as controlling as her Dad, as fierce with his ignorance. Where did all that intelligence go when his emotions started to rise?

"Dutch earned his rank." She tried to defend him. "He got the fastest time in the flag tower run and…"

"Right I've heard that story and I no longer believe it." Lazio pointed a firm finger at her head. "Think about it Becca. He was shot in the chest and then drowned in quicksand and we're supposed to believe that he escaped? We're supposed to believe that Dutch has this superhero, Houdini like ability to thwart any attacker and evade capture? That sounds like storylines out of a comic book. All he did when the police arrived was run away. He hid in the woods like a coward until the cops left and then we had to take him out of Avon in the trunk of John's car. Where's the heroism in that?" He took small steps towards her with every other word until Becca was backed up against her bedroom door.

"He's still the General, no one else can do it." She was not going to turn coat on her leader even if she was mad at him.

"He's a fraud and he doesn't love you…" Lazio reached for her shoulder, "Not the way I do."

"Lazio?" Becca was trying to push him away as Lazio leaned in to kiss her. "No, Lazio no!" Becca couldn't get him off he was too large, too insistent. Instead she reached behind her back and turned the knob. She fell backwards into her bedroom. He reached down to help but she mistook his kindness for aggression and bit his hand.

"Oww, what the hell? I thought you liked me?" Lazio pulled back suddenly, the withdrawal didn't make any sense to Becca who jumped to her feet and shut the bedroom door in his face.

"Leave Lazio, leave right now or I'm calling the police!" She clasped the latch and backed away half expecting him to try to break it down.

"He doesn't love you!" He said with authority. "Listen," His voice came down to a strange whimper, "I wanted to tell you for a long time and with Dutch out of the picture…I thought that we could be together. I can do things for you that he never could. I will use my magic even though I'm not supposed to. For you…I'll do it."

"Get out Lazio I'm dialing the police." She grabbed the phone from next to her bed and started pressing buttons so he would hear.

"Rebecca, don't make me do this."

She moved away from the door, "Do what?"

"I can *make* you love me! I have the spells." The strength of his convictions returned as his anger rose, "I would kill for you! I would die for you! Open the door!"

"Lazio I'm asking you to leave, will you do that for me? If you care about me then leave. That's what I really want right now."

Two heavy steps retreated from her door.

"We'll talk later...do you promise that we'll talk later?" He asked expecting that she would eventually understand that she needed him.

She didn't want to make any promises. Becca stayed quiet and waited. Moments later she heard the kitchen door close softly.

Exhausted she slumped to the floor, "First my boyfriend gets beat up by his best friend and then an evil Christian hating witch wants to cast a love spell on me. Forget it, I'm not dating anymore."

SHOWDOWN AT HARRISON BOULEVARD

CHAPTER 49

▼

"Its 6:35 where are you Lelaine?" Aubrey sat six houses up the street from his ex-wife's apartment. Lelaine, Peter's Mom, usually left for work at six thirty in the morning. She was five minutes late but Aubrey was spitefully patient.

Lelaine had woken up on time. The setting on her alarm clock hasn't changed in fourteen years. Ever since Aubrey left for a girl half her age, Lelaine had to become the sole support for Peter and his younger brother Ben. Peter, who had seen and been affected by the wrath of Aubrey became a troubled child almost immediately.

As a kid Peter hung out with TC, Dutch, Erik, Gary and a few others who had already garnered a reputation for getting into trouble. An incident arose where they were exploring an empty building downtown when several older teens blocked the doorway and trapped them inside. Most managed to escape but Peter and Erik did not. Over the course of three hours they were physically tortured and left to die. While his father's beatings provided the cocktail of his scarred psyche, this incident was the match; it was the final catalyst that brought his anger out into the world. Peter and Erik made it out of the building but their lives were never the same.

In the ensuing weeks he had to endure the ribbing of his parents for being there in the first place and then the humiliation set upon him by the press and the trial. Erik had also suffered but Peter lost track of him. He was angry at the person who led them into the building in the first place, the leader of their group of friends at the time—James Ballum.

Ben, on the other hand, was quiet and unaffected by anything his mother or father did. Ben was 'a good kid' as Lelaine kept reminding Peter though they were never sure how he managed to survive so easily.

The night before this one Ben had stayed at a friend's house. He always arrived at school on time and performed well in his classes despite parental negligence. With Ben out of the house, Peter and Paul stayed up until nearly four in the morning before they finally passed out. In the next room over Lelaine woke up on time but discovered that her car was covered in a hard layer of wind drift ice that did not want to break off. She chipped away at the frozen shards until all of her windows and her driver's side door handle were clear. Her car had been warming up the whole time and that helped to loosen the ice from within.

Her driveway was at an awkward slant. It rapidly dropped down to Spring Street at the corner of East Main. In order to properly stop at the blinking red light she would have to back down the slant slowly, nearly to the intersection itself and then back up the hill so she could face the red light and see if any traffic was coming. There were many pitfalls to this stoplight the worst of which presented itself when the road was slippery. A car coming down the hill would not be able to stop before reaching the light and could slide out of control into oncoming traffic. It had happened before. Her driveway was a death trap but the town was not going to rebuild the road for the sake of only one resident so it had remained this way for as long as she could remember.

Everyday for the past fourteen years Lelaine Truelson had carefully backed down the driveway and backed up the hill to get a clear view. Today the crossroad and the driveway were covered in the same wind swept ice. Today she had to maneuver her car as if it were the space shuttle on a launch pad, crawling one cautious inch at a time.

"Here we go," Aubrey checked the clock at 6:41 and pressed lightly on the gas. His stolen white Crown Victoria rolled through the snow towards the top of the hill high above the driveway, high above Lelaine.

Down below she carefully checked her speed and adjusted the mirror as her nearly bald snow tires reached the sloped end of the driveway. Adding a little gas her tiny Subaru hatchback backed up the hill but almost immediately started to slide towards the intersection.

"No shit." Aubrey watched with glee. He may not have to do anything after all. The ice might finally take care of her for him. She was sliding helplessly towards the early morning traffic.

Lelaine grabbed her second shifter and jerked the car into all wheel drive then tapped the gas. The hatchback jerked forward, slid another couple feet and then started to rear backwards. All four tires were working against gravity and pulling her slowly back to safety.

"Fuckin foreign cars." Aubrey swore as the Subaru had saved his ex-wife yet again. "That's it, she's done!" he dropped his boot on the gas pedal.

The crown Victoria topped the hill and picked up speed on its way down. He half sped, half slid right into the back of her car. Lelaine's head snapped back against the headrest and then hit the steering wheel. She lost consciousness as the car fell out of gear and rushed down the hill into the middle of oncoming traffic.

"What the fuck was that?" Peter jumped out of his bed. "What was that? Did you hear that?" His nerves had kept him close to wakefulness all night. He was waiting for Aubrey to come for him, to hunt him down. Was he here?

In the night they had switched positions and Paul had fallen asleep in the chair by the window. He lifted his head to look around and caught sight of the Subaru outside in the intersection. "Peter, it's your Mom."

He ran to the window and caught full view of the accident. His Mom's Subaru was struck broadside by a speeding van doing fifty miles an hour, it spun her hatchback one and a half times before the front left wheel hit a pothole in the cement and flipped the car on its roof. Not far behind the hatchback was a white Crown Victoria that had also slid into traffic. Aubrey jumped out of the front seat onto the ice-covered pavement. He made it out of the way just before a Bat bus hit his car and tore it in half.

"Fuck no! No! Mom!" Peter screamed as he ran out of the house slipping all the way towards his worst nightmare. He hadn't seen who the man was that had jumped from the other car, all he knew was that the one and only person in the world who cared about him was hanging upside down by the seatbelt of her shattered Subaru in the middle of a four car wreck.

CHAPTER 50

▼

"Thomas Charles Robbins! Get down here right now!" Martha shrieked at her son from the downstairs living room.

"What?" He screeched back and made his way to the top of the stairs but stopped short of trekking them.

"Get down here!" She blasted back at him.

"Ok, ok, I'm coming." His heavy footsteps shook the brittle wooden staircase as he thudded to a halt before his parents. He wasn't necessarily in trouble they did this for nearly any occasion.

His Mom was tired from a long day of office work at Reebok headquarters so she had good reason for never budging from her chair once she got home. His dad hadn't worked in years. A former Marine and Korean War veteran who survived off a workers disability fund, Tom Sr. was a grumpy but often emotionally distant jarhead.

"What's so important?" TC crossed his arms and looked disapprovingly at both parents who met his glare with equal derision.

"There was an accident down at the Spring Street crossing, a bad one." His mother informed him.

"Yeah so…there are always…"

"Your friend Peter might have been involved." Tom senior growled having shifted his sights back onto the television. Professional wrestling showered the screen with colorful grunts and slams. Tom Senior has always been convinced that pro wrestling is real and no one was going to talk him out of it. "How can they fake a fall?" He would say every time TC's friends came over. So these matches were clearly more important than finding out who might have died down the street.

TC took exception, "First of all Peter is not my friend and second..." The red light on the police scanner next to Tom senior flashed repeatedly and then stopped before a voice blared out in scratchy staccato.

"We have a fatality...roger that, EMS is on its way...Mr. Truelson was in the second car..."

TC's eyes went wide. "Um...on second thought...I think I'll go check that out."

Both his parents approved. They didn't keep up with TC's friends, but they did want to remain an integral part of Avon's forever chugging gossip train. If TC arrived on the scene then they would be privy to first hand account of what had happened and could use these recollections to demean or prop up other town folk that they liked or despised. They never intended to manipulate information in this way, few people do. It was a sort of community defense mechanism. It was a way of positioning rhetoric to ensure that the focus of oncoming rumors was parried away from their own lives. TC was often the conduit for this type of intelligence work.

Like a superhero racing to the scene of a crime he grabbed his ten-speed bike off the front porch, carried it to the street and took off down the hill at incredible speed towards the accident.

Hardly five minutes later, having been passed only by an ambulance, TC arrived at a corner of the crossroads and couldn't believe the carnage.

"Stay back son, get off the street." An officer urged him onto the sidewalk in front of a red brick realty office. Being behind the police car didn't hamper his view one bit, at six feet five inches tall he could see clear over the barrier of vehicles that was being used to block the roads and divert traffic.

"Unbelievable..." He gawked at the center of the white, slush arrayed crossroads where stains of red blood and black oil sheen across the snow. A yellow ford van sat sideways in one lane, its front end flattened, its occupant had already been carted away in an ambulance that was disappearing into the distance. A single red and white Bat bus rested in the middle of the intersection with a twisted lump of steel wrapped around his front bumper. Inches from the bus emergency medical workers were hurrying to remove a woman from an overturned white car that TC immediately recognized as Lelaine's Subaru.

"His Mom got hit. So then that must be..." TC's scanned the opposite corner where he could see Peter on his knees on the sidewalk, his hands covering his face. The police wouldn't let him come any closer. Paul was by his side trying to calm him down. "No fucking way. And who is that?"

Only fifty feet from Peter, a man was struggling against the grip of two police officers. Despite being pushed face first up against a cruiser he managed to get an arm free and elbowed one cop in the face busting his cheekbone. The man pulled the other officer closer and head butted him in the nose. Then he made a break for the open road but his left leg had a severe limp that slowed him down. That's when a third police car took a sharp left off Harrison Boulevard and slid in the snow blocking the limping escapee's route. An energetic officer Gillman leaped out of the car and grabbed the perp by his jacket.

"That's Aubrey...and...Gillman?" Now TC recognized both of them and couldn't believe his luck. This was a classic moment, he knew that Aubrey was a longtime street criminal with a vicious reputation and now he was in the hands of Officer Gillman a tenth degree black belt. The baddest cop in Avon was about to fist fight with one of the toughest crooks in Brockton. This was going to be great!

Aubrey was not going to be manhandled by anyone he threw a wide right hook at the tall, disciplined officer. Gillman saw the telegraphed punch coming and he rolled his shoulder underneath it. The missed punch threw Aubrey off balance and he fell into the grip of Gillman's left arm just as the pointy bone of an elbow shot up under Aubrey's chin. This Shotokan move, known as the Atemi waza, snapped his head upwards. For one dazed second all Aubrey could see was the sky above him. All he could feel was a pain shooting through his jaw like it had been split in half. Then he was tugged off balance by his wrist. It was pulled forward and then twisted back causing an agonizing pain to lock up the muscles in his arm. He screamed out loud and used his free hand to grab at Gillman's face but the officer was not going to let him get a hold. Aubrey reached inside his own jacket and pulled out the stolen police revolver. Gillman shifted his weight yet again, knocked away Aubrey's weapon and cracked him with three stunning punches before throwing him face first into the snow. Again Aubrey reached into his jacket but a knee sunk into his back crushing his hand under his body and against the cement. With his opponents face in the slush Gillman pulled out his handcuffs and locked one wrist into place. Aubrey rolled to the side and slung out his knife but Gillman's right shoe stomped on his hand forcing him to relinquish it. That's when the two injured officers arrived to help out.

"You're too late." Gillman reprimanded them for letting Aubrey escape in the first place. He locked the other wrist behind Aubrey's back but kept his face in the slush.

The officers were apologetic and as if to prove their worth they were extra rough as they lifted Aubrey and threw him in the back seat while reading his rights. They also made sure to secure him to the interior of the car so he couldn't escape again.

"Well I'll be." TC was beside himself. The chain of events at this one accident scene was the most amount of action and confusion that Avon has witnessed since the HAWKS found the wolf house. "I never thought I'd be cheering for Gillman or feeling sorry for Peter. This town is going to hell." Then he thought to himself, *I'd better report to Dutch—this changes everything.* He climbed back on his bike and sped away to deliver the news.

CHAPTER 51

▼

Tyrone stayed behind the gathering crowd as he watched the E.M.T's drive away with Peter's Mom. He lingered just out of sight as Officer Gillman's car drove by with Aubrey Truelson handcuffed to the back seat. A telephone pole blocked his thin form when TC took one last look around from across the street before riding away on his bike.

"Darius is gonna flip." He whispered to himself and then realized, much like TC must have, that the excitement was over. He walked back to his aunt's house, only four doors down, where he had been staying for the weekend.

His Aunt's house was a white, three-floor colonial hidden from the street by a wall of bushes. It sat so close to the intersection that Tyrone heard the crash despite the music that was blasting into his headphones. It was this close proximity that allowed him to meet Peter years ago when Tyrone was first sent to Avon by his parents. They wanted him out of Brockton during the summer in order to get him away from the gang scene. They especially wanted him gone when the Brockton fair came to town. Year after year gangs had overrun the fair causing riots and shootings, nearly every summer resulted in a handful of deaths. His parent's plan worked as his older brother Darius ended up in DYS while Tyrone had yet to be arrested. Not that he really did anything but that hardly mattered in the so-called city of champions.

Inside the colonial the rooms were so dark he often wondered if they merely forgot to pay their electric bills. Tyrone climbed into a big comfy living room chair, grabbed the phone and dialed his brother.

"I think Peter is out of the picture." He projected a sorrowful confidence to Darius who had only been released the day before.

"For good?" Darius was doubtful that anything, even a tragedy so personal, would stop Peter from attempting to purge his ambitions. That kid went through a lot of trouble to kill off Schmel. Now that Rafael had told the story of how it happened, the word spread fast. Darius wished that Raf could have kept his mouth shut. By speaking up about Peter's success in offing the SSP's previous leader, people would know who had the right to run the gang. All Darius could hope to do was persuade his brothers on the street that Peter was to be hated, not admired. Peter was to be the object of their revenge, not an icon for their future. Considering his skin color it wasn't going to be a hard sell. But one thing he knew for sure, Peter had no parachute. His friend Paul had a job and some work skills but Peter had nothing. He had committed himself to a life of crime so he wasn't going to give up now. He couldn't, he had nowhere else to turn.

"His Mom's in the hospital, his Dad's in jail...he was on the sidewalk balling his eyes out. He's got nothing going." Tyrone wanted to believe otherwise.

"He also has nothing to lose."

"I guess."

"Tyrone, who else knows about this?"

"TC was down here so Dutch will know."

"No I'm talking black."

"You mean like Raf?"

"Yeah."

"No, I mean it might get back to Raf eventually but he doesn't have any contacts here in Avon."

"What about Damian Burke? How is he coming along?" Darius really didn't know what to think about his lock-up buddy Sly. Damian could talk his way into or out of anything, he had proven that but did he have loyalties? Could he be trusted? Were his sincere faces always a temporary lure to catch whatever sympathy floated his way?

"Sly fought Dutch just as you wanted."

"Word up?" That was unexpected. "Did he win? More importantly, did it crush his boyz?"

"Yeah, I mean it was broken up by the cops but I'll say this, the HAWKS ain't shit if Dutch is their best fighter. But then again," Tyrone caught himself. "I've seen this kid before. He's hard to get a handle on. This is the kid Peter shot in the chest back in the day. He hit me in the face with a brick that night. He ain't scared of nobody. Even against Sly he threw the first punch."

"So he is dangerous." Darius said taking note of how formidable anyone would have to be to pull off so many legendary escapes. "And he got away again?"

"Yeah I guess, but his boyz weren't impressed, they were embarrassed I can tell you that. Some of them think he's a fraud."

"Do you?"

"No."

"Why not?"

"Cause Dutch is fuckin crazy. Who attacks five people with no weapons and no back up? Who tries to knock out his own best friend? He came to Avon even though he knows that the cops are after him. Who does this shit?" Tyrone didn't realize until now that he had accumulated so much respect for a man he had only seen twice.

"Alright, you sold me. Here's what we have to do. Peter and Dutch are rocked back so we got to take advantage. We got to keep them off guard." Darius paused as he struggled to put the pieces together. "We can't find Dutch so until he surfaces we have to hit the only visible target. I want you to contact Sly for me. Tell him about what happened to Peter and that now is the time to strike."

"What are we gonna do?" Tyrone got a little nervous. He had always stood at the edges of these schemes; he was never a central player. With Darius out of DYS, Tyrone was now at the tip of the sword. He would listen to his brother but not if his commands were going to land him in jail. Unlike the rest of them Tyrone was not a warrior, he had his limits.

"It doesn't take long to fully fuck-up a person's life. Peter lost his Mom and Dad, now he needs to lose his best friend."

"Paul?" Tyrone's mouth hung open. He was glad that Darius was not there to see his reaction. He swallowed hard. He could understand why they would want Peter put down but...

"That's right, we'll kill off Paul and *that* will push Peter over the edge. He will have lost everything. His mind will snap. His world will bust open. He'll do something stupid, something huge that will get him killed. I don't care who you are, when you lose that many people, you never recover."

CHAPTER 52

▼

Damian was dumbfounded. He was wasting time on his walk home after meeting Tyrone behind Christopher's sub shop on West Main Street. The secrecy required for the discussion was understandable and they wouldn't get any privacy if Tyrone had come to the Burke household. The tales of parental abuse coming from that place would make any kid wish they were an orphan. Besides, it was better if very few people knew that they were working together. Instead Tyrone and Damian met behind the business-plex where they sat on a rear staircase far below the store and out of sight.

Damian rewound the conversation in his mind looking for a way out of what had been asked of him. The fight with Dutch was hard enough but there were some things he absolutely would not do and being part of a murder was one of them. He walked slowly in a daze of disbelief...

"We'll set the trap," Tyrone had promised as if giving Damian less to do was going to make his part any easier. "All you have to do is deliver the message. Paul still trusts you."

"And they don't trust you?"

"Not anymore. Darius is my brother and he's out of jail. They'll assume I'm on his side."

"Are you?"

Tyrone punched the wooden rail to the staircase risking a splinter. "I'm on my own side."

"You don't have to be." Damian saw an opening to reach out to Tyrone; maybe this was his chance to pull him away from the falls. If not, if Damian didn't try, it was inevitable that Tyrone would be too close to the action when things finally went wrong.

"You can walk away from this…"

"Bullshit I can!" He exploded on Damian's premise. "This is my own brother versus my friends! How can I choose? How can I walk away? This is my old neighborhood tearing itself apart. How can I let it crumble?"

"But you can't stop it."

"Yes I can, the SSP can pull this together!"

"Tyrone, it's chaos. It's everyone out to kill everyone else. You can't control that, no one can. It has to run its course. You'll either be a victim or a bystander, there is no in between."

"I can try to shape it. I have to try! Now listen, here's the plan." He reverted back to his street slang and pushed away any semblance of practical reasoning. Much like Darius back in DYS, Tyrone was falling into the same trap of believing that he was far more powerful than this world would allow. "Listen, Paul will roll up to the gate at the old Drive-in on the south side of Brockton, you know where the outdoor movie screen is? One of my boyz lets him in and we lock the gate behind him. Then it's going to be a shooting gallery. We'll aim from the roof of the popcorn stand and blow his car to pieces as he tries to find a way out."

Tyrone had already filled Damian in on Lelaine's car accident, Aubrey's arrest and his phone call to Darius. Damian shrugged off all of it. He still wasn't given any time to heal. He felt the bumps on his face from the fistfight with Dutch. His ribs were bruised on his left side and he had a long red scar across his neck. At the most he knew enough to fake an acceptable level of comfort during this macho façade. If Tyrone wasn't going to snap out of it then Damian still had to maintain his own discipline, he had stay in their circle of respect until he could find a way out.

"What if the bullets don't hit him?" The plan was haphazard at best. This wasn't a clinical murder it was a game, a way of toying with their enemy. It would be messy, incomplete, and was likely to fail on many levels.

"No worries, there's no other way out. He'll crash into the gate, or drive into the woods but he won't get far. A nasty swamp, thick trees and bushes surround South Side. You can barely walk in there. Besides I'm talking about a shower of bullets. Trust me, Paul won't get away."

Damian wanted to suggest a more definite way of killing Paul but he was afraid they might take him up on it. Besides he really didn't want to kill anyone, not yet anyway. It was better to let these gangsters trip over their own feet, why be implicated for making a suggestion? He kept his mouth shut and listened to every deranged detail.

One night he would get a call to find out the date of the event, then he would deliver the message to Paul and the games would begin. It's as simple as that. However, one thought did bother him more than any of the others. Tyrone said there would be a shower of bullets. How? How many people were going to be there? How many guns did it take to produce a shower of bullets? And why did they want him to attend this duck hunt if his only job was to deliver the message? How big was this event going to be?

Damian switched into Sly mode, squinting his eyes as if giving this plan the utmost of attention. "If you're going to make an example of Paul, then you'll need a lot of people to see it happen. A show of power is no good if it goes unseen."

Tyrone smiled. "Don't worry brother, you ain't never seen so many nigga's with guns as you will on that day. Bank on it."

He accepted the slight and they went their separate ways. It wasn't until Sly reached Feeley Street that the absurdity of his situation dawned on him.

"What the fuck am I doing?" The more he pondered the more he wished the circumstances were different. Being on the inside of a teenage criminal syndicate was sure to land him right back in jail. He didn't want to count the days until Darius got paranoid enough to place him on his hit list. He just wanted out, but how? Ten minutes ago he thought he could help Tyrone walk away but how is *he* going to walk away?

The last glow of a fading blue sky was disappearing behind the trees. Damian crossed the street and walked closer to the woods, there was no sidewalk on this part of the road. As soon as he reached the woods, he caught another view of the trees. Among the lightly frosted evergreens was the dark figure of a man approaching him quickly. Damian reacted too late.

"Get over here punk!" The man bound out of the woods, grabbed Damian's sweater and yanked him into the branches with one overwhelming pull. Damian stumbled forward and tripped to the ground as a heavy knee landed on his back. Did he see orange hair?

"Where is he Burke?" A solid emotionless voice commanded an answer.

"Where is who?" Damian tried to lift his head but the man's palm came down on the side of his head crushing his face into the wet leaves. Damian could only see the blurry white of dirty snow.

"Where is Dutch? The leader of the HAWKS gang, where is he? C'mon you little shit, you're his best friend, where is he?"

Damian's right hand was free and out of instinct he formed a claw with his fingers and grabbed a hold of the skin on his attacker's lower leg digging his untrimmed fingernails into the exposed flesh of an ankle.

"Aaaaaagggghhhh!" The man screamed and pulled back but then dropped all his weight down on Damian's injured ribs.

"Ooowww!" Damian howled in pain but then lost his breath. The man was crushing his lungs; he couldn't inhale. He was struggling to breathe and couldn't hear a word the guy was saying. He caught the green of a Celtics jacket out of the corner of his eye.

"Gary?"

"Where the fuck is he Burke, I'm tired of playin with your type, ya hear?" A more honestly flawed South Boston accent spilled from his lips. He had fallen out of character. This was his true voice. Damian had thrown him off guard with his attack forcing a deep, authentic frustration to pour out of the man.

"Where the fuck is he?" Roared the southy accent.

Damian tried to respond but his wind was gone. "Can't breathe...can't." The weight of his foe was crushing his body; he was quickly losing consciousness. No matter how bad he was hurt, he would never give up anything about Dutch. He had put his friend through enough grief to last a lifetime. Sly would be defiant to the end.

"Fuck you asshole." He wheezed.

The last thing he felt was a brick hard fist dropping like a sledgehammer into the soft skin of his right temple. The world exploded in white sparks and then the darkness fell like ashen snowflakes until he could see nothing at all.

BAD MR. FROSTY

CHAPTER 53

▼

Dutch awoke the next morning with a tight pain in the side of his neck, a crick from sleeping on his Mom's living room couch. Throwing off the spare blanket he sat up and struggled to open his aching red eyes to a new reality. The Middleboro apartment was silent, quite the opposite of his last abode on a busy street in Norwood. There he could hear cars driving by all night but here he heard none. This town had a peaceful quality to it that did not go unnoticed. The apartment was also particularly silent compared to last night when he first arrived.

His parents insisted that Tim, 'Psycho', come in to say hi to everyone, John came in as well. When they said everyone, what they really meant was for him to say hi to Lucy who had arrived in Middleboro a few days earlier. They had always liked Psycho and hoped that someday he might become a part of the family, an inference that made Dutch sick to his stomach. Not because he didn't like Psycho but because they were practically selling off their only daughter like this were the Middle-ages. How counter-progressive could they be? Their kindness was simply a modern day version of a pre-designed marriage acting as yet another instrument that confused Lucy into thinking she is more independent than she really is. It was the approval part that bugged him so much. Why should his parents, who have a rotten relationship in his opinion, be the ultimate deciders of who Lucy falls in love with? That's like a high school drop out teaching a current student the best way to graduate. Dutch wouldn't presume such arrogance so why did his parents do it? The whole thing reeked of hypocrisy.

Sitting ignored on the opposite side of the room he watched them talk up to Tim as if he was their own. Dutch cringed at his progenitor's false friendliness. It wasn't that they weren't good people but they were definitely bad parents. They had no plans for him or Lucy; no college money put aside, no blue or white-collar skills to teach them, hell, no colored collar at all. This lack of preparedness always made him a little hot under the um, t-shirt. It felt such a foreign concept when Mom and Dad acted like they really cared.

As Psycho and John reluctantly accepted praise and smiles Dutch sat brooding waiting for the faux orgy of platitudes to end. He knew that the moment his friends left, the second that front door clicked shut his parent's gleeful personalities would also disappear. Minutes later after they had gone, his prediction proved true. They didn't ask about his injuries or mention the mess that had become of his face. They didn't say another word, he was handed a blanket and a pillow for his first night on the living room couch.

Last night now felt like a snippet of a bad dream. On this new morning in a strange town, with daylight filling the room he got a real good look at the new, though undoubtedly temporary domicile that his parents had picked. The house was three stories and white with a rounded driveway that curved up like an over-sized speed bump. His family had the first floor. It provided a good view of School Street that ran three blocks down to Middleboro center. The location was simple, suburban, not too crowded but very far away from the friends he had grown up with. Outside the window he could see the outline of what was soon to become his first vehicle. A large black dodge van with silver hubcaps, it took up a good portion of the speed bump and cast a shadow across the yard. It was black on black, dark as dark can be, ominous to a tee and perfect for his needs.

He stumbled weakly to the window and looked out at this masterpiece of American automotive hardware. "Well, it's a piece of junk but it's *my* piece of junk." He could feel a little pride swelling up in his chest and then, without notice, almost against his better judgment, he smiled.

"I knew you still had a little happiness in you," His Mom walked into the room with her coffee and sat down in a chair by the window.

Dutch hid his smile but she had already seen it. "This is, um, the van—I like it."

"Well," she looked at van with a scrupulous grin, "it needs work. Maybe a lot of work but the guy assured us that it has a good dependable engine."

Dutch nodded. He was willing to work on it, in fact he wanted to fix it with his own hands but his knowledge of cars was somewhat limited. Other than one semester of basic combustion theory taught to him by George Hatch back in Crowley Middle School, he didn't know a camshaft from an alternator. Could this be too complex? Could he be stuck here, the victim of a parental trick? Had they lured him with the promise of a vehicle knowing full well that he was incapable of reviving said mechanical beast? Were they so devious or was he just being paranoid?

"What does it need, exactly?" He asked.

"Well Lucy's new boyfriend says that..."

"She has a new boyfriend already? She's only been here a couple days."

"Well, you know your sister." His Mom disapproved but felt that there was little she could do to stop her.

"So what about her boyfriend?" Dutch was waiting to hear about his police arrest record. She said he knew about cars but in Lucy's language that might mean he's good at stealing them. She always seemed to pick the biggest losers.

"He said that you need a new alternator, maybe a fuel pump and definitely a tune-up."

"Oh, that's not so bad." Damn it! It had to be one of the things he didn't know about.

"Can you do it yourself?" She asked responding to his false confidence.

"Um, no not entirely." He had to concede that he did need Lucy's boyfriend if he was going to get this thing running sooner rather than never. At least the guy couldn't steal it until it started working. That gave them both an incentive to put it back together.

"Ok, well, her boyfriend will be coming here after he gets out of school."

"Fine." Dutch rolled his head around to loosen the pain of sleeping sideways.

"James, you're face looks pretty bad."

"Thanks Mom."

At the bottom of his neck rotation with his head hanging low, he asked, "Oh, what's his name anyway?"

"I don't know." She sipped her coffee waiting for a tirade from her oldest child.

"You don't know?" His voice descended into condemnation but in appreciation for what they had done in buying the van he stopped and asked calmly, "What do you call him?"

"He has a nickname, like you do."

"And that is?"

"We call him Zombie."

CHAPTER 54

▼

"What is that noise?" Dutch stepped away from the hood of the van where he was listening to clicks and drips of an old engine, he wasn't sure what he was listening for but he didn't want to appear unprepared when Zombie arrived. Thus far he had unsuccessfully tried to start it, twice. The engine made a hearty attempt at running but failed to comply with his wishes. Dutch had borrowed his father's tools, a collection of assorted items purchased at Sears over the years. Then he laid out an oil sheet under the engine, a dirty bed sheet really, and he had only started to investigate the van when he heard another sound, a thunderous quake. It took only a few seconds to realize that it was not coming from his van, the ground or the sky but rather from down the street.

"You've got to be shitting me." He stood in awe as an enormous day glow orange pick-up truck with an oversized snowplow drove up School Street. The roof was festooned with a collection of heavy-duty overhead lights of such size and variability that they could probably turn night into day with the flick of a switch. Across the top of the dark windshield written in bright orange angry letters was the name of this snow-eating monster, it was called—Bad Mr. Frosty.

This behemoth of a vehicle stopped at the bottom of his parent's driveway and the passenger side door opened.

"Sup bro?" Lucy jumped down to the cement far below her door. "What do you think?" She gave a know it all grin as she swung her book bag over one shoulder.

"Whose truck is that?" Dutch stepped a little closer. It seemed silly but he could swear that the plow had teeth on it. Festooned in cartoon colors with a vibe so close to life he half expected it to talk to him, this vehicle had a personality of its own. He might not have been surprised if she said it drove her home because it wanted to.

"It's my uncle's but I operate it," An almost drunken voice dangled in the air as a man walked around the plow and ran his fingers over the truck's iron teeth. "Been doing a lot of work this year."

Lucy was so proud of her new man, "Zombie got a contract to plow the VFW parking lot."

"Doesn't the town do that?" Dutch asked.

"They do," Answered Zombie who stopped at the bottom of the driveway, "but they save it until after they get everything else done. Diddleboro has two hundred miles worth of roads." Zombie's voice was jerky, almost humorous in the way that it slurred some words and hiccupped others with no clarity or syntax. He clearly wasn't drunk but he sounded like a man who was faking intoxication in order to disarm any would be pedants.

"James this is Zombie, he's going to help with your van." Lucy stood between the two, looking back and forth as neither one moved, neither knowing what to think of the other.

"Well I'm gonna put my books in the house so...have fun." She scuttled away.

Zombie was about five foot eight, an inch shorter than Dutch, just as thin but with a scruffy beard. He didn't look like a high school student, how many juniors have full beards? He started to wonder if his sister was pulling a fast one, dating a thirty year old and giving Mom a fake back-story on him.

"How was school?" Dutch asked testing the waters.

"Diddleboro high sucks dick. Just like any other school." Zombie looked past him focusing on the van as he talked. "I'll get out of there eventually." He instinctually walked towards the open hood.

"You're a junior?" Dutch tried again.

"Yeah but I'm on the five year plan."

"Oh," Dutch gave a hint of disapproval.

"But," Zombie caught the disquiet of his tone, "at least I'm gonna graduate. Late is better than never."

"Yep..." Stumped by the parry he moved aside so that Zombie could look at the gritty, grease covered six-cylinder engine.

"This is only part of it." Zombie said peering into the limited opening. "The rest of your engine should be accessible from inside the cab."

"Oh, that explains a lot." Dutch couldn't find several parts of the engine when he first took a look.

Zombie reached deep inside and made some minor adjustment. Dutch couldn't see what it was.

"Hop in and start it up," Zombie said with a clinical air like a doctor assessing a patient.

"But it won't start."

"Press the gas pedal down half way, then turn the key."

Dutch climbed in the cab and gave it a try. He was surprised when the engine revved to life. "It actually runs, I thought it needed a lot of work."

"What?" Zombie asked over the loud idle.

Dutch climbed out and repeated his surprise. "I can't believe it runs."

"Yeah, for now anyway."

"What do you mean?"

"The battery is good, the plugs are old but still useable so they spark up, your carburetor is filthy but not yet garbage. The fuel pump is leaking but it's not clogged. It'll run for a while but with a bad alternator the battery won't be able to stay charged and it'll stall on ya."

"You know all that from one adjustment?"

"No, I looked at it yesterday before you arrived."

Dutch nodded, "So can it be fixed?"

Zombie smiled with all his crooked teeth, "Sure, you got air, fuel and spark, it just needs a little lovin. I'll scrap it together so long as your pops can pay for the parts and you help me do the work."

"No problem," Dutch held out his hand. "Is that all you want?"

"Well, you could buy me a sub sandwich."

"Deal," Maybe this guy wasn't so bad after all but Dutch had to ask one question that had been knawing at him all day, "By the way, why do they call you Zombie?"

Zombie maintained his smile and Dutch could see the mischief rising in it. "Because...Satan's my man." He was genuinely happy that someone asked.

"And what does that mean?"

"It means what it means. I worship the devil."

CHAPTER 55

▼

"No that's ok, you guys can go." Lucy waved away Zombie as they stood in the kitchen.

Dutch had just received money from his father and they were ready to head to Auto Zone in Raynham to buy the parts needed for the van.

"Are you sure honey?" Zombie was surprisingly sweet as he whispered to Lucy who cast off his kindness by shooing him away.

Dutch took note of his consideration. He hadn't quite figured out what to think of a Satan worshipping auto mechanic who was skilled in pillow talk. Was this social progress or the first sign of Armageddon? Zombie did take the time to explain that he was a member of the First Church of Satan. He had a colorful membership card and everything. He said that Satanism is more like atheism than demon worship; it's based on self-interest rather than self-sacrifice. Dutch nodded his way through the lesson in religious oddities but didn't really care either way.

"Let's go amigo." Dutch prompted as he left the room and walked out the front door leaving it open for Zombie to follow.

Minutes later they were cruising down North Street toward route 44. A small, curvy pot holed road Dutch watched as every car passed Bad Mr. Frosty very carefully avoiding the fearful painted teeth. Each passing motorist was forced to edge only inches away from the menacing blade as Zombie kept his foot heavy on the pedal.

"How did you meet Lucy?" Dutch asked from the well-worn suicide seat. He made sure to put his seatbelt on after they took an absurdly fast corner in this civilian winter tank.

"Lindo's sub-shop. We were both getting munchies and I guess she saw me drive up in Bad Mr. Frosty so she asked about the truck. Three hours later I let her drive it."

Dutch caught sight of the long, black, angular tube coming up from the center hump and the third pedal on the floor. "My sister can drive a stick?"

"Impressed the shit out of me," Zombie smiled. No wonder he liked her, Lucy had always hung out with grease monkeys, maybe some of their knowledge rubbed off. A long time social misfit and rebel, she leaned precariously towards the wild side so perhaps she was right up his alley.

The truck took a hard right onto Nemasket Street and barreled down a sloping hill. Dutch cautiously put his hands on the dashboard.

"You don't trust me?" Zombie watched him slowly release a tentative grip.

"I don't know you that well." Dutch said respectfully.

"Listen, I like to crash cars because I don't care what happens to me but I would never hurt another person who didn't deserve it."

Dutch swallowed, "That's reassuring but what if another driver gets in your way?"

Zombie saw the car tearing out in front of him. A gold Pontiac Trans-am was spinning its wheels on the icy road as it came out of a side street. Zombie pulled his truck to the right pumping the brakes but the truck was simply too heavy as it continued to roar down the hill.

"There's another car coming." Dutch yelled as a red Chevy Camaro, apparently following or chasing the first car, took the same corner. Its rear end jerked sideways before straightening out and bolting across the bridge before them.

"It's not stopping!" Dutch's hands returned to the dashboard as Bad Mr. Frosty changed directions and slid to the left towards a snow bank on the side of the road.

"I can stop it." Zombie smiled and grabbed a yellow level to the left of the steering wheel. They were careening towards a snow embankment that barely hid a solid rock wall. Just as the truck was about to crash Zombie pulled the lever and dropped the plow into the snow bank. The big blade dug deep, driving up a huge pile of wet drift onto the windshield. It brought them to a sudden jerking halt.

Dutch felt the seat belt hold him back; his hands would have done little good against such an erratic impact.

They sat staring at the snow dripping down the glass. Had they gone through the bank this huge monster of a vehicle would have decimated the wall and sent them soaring off a thirty-foot hill into the water below.

"Good thinking." Dutch squeaked as the breath began to return to his lungs.

"No problem, just hope I didn't break anything. I got to check the truck." Zombie opened his door and crunched through the snow looking under the front end. He returned with the smile still gleaming between the black hairs of his beard. "It's good to go."

"Tough truck."

"Hell yeah, this is Bad Mr. Frosty!"

"So who the hell were those people?"

"Fuckin Jucketts."

"Jucketts? What's a jucket?" Dutch instinctively grabbed his seat as Zombie raised the plow and started to back the truck up to get it in line with the street.

"They're a bunch of kids from Juckettville, it's part of Diddleboro. They're stoners and shit."

"Druggies?" Dutch's curiosity caught fire at the prospect of new enemies living in the very town his parents decided to move to. Even in the peaceful backwoods of Middleboro there was a drug culture. Now he knew that there was no safe place he could go without facing these chemicals demons. If they were rampant in this rural town then it was official, they were everywhere. "Do they deal drugs too?"

"Yeah, they're trouble makers. The gold bird belongs to Hades but I don't know who was in the other car." No sooner had they driven ten feet towards the beginning of a large rock bridge over running water did another vehicle come flying down the same side street towards them. Zombie stopped Bad Mr. Frosty right in its path. "They ain't making me crash twice in one day."

The vehicle screeched to a halt. A fat baldhead poked out the driver's side window of a lifted, blue and white Ford Bronco. "Get the fuck out of my way Zombie!"

Zombie rolled down the window in time to hear the comment. "Go find your own road!" He yelled back at him.

"Did you see two cars go by?" The fat man asked belligerently.

"I saw your momma go by in a Yugo!" Zombie rolled up the window as the fat man gave him the finger and backed his truck up the road. At first it seemed that he might speed up and ram them but with no more tussle he turned his Bronco around and left the way he came.

"Ok," Dutch wiped his forehead, "And who was that?"

"That was Taco, he's one of the Manson gang." He said the gang name the way a clown would repeat a child's name just to remind the birthday brat that there was still an adult behind the squishy nose.

"Is he a Juckett too?"

"Yep, whole bunch of losers."

"But he didn't pull out a gun or anything."

"Nope and he won't because I got three big, mean ugly uncles, spawns of evil who drive Harley Davidson's with the Hell's Angels. People around here know better than to fuck with me."

"Is that all true?" Dutch unzipped his coat, it was thirty degrees outside but he was sweating from all the excitement. He thought they were going to Auto Zone, not playing demolition derby with the locals.

"Hmm, partly. As long as they think it's true then I got nothing to worry about." Zombie drove the truck across the bridge as Dutch got a good look at what they were passing.

Down to the left, beyond the wall they almost crashed through, was a small reservoir of water that emptied into numerous tiny waterfalls between a collection of rock walls. These miniature tributaries then reformed into a wide flowing river. The snow had lightly peppered the rocks and formed crescents of ice at the edges of the moving water. It was beautiful, like a postcard. Dutch found himself mesmerized by the sight.

"What is that place?"

"It's Oliver Mills Park. It's a herring run, you know where the fish go upstream to lay their eggs and their spawn is washed downstream, blah, blah, blah...the circle of life and death." Zombie grinned again but this time it was both evil in appearance but lighthearted in intent.

They crossed the bridge and took a left onto route 44 heading toward Raynham.

As Dutch took his eyes away from the sprinkling waterfalls they landed on Zombie's smiling face. "I got to say, if all Satanists are like you then I think I found my new favorite religion. Are they like you?"

"Don't know."

"Why not?"

"I've never met another. In this town I'm the one and only." Zombie smiled all the way to Raynham.

CHAPTER 56

▼

"Will that do it?" Dutch's hands were black as tar but twice as shiny as he let go of the alternator that Zombie had tightened into place.

"Yep, I just got to double check everything and we can give it a go." With his coat sleeves rolled up Dutch could see the huge tattooed forearms on Zombie, he was like Popeye with an easy-grip wrench.

"I'm gonna go clean this shit off my hands."

"Oh wait up, you're gonna want to use this." Zombie reached down to his red tool chest and pulled out a quaint circular plastic container. "It's Orange goop, it can get anything off your skin."

"Thanks."

Lucy walked out of the house while he was walking in. "You guys aren't done yet?" She chided.

"I don't see you helping."

"I would have been done hours go. I want you to learn for yourself."

"Whatever..."

"You doubt me? I once changed an alternator by myself in under forty minutes."

"Bullshit." Dutch snapback but he glanced at Zombie for confirmation.

"Don't look at me. I wouldn't doubt her."

Dutch didn't want to see their displays of redneck affection so he quickly slipped inside.

Lucy circled behind Zombie and grabbed him around the waist.

"Hey hon. Are you gonna adjust my alternator?" He chuckled.

"You wish. How's the van coming?"

"It's almost done, that slant six will run forever if he takes care of it."

Lucy peered into the open hood. "Why?"

"It's a good design. The engine is in there sideways so the oil slowly slides down the pistons taking much longer to settle at the bottom. Everything else will go before the engine does."

Lucy started picking up loose tools and putting them back into his toolbox. "Are you guys getting along?" It was a trick question. Lucy often rebelled not only against her parents but also against Dutch. If he and Zombie were becoming friends then she might have to start looking for another lover.

"Yeah, you're brother's a cool shit. He doesn't mind my crazy driving or my devil music."

Wrong answer.

"That does take some getting used to," She sourly noted that Bad Mr. Frosty had snow stuck to its teeth. "Did you guys plow something?"

"You could say that." Zombie smiled at her but wouldn't elaborate. He was already sharing secrets with her brother, isn't that cute.

"Ok, let's fire her up!" Dutch jogged out the door and up to the driver's side. He pulled the lone key out of his pocket and cranked it in the ignition. The engine roared to life and now it was Dutch who had to smile. The HAWKS first official vehicle was at least mechanically ready for action.

"So what you guys going to do?" Lucy closed the toolbox and carried it over to the breezeway.

"Joyride." Said Zombie as he waited for Dutch's agreement.

"Yes we do have to test it but then I'll need to make some modifications."

"Joyride first." Zombie climbed into the passenger seat.

"Hey I want to go." Lucy begged as she caught the absence of any rear seating.

"Sure but you'll have to sit on the spare tire."

Lucy turned it down. If they were going to race around on Middleboro's icy streets then she would end up bouncing around the back of the van like a rubber ball.

Zombie guided Dutch through the back roads as they talked about these so-called modifications. Beyond adding a couple love seats for people to lounge on Dutch did indeed have some big plans.

"You want it to be bulletproof?" It wasn't what Zombie expected to hear. He had imagined that he might want a supercharger or a sunroof, something fancy or faster but bulletproof? "No problem bro, I can do that."

"You can?"

"Sure," Zombie reached in his pocket and pulled out his truck keys. Attached to the main ring was a piece of thick rubber. He threw the keys to Dutch. "Take a look."

"What am I looking at?"

"That's a synthetic fiber in a super dense weave. It's bulletproof. You probably know it as Kevlar."

"Kevlar?" Dutch heard of it, the most current and high tech way of protecting the human body from bullets in a war zone was to wear Kevlar padding. But how did Zombie know about it? His skepticism was growing. Did Zombie have a penchant for lying? Was he trying to impress Dutch or was this real? "What do you know about Kevlar?"

"Are you kidding? They invented the stuff in the sixties as a way to toughen truck tires for the army. They wanted to make them unbreakable." Zombie accepted his keys back and felt the tough material between his coarse fingers. "This piece came from a tire I stole off an old two ton army truck they had at Diddleboro auto-salvage."

Dutch blinked in disbelief but figured that even if it was only partly true he still had to have some kind of protection for people riding in the van. A partial plan was always better than no plan at all.

"So, do you still have the rest of that tire?"

"Bet your ass I do. We can nail it to a couple two by ten inch planks and line the interior with them." He was thrilled about working on such an ambitious project but needed to know a little more about what they would be defending against. "Um, it's none of my business and all but since we're talking about it. I heard that you are in a gang?"

"My sister exaggerates a little."

"Your Mom told me."

Dutch shook his head, what his Mom must think of him? "To be accurate I'm the leader of the HAWKS Foundation and we..." He glanced at Zombie remembering that he was talking to a happy Satanist, this was clearly the kind of person who would understand what Dutch was doing and more importantly, why. "Ok, we are a military squad dedicated to killing drug dealers. We're guided by a malevolent philosophy that also acts as an oath and a bond to keep us together and on track. After high school we're all going to join different branches of the military to learn the skills we'll need to wage a silent war on America's streets. Our tactic is called Stealth Justice and, well, that's the short version."

Zombie sat silent through Dutch's explanation. Then he lifted his chin. "So it's not a gang, more like a platoon or something?"

"In military terms we'd be more of a squad but yeah."

"And you only go after jucketts?"

"We call them druggies but yeah I guess it's the same thing."

Dutch decided to use Zombie's own words to make the connection, "We go after those who deserve it."

"Ok, I see that. In fact I can think of a few evil fuckin Jucketts that the world could do without. A couple of those Manson gang assholes beat up my nephew about a year ago and it was all about drugs too."

"You're uncles didn't do anything?"

"Nah, my uncles mostly scare people. Sounds like you guys actually hunt them down. I can dig that."

A wide smile broke across Dutch's face, "So you'll help me with the modifications?"

"Hell yeah, sounds like fun."

DAISY DRIVE-BY

CHAPTER 57

▼

"What the hell is he doing here?" Lazio was beside himself. Of all the people who might climb out of Dutch's new team van no one expected to see Damian. He appeared smaller, worn-out, like he had lost weight. His face was bandaged on the right side in front of his ear; his eyes were slits with dark lines beneath them. Sly was deeply tired. Despite a beaten exterior his charisma and pernicious confidence remained the same.

"It's good to see that I'm still loved by so many." He said stepping past a confused Lazio to shake Psycho's hand.

"Good to see you," Psycho said with little fan fare, "But I don't get it, what's going on? How did you guys reconcile so quickly?"

"Dutch will explain."

Several hours earlier Dutch made a series of phone calls from Middleboro. He contacted each member of the HAWKS individually with a specific request so that they could meet on this night to take care of some secret business. Lazio, Psycho and John came out of Lazio's house the moment the black van arrived carrying Dutch and Sly but Becca was nowhere to be found. She had never been called.

Dutch stood before them and captured their most intense concentration. His face had healed evenly over the past week and while he couldn't erase the screw-ups of the past he could certainly provide a new hope for the team's future. That was what it felt like, all of the present members felt elated despite the confusion because beyond it was a growing sense of purpose. This was a new beginning and now Dutch would encapsulate that vision in one of his inspiring speeches.

"My fellow HAWKS, there are actions that we can control and reactions we wish we could change but now is not a time for regret, instead…it is a night for vengeance."

"Alright!" Psycho cheered him on. "Let's hear it."

"Tonight we will exact due measure against one such person who has caused us trouble here in Norwood. John," Dutch turned his portly friend, "Did you get what I asked for?"

John nodded reluctantly, "I spend so much money on you guys but…*this* should be entertaining." John walked to the back of his Cougar and popped the trunk open. The team gathered behind it mouths open in disbelief.

"Are those…?" Sly was about to ask but Dutch anticipated the question.

"No, they're not real guns."

Psycho let out a disappointed breath, "But they look so real, are they toys?"

"Expensive toys," John said as he reached in and handed a rifle to Psycho.

"It's a BB gun." Psycho said as he felt its lightweight hollow plastic stock and noted the extra small nozzle opening.

"Wrong, it's an air rifle," John corrected handing a shorter blue stocked gun to Lazio.

"What's the difference?" Lazio asked as he cocked the rifle by folding it in half and then back out to the fixed position.

"These cost more." John grumbled.

"You'll get your money back, I promised." Dutch said from behind the crowd.

Each member took an air rifle and spent the next few minutes figuring out how to cock and load them. Then they fired a couple shots into the air to make sure that they all worked. None had a sound any louder than the pops made by squishing bubble wrap.

"Stealthy," They had all but forgotten about Sly's presence. He handled his weapon with ease. "I had one of these when I was younger but this one is far superior."

"You get what you pay for." John was proud of his purchase and showed off his F.I.D card. "I can get as many as we need."

"Why didn't we get real guns? Shotguns and rifles, that card…" Lazio had fallen behind the pack.

"Cost," John said sternly. "These cost thirty a piece, one shotgun costs a hundred and twenty bucks."

"And," Dutch patted John on the shoulder, "We want to avoid suspicion whenever possible."

"I have to admit, this is pretty cool." Psycho's skepticism was overcome by the feeling of power that even a less damaging weapon can bring to its user.

"Ok so we're armed, kind of, now what is he doing here?" Lazio aimed a suspicious eye at Damian. He hadn't forgotten about the blonde turncoat and couldn't fathom why they would be talking to him, let along working together with this Benedict Arnold after what he had done.

"Lazio, that was the other part of the plan." Dutch stood between them. "Remember there was a part I couldn't tell you guys about? Look, we didn't know if it would work so Damian and I; excuse me, Sly and I took it one step at a time. He contacted me when he got out of DYS, two days after he talked to John. He explained that the SSP wanted to draft him but only if he destroyed the HAWKS first. This required that he beat me in a street fight in order to demoralize all of you."

Lazio lowered his eyes to the ground in shame. He had been demoralized and had acted righteous about it. He bought it hook, line and…"Wait a minute. Why would you want them to think we were destroyed?"

"Having someone on the inside provided me with an opportunity to know everything the SSP was planning. Sly was a spy and it worked, they trusted him."

"So the fight was.?" Psycho almost had it.

"Yes, it was staged, partly fake, mostly sloppy but it did the trick. They believe that he is one of them." Dutch was proud of their scheme even though he had to look the fool as it played out.

"I thought something weird was going on." Psycho said. "You never did throw your karate kick."

"You convinced me, I was scared." John said honestly.

"It almost didn't work." Sly explained. "Dutch was so nervous that when he threw that first punch I had only a split second to react to it. He nearly took my head off with that right hand. If it landed, I would have been out cold and that would have blown everything." He ran his fingers gently across the scar on his neck where Dutch's glove scraped a long gash.

"So that's why you guys were talking during the fight." Now Psycho understood. It looked suspicious at the time. It made much more sense that it was an improv act with an audience who thought they were watching the real thing. They were pulling their punches and whispering instructions under the grapples, now it all made came together.

"So what good did it do?" John asked. "They trust him but what does that mean for us?"

Sly was about to explain but Dutch stopped him, "John, the SSP confided in him, they told him who their next target is going to be and how they are going to kill him. He got the phone call tonight, he knows when and where down to the last detail. Gentlemen, we have five days before the SSP sets themselves up for a fall. Thanks to Sly, we can be there when they try to commit murder."

He stepped into the crowd of armed teenagers. "But tonight we will practice our skills with the air rifles. We will hone our abilities to ready ourselves for the SSP."

"How?" Lazio shrugged. So far their plans hadn't worked so well.

"By going after our local adversary—D-Rod. We need to let him know who he's dealing with. Then, using the information Sly has been entrusted with, we can plan the extinction of the Spring Street Posse."

Dutch exchanged handshakes with Psycho and John but stopped before Lazio who was less than enthusiastic.

"How are we going to outsmart D-Rod? He's tricked us twice." Was Lazio displaying a little empathy for his old friend? Then he blubbered a passive warning, "But he has *real* guns."

"We're not going to hurt him." Dutch tried to figure out what was really bothering him, "Look, I had to lie to you about Sly."

"But why?" He didn't like being left in the dark, he didn't like feeling like a junior member of the team on the outside of all the important decisions. He was also afraid that Dutch might have called Becca and found out what happened between them. His paranoia was escalating.

"Because I needed your reactions to be authentic. I needed Tyrone or whoever else they brought to be sold on the fight." Dutch moved closer so that only Lazio could hear him, "I needed our enemies to see the disappointment on your face when your fearless leader ran away from a battle." Dutch looked him dead in the eyes. "It worked Lazio, it was huge and complicated and brilliant and fucked up. The pieces didn't fit exactly the way we wanted but in the end, it worked. The SSP think we have disbanded. They'll never see us coming. We have the element of surprise."

Lazio nodded, "Ok, I get it, but D-Rod will see us coming."

"Maybe, so what we'll do is make sure he can't stop us. Not this time." Dutch didn't detect anything more than the shock of being lied to. He reached into John's trunk and lifted the last rifle. It was Daisy sharpshooter with a real wooden stock and eagle eye sight. It was a sniper's weapon of choice, provided the sniper didn't want to hurt anybody.

"So what are we going to do with these?" John finally asked. He had spent a lot of money and deserved to get some answers.

Dutch walked past him and hid his rifle behind the love seat that sat long ways inside the back of the van.

"Hide your rifles men." He said before looking at John, "These," He snagged the toy from his hands, "are going to bring a lot of unwanted attention to our enemies."

John was stumped.

The remaining ammunition was packed in a black cardboard container that looked like one pint of milk from a school cafeteria. Sly placed it in a sliding drawer under the passenger side seat. Psycho was holding the door open for him when he noticed the small bandage on the right side of his skull.

"Was that from the fight? I thought it would have healed by now." He whispered.

Sly glanced around and whispered back, "I got jumped. This is from someone who is looking for Dutch. We've got bigger problems than the SSP. This mafia gang war shit is real; some high profile enemies are determined to get their hands on the General."

"But do we even know who we're fighting?" Psycho asked lured in by what must be a confirmation of all the rumors he had heard ever since they found that dead body in Avon the year before. The loose and presumptuous connections between La Cosa Nostra, the SSP and the decapitated body were starting to form a grid of clear implications instead of a blur of hazy imaginings. Psycho nudged him again as they climbed in the van, "So, who is it?"

"No, Dutch can't handle all this right now."

"Sly, I won't tell him. I promise."

Damian considered the way Dutch might respond if he found out they were keeping secrets but this was just too real. "Well, fuck it. The guy who jumped me tried to hide his accent but when he gave it up, I knew right away. It's Gary's uncle Vinny. I met him once before. He works for the Boston mob and he's seriously pissed off."

CHAPTER 58

▼

"Yes officer, I heard what sounded like gunshots coming from inside the apartment, no, *inside* the apartment. Someone was shooting and blew out the windows. There's glass all over the sidewalk in front of the building." The caller was shaken but the officer tried to keep the timid voice on the line.

"Can you tell me your name son?" The officer asked.

"I...I live on Washington Street...I...I don't want this coming back at me...sorry." *Click*, the line went dead.

Sly ran from the phone, jumped into the open back door of the van and sat on the end of the love seat before eager faces.

"How did it go?" Psycho asked.

"It wasn't my best performance but they bought it. There's a cruiser on the way." Sly reached behind the love seat and pulled out his rifle.

"Ready back there?" Dutch asked from the driver's seat.

"It's a go General." Psycho grasped his rifle cocking it one last time to make sure that it was pumped to its fullest pressure.

The van drove half a mile down the street and pulled into the parking lot of a convenience store that sat opposite their target, a three-story apartment building. The van's enormous darkened windows blocked the rear view towards the store. The right flank of the van ran perpendicular to the house allowing for a perfect line of sight. The sliding door wrenched opened wide as five gun barrels aimed up at the third floor where D-Rod lived with his mother. She had already left for her night job so there was only one person likely to be home.

"Fire!" Dutch gave the command allowing all five gunmen to crack off their first shots. Pellets blistered through the air mostly ricocheting off the glass windows.

"They're bouncing off!" Lazio noted as one of the small golden pellets nearly rebounded all the way back to the van. It was his own shot that had gone astray. Lazio couldn't aim worth a damn and hit brown wooden shingles instead of a window.

Dutch wanted to slap Lazio for what looked like a deliberate fuck-up.

"Not all of them missed." Psycho's pellet split a pane of glass in two. He had hit it dead center.

Dutch saw the crack and redirected their aim as everyone pumped their guns and set to fire again.

"Aim for the main living room window. Hit it!" He commanded. Another rally of shots shattered the window. Its crystalline pieces tumbled over each other down to the bushes below.

Meanwhile Psycho had moved onto the next window and cracked it as well.

"Again, next window!" Dutch pointed to the left.

The second wave of projectiles separated the cracks sending huge shards of the window down in jagged pieces that broke with resonance on the sidewalk. If anyone was in that apartment, they would have heard it.

"Good, do the same with the next one." Dutch pointed to the kitchen window.

One by one the windows cracked, shattered and fell. Each one breaking away more violently than the next as they all improved their targeting, all except for Lazio whose gun had mysteriously jammed? Regardless of his incompetence, within less than two minutes the third floor had more holes in it than a screen porch. Every window had been blown out of its frame or was nothing more than sparkling icicles dangling from damaged sills.

"Silhouette in the kitchen!" Sly saw a figure hide behind the refrigerator.

"Ok, let's get out of here!" Dutch jumped back into the driver's seat, all the barrels were tugged back inside as Lazio slammed the door shut.

"He's coming!" Sly saw a lone man with what looked like a pistol in his right hand. "He's armed! GO!"

The van tore away but not before the sound of actual gunshots filled the air. The man in the open window fired down at the van but it quickly turned the corner, almost tipping over and disappeared from view. No one saw for sure who it was but they had a good guess.

CHAPTER 59

▼

"Sir what did you put in your pocket?" Matt Verde was the first police officer at the scene. He saw broken glass on the cement in front of the building and the missing panes on the third floor. The caller had given an accurate description of the shooting so they had to assume the worst. He quickly called back up and waited at the end of the driveway. It was then that D-Rod came racing out of the house. In the split second that he saw the cruiser he slipped a shiny metal object into his right front pocket.

"What? Nothing..." D-Rod took a half step back.

"Put your hands above your head!" Officer Verde rested his right hand on his sidearm.

"I didn't do anything, they were shooting at me!"

"Who was shooting at you?" Matt asked taking two steps forward to every half step of D-Rod. "Stop moving sir."

"I don't know, a van full of army guys, they were dressed in black, they had rifles with scopes and shit..." He had a theory about who they were but still wasn't sure. Unfortunately saying it all out loud did sound a little crazy.

"Sir I'm going to ask you one more time to put your hands above your head and stop moving." Matt unsnapped the leather holster allowing his Berretta to slide into the palm of his hand. "Put them up sir!"

"Fuck!" D-Rod muttered as a second police car pulled in front of the house careful not to run over the broken glass. D-Rod cautiously raised his hands. He didn't want his Mom's driveway to be the last place he ever stood in this world. He didn't want her to come home from her night job to see bloodstains painted across the garage door but he also didn't want to go to jail.

"Fuckin HAWKS!" He exclaimed accidentally.

"You know who did this?" Matt closed the gap, "Is it a rival gang?"

Two more officers rounded the corner and immediately pulled out their guns as they saw the tense situation.

"Ok, ok, my hands are up...there, see..." He reached for heaven and closed his eyes sure that they were going to take the easy way out and end his life right now. Who would even care? D-Rod was a high school dropout with no father, no job and no future. As soon as they went up into his apartment they would find enough evidence to be justified in their actions. He might as well get it over with, "Just shoot me." He whispered thinking that none of them could hear.

Matt was the youngest officer on the scene and still the closest to D-Rod, he caught the whisper and quickly walked up to grab his arms and handcuff them behind his back.

"The glass is from my Mom's apartment," D-Rod said to the two officers so they would lower their guns. They clarified the correct floor and rushed upstairs. Now a third police car had pulled out front.

Matt carefully reached into D-Rods pocket and pulled out a silver 25-caliber pistol. "Is this all you have?" He asked with a surprising sliver of sympathy.

"Just shoot me man. If my Mom is going to have to visit me in jail for the rest of my life, I'd rather be dead."

"What do you have up there?" Matt asked as he patted him down for any other weapons. "You got more guns? Or is it drugs? Were the shooters friends of yours? Did you rip them off, was it a deal gone bad?"

"Just shoot me," D-Rod pleaded half-serious as his whisper faded into a somber murmur.

One of the officers came down the stairs yelling out orders in his CB radio as Matt asked what he found.

"In the back of his bedroom closet there was a false wall made of cardboard, we're talking AK-47's, Uzi's, a Law rocket launcher, sticks of dynamite, about twenty Glock handguns. Most of it's pretty old but this is a huge stockpile of military weapons. This kid is *not* the head of this operation..." The officer stood right in front of D-Rod and asked him straight out, "Who are you working for?"

D-Rod glared back at him with outright disgust, "That's my stash motherfucker! I found them all fair and square!"

"You found them? Bullshit! Who are you hiding them for, you can either tell me or you can tell the judge."

"I found them asshole!"

"Ok," Matt was willing to play along, "Where did you find them?"

Matt's tone was calm, sincere, so D-Rod figured fuck it, he's going to have to tell them eventually, "I found them in a cave."

"Bullshit! A cave in Norwood, where is there a cave in Norwood?" The other officer yelled so loud and so close that spittle landed on D-Rods sweater.

"Yo fuck you man!"

The loud cop waved him off and headed back upstairs excited by the enormous cache.

"No, wait." Matt spun around D-Rod to face him, "What's your name?" He whispered with respect and patience.

"D-Rod."

"Ok, D-Rod. Seriously, where did you find these guns? Are there any left? The public could be in danger and if you tell us up front it will help your case. I'll believe that there's a cave if you can tell me where it is? Was it at someone's house?"

"No, I…" D-Rod wanted to run, to make a break for it but two more officers were coming up the driveway. Matt was the young cop, the one willing to listen, the others may not give a shit what he says but Matt, the arresting officer was actually giving him the benefit of the doubt. He had only a few seconds to take advantage of it before a superior officer took over.

"It's under the railroad tracks, it's um…the name is stupid you won't believe me. It's behind the warehouse on Guild Street. I found the cave when I was a kid, the guns have been in my closet for years."

"Did you sell any of them?"

"Well…"

"Be honest, you're looking at twenty years."

He thought again of how this was going to hurt his Mom. "Yeah, maybe I sold a couple. Today I…I sold some dynamite but that's all, I swear."

"Does anyone else know about the weapons?"

"An old friend of mine knows about the cave but I convinced him that it was full of monsters so he never went down there." Then he stopped to consider Lazio for a second. "He's one of the motherfuckers who shot my windows out!"

"Does he have guns from the cave too? Is that what he shot your house with?"

"No, he's afraid of the monsters. I gave him a big long tale about a secret society run by the god Baphomet."

"And he believed you?"

"Yeah he's got mental problems."

The two officers arrived, one of them was a lieutenant who demanded a situation report and insisted that D-Rod be locked in a car. Matt took D-Rod by the arm and brought him down the driveway.

A voice yelled down from one of the broken windows, "Verde?"

"Yeah?" he turned up to face the officer.

"We've got BB pellets all over the floor up here. The windows were shot out with air rifles."

"Ok, got it." He opened the backseat of the cruiser and gently placed D-Rod inside. Before closing the door he tucked his head down, "I have one more question."

"Are you really going to help me?" D-Rod shot back. Was he answering all these questions only to be hung by them later on? Was this a cop trick?

"I'll help but you've got to stay honest with me. Just answer me this, do you know who was storing the weapons? Did you ever see anyone in the cave? This case is far bigger than you alone. I realize that. If we can identify the people who were stockpiling the weapons then you might be able to testify against them."

"I know who ran it. They were Teamsters, truck drivers and such. They used to load shipments from that warehouse."

"Teamsters..." Matt was putting the pieces together. The Norwood police chief had recently warned him that the FBI was investigating mob related activity in the Teamsters. This meant that all the assets associated to the Boston unions could be a part of the investigation. If this kid was telling the truth and the union just happened to own that particular warehouse then Matt may have hit the jackpot.

CHAPTER 60

▼

"That was just about the coolest thing we ever did, I can't believe it worked." Psycho sat on the very bottom stair at Becca's apartment while she sat three steps up from him staring off into space. Dutch had deliberately left her out of the mission. He didn't even call. It was exactly what she feared might happen if she got too close.

"What happened to D-Rod?" She asked without emotion. She really wished she could have been there if only to be a part of the action but the General didn't trust her anymore. Psycho said that Dutch thought she had lost faith in him after losing the fight to Sly. Now that the fight turned out to be a fake, she sunk into a pessimism driven by guilt. Dutch said he needed his men to stay loyal through thick and thin. Becca failed that test.

"D-Rod got arrested. They snagged all of his guns from what I hear." Psycho turned to look up at here. "You don't really care about what happened to D-Rod."

"No."

"Do you want to hear about Dutch?" He didn't want to tell her anything but as always he enjoyed talking to her or simply being in her presence. They were relaxed around each other and had become good friends.

"Yes, if you don't mind."

"It's ok."

"So," Becca moved down one step. "Dutch planned the whole fight in advance?"

"Um, yes and no, the fight with Sly was arranged but not practiced. They really did hurt each other but it was done with a certain amount of restraint."

"Sly was a spy the whole time." She couldn't believe it. It was such a remarkable plan, so good that no one suspected anything and yet..."I doubted him."

Psycho was listening but not really. His mind was on last night and the drive by. "If he really has all the guns he claims to have..." Speculating with awe, "That kid is going to be a permanent resident of Walpole."

"Prison?" She said not listening to him either.

"Maximum security."

"Should I call him?"

"D-Rod?"

"No, Dutch, James, the General...I have his Mom's number in Middleboro...but should I call him? Maybe I should apologize? Or maybe I should tell him about Lazio and what he did?"

Psycho thought about it for a long moment. "No, let me do that, eventually. Listen Dutch got a team vehicle, plus the guns. He just got his act together. If you tell him that Lazio is, well, stalking you then he'll have yet another enemy to go after but this time it will be one of our own people."

Becca moved down another step so she could see Psycho's face as they talked. "Who's going to protect me from Lazio? Who's going to...?" She started only to be cut off by his most stern admonition.

"We can't have a war within the HAWKS. I'll make sure Lazio stays away from you and I'll tell Dutch when the time is right." That was the end of the discussion. On any other issue he would easily fold to her soft voice and sweet smelling skin but on this he was adamant. They could not go to war with themselves.

They both fell awkwardly silent. The tension that began their friendship as teammates had changed as time went on. Psycho was allowing her to confide in him. Becca had figured out that Psycho didn't hate her after all. He was only concerned for her safety. He really cared but it wasn't like the attention she usually got from guys, it was respectful. In fact, right now, he seemed to care far more for her than Dutch ever did but Becca couldn't get Dutch out of her mind.

"So how did James know about Kaitlin?" She had followed the story all the way to its not so happy ending. The Brockton police arrested Aubrey Truelson to great fanfare even though Avon's officer Gillman got most of the credit. The remaining praise belonged to the person who called in the crime, a teenager named James Ballum. Previously wanted by the Avon police, they had stated that his brave conduct in ratting on Aubrey might be enough for the police to forgive his past adolescent foolishness. The happy part was that Kaitlin Mason is alive and recovering from her wounds. Unfortunately Aubrey killed the little girl's grandmother the day before he was captured and now her mother Michelle was missing. They were investigating to see if Aubrey had kidnapped her as well. It was still unclear what he had against the family.

"Kaitlin? Oh, the little girl." Psycho shrugged. He was pretty sure that Dutch didn't know or care at all about the little girl. He asked Dutch about it who simply ignored the inquiry.

"That was so…" She beamed with her elated image of Dutch as savior. "It was so brave, so selfless. I didn't know he had it in him."

"Yeah, neither did he."

She saw that Psycho was getting jealous again. "Hey, listen, I want to thank you." She said with certainty moving down one last step. Now they were touching leg to leg. "You have been listening to me complain ever since the initiation and I know how you never wanted me on the team and…"

"It's not that. I mean I have nothing against you personally, I didn't want…what I'm trying to say is that I could stand it if someone else got hurt but…"

His unusual kindness fell into a stumbling embarrassment. Was he trying to apologize or was it something else, a feeling more tender?

"You can say it…you can tell me anything."

"There's a level of trust, a bond and…" He stumbled again.

"Psycho, I'm still a HAWK. As a friend or teammate, either way, you can trust me."

He nodded, it was true whether he liked it or not. He could trust her; he had always been able to, so why should it change now? Psycho leaned his head back against the wall, closed his eyes and said, "I couldn't stand it if anything ever happened to you."

Becca felt her face go flush, a slight tickle lingered down her spine as she instinctively moved a little closer to him.

Psycho kept his eyes closed. He didn't want to face the consequences of what he said. He was loyal to his team, to his country, to his General but shouldn't he also be loyal to his heart? "I should probably go." He stood up still facing away from her. Those deep brown eyes would make him fold like a lawn chair. He avoided them at all costs.

Becca stood as well, reached around him from behind and hugged his thick shoulders. "Thank you." She planted a light, friendly kiss on the side of his neck before he could do anything about it.

Now it was Psycho who felt flush, "Ok, my snow is in the car, not my car I don't have a car…I, um, I mean it's snowing and John has to get home…I really have to go. Good night Becca." He walked to the door tripping on the carpet but catching his balance. He straightened out his stance, lifted his head high and waved as he exited.

Becca sat back down on the stairs and watched him stomp through the snow. She thought about what he said. Dutch was always going to be a pile of uncertainty fueled by ambition and masked with bravado but he was their leader and they needed him. Psycho on the other hand was sweet, sincere and steady. He could afford to care. But, because of Lazio, no matter what she did or did not do, the HAWKS were going to crumble from within right at the moment when they appeared to be the strongest. Lazio could ruin everything. He was jealous of Dutch, obsessed with her and might turn a dangerous situation into an unfortunate opportunity. If it all went wrong, this disintegration might be blamed on her presence as a member of the team. They might think that she provoked his attentions. Psycho believed her and promised to do something about it but she never wanted to pass it off on someone else. Why did it have to be so complicated? More importantly, how could she stop the inevitable from happening?

She snapped her fingers as the most obvious idea announced itself, "This is my responsibility. I have to get rid of Lazio myself."

SHOTGUN CREW

CHAPTER 61

▼

"He wants to meet with you, in person." Tyrone had become the in-between in Darius's growing underground constituency. He proved his worth by sticking with Sly and creating the downfall of the HAWKS. Then he reported the news about Peter's personal tragedies that spelled the end of his immediate ambitions. Soon after, Sly reported that he had been in a car accident and would be unable to participate in any further plans. That was it; Dutch, Peter and Sly appeared to be incapacitated. As far as they were concerned the tiny Avon gangs were no longer a threat so now the two competing factions of the SSP could sort out their own in-house affairs.

Tyrone stood in the doorway of Schmel's old top floor apartment that had often been used as the SSP's headquarters. Now it had become Rafael's main base. Raf had always maintained a small one bedroom apartment on the first floor where he and his girlfriend spent time so even he felt out of place up here. She was in the building tonight but he didn't want her involved. If they knew about her then she'd be their first target. He knows how Darius's mind works and had to make sure that each of his moves was a calculated defense.

Tyrone, due to his familiarity and new stature, was able to by-pass seven sentries on his way to the top floor. He was comfortable with his approach, confident even as he passed by friends who were still undecided about who they should follow, but now standing before his brother's competitor to the throne, he started to sweat.

"Have a seat." Rafael sat opposite him on the right arm of a plush red sofa while Tyrone was seated on a wooden chair waiting for a reaction, or an answer, anything. His calm air faded with each passing second.

Raf walked away from the couch, picked up a large brown bottle of beer and returned. He sat lightly and took a long swig but kept himself from facing Tyrone directly. He was thinking three steps ahead, trying to gather his cards and strategize the best way to play against Darius. This was a hard call, Darius was a pro, a long time standing member of the Posse with intricate ties. Darius could have men in the building setting up a late night raid or one of his own bodyguards might be willing to switch sides for a proper barter. Much like Tyrone, Rafael was also in over his head. Maybe he should let it go, his family lived in Taunton, he really didn't have turf to fight for. If anyone could walk away it would be him, Darius was going die fighting on the city streets. It wasn't a prophecy so much as a life long dream, his decided fate. It was pathetic really, Darius and many of these thugs simply couldn't imagine any other way to live so they celebrated the only path that appeared viable. In that way Darius was more like Schmel than Raf was but was it reason enough for that vagrant to inherit all the spoils? The SSP brought in one hundred thousand dollars a year, maybe more. They had a system of businesses, in seven towns linked together by family ties and a network of friend-to-friend dealers. Why should Darius, the constant felon, the backstabbing alley thief that he is, why should he get all of this? Then again how could Raf beat that level of commitment except to be the person who kills him? This was adding up to become a no win situation. Raf changed the subject.

"What's the word on Peter?" He asked testing Tyrone's awareness of the current battleground.

"He's living with a handful of people in his father's house. He takes daily trips to the hospital to visit his Mom. We're watching him but he's an emotional mess. He's harmless."

"Is he armed?"

Tyrone nodded, "With his Dad's shotgun for sure and whatever else the police might not have found in that shit hole when they gutted it for evidence."

"Six people, one weapon." Raf took another swig and considered Peter's momentary weakness. It could be considered an act of strength if he took down the Shotgun Crew. They were battered and inconsequential but a show of strength was expected. Who better to beat down than a lame dog? Then again he was sure that Darius was thinking the same thing.

"Are you guys going after him?" Raf wobbled to a window and peered out at the streets. The liquor was going to his head. He shook it out and considered his options. This was his turf or could be if he put up a strong enough front. It still didn't feel real, all the power that would come, all the people who would look up to him. Was he ready for it?

Tyrone answered in delay, "Word up, it's just a matter of time before Peter's capped. Loose ends and all."

"How do I know you won't recruit him?" He watched tiny shadows move in and out of the alleys below. Those would be his phantasms of black market commerce. The menacing streets of Brockton would remain feared under the cloak of his intimidation. But first he had to show enough strength to intimidate.

"You don't, we take what we want."

"We?" His eyes went wide.

The statement had been bold, audacious, maybe a little over the line considering where Tyrone was sitting. Now he got really nervous. The more he gave the impression that he was making decisions with Darius, the more he was at risk of becoming a cold, dead example of what Raf might do to his enemies. As a courier he was really a small cog and carried little influence but if Tyrone were going to ascend to second in command then it would be in Rafael's interest to make sure he never leaves this building. A wrong perception can be more dangerous than the true reality.

"I meant to say, Darius will take what *he* wants."

"And you?"

"I'll report to him whatever you want me to say." He felt like a pussy for backing down but what could he do, Raf had his life in his hands. All of his previous confidence was gone; he just wanted to get out of here alive.

Raf finished the bottle with the third swig. His mind was rolling just behind his eyes, the alcohol had loosened up his hesitation and now he was ready to speak with authority.

"Here is what you tell Darius." He stood directly in front of Tyrone playing his role better than expected. The courier was exceedingly nervous as the words were drooled on top of him like a stream of arid hate. "Schmel was my cousin, his father was my uncle, his family is my family so the SSP is in *my* blood! If Darius wants to die a thug, then he's going to die by my hands. If he wants to run a war against me, then let the war begin."

Raf raised the empty bottle high as Tyrone cringed expecting it come crashing down on his head. Instead Raf poured three drops of smelly ghetto beer onto Tyrone's hair.

"Can you remember all that?" Rafael's breath swooned down on him. Tyrone wanted to puke. He held his breath an answered quickly.

"I got it."

"Good. Now get out!"

CHAPTER 62

▼

"We've got them?" Peter nearly fell off the pile of milk crates that he was using as a chair in his father's kitchen. His hands were filthy, his face covered in sweat. The police had made quite a mess out of the house when they searched the place for drugs and guns. Luckily, they hadn't found all of them.

Paul carried the cardboard box over to the counter top and set it down as carefully as he could, as if the contents could explode if handled too roughly. He had been gone for days trying to negotiate with his dealer over the price of a certain necessary group of items. Even after he managed to purchase what he needed there was another delay. On his way back to Brockton his Camaro spun out on a patch of black ice and sideswiped a telephone pole. He had to stop in Avon and spent several hours kneeling on cold cement replacing his rear right tire. The next day he drove to Brockton with the cardboard box in his trunk.

Meanwhile Peter had spent the same night digging a steel safe out of the far right corner of the backyard. In it his father hid two shotguns, ammo, some canned food and a stash of weed. It was actually very poor planning because he didn't include a can opener or a lighter. It took six hours for Peter to find the right burial spot and then another three hours to break enough frozen dirt to get the safe out of the ground. Now the old rusted safe was lying open on the floor next to his feet. The guns appeared to be in workable condition even though he had nowhere to test them.

Paul took the tape off of his box. He got the price he wanted, plus some. "We have more than enough."

Peter stood next to him and opened the flaps but his expression fell from tired to disappointed. "They look old, are they gonna work?"

"Yes, he assured me that it's the ingredients that matter, not the age though he was in a rush to get rid of them."

"A rush?" Peter didn't know anything about the deal except that Paul knew a guy, well, a kid who was supplying what they needed. The kid had a wild reputation for producing some amazing items.

"Yeah, in fact I called him when I got back to Avon but a cop answered the phone. I think he got nailed."

"Where does he live?"

Paul hesitated. He promised his contact that he wouldn't tell anyone who he is, not even Peter. "North of here…I can't…"

"Why can't you fuckin tell me, does he think I'll go after him or something?" He didn't appreciate the secrecy but otherwise there would have been no deal.

"It's not that, it's just…he's a supplier, he sells to everyone. He could be playing six sides of the same dice, you know?"

Peter shook it off, "It doesn't matter. In a couple days we'll flatten that dice. When this is over there will only be one side left, ours."

"I'm sure this will work," Paul said protecting both his position and the product at the same time. "But when it's over, what are we going to do about Dutch?"

Peter slammed his fist down on the cabinet next to the box. He was so sick of hearing about Dutch. They were in a turf war against two halves of the Spring Street Posse and Paul was worried about Dutch?

"Careful," Paul said under his breath. "I was lucky that the car accident didn't set these off in my trunk."

Peter had no response. Dutch had all but disappeared from the face of the earth. Even the mafia couldn't find him. What was Peter, with his limited resources, supposed to do? "Dutch…" Peter bit his lower lip in frustration, "I'll kill him so slowly…"

"Ok, well, I'll just hide this stuff downstairs until we're ready to use it." Paul went to pick up the box but Peter blocked him and set it back down.

"Why wait?" He said leaving his mouth partly open, his teeth showing. He wanted to prove himself right now. He wanted to pre-empt this war to demonstrate that the Shotgun Crew, though small and poorly financed, was just as furious and deadly as any clique in the Posse.

"You want to plant the dynamite now?" Paul could hear music coming from upstairs where three of their new members were passing around a joint while listening to NWA. "I guess we have enough men but…"

"But nothing. We've got the firepower, the ammo, and the explosives, why wait? The sooner we conquer Brockton, the sooner we can hunt down Dutch.

Tonight…tonight we are going to burn the Renaissance to the ground along with every member of the Posse who gets trapped inside. We'll show them that we matter, that we should be feared. Let's chop the fucking dice in half!"

CHAPTER 63

▼

"They're moving." Lamar sat in a dark second floor window and watched the street below as Peter, Paul and Apollo climbed into Paul's car. They had carefully placed a box in the trunk before jumping in and driving towards downtown.

"Where are they going?" Darius asked on the phone line.

Lamar was using the upstairs of his older brother's apartment to watch Peter's movements. Day after day Peter had kept the house very quiet allowing his friends to enter and exit only through a hole in the back fence. Lamar watched Peter dig up the back yard to uncover a large metal safe. He reported everything to Darius who was staying at Geo's apartment, which was being used as a temporary headquarters.

Other than the digging, everything had been quiet; that was until Paul drove up tonight handling a suspicious cardboard box. Whatever the Shotgun Crew had been waiting for had finally arrived.

"They're heading towards Main Street but when they hit the hill I couldn't see which direction they turned." Lamar pressed his face up against the glass and tried to see the reflection of brake lights or a blinker to guess where the car was going. Only the faintest yellow flicker gave him a hint but not a solid one.

"They took a right, I think."

"Lamar, if you had to guess..."

"I dun know. They were being careful with the box, like it was fragile."

"I thought you said the safe had guns in it?"

"It did, two shotguns."

"Then why would they need more? And why keep them in the box?"

"I don't..."

"Maybe they got bottles?" Darius asked trying hard to imagine what Peter could be trying to pull off, "For Molotov cocktails?"

"Maybe, it's fragile, it's big, heavy..."

"Thanks Lamar, call me if they come back." Darius hung up the phone and turned to the card table where his top five inner circle leaders sat arguing over the value of a 24-karat gold butterfly knife.

"Geo, you're downtown right?" Darius asked a tall broad shouldered twenty-something in a white wife beater who had a gold handkerchief wrapped around his head with a small flap hanging down in the front just above his eyes. Darius had been chiding him for not wearing the gang colors of gray and blue. Geo's fashion sense was going to get him killed.

"I got Main Street bro." He responded dangling the open knife out for the others to bid on. Again with his arrogance but this had been going on all week. Darius had to ask him for a place to stay, this was Geo's apartment and he didn't let anyone forget it.

"Geo, get over here, call your lookouts, get a bead on Paul's Camaro." Every head at the table turned to Darius who finished with flare, "Peter's moving, something's going down tonight. We have to find out what."

Geo athletically leaped over his chair and grabbed the phone. Every move of his body was showy, every gesture demonstrated boldness in the face of Darius's authority. He was testing his limits but he was also doing his job. Seconds later he had an answer, "Darius, Peter's crew is heading towards Spring Street." He held his hand up in the air as the line chirped at him, "No wait, they're heading right to the Renaissance."

Darius turned back to the table as Kelvin folded his cards and got to his feet. Standing at only five foot eight inches Kelvin wearing a gray Gold's gym sweat-shirt with cut off sleeves was nearly two hundred and fifteen pounds of iron-crafted muscle. At twenty-eight years old he was the gang's senior member, a man who used to run with Schmel's father. His selected area of the city was the Renaissance itself.

"I got this," He confidently punched in his numbers as Darius listened on. Kelvin was silent for a long time only saying uh huh, yep, get someone on the second floor to a window, yep, uh huh, ok. After a minute and a half of mumbling monosyllables he held his hand over the receiver and bent his mouth towards Darius, "They parked at the senior center behind the building. I think they're going in."

"Going in?" Darius shot to his feet and walked to the table. Everyone stopped playing and waited for his next move.

Only Geo wasn't surprised that the Shotgun Crew was risking an all out attack. "Let's shut them down. Let's do it now."

"I guess they're back in the game after all." Granted Darius didn't want Peter to succeed at anything but maybe this was going to work in their favor. "Sit down Geo, we can't hit them tonight. We're twenty minutes away, by the time we get there it'll all be over."

"But..."

"Sit down!"

Kelvin was still on the phone giving instructions to his men to keep a constant eye on Peter's crew. It didn't take long for more information to flow back to him. "One of the crew went to the front door with a chain, the rest went in the cellar and they're armed."

"Do they have the box?"

Kelvin whispered hushed tones but got an immediate response. "Yep, a big one. Do you want to warn Rafael?"

"No, Raf is a bigger threat than Peter." Darius leaned against the card table trying to figure out why Peter would sneak a couple of hoods into the palace headquarters of Rafael's Spring Street Faction. "What does he have in the box? He's either committing suicide or..."

Kelvin waited as the wheels in Darius's mind burned with concentration. What was Peter doing there? Had he struck a deal with Rafael? Was he trying to raid the place? Why was it so delicate, so fragile, so...? "Explosives," Darius said it out loud even though he still didn't believe it himself. "The box has explosives in it. That's why they were being careful; they're going to burn the fuckin build-ing down! Kelvin, tell your men to find Tyrone and get out of there. Tell them not to make a scene of it but they better get some distance."

The teens at the table stared down at their cards only occasionally looking up at Darius. They didn't know if they were going to fight tonight or just play poker.

Standing over them Darius mumbled, "Peter found a way to kill Rafael."

"So are we going to let him do it?" Kelvin asked.

"That building has bad wiring, old insulation, a rusty fire escape. Anyone trapped in there is fucked especially if Peter chained the front door shut."

Kelvin hesitated on the order, "Darius, we got friends in there. People who don't have nothing to do with this are gonna git hurt. Families..."

Darius left the table and stood over his friend who was hunched down next to the phone. "We asked everyone in that building to join us, we asked every family, every friend and they picked Rafael. They made their decision and now they have to live with it."

"But they couldn't just move out, they'd have nowhere else to go…" Kelvin tried to reason with him.

Geo jumped in between them and screamed down at Kelvin, "Yo fuck the Renaissance, it's just a fuckin building, we got my pad now! I say let it burn! Let it burn!"

Kelvin looked around Geo to Darius who was slowly nodding his head up and down in agreement. After a lifetime of bad deals, poverty and sad memories that building had produced little more than tragedies in their lives. The Renaissance represented their failure to rise above it. They had to face that it was time for the SSP to move on. Darius leaned down to Kelvin with cold victory in his eyes and said cryptically, "Let…it…burn."

CHAPTER 64

▼

The fire alarm blared through the hallways with a piercing echo that challenged the eardrum to stay intact. Tyrone raced down the stairs all the way to the third floor when a door opened in the hallway and three people pulled him into a dark apartment. A split second later Rafael raced past the open door down towards his old place on the second floor. His girlfriend was still down there.

"What the fuck!" Tyrone roared trying to scramble away from the clenching hands. "Let go!"

"Chill Ty, it's us." One darkened figure assured him as his grip loosened around Tyrone's arm. "Don't worry Raf didn't see anything."

He recognized the voice but couldn't remember the name it belonged to. "Who are you guys?"

"Kelvin called five minutes ago, said that you were still in here, said we should get you out." The same voice explained as the hands guided him through a second room towards an open window. Either the apartment had no lights or the power had gone out he couldn't tell which.

"What's going on here? Is there a fire?" Tyrone asked of the voice.

"A big one, the Shotgun Crew is making their move against Raf."

"And against us?"

"No, they don't even know we're in the building. Kelvin said to get out fast. We're gonna let the place burn, not that we can stop it."

"Ok, how do we do this?" Tyrone followed his captures out onto the fire escape. On the floors above him several people were testing the sturdiness of the old metal, only a few were coming down. Below him was a forty-foot climb on rusty grates that everyone knew fell far below the fire code. "This is not such a good…"

A shot fired out from below hitting the side of the building. Tyrone and his handlers dived back into the apartment.

"Who the fuck is shooting at us?" Tyrone screamed out. Now that he had been outside the air in the apartment was noticeably different. His nostrils started to sting from the smoke coming under the door or through the vents from the floors below. They were already breathing in a dense acrid smell like paint burning. "We have to get out of here!"

On the street below an argument had broken out between two officers. Officer Degan, who had only been back on the streets two days since his suspension for killing Schmel, was holding his pistol at the ready having expelled only one shot. "He had a piece, I swear I saw one."

The other officer stood next to him watching the window for movement. "Degan, I didn't see shit. I saw three or four kids trying to escape a fuckin fire. I didn't see a weapon."

Degan's eyes stayed locked on the window. He knew what he was shooting at. For weeks he had been sitting at home waiting for his chance to get back on Spring Street and finish what he started. His temporary suspension did not force him to face his itchy trigger instead it angered him that the Brockton police force was not serious about ending gang violence in the city. Schmel was the SSP's leader and everyone knew it. He should have received an award, a medal of honor for killing him not a suspension from duty. Degan had also seen the other gang member who escaped that night, Rafael was well known as a blood relative of Schmel. His contact assured him that Rafael had taken over the Posse. Degan knew that he was under a heavy thumb, he knew the chief would put him on trial the next time he kills but so long as he had a badge he was going to do what he set out to do. He was going to assassinate the new leader of the SSP. They may never thank him for this but it had to be done and the city would be better for it. Maybe this time it would settle the pain he still felt for the loss of his wife. The pain that just wouldn't go away.

"Where the hell is the ladder," A third officer came up to the lead man, "And why isn't anyone coming out?"

The bottom floor of the building had flames flickering out two windows while heavy smoke leaked upwards through twenty cracked or open windows on the second floor.

"You are guys are useless," The third officer fed up with being cautious ran up to the front door and found the chain. "It's locked, it's got three fucking pad locks on it." He could hear banging from inside as people tried to escape. "Get the fire chief on the horn we're going to have a disaster here!"

"I got it," The second officer ran back to his car giving Degan the opportunity to sprint towards the side of the building. He thought he saw Rafael up on that fire escape and his single shot missed but if this was going to be his last day on the force he was going to make it count. Degan jumped a small brick wall, pulled down the metal ladder and started his climb towards the third floor.

"Did you hear that?" Paul stood as a sentry in the cellar by the back door firmly holding a shotgun at the ready. Peter and his comrade were racing towards him ducking pipes and wires, gasping heavily to reach the fresh air. "I think the cops are here!" He yelled to Peter in the confusion.

"Sirens?"

"No I heard a shot out there."

Peter passed Paul checking the back alley. The barrel of his 11-87 leading the way, "It's clear!" He ran up to the edge of the building and saw two police cars with flashing lights sitting in the street blocking traffic. Even with his adrenaline pumping he felt the first flashes of a vicious headache caused by the smoke. He took a deep breath of night air and peeked around the corner. "It's good let's go!" His command echoed off the towering senior center.

Tyrone heard the echo up above, "Peter?" Was he really here? They said the crew was responsible for this inferno but he had trouble believing it. Maybe Ty could talk his old friends down from this, maybe he could reason with them?

"I gotta see if that was Peter."

"No don't!" They didn't stop him in time.

Tyrone lifted his head above the trim of the window and looked right into the barrel of a pistol. The blast was a muffled echo that shook the walls of the apartment. Kelvin's three inside men were showered with an array of bone chunks, blood and brains. They all ran from the room back into the hallway and raced up the stairs away from the rising fire. They passed Rafael's personal bodyguard who was running down three steps at a time.

"Where are you going?" One kid asked.

"Raf is down there!" The bodyguard yelled not even slowing down. "I told him not to bring that bitch here!" He disappeared into the smoke.

Back on the third floor Tyrone's body had slumped onto the windowsill as a steady trickle of blood dripped from his open skull down the side of the building weaving its way along the bricks.

Meanwhile tires screeched out of the senior center as Peter, Paul and Apollo used back roads to leave the scene unnoticed. The old style dynamite didn't explode as they had wished. It's simple design of sawdust soaked in nitroglycerin and wrapped in flexible paper was extremely unstable. It had been stored under bad conditions and the nitro had started to leak out but it did start an uncontrollable fire that would be nearly impossible to extinguish. The structural damage to the building would be incalculable. Their plan was completed and done so at a level they never dreamed possible.

Pagan Predator

CHAPTER 65

▼

The door slammed hard waking Dutch from a terrible nightmare. Once again he was a little kid stuck in a doorway being pushed into an abandon building by an older teen. Then suddenly Gary threw a rock at the teen allowing Dutch a chance to push his way out the door to freedom. The two of them escaped on foot but there was something missing, he felt like someone had been left behind. Painfully awake Dutch was sitting up in the middle of the couch at his parent's apartment. Zombie sat in a chair opposite him.

"Had a bad dream?" Zombie asked as Dutch rubbed his knuckles into his tired, red eyes. He got home very late, the drive from Norwood and residual excitement left over from their air gun drive-by kept him up until nearly five in the morning before he calmed enough to fall asleep. Since then he strategically placed a pillow over his eyes to block out the rays of day.

"Shadow of a memory." Dutch said poetically without explaining.

"But a bad one?"

"Yes." He asked about the loud noise that woke him. What had snuck into his dream giving it real sound effects, what from the world of the wakeful?

"Your sister is pissed at me. She slammed her door and locked it. It's fuckin stupid." Zombie stroked his beard.

"Don't take it too hard she's not one to keep a boyfriend for very long. It's her short attention span." He turned so that his feet fell on the cheap blue rug. His head rose up along with his arms to stretch out the aching chest muscles that had repeatedly pumped the air guns for maximum power. Now those muscles repaid him with delayed onset muscle soreness.

"Yeah but...I guess a friend of hers died and I didn't...I don't know what I said. Doesn't matter."

Dutch shrugged his shoulders; he didn't want to get involved. He probably didn't know the friend and really didn't care. As for the relationship, Lucy was going to break up with Zombie the same way she did with everyone, she'll get pissed at him, accuse him of things he cannot change and finally cheat on him with the next guy in line. He hated the way she treated them and even if some of the guys deserved it, not all of them did. Zombie certainly didn't but it wasn't him it was the relationship. Anyone could see that it wasn't based on love; it was more like an easy opportunity, for both of them.

"The van worked well last night, though the steering was a little stiff. I almost tipped it over."

"You've got bigger problems." Zombie nodded to the window.

"What problems?"

"I'm guessing the bullet proof interior worked?"

"Why? I mean yes it did I suppose but...oh." Dutch jumped off the couch and opened the curtains. On the exposed side of the van, just behind the side door but luckily above the rear right tire were two bullet holes. "Fuck! How am I going to hide those?"

Zombie stood and walked to the door. "Go get dressed, I'll take care of it by the time you get outside."

"What are you going to do?"

"Trust me, the power of Satan is great."

"But..."

"Just trust me." Zombie smiled his evil but happy grin and walked outside.

Dutch's Mom was sitting at the kitchen table with a coffee in one hand the Brockton Enterprise newspaper in the other.

"So a friend of Lucy's died huh?" He asked expecting to hear a name foreign to his ears.

"Yes," She spun the paper around so he could see the cover story. "James, did you have something to do with this?"

The title read 'Renaissance Arson, Three Dead.' Dutch sat at the table with his mouth open. His eyes scanned the page for information that might ring a bell. He'd heard of the building's reputation but didn't know much about it or anyone who lived there. Surprisingly the sentences jarred his memory with familiar names...Tyrone Waters was shot by the police as he tried to escape the burning building...Officer Degan Malone has been permanently suspended despite claiming that he had misidentified a gang leader...Rafael Keynes and his girlfriend Michelle Mason were burned to death, they had been living on the first floor directly above the location where the fire had started...Michele was the mother of Kaitlin Mason the little girl who had been rescued only a week before...Seventeen people, who suffered from smoke inhalation, were dragged out through the front doors after the fire department axed them open...Several witnesses claimed to have seen three teenagers, two white and one black, running from the inferno.

"I don't believe it." Dutch reread the parts that stood out the most. Two white teenagers? Peter and Paul? Was it possible that they took the initiative and attacked the SSP? Tyrone is dead? Holy shit! His face displayed every emotion he was feeling.

"James look at me," His Mom was angry and serious, "You were out all night...did you have something to do with this?"

"No, no I swear I didn't go anywhere near Brockton. I visited Tim and Lazio in Norwood. They can vouch for me. This is news to me, I can't believe it."

"James I swear if you're not telling the truth..."

"Mom? Here..." He held up the newspaper article, "Look it says there was a black kid running away. The HAWKS don't have any black members. Not that I would mind, we just don't happen to know anyone."

Her eyes softened a little. She didn't want to believe that her oldest child could be responsible for such a tragedy but she didn't understand him lately. She didn't know where he went or who he saw. The rumors around Avon were unbelievable. Her family heard that he was wanted by the police and they suspected it might be concerning drugs as his eyes were always red, bloodshot. Was her oldest child on drugs? Now that she had him at home she had to find out.

"James, are you in trouble of some kind?" It was time to get to the source of these problems.

"No..."

"Let me see your arm?" She reached for it but he pulled away.

"What? Are you serious?"

"Tell me, are you on the pot?"

He wanted to laugh at the way she worded it but he was too busy being angry at her presumptions. "Mom, I'm the most anti-drug person you will ever meet. Trust me on this."

"James, it's getting harder to trust you when I don't know what's going on."

"And you're all of the sudden going to take an active interest in my life? It's a little late for that."

"I just want you to be safe."

"I'm fine!" He stood in a fury and stormed out of the room. What was she thinking? He hated the druggies who are destroying this country; they had tortured him for years. Why would his family even consider that he was one of the enemies? What's wrong with these people? Dutch didn't set the fires and he wasn't in Brockton last night. He was being accused of everything! "I'm fine!" He roared before stomping into the bathroom and swinging the door shut.

His Mother shook her head in defeat. "I wish people would stop slamming the doors."

Dutch didn't say a word when he sped by her in fresh clothes to check on Zombie's progress in the driveway. He couldn't believe she checked his arm! He had been telling her for years that he had a sleeping problem, that's why he had red eyes all the time. She must have believed him to be lazy on all those mornings when he trudged out of bed and wobbled like a mummy out to the bus stop. Then came the bullies. Right from freshman year he told her that he was not getting along with his classmates but even after being thrown out of high school she still doesn't believe him. There was no point in trying to explain. If she really wanted to get involved she should have it done it during those first few nightmarish years at high school, that's when it would have made a difference. It was too late now, his path was set, the pain inflicted. A desire for revenge was fueling nearly every action he took.

Dutch snapped out of his rage by the time he reached the driveway where he witnessed a very unusual sight.

"Ta Da!" Zombie flicked his wrist like he was waving a wand. "No more bullet holes."

The van was decorated with a streaming line of black and gray stickers that were shaped like bullet holes. They started from the right front fender and rolled like an ocean wave up and down the side of the van with such artistic grace that Dutch couldn't tell where the fake holes ended and the real holes began.

"It's brilliant Zombie, I'm impressed."

"I bought the stickers at Auto Zone, I was going to use them on Bad Mr. Frosty but you needed them more."

Just for fun Dutch asked another question, "Can we do the same thing if I run someone over?"

Zombie stroked his chin playing along with the joke, "Hmmm, we can try."

"What would you have in mind?"

"We could glue a bloody wig to the grill and then dangle an eyeball from the exhaust pipe."

"Now we're talking."

CHAPTER 66

▼

"It's true, Tyrone's dead, Rafael's dead and the word is that Peter started the fire." TC heard some of it on the police scanner so he made a quick call. His parents were both out for the afternoon so he had the rare run of the house and the even rarer use of their only phone.

"I know I read the article five times. My Mom accused me of doing it."

"But the HAWKS don't have any black members?"

"That's what I said but with Lucy crying her eyes out in her bedroom, I think Mom just wanted to blame somebody." Dutch sat by the window; he was still ignoring his Mom. He vowed not to speak to her all day. It might take that long for him to calm down.

"Why does your Mom care? He was a gangster? That dingbat always ran with the wrong crowd, this was bound to happen."

"I don't know. Lucy keeps defending him, saying that Tyrone was only in the gang because of his brother. She said he never earned anything. He never killed or shot anyone. She said he wasn't a thief or a crook, blah, blah, blah," he sighed. "Have you heard any different?"

"Nope but he's a Brockton kid so..." TC could care less about Tyrone but he felt bad for Lucy. He did nothing to hide the hint of disdain he held for those who grew up in next city over. TC and Dutch encountered many kids from Brockton over the years that turned out to be rotten to the core and it tainted their perceptions. "I can ask but..."

"No forget it, it's not important. Let's just concentrate on the showdown at South Side. This is too big an opportunity for us to miss. Now with Rafael out of the picture and the focus shifting to Peter, our presence will be completely unexpected. But there's one thing,"

"What?"

"We're going to need you there."

"But I have to work that day."

"TC, I wouldn't ask if I didn't absolutely need you."

"Why me though, you've got a full crew."

"No I don't, I have Damian, Psycho and John."

"What about Becca and Lazio?"

Dutch exhaled in frustration, "Becca is not talking to me and there is something weird going on with Lazio. Despite the fact that he's a lousy shot and this is a sniper mission, I just can't trust him."

"Is it because of his beliefs?" TC asked. He had taken a liking to having another pagan on the team even if Lazio was a bit on the extreme side.

"No, you're a witch and I don't mind. Hell, Lucy's new boyfriend Zombie is a Satanist and I could care less, he's a great guy. It's not his religion. I just get a feeling of disloyalty, like he has other interests that are more important, like he could turn on us."

"You're being paranoid. You thought that Gary was trying to take over the team and nothing ever happened from that. Now you think Lazio is what? A spy for Baphomet? A Nightbreed double agent? Even I think that's kooky."

"It's not paranoia. I can't put my finger on it but this is a dangerous situation. I want to be surrounded only by people that I can count on. Besides, like I said, he can't shoot worth a shit. He hit D-Rod's house and the pellet ricocheted back at us. Then he jammed the BB gun. How the hell do you jam a BB gun? The point is that he sucks. I need a real marksman. I know you can shoot because we used to steal your brother's gun and hit targets in the woods."

"Yeah I remember that. That's when my brother tried to stab you."

"So will you do it?" Dutch had counted on him for years and this was one of those times when loyalty meant everything.

"I can ask Jimmy…"

"No, there is no maybe, I need you there!"

"But I've never held a job this long before and he'll fire me if I…"

"TC do you realize what we will be doing? In one night, using our greatest skills, we can take down the Spring Street Posse for good. We can clean the streets by dismantling the largest criminal organization in the Brockton area. Stealth Justice TC! We've never done anything at this level before. Peter won't be there but we'll nail Paul and Darius in one afternoon! Think of how many lives we will save."

The line fell silent. TC breathed a little deeper through his nose, he was pouting. He really didn't want to call in and risk losing his job. It took him so long to find work where he fit in. Granted he still had to deal with occasional harassment from the many town residents who harped on him because of his family history but he was handling it well enough. It was that same family history that made his existence in Avon so difficult. Jimmy took a big chance when he hired TC, he may never take that chance again.

"TC," Dutch implored of him, "Please…if this goes wrong and we get killed in a cross fire between the police and the SSP, would you want to live with knowledge that you weren't there to watch my back?"

"So you are calling the cops?"

"Yes, but that's only part of it. We have to make sure this goes down the right way."

"That's not fair. No one is making you do this."

"You know we have to. No one else can, no one else will. This is what the HAWKS are all about, please come?" He was begging now.

"I'll ask Gaia and then…"

"Fuck Gaia, tell me now!"

TC was bit with a vein of anger at his best friend, not because he didn't want to be a part of the action but because he knew he couldn't refuse. He couldn't live with himself if anything went wrong. Even with the blasphemous expletives put aside, the guilt trip worked all too well.

"Fine, see you Thursday!" TC yelled back at him.

"Fine." Dutch replied with force.

"Good bye!"

"Fine!" Dutch slammed the phone down on the receiver. It was done. The HAWKS Foundation would be ready for their biggest and most dangerous mission. TC, and hopefully Gaia, would be there to watch over them all.

CHAPTER 67

▼

Peter saw the headlights flash through the cracked yellow shades of his father's living room. He jerked up to lean against the wall and peeked through a tattered shade as a shiny black Cadillac took a quick u-turn and slowed before the front gate.

"Guys, get ready." He said to Paul and the three other members of his immediate gang. Two of them grabbed their shotguns while the third grabbed a modified baseball bat. This lightweight wooden slugger had several five-inch nails sticking through its head, each jutting out in a different direction. They were expecting payback for what they did to the Renaissance but something different was happening outside.

The passenger side window of the Cadillac eased down and a light yellow envelope was thrown over the fence and onto the weed-strewn walkway. With tires smoking and a radio turned to full bass the car abruptly tore away turning down Nilsson Street.

Peter stared at the envelope through the shade, waiting for it to explode. Two whole minutes passed and nothing happened.

"You want me to get it?" Paul asked figuring it to be nothing other than it appeared.

"No," Peter pointed to the third black kid, the one holding the modified baseball bat, "You get it."

"Fuck," Apollo dropped the bat on a couch where it stuck into a cushion. He took a place by the door readying himself for a sprint when it opened. Being the youngest member always landed him the most dangerous jobs but if he didn't do it he'd be tossed from the crew in a second. Having no home, he couldn't afford

- 272 -

to leave the gang unless he got a better offer from somewhere else so in the meantime he'd accept the abuse and take the risks. He took his nickname from Rocky's nemesis Apollo Creed in the boxing movies and as a result he was always given the most athletic assignments.

Steadying himself, he drew two quick breaths, pulled the handle and sprinted outside. Grabbing the envelope he spun in his sneakers to dart back but instead he thudded into a shut door. Peter had locked it from inside just in case.

"Pete what are you doing? What if they come back? They'll fuckin cap me out here?" He whimpered while standing exposed in the cold night air.

"Read it!" Came a roar from behind the door.

"It says 'To the Shotgun Crew.'"

"At least they got our name right." Paul quipped while watching through the door's dirty window.

"Open it," Peter commanded through the mail slot.

"Come on man, it's cold out here." He was holding it between two fingers away from his body like it was a dead rat. Truth is there was no telling what was in the envelope. They did the Renaissance job only two days before and people did see them run away. This envelope was bound to be retribution for what happened to the building. They might even blame the Crew for what happened to Tyrone. Darius would no doubt be enraged at the loss of his younger brother but how far would he go? As a narcotics dealer he was privy to various chemicals and drugs, so what might he come up with to make this envelope so deadly?

"Please Pete, don't make me…"

"Open it!" Peter screamed.

"Ok, ok…alright now." The kid squatted close to the ground pinching one side of the envelope with two fingers. Then, with his eyes clenched tight, he tore off the top. "Nothing happened," He said while watching the open package lay there innocently.

"What's in it?" Peter asked more calm than before.

A single piece of yellow legal paper shone bright under the pall of the streetlight. "It's a letter," Apollo started to read it to himself when Peter opened the door and took it away from him.

"Get back in here."

Safely inside Peter grabbed Paul by the arm as they went into the silence of the kitchen, his eyes never left the paper. Peter's face grew red as he finished reading and surprisingly he handed it to Paul. "It's addressed to you."

"Really?" Paul read it just as fast but he was overtaken by what it said. The top of the letter was addressed to Paul, leader of the Shotgun Crew, but the rest was a bizarre appeal to peace and respect, "Darius knows that we torched the Renaissance…he thinks we're worthy adversaries…he says Rafael deserved to die in the fire…we did him a great service…and he wants a truce. A truce?" Paul watched Peter's face contort.

"Paul," He said holding a strange measure of restraint, "Why does Darius think that you are the leader?"

"I don't know," Paul lifted his shoulders.

"You don't know or you're not telling me?"

"I swear to god, I don't know. He's just mistaken, hell we only know this guy by reputation, it shouldn't be a surprise that he got us confused."

Peter lifted the letter again, "But he wants to meet you at the South Side Drive-In, if I show up instead…"

"What should we do?" Paul could tell by the determined gleam in Peter's eyes that he wanted to go through with this. Peter, secretly, wanted a truce. He wanted to be in the inner circle of the SSP especially after having seen in the last few weeks that hundreds of black Brocktonians are not going to follow a white kid from Avon no matter how many gang leaders he kills or buildings he incinerates. His plan for domination was becoming unrealistic; it had failed the moment he moved to Brockton when only three teens showed up to work for him. This letter was a subliminal ultimatum. Either Peter accepted the offer to join them or two hundred gun toting Posse members would be knocking on the door to eliminate the competition.

"You'll go," Peter said crumpling the paper in his hand. "Explain everything…they can kill us whenever they want to…its already over…we have no choice."

"But we nailed Rafael. They must be afraid of what we'll do next. The job at the Renaissance was brilliant. They respect us."

"Sure if you believe them."

"You don't?"

"It doesn't matter. They know that we did it, they know they outnumber us, out gun us. They know where we live. Darius could come here tonight and burn down this house with us inside it and if we ran out the door we'd be shot down in the street. They're ten steps ahead of us and we haven't got a clue where they are. How do you beat someone you can't find?"

"You just wanna give up?" Paul lowered his voice so the others couldn't hear his hesitation. "Peter, because of us Schmel is dead, Rafael is dead and their headquarters is partially destroyed. Why stop now?"

"Because we can't win this right now. Let's go along with the truce and then, when we're on the inside, we can come up with the next plan."

Paul's shoulder's slumped, "Sure, if they let us live."

Peter stared down at his long time friend with cold eyes. He knew he was handing him over to the enemy but he was not about to risk himself. Just like the three teens in the living room Paul was also a pawn of Peter's ambitions. "If they let you live we'll take the next step."

The words hit Paul like a shoulder block to the chest. He had never wanted to quit the Crew before this moment. He had never before questioned their goals but this time Peter had gone too far. He was willing to let Paul die at the hands of their enemies for the chance, the slimmest opportunity, that they might be let into another gang.

"Pete, this is the last time."

"Meaning what?"

"If this doesn't work, if these fuckers try to take me out…I'm…out of this. I'm serious. I'll fucking quit. Unlike you, I've got a job. I can make it on my own. I don't need this shit."

Peter didn't even blink. His face froze like a statue that would not admit defeat despite years of acid rain pouring down on it. After all the pain and suffering he had endured what did it matter if his best friend walked away? Was it all worth nothing if he had no one to share it with? With no job, incomplete schooling, no saleable skills, one parent in jail and the other in the hospital could he really afford to let go of his one last true friend? Was Peter being neglectful or was Paul trying to find a way out?

Peter decided it was the latter. He nodded his understanding of Paul's declaration, "Fine, just do it. Get it over with."

CHAPTER 68

▼

"Do you want to break it to him?" Psycho asked as John's Cougar pulled onto Lazio's street.

"No, didn't Dutch ask you to? I don't want him casting a spell on me or doing the evil eye. He's creepy. I don't even know why you guys wanted him on the team."

"That would be my fault." Psycho leaned his head against the window. "He hasn't done anything against the team, he's a bad shot but he's been a good soldier. I think we should bring everyone that we have, you know, strength in numbers."

"Even Becca?" John asked looking to his left as the top of her father's apartment building appeared over a fence of bushes.

"Well…" His voice trailed off. Psycho knew he had to have a serious talk with Lazio in relation to how he scared Becca but that would be a blow over and above the fact that they were cutting him out of the planned attack at the drive-in. Psycho had been friends with Lazio for too long, that coupled with his budding feelings for Becca, left him in a sweeping state of doubt and confusion. If only there was a way to get out of this.

John brought his car to a full stop at the intersection and didn't move.

Psycho didn't hear any cars pass as he closed his eyes for a brief moment. "Why did you stop?"

"Take a look." He pointed to Lazio's house. Five vehicles were sprawled haphazardly across the sidewalk blocking the driveway. The police car was the most noteworthy, next to an unmarked police car, a large white van with black writing on its sides and two other professional looking vehicles.

"Oh Shit. Did they find out about us? I bet you D-Rod turned us in."

"What should we do?" John asked as the front door of the house opened.

"Take a left, quick, go!" He slapped the wheel as John spun around the corner. Psycho watched a policeman and two other men guiding Lazio out the front door in handcuffs.

"He's under arrest." Psycho said plainly, not surprised. Maybe D-Rod only turned in Lazio? Perhaps he didn't want to sit in jail by himself?

"Where do we go now?" John stopped at the next stop sign, they were facing Becca's house dead on.

"Fuck it, drive around the corner and park in the grass behind her building."

Moments later they had climbed to the third floor and knocked on her door.

"Oh my god I'm so glad you guys are here!" She nearly knocked Psycho over with a gracious hug and then dragged them both inside.

"What the hell is going on?" John said out the side of his mouth as he neared the window. He watched them put Lazio in the back of the unmarked police car as the men stood on the sidewalk talking in a semi-circle. One of the men pointed towards Becca's house.

"I think they might come here." John mused.

"Why?" Psycho asked looking over his shoulder.

"They pointed this way."

"Yes, they might come back," Becca had Psycho sit at the kitchen counter.

"Come back?"

"Yes, just listen. I learned a little more about Lazio. He's not as innocent as you think. Last night, he broke into the apartment and…"

"What apartment?" His face showed a true and honest confusion.

"This one. Lazio broke in here, he was coming after me."

"For what?"

"Remember I said he attacked me one night, he tried to kiss me and then he tried to force his way into my bedroom? Well, I told him I was going to call the police if he did it again but…"

"You're serious?" John stood in the middle of the kitchen his normally innocent pink face now had a scowl that was wholly out of place. He had somewhat unconsciously become protective of her, just as Psycho did. Being the only girl who had ever become a HAWK, she was likely to end up with nearly everyone's affection but this had only donned on John in the last few moments.

"So *you* called the cops. This has nothing to do with the HAWKS. D-Rod didn't turn us in? They're not after us?" Psycho asked hopefully.

"Yes, I mean no. No one mentioned anything about D-Rod. When the police showed up they knew all about Lazio. They knew where he lived, they listed his past offences, I guess he's done this before."

"Oh my god," Psycho rolled his head backwards, suddenly it all made sense to him. "When we were kids he used to tell me that he used magic to sneak up on people and he told me once about a Russian girl…"

"Sonia," Becca named the girl. "She was his last victim. He had been following her around and watching her through her bedroom window for years. They warned him to stay away. I guess he tried to cast love spells on her and when none of them worked that's when he got really aggressive. He attacked her one afternoon on her way home from school and tried to rape her in the bushes beside her own house."

"Did he ahh…" John was afraid to say the word.

"Go through with it? No, her parents saw him pull her into the woods and they ran out to save her." Shaking off a chill Becca tried not to imagine it happening to her. "The police said they have had many calls but he's usually gone when they show up. Because of his elusiveness they said it's important that I make sure he gets sentenced."

"You're pressing charges?" Psycho wanted to touch her hand, to reassure her that she was safe and he was going to keep it that way but he remembered hearing that sexual harassment victims were often weary of anyone touching them so instead he made a fist.

"I don't have to," Her hand rested easily on his knuckles, she needed a reassuring touch right now but didn't want to say the words aloud. Besides it was Psycho, she could trust him, she always had. "Lazio is crazy, that's what they said in so many words. I guess he takes the pagan stuff too far, they said he once tried to fly."

"Let me guess, off a building?" John asked.

"I don't know but he's going back to wherever they were holding him before."

"That makes my job easier." Psycho breathed out a little guilt. If he had only talked to Lazio earlier, warned him of dire consequences, told him that he was kicked off the team then maybe…

"Sure does," John nodded.

"What was you're job?" Becca asked hoping to be let back into the veil of team secrets.

Psycho and John looked at each other and then back at her. Dutch had given them very explicit instructions and of them silence was one they most needed to maintain. Psycho mumbled, "We can't tell you but it doesn't matter...well, we just can't tell you."

"Will he still go through with it?" She asked about the up coming mission but smartly didn't want to be there. In fact, she wished they would abandon the whole thing.

"Knowing Dutch, we'll do it no matter what."

"What about his plans for the school?"

"We all have to talk to him about that one." Psycho nudged John who vehemently agreed. "It will take a lot of convincing but maybe, if all goes well. It won't get that far."

"Ok," Becca hugged Psycho again and held on tight, this may be the last time she ever sees him. The incident with Lazio was just another in a long line of screw-ups precipitated by Dutch. Her anger against his overreaching ambitions had grown as she sat in isolation thinking about everything that he had planned. In retrospect she was far more upset about the things she had not been privy to. Now her instincts told her that Dutch was going to lead this suicidal mission with a total disregard for his friend's safety. She was absolutely sure that he was going to get them all killed. Once again her lack of faith was showing.

FUNERAL PREPARATIONS

CHAPTER 69

▼

"This won't end the Brockton Street wars but it's our equivalent of D-Day." Dutch relaxed in a wooden chair on the front porch. He and Zombie finished putting a new steering wheel on the van, one that was smaller and able to turn quicker for defensive driving. Zombie rested in the chair next to him watching kids play basketball across the street. The neighborhood was a peaceful distraction for Dutch but Zombie was getting a little bored. He had done most of the work on the truck and was happy to be a part of the effort. Now he was interested in a more active role.

"Who are the players?" Zombie took a swig of his beloved Mountain Dew.

"Rafael died in the fire so it's down to Darius and Peter, well, they invited Paul but who knows who might show up."

"And Tyrone is dead. You're sister said he was a good guy, did you know him?"

"Kind of, when we met I hit him in the face with a brick."

"That's one hell of a first impression."

Dutch chuckled but continued the memory, "And the second time we met he was there to make sure that my best friend beat the shit out of me."

"Oh, so you guys were close."

Dutch smiled hard but it might have been more from his nerves than an impending good mood. He feared becoming too relaxed and blamed the town for his ease. Middleboro was starting to grow on him. It was a disarming place to exist, the mellow trickle of Herring runs, and the thick green trees along nearly every street. Avon had been a small, cramped place to live; Norwood even more so but there was something soothing about the natural elements in Middleboro that made Dutch yawn.

"Tired?"

"No." He shot back.

"So anyway, Lucy said the Waters family went out of their way to keep Tyrone from getting in trouble."

"I guess they failed."

"Yeah, Lucy said he couldn't walk away from it all. She said he moved to Avon and became friends with Peter and that's who dragged him back into the gang thing. Sound right to you?"

"Peter is…who knows what part he played. I can tell you from personal experience that he doesn't give a shit about his friends."

"You guys got a history?"

"A long one but it all ended in Middle school when he attacked me one day after the final bell."

"What did you do?"

"I defended myself. I humiliated him in front of the whole student body."

"No, I mean, why did he attack you?"

Dutch scratched his chin and adjusted the notebook on his lap. "I never really found out." He flicked the pages of his journal and seemed to be reaching into his memory for a better explanation. His feud with Peter never fully made sense to him. It was like the old fable of a kid who gets in a fight and loses so he gets his older brother to come along. The brother fights an uncle who fights a father who calls more friends. The battle of siblings escalates until someone ends up dead. Along the way the original offense is forgotten.

Zombie felt uncomfortable probing any further, "So Darius is the top dog?" He asked as Dutch reached for his Snapple iced tea. He carefully lifted it to his mouth and then awkwardly put it back down as a slight tremble gave away his nerves. His eyes drifted away, he never answered the question, embarrassed at his queasiness.

"So what's in the notebook?"

"Big plans." Dutch opened it and looked down at his work. The pages that started as a diatribe about his tragedies had transformed into juice for the most diabolical theories he had ever conceived. Between mechanical grunt work and exercise he had collected information about Blue Hills. Schematics and fire regulations, wiring and door locks. All the logistical details necessary to light up the sky with a blaze of student body parts. Zombie didn't need to know about this. Some things were better kept secret until the last moment. If the HAWKS were given time to think about it, they might refuse his orders. He didn't want to have a mutiny on his hands.

"This happens tomorrow right?" Zombie probed again not expecting an answer, maybe just a nod. "You're van is ready, I'll swear to that. It's an A-team rigged urban personal carrier and so long as you don't flip it over taking a tight corner at seventy miles an hour, it should be formidable. We already know its bullet proof."

"You think?"

"Well, bullet resistant."

Dutch nodded. He wanted to ask Zombie for a favor but that was something he was not accustomed to. With his current crop of friends he simply gave orders and they listened but Zombie was not a HAWK. He could not be pushed around and Dutch owed him so much already.

"You alright?" Zombie leaned forward in his chair. He didn't wait for an answer using this moment to test the waters of his own possible application for the team. "Dutch, I um, look you and your guys are about to agitate a battlefield, I don't know if that's the right word. Look, I understand why you're doing it so I want you to know that I'm behind you. If you need anything…"

"We lost a member yesterday. Lazio was arrested or locked up. He may be in an asylum. I didn't get all the details."

"Lazio was the witch right?" His curiosity allowed him to keep a running mental list of the team members. "But you didn't trust him."

"I didn't and we weren't going to use him anyway but…we can't be short one man…this mission is too important. I already called in TC, he put his job at risk but we need one more."

"Just ask mon, it's cool." His smile said yes before Dutch could even bring up the courage.

"I need a driver." It was a soft request but it was enough.

"You got it." There was no hesitation in his response.

"There might be repercussions…"

"I know, jail, getting shot at, being run down, I know what could happen. I think that what you are doing is pretty ballsy. Let me tell you, if the HAWKS lived in Diddleboro a couple years back I have no doubt that Juckettville would be a harmless cross roads instead of a drug filled haven for the fuckin Manson Gang. If we had the HAWKS here when it all started, there would be no dangerous neighborhoods in this town."

"I appreciate your confidence."

"That's what's going to win D-Day right? Confidence." Zombie's infectious optimism electrified the conversation and reanimated Dutch.

"You're damn right! That's why we're going to kick some ass!" Now he was ready.

THE BATTLE
OF SOUTH SIDE

CHAPTER 70

$$\blacktriangledown$$

"Geo come here man," Darius pulled the tall kid aside, they walked behind the faded white washed snack bar before Darius ripped into him. "What the fuck man? You can't be second guessing me in front of everyone, that's gonna git you killed!"

"Why you buggin?" Geo had ignored the order to wear gray colored clothes to blend into the rolling concrete hills of the drive-in. Then he was further confused when Darius shifted gunmen off to the far sides of the lot leaving only himself, Darius and Kelvin to stand in the middle. His protest was happening in private behind the snack bar because Darius didn't want anyone else to get any bright ideas. Even here Geo broke rank, "We'll look weak, we need to show our numbers, we need to show our strength. We've got about a hundred guys here today and we're hiding? This is a message of fear..."

"Shut up Geo, I know you're trying to think but it's hurting my fucking ears!" Darius cornered him up against the wall. "I don't need to splain myself to you. I have tactics, that's all you need to know. Now get up on the fucking roof and take your position!"

"Tyrone followed orders and look what happened to him."

"Shut the fuck up about my brother!" Darius grabbed him by the collar of his gold sweat suit and pulled his face real close.

"What up?" Geo was brooding like a child but he folded as Darius got up in his face.

"Don't you ever mention him again! Ever!"

Geo nodded as the grip released. He was pissed at being bossed around but he did as he was told climbing an old freezer unit and disappearing over the lip of the roof.

"They all set up D," Kelvin returned from the front gate. Three members were hidden by the entrance to let Paul through when he arrived. They were actually Geo's men but Kelvin was asked to double-check everything that Geo did. The gatekeepers had orders to chain the barrier behind Paul and make sure no one else disturbs the proceedings.

"Good Kel, and the flanks are ready?"

"Flanks?" Kelvin's head bent back to look for where the other guys went.

"You couldn't see them?" Darius almost laughed.

"No," Kelvin said feeling stupid.

"Good, that's means they're well hidden. C'mon let's get up top."

"I was just wondering, what if he brings more people? What if the Shotgun Crew goes Kamikaze? When they torched home base that was, well, gutsy, real fuckin gutsy."

Darius waved away the story as if it were an irritating fly, "They lit a match and ran, any coward can do that. This time we've got an army to shred those motherfuckers! They're gonna need more than fireworks to make us flinch. They can bring all the people they want. We'll make em pay for what happened to Tyrone." Darius had it all figured out. On this day he amassed the largest gathering of Posse members in the history of the SSP. Just by commanding such a huge force to show up he proved that he is, without a doubt, the leader of Brockton's most lethal gang. Slaughtering Paul or every member of the Shotgun Crew was now a matter of revenge. It would be a cathartic experience that strengthens their collective will and cements the SSP together under one great motivator, one unquestionable leader.

CHAPTER 71

▼

"I'm gonna die, I'm gonna fuckin die. This is so stupid." Paul's mantra of helplessness was like a nervous tick that he could only wish to contain. Peter bought the story of a truce and in an act of either cowardice or effrontery, Paul hadn't yet decided which, a single man would face Darius as was suggested in the letter. "It had to be me?" His hand reached underneath the brown coat lying on the seat next to him, he was hiding a sawed off shotgun. It was his only weapon and he had no back up.

Paul stopped in the parking lot of K-mart, only a hundred or so feet from the gate. The entrance to the drive-in sat behind a plaza building hidden by bushes and old tattered signs. His breathing was short, bursting out in staccato breaks forcing sweat to gleam from his forehead. It was March, still cold though there was no longer snow on the ground, and he was sweating like a guilty man on death row in Texas. In all of his wildest imaginings he could not envision a way to get out of this alive.

He placed the shifter in drive and started across the lot towards the entrance. There were no visible sentries, no guns in the weeds so far as he could see and unfortunately no police in the immediate area. Maybe they had forgotten? Maybe Darius was playing games with him, trying to provoke a little fear? If that was his test balloon, it had worked. Paul was ready to quit the crew, tell Peter to go fuck a pig and exit Brockton for good, maybe live with his uncle Roy in Florida. Yes, Florida sounded good right now. The warm sun, palm trees and beaches would be a welcome reprieve. Most importantly no one in the sunshine state knew anything about him. He could start over. Paul stopped the car fifteen feet from the gate and gave Florida a pause of real consideration.

"I can turn around right now and..."

Three black kids dressed in jeans each with a gold bandana wrapped tight around their right arm ran out of the bushes and manned the entrance gate. Paul knew little of the inter-gang affiliations so the color gold meant nothing to him. He saw only the enemy.

"Fuck..." And now they had seen him. In puppet fashion two of the three had their hands deep in those jean jackets. Either they were fingering weapons or they were faking it with the utmost of arrogance. Forget Florida, now he had to proceed.

Paul pulled his Camaro forward but stopped five feet short of the gate. One kid ran up to his window.

"You Paul? Shotgun Crew?" The name of the team gave Paul a slight sense of belonging but he was forced to remember that his affiliation was also the reason they might want to kill him.

"I'm Paul, I'm here to meet..."

"Open it." The kid didn't wait for any further explanation. They had their orders, let Paul into the gate and lock it behind him. No more, no less and absolutely no deviation. Unlike Darius who acted on a higher plain of reasoning, Geo always told his men what to and not to do, to the letter, so they understood. Luckily he forgot to tell them to disarm Paul or search the car for hidden weapons.

"Thanks," Paul mumbled as he rolled up his window and drove cautiously through the opening. In his rearview mirror the metal bars of the swinging gate clanged behind him. A chain was reinserted via a figure eight coil and secured with a bike lock. It was like watching a prison door shut, his execution was at hand but at least he was armed. Worse case scenario, he would take some of them with him.

CHAPTER 72

▼

"He's in sir, do you want to give the order?" It was officer Pergola's first day on the job. He graduated near the bottom of his class at the academy so a position with Brockton's under paid SWAT team was the best he could manage.

"Make sure all three vehicles are in place and call in our location." Officer Baravella was a barrel chested brute in his mid thirties with a Sicilian complexion though no one dared ask his heritage. He practically founded Brockton SWAT, or BRAT, as it was known downtown. He had kept up with current events surrounding what was rumored to be a gang war based on Spring Street and even though he was well aware of the SSP he assumed their vast numbers to be heavily exaggerated. Maybe it was twenty or thirty kids, a handful with stolen weapons that they barely knew how to use, BRAT could handle that level of aggression with no problem.

"The chief says it's your call." Pergola held his walkie-talkie up in the air waiting for an answer. He was eager to be a part of some real action, to prove that his poor scores at the academy had nothing to do with his courage under fire.

"Bring red team up to the front." Baravella was calm and professional as he gave the order.

Officer Pergola called in the first strike with relish. He stood to the side of the van and watched as four BRAT members rushed out of the parking lot. In seconds they both tackled and disarmed the three teens that were guarding the chained gates. It was over before they even knew what hit them. Geo's crack squad was nullified; face down in the cement wearing handcuffs. One of them carried a switchblade but none had firearms.

"Good, good. Now pull back and let another squad take them away." The BRAT advance was going as expected, with very little resistance.

Pergola nodded and resumed his chatter. Like clockwork two cruisers silently pulled up to the corner of K-mart opened the rear doors so the captured teens could be thrown in and then they drove off just as quickly. There were no flashing lights or sirens. The gang members would be hauled directly to the lock-up while their friends knew nothing of their disappearance.

Pergola watched the cars drive away but something struck him as odd, "Why didn't we wait until we have all of them under arrest? Wouldn't it be better to keep more officers available?"

Baravella was checking his Magnum one last time as he answered the neophyte, "We reduced their numbers, now we don't have to worry about leaving people behind who may escape and shoot us in the back."

"But what if we don't have enough guns?"

Baravella gave him a sobering stare, "These are teenagers, not soldiers. They are drunk on power, short on promise and absent of training. We have enough men."

Pergola accepted his premise, outwardly at least, on the inside he started to worry that maybe, just maybe, BRAT was underestimating these kids. They'd find out soon enough.

CHAPTER 73

▼

"I counted forty-eight guys." Psycho crept up to Damien's camouflaged position at the center of the moss-covered log overlooking the battlefield. They had a perfect view of the drive-in's parking lot and all the street gangsters who were spread across it watching Paul's silver Camaro's long creep towards the snack bar from behind the rolling concrete hills. The HAWKS ground position was distant, elevated and invisible.

"I got forty-nine but that's not counting any that might be on the other side or at the front gate or in K-mart's parking lot." Damian was unafraid of the numbers but seemed a little irritated by the black and green make-up that hid his face. "They're not all armed though."

"Well that's it then," John sat up from out of the newly growing ferns, "There's too many of them, we are outnumbered. We have to get out of here."

"Get down!" Damian grabbed him by the back of his camo jacket and pulled his head back behind the log. "Wise up John, you're not getting us killed today!"

"They can't see you John," TC said calmly, "I can barely see you."

"But we're outnumbered, if they find us…"

"Shush, just shut-up John! Shut-up!" Dutch rolled out of the greenery coming right up in his face. He grabbed his friend's BDU's near the throat and squeezed forcing John to stop talking immediately. The anxiety was getting the best of John but this was a military mission, they had their weapons, they had a get away vehicle and most importantly they had a plan. John's face started turning purple.

Damian got Dutch to release his grip and then tried to reason with their reluctant compatriot, "Listen, we're not here to confront anyone. Think of us as ghosts, we're like poltergeists, we're just going to instigate a tense situation and we're going to do it without ever being seen. That's why we're at a nice safe distance. Right Dutch?"

Dutch turned away and merged back into the ferns.

John adjusted his glasses and peered over the moss. He wasn't about to give up, "If they turn around and shoot I guarantee their bullets can reach this log. When a gun is involved there is no such thing as a safe distance." After all the times he had allowed himself to be talked into these deadly scenarios, he figured he would have learned by now. With Dutch around, nothing is ever safe. Dutch wouldn't do it if it were safe; he thrives on the risk being taken.

"They can shoot but they can't aim, not from this far away." Psycho explained to deaf ears. John was having none of it. He was here to stop them not to help out.

"C'mon Tim, we called the police, we did our part so lets leave before one of us ends up dead." He wiped guck from the corner of his eye smudging his loam green mask. "Besides, we don't know what kind of guns they have."

Damian, holding the binoculars, watched the roof of the snack bar, "I know all about these fools. The guy wearing the gray sweat suit is Darius he has a 44 Magnum, he's only fired it once and the recoil almost broke his wrist. He's afraid to fire it again but he will if he has to. You see the other gang members don't know that he can't shoot and he doesn't want to look stupid."

TC chimed in, "There was a drive-by a few weeks ago in Brockton. The gunman had a Mac-10 machine gun. So we know they have at least one of them, probably more." He squatted at the end of the log where his brown face paint made him blend so naturally with the trees that he was only clearly visible when he spoke. "I heard about the weapon on the police radio."

"Thanks TC, see that's what I'm talking about. They have a machine gun, they can hit us with a machine gun." John said frantically. The only reassurance in his arsenal was that Zombie was fifty feet away up the hill sitting in the van with the door open and the engine running. Zombie scared John when they first met but he also impressed him with his knowledge of Brockton's city streets. It was their new Satanist friend who knew how to reach this dirt road behind the woods of the Drive-in. Dutch had planned on there being woods in the area but it was Zombie who found a hilly overlook thick with early spring brush. Another dose of confidence came to John when he actually rode with Zombie as he drove the new HAWKS vehicle. His driving skills were formidable; he could corner and swerve the thirteen-foot van as if it were a racecar. If anyone could outrun a gang member or a cop car, it was Zombie.

"But they missed." Dutch settled back into the greenery and aimed his pellet rifle at Darius, watching for a hint of movement through his scope.

"Who missed?" John asked.

"The gunman with the Mac-10, they drove up to a guy on the sidewalk, fired a full clip and filled the house behind him with lead as the guy ran away."

"So he was a bad shot."

"No John, the Mac-10 has a short barrel and single hand grip, it's designed to spray a target at close range but only if the user knows what he's doing. Way out here," Dutch adjusted the sight on his rifle to focus on Darius, "Out here John, it wouldn't hit a fucking thing with any level of accuracy. We're too far away and those are untrained teenagers."

The team calmed a little after Dutch's diagnosis of their enemy. TC elected to find a tree so he could get a better downward angle, Psycho moved to the other end of the log stealing the pair of binoculars so he could watch the gate. Damian settled down next to John to keep him calm. They talked in whispers under the cover of the log. The HAWKS collective confidence was returning. The woods embraced them with a fragrant breeze and the knowledge that at the very least they were in their own element. No one could best the HAWKS in the woods; this was where they reigned supreme.

"Now we need the cops to show up before Darius gives the order to blow Paul's car into a chunk of twisted metal." Dutch whispered. "I hope they believed you Damian."

"If not we're gonna run out of pellets trying to fight these guys off." Damian joked patting John on the shoulder.

Psycho removed the binoculars disbelieving but then looked through them again to confirm what he had seen. "General, you don't have to wait any longer. Not only did they bring Brockton PD, they brought a SWAT van," Psycho talked while watching the rush of activity at the front gate, "And here they come, they're driving in right behind Paul!"

CHAPTER 74

▼

"What am I doing?" Paul's jitters reached an apex as he got to within twenty feet of the snack bar. He could see Darius on the roof with two of his lieutenants, a muscular guy to his right and a taller kid decked out in gold. They all had menacing stares but didn't appear to have any weapons though he knew they were armed. Paul watched their faces when he saw the kid in gold flick his eyes to the far left. What was he looking at?

"No fucking way!" Paul followed his flicker to the hat of another person hiding behind one of the humps in the parking lot. Within seconds he saw another person's elbow resting on a hill and finally he saw the barrel of a gun aiming his way. A fourth head appeared, then a fifth, sixth seventh…"Kiss off assholes!" He stepped on the gas and spun the wheel sharply to the right. His tires ripped out with a screech as his Camaro deftly jumped the first hump. It was a trap, exactly what he feared. Paul knew that he was surrounded and there was only seconds before the SSP was going to open fire.

"We've got one on the run, car three stop that Camaro!" Baravella ran the operation from inside the passenger seat of the white BRAT van that led the charge. Two Brockton cruisers followed close behind, the second in line broke off to the right to head off Paul leaving the others racing towards the snack bar.

"There are only three of them up on the roof." Officer Pergola confirmed from the driver's seat. "You were right. This is small time."

"Let's not get ahead of ourselves." Baravella was wondering why the Camaro was racing away. Was the driver really scared of only three people? They were armed for sure but the abrupt turn around seemed out of place. Three young hoods not enough. He had expected a small force of maybe ten or even twenty but three? Something wasn't right here, where were the others?

"It's the cops!" Geo nearly jumped off the roof as the three men in charge raced to get out of view. Once behind the building Darius pulled out his 44 and tried to signal to the men hidden on both sides. He wanted them to open fire, on Paul, on the cops, all out, every gun blazing! Guys from both sides were watching the vehicles advance but those who saw Darius waving his arms around had no idea what he was trying to say. Did he want them to stay hidden, to run or what?

"That's it? Three vehicles, that's all the police brought? Are they crazy, they'll get killed!" John woke up his friends to the potential slaughter before them. His observation was right; if the SSP opened up first those cops would be eaten alive in a full-fledged crossfire. Even if the van were armored the police inside of it would be trapped, unable to get out unless they barged into a field of incoming lead.

Psycho dropped the binoculars and adjusted his rifle but didn't know where he should be aiming. "Who do we shoot?" He waited for directions.

"Dutch? Dutch what do we do?" Damian snapped at the General. This was a crucial decision. They could save the lives of themselves or Paul or the cops or they could fuck it up and get everyone killed. All of the HAWKS looked to Dutch who had not said a word. He was still studying the landscape before them trying to figure out how best they could make a difference.

"Dutch, maybe we should bolt before the bullets start flying." John pleaded with him thinking that the General might be in over his head. He had after all, frozen in the field before. There had been times when Dutch didn't know what to do and hesitated at critical junctures. He usually redeemed himself in these lesser scenarios but this was not a lesser scenario, this was a war zone.

"No. No one leaves." It was his only response.

"But we can get away clean if we go right now." John tried again and Damian did nothing to quiet him. None of them were sure what to do.

"No."

"Dutch." Now Psycho spoke up, "What's the plan?"

The General appeared to have frozen but TC knew otherwise. Quickly climbing down from the tree he snuck up behind his old friend, "James, look at me." Dutch turned his head to face his friend fully. "Look in my eyes. Forget about everything around us and let your instincts guide you. Now tell me, what should we do? Don't even think about it, just spit it out, what should we do?"

Dutch felt the words spill from his mouth but he almost didn't believe what he was saying, of all the possible targets, Darius, Geo, Kelvin, Paul, he selected none of them instead he commanded "Shoot the truck."

"Are you sure?" TC read an underlying certainty.

"Yes, shoot the truck." Dutch took his rifle off his shoulder and exchanged weapons with Psycho.

"Take it."

"Why?"

"Because you're the best shot and I want you to hit the passenger side window." Dutch spoke louder to address them all, "HAWKS, the cops are driving into a trap and we have to warn them. Shoot the truck!"

"You got it," Psycho set the butt to his shoulder, balanced the weapon in his hands lightly, looked through the scope and pulled the trigger. He could hear the compressed air release and blast a single golden pellet out into the open air.

Following his lead all of them aimed at the police van and fired at will.

"I sure hope this works." John whispered as he applied pressure as the last person to fire. To his surprise, the target was easy to hit.

CHAPTER 75

▼

"But I can get a shot off before they even draw." Geo aimed around the corner from behind the snack bar.

"No you idiot, we need to bail!" Kelvin's voice cracked as he stumbled back away from the snack bar. He was getting ready to run terrified because he recognized the Brockton SWAT van. There was no doubt that Baravella, a cop bearing a brutal street reputation, wasn't far behind. "They have body armor and semi-auto rifles, you'll cause a shoot out! We'll lose everything!"

Darius was waving his arms furiously to his men trying to get them to pull back or to fire, still they didn't know which. This was supposed to be a display of power on a battlefield but now he might very well lose his newly assembled force to the accuracy of police trained marksmen.

"Come on!" He yelled but most everyone's eyes were locked on the van that had come to a full stop. They weren't going to bail as Kelvin hoped and yet the men had waited too long to fire, they were losing a tactical advantage.

"Darius? What do we do?" Kelvin panicked.

"Fuck!" He had already lost control of the situation. No one was responding to him.

"I know what to do." Geo left them behind and circled into the open with his rifle drawn.

"Stop here." Baravella had a bad feeling. He momentarily thought he was being paranoid until Officer Pergola offered up a frightening possibility.

"I think we're surrounded."

They both sat waiting in the van. "Did you see more of them?" He asked his second in command.

"Uh, I think so, on both sides. What should we do?"

"Where?" Baravella asked him to point one out but they were still looking in the general direction of the snack bar.

"I don't know, maybe I'm wrong." Pergola swallowed hard, there were only two ways to face this crisis, strike out and risk being gunned down or pull back in the face of an imagined enemy. Baravella had to choose fast.

"Why aren't they shooting?" He thought he had seen at least one gun barrel other than those carried by the teens that were hiding behind the snack bar.

"Let's not encourage them…" Pergola was feeling the fear of being in someone's sights. This new sensation felt like a little angel yelling his year for him to run, to hide, to stay alive. If ever he wanted to prove his courage under fire, he might be about to get his chance. He stuck to his seat, gripped his pistol and waited for Baravella to give the command.

Suddenly a handful of hard thunks ricocheted off the right side of the van freezing everyone within it. The first pellet cracked the window next to Baravella's head.

"They're shooting!" Pergola concluded a little slow.

"With silencers?" Baravella didn't believe it, those weren't gunshots, were they? It didn't matter. "They're attacking, lets go! Deploy!"

"He's not getting out of here clean," Geo was eyeing Paul's car as it bounced over the hills. "I can hit him." Geo had his rifle aimed. He had the Camaro in his sights as the car inadvertently took a left turn.

Paul saw that the police had a car guarding the exit so he turned away from him giving Geo a clean view of the broadside of his car. Geo aimed at the driver with shaky hands.

"Put it down! Get back here!" Darius was still trying to signal his men. "They won't know what to do without orders!" He pleaded with Geo, "Someone might take a shot and start a chain reac…"

A single blast broke the silence. Geo had fired on Paul and done so in full view of the police van.

Paul was turning the steering wheel to come back around when he heard the shot. The bullet hit the cement just behind his front left wheel. It bounced off the concrete and up into the floor of the car. A searing white hot flash of pain forced him to cry out as the bullet passed cleanly through his left ankle and lodged itself into the underside of the dashboard. The electrical system short-circuited forcing him to lose control.

"Fuck, aaahhhh, NO, Fuck!" He swerved the car fish tailing the rear end. Turning back to his right and seeing the gate ahead of him he slammed on the gas with his other foot just as a patrol car came into view. It was driving right at him and there was no time to turn. The two cars slammed together nose to nose with a god awful smash.

Time seemed to stop as everyone on the field of battle turned their heads to see the two vehicles mesh in a gripped collision. The sound shocked them all like a thunderclap on an empty plain.

Paul was knocked unconscious when his head hit the windshield. A sparkle of glass spider webbed its way across his face washing over his vision with white light that was followed slowly by the dripping of liquid red.

The HAWKS watched the surreal accident unfold but a split second after the moment passed Psycho pointed to the doors of the van, as they swung open from behind. Eight men dressed in black Kevlar, carrying impressive machine gun style rifles broke off four to a side. The ones closest to the HAWKS hit the ground and aimed at the hills. The other four disappeared behind the van presumably doing the same thing on the other side. The two officers in the rear car swung open their doors pulling out their side arms at the ready. No one fired right away, they waited to be fired upon but it was going to happen.

"He's getting away." TC focused on Darius who, with Kelvin at his side, was sprinting towards the farthest woods trying to escape the inevitable barrage. Geo, the tall kid in gold was still standing out in the open. He had raised his weapon again, this time directly at the police van.

"Fuck you pigs, Gold team throws down!" They heard him scream.

Geo pulled the trigger for a second time. The synchronicity on the part of the SWAT team was outstanding. They all aligned their guns and shot center mass in uniformity. This set off an avalanche of desperation. Geo, the SWAT team, the Gold team men in the opposite woods, the gangsters behind the hills and the plain clothes officers at the car all opened fire. The air split and whizzed with bullets flying in every conceivable direction, the echoing snap of multiple shots was deafening.

At first the HAWKS were gawking open mouthed like tourists at a Disney ride gone mad, until John awoke them. "Ah guys, maybe," He got to his knees and stared with horror as Geo was cut down by no less than fifteen semi-auto shots that pierced his chest, stomach and arms. He bounced like a puppet on strings as each shot pushed him a little further backwards. A clouded spray of blood filled the air like a vapor as the strings were cut and his body crashed to the ground.

"I'm rethinking that safe distance idea." Damian said as he crawled back a few feet, his eyes still unable to break off from the carnage before them. The white van shook from a thunder of a hundred shots fired from both sides. The SWAT men, conserving their ammo, had to fire selectively at whoever was at least partially visible. Their more patient targeting was paying off in spades. Some of the gangsters, mostly the ones without guns, were running away from the scene. A handful them were running towards the woods.

Dutch could see the SWAT men aiming at the running gangsters in the same line of sight that he was in. One missed shot and, just as he was thinking about it, a bullet hit a tree above them.

"Ok, I think we've done enough. Fall back!" Dutch and Damian grabbed John and hauled him to his feet as the HAWKS blazed a trail through the woods. The faster they ran, the more bullets seemed to pierce the trees around them, the firefight was accelerating. The further away they got, the louder the echoes resonated.

When they reached the van Zombie was sitting in the driver's seat, engine revving, ready to go. "Are they shooting at you guys?" He yelled out the window.

"Not yet." Psycho replied. "But lets not tempt fate any longer than we have to."

They dived inside the open doors and shut them tight as the truck tore away down the dirt road. Dutch was pissed at the one thing he was sure went wrong.

"What's the matter?" Damian asked while wiping the camouflage off his own face.

"I think Darius got away."

"Dude, there is no making you happy. We survived, that should be good enough." Damian lifted his head to the window and looked for the missing gangster. As the HAWKS van turned off the dirt road he could see a black car with tinted windows parked further down the street but no police were coming. He turned back to Dutch, "Maybe it's not too late to go after someone else."

"Like who?"

CHAPTER 76

▼

"That was great, I mean, I never imagined we would be a part of something so…" John was shivering in a state of awe. "I mean, we were actually running through the woods dodging bullets, how cool is that? How many people get to do that?"

Psycho wanted to quiet him down, "Soldiers do it all the time, so get a grip."

The black HAWKS van was bouncing its way through Brockton's streets as the team collected itself. Zombie nodded his head and smiled once in a while during John's raptured ramblings but no one else was talking, at least not very loud.

Back behind the seats another more calculated conversation was taking place, "Where would he be?" Damian asked Dutch as the others stared out the windows half expecting lights and sirens to come railing up behind them.

"At his father's house," Dutch glanced out the window to see where exactly they were, "we could be there in five minutes."

"I say we do it, he's only one man and he doesn't know about the van. We have surprise on our side. It's perfect timing, this is our chance." He pushed his sweaty blonde hair off his forehead. Damian had already wiped the camo make-up clean away, he was afraid it would close his pores and give him pimples if he kept it on for too long.

Dutch considered the idea as Psycho scooted up next to them. "What are we talking about? Our chance to do what?" He was excited by their success even though he wanted to act humble on the outside. On the inside he was up for anything just so long as he didn't have to listen to John marvel over it.

"We want to pull a drive-by on Peter's headquarters." Damian told him with growing certainty.

Psycho was careful to watch Dutch's reaction before he reacted himself. Dutch was cautious, they had escaped one dangerous situation already, they had one big win for tonight so should they be pushing their luck?

"Ok, let's do this." Dutch nodded, "I'll go tell the driver." He climbed to the front and tapped Zombie on the shoulder.

"What's up gangster?"

"We're gonna hit a house, is that cool with you?"

"No problem mon," Zombie's voice fell into a Jamaican accent, he was having as much fun as Psycho, "Just point the way mon."

"That settles it." Dutch leaned back against the couch and started pumping air into his rifle. "We're going for the jackpot, orchestrating the downfall of two gangs in one night."

Psycho reached under the seat to pull out a box of BBs but found something else. It was Dutch's revenge journal with his plans for Blue Hills sketched across several pages. Psycho took a quick glimpse but then shoved it back underneath. He reached again and found the BBs. He didn't want Dutch to suspect anything so a big grin split his green and black complexion. "This is going to be so much fun."

SUBURBAN APOCALYPSE

CHAPTER 77

▼

"C'mon, we're outta here." Kelvin held the door open as Darius jumped into the odorous back seat of the black Cadillac. They had escaped from the far side of the woods nearly a block away from where the shooting continued.

"They got Geo," Kelvin told the driver as he held his nose. Darius grimaced at the scent of gun power and smoke. He knew that kid was going to blow his wad. Geo couldn't keep his cool, he was too quick to judge, too quick to aim.

"He killed himself, and what was up with his boyz?" Darius stared at Kelvin looking for an answer to what was nearly a conspiracy on the battlefield.

He met a dumbfounded look in return, "Whatever he planned; it had nothing to do with me."

"Geo was trying to make his move," Frustrated he snapped out of his reverie to command the matter at hand. This wasn't the only front in the war. "Did you guys get it done?" He asked the second man in the suicide seat.

"Clean," was the response.

"And our man on the inside?"

"Kept his word."

Darius didn't like to take anyone's word especially after what Geo had just pulled, but he had to believe that loyalty would prove true for the rest of his men. Maybe they'd learn their lesson after seeing that the only person who had miffed his responsibilities and succumb to the passion of ambition was riddled with bullets and bleeding his last flowing drops into the dead earth of a long abandon drive-in.

"Such a fucking…" Darius spit under his breath.

"It wasn't your fault G, he wanted the juice. He just didn't want to earn it." Kelvin was trying to be helpful.

"I know but with the Shotgun Crew cut down there ain't no one else to blame."

"What, we need an enemy?"

"To keep us tight, to hold the posse firm, yeah we need an enemy."

"No problem boss," The driver responded to the backseat conversation. "We saw a black van come tearing out of the woods just after the shooting started."

"Someone else was there?" Kelvin couldn't imagine why.

"Did you get a good look?" Darius prodded.

"No, but judging by the way it took the corner I'd say it was heavy."

"Full of people?" Kelvin asked again falling behind the train of thought. "But not cops?"

"No," Darius knew what was up. It made sense that the police would be there. It made sense that Paul was surprised to see them. It made perfect sense if, "It was another gang. Did you see any of them?"

"Yeah, one. Blonde hair, stuck his head up to a window for just a second."

Darius bit his lip, "Blonde hair. There was only one mother fucker who knew about this that didn't show up like he was supposed to."

"Damian?" Kelvin asked.

"Damian, he fuckin turned on us. I bet he's hanging with his old crew, those crackers from Avon." He did little to hide the malicious delight behind his usual scowl. They did have another enemy; the posse had a reason to stay tight. "Boyz we got turned in by the HAWKS Foundation. Looks like the war ain't over just yet."

CHAPTER 78

▼

"Take a right up here, ready guys?" Dutch manned the side of the van as Zombie took a sharp turn into the cul-de-sac. Tearing around again, this time to the left in a wide arc he slammed on the brakes right in front of a small metal gate. Dutch pulled the door open, five guns lined up to fire at Aubrey's house but no one pulled the trigger.

"Looks like someone beat us to it." Damian noted as he lowered the barrel in shock of what he was seeing.

"My god, what kind of firepower does it take to do that?" John slumped onto his butt staring confounded at the mess before them.

Aubrey Truelson's tattered house spilled a lazy gray smoke upwards through over three hundred holes that crucified the second floor face. There was not a window left to speak of. It reminded Dutch of the pictures he'd seen of Britain in the 1940's after the German's carpet-bombed the cities. He could hardly tell where the house ended and the rubble began.

A small dwindling fire surrounded by broken glass held its own on the right side of what had been the front porch, a likely victim of a Molotov cocktail. This half of the house was now an ashen pile of cracked boards and glowing embers. It lit a rubble-strewn walkway that once led to a solid front door, now torn from its hinges. The house was crumbling as they watched. The crackle of a fire deep inside of its jagged guts was fueling its ultimate demise.

John couldn't speak. The awesome carnage gave him a momentary flashback of the wolf house they had found in Avon only six months ago. It seemed to be forever their destiny to stumble upon places of destruction. He only stared as the other members dissected the scene with questions of plausibility.

"Do you think Peter was in there?" TC asked sounding concerned.

"If he was..." Psycho watched the steady flow of smoke pouring out from a doorway deep within the structure. "He's got to be dead. I mean, do you remember that part in the movie Predator when they filled the jungle with so many bullets that even the trees fell?"

Dutch numbly nodded his head. He loved that part of the film but he never thought he'd see it happen in a city. "Someone blew away this house. They just...obliterated it with firepower." Now he understood why they set up the meeting at the drive-in, "They were trying to kill both of them at the same time."

"Both of who?" John was regaining his senses.

"Peter and Paul," Damian concluded. "I get it. They set up the meeting across town to kill Paul but that left Peter at the house all alone. It's divide and conquer. Peter was probably waiting for Paul to return when the Posse drove up and blew the place to hell."

"Should we go look for him? For Peter? I mean, just in case?" TC's concern for human life was overriding his hatred. This act of vengeance was too much for any enemy. This was overkill. This was unfair. Peter didn't stand a chance. No one would have.

Damian reluctantly put his hand on TC's shoulder, "We need to get out of here."

"But if he's..."

"No, Damian's right," Psycho reached for the door handle. "The porch is still smoking. This must have just happened so the police should be here any minute. We can't save anyone."

"Wait I think I saw..." John caught a glimpse of movement through the doorway but the black tinted window shut in front of him.

"John saw something." TC chimed up louder so they would listen. "Someone might have survived."

"No," Damian tired to quell the rescue mission before it could start but he wouldn't need to.

"Guys," Zombie tapped on the butt of Dutch's rifle, "We got yowlers on the way."

"Yowlers?" John asked.

"Cops, sirens." Dutch explained as he slid into the passenger seat. "Let's go Zombie, get us out of here as fast as possible. If Peter is in that mess then they'll have to help him."

TC sighed deeply and watched the house with regret as the van took off. For some reason he didn't even flinch when Geo was shot to death right in front of him but the thought that those same gangsters got their hands on Peter was bothersome. If TC or Dutch killed Peter it would be justified, understandable, easy to accept but not even their archenemy should suffer at the hands of these gangsters. They had no right. Not even Peter deserved to die like this.

CHAPTER 79

▼

Peter had seen duel beams flash across the ceiling, a dull illumination that briefly sliced the blackened smoke. His head was swirling with distortion, a fit of coughing contorted his muscles but it was nothing compared to the searing whip of skin across his back where the bullet had grazed or pierced, he couldn't tell which. Lying on his stomach by the kitchen stove he crawled towards the doorway in time to see movement outside. Dark painted faces, soldiers with guns stared at the house while he tried to clear his blurry vision. Smoke stung his eyes, splinters from the torn up floor poked into his hands as he pushed himself a little closer. The faces were real, in fact, one of them looked very familiar.

"Dammmiiiaaannn…." His breathing was weak. He'd been inhaling smoke for god only knows how long. The loss of blood from his open wounds caused further dizziness. Popping sparkles of light reminded his brain that he was not fully conscious. A trickle of liquid salt dripped down his mouth and he spit it away. With one eye swollen closed he forced his mind to concentrate on the busted open doorway. They were still there; the soldiers were watching him crawl towards them. No, they weren't soldiers. He saw Damian. He saw the blonde hair, the bright eyes and so those were, "The HAWKS."

The faces were real, he couldn't see any expressions through the make-up but they were the HAWKS, of that he was sure. Peter blinked the tears away and coughed up a layer of black phlegm from his fading lungs, in those convulsive seconds he heard a loud squeal and lifted his head. The faces were gone. He was alone again. They had shot his father's house to ribbons and left him for dead. That's all he could imagine. Dutch finally had his day. Peter had been bested by the HAWKS.

He shook his head but it only stirred about a mulling headache. He was able to roll up to a sitting position, his back against the wall. The pain of the gunshot wound froze him in place. He couldn't move, he could only think. What had *really* happened? How did he end up on the floor? How did they get inside the house to attack him? He remembered sending Paul off to meet Darius and the long wait for his return but his best friend never came back. He remembered hiding his most recent stash of marijuana under the sink where…

"My weed?" With a sudden burst of strength he crawled on his hands and knees to the sink, opened the doors and pulled out a cinder block. Inside both of the holes were paper bags from a grocery store but where…

"They stole it!" He managed to scream out his rage but even that small effort magnified another pain, this one coming from the back of his head. His hand gently patted the back of his skull and under the red locks he found a lump the size of half an egg and holes that bled furiously down his neck. That's right, he had been hit in the back of the head, now he remembered. Again he sat down this time watching flashing lights reflect off the one remaining unbroken lamp swaying from the ceiling.

"The cops." Maybe his eyes were playing tricks again but the flashes flickered colors and varied like those of a police car or hopefully, an ambulance.

Rubbing the bump he traced a small line with his fingers, a point of contact. He remembered being hit but who did it? Left alone with the three members who had crossed over from the SSP he was anxious for Paul to settle the meeting quickly. Peter no longer trusted these punks feeling that they would be more likely to side with the winner of a gang war rather than have any loyalty to the Shotgun Crew. Perhaps he was right. The HAWKS may have turned his headquarters into Swiss cheese but he wasn't so sure that they had anything to do with his missing weed. After all, where were his men? Where were Apollo and the others? Did they flee?

Before he blacked out Apollo had watched him tuck away his stash. It must have been him. That ungrateful brat must have hit Peter on the back of the head with something heavy and judging by the deep holes in his neck, it was also very sharp.

"The baseball bat," Another flash came back to him. Peter remembered hitting the floor out cold but on contact with the linoleum he awoke just long enough to feel the gunshot slice open his skin. Apollo grabbed the weed and ran out the back door as a rhythmic thud of gunfire blasted every inch of the house.

"Fuckin HAWKS!" He swore of his enemies, "Fuckin traitors!" He swore of his own men.

After the punk kid ran and bullets started flying he had faintly heard the breaking of glass as Molotov cocktails smashed against the front porch and through the remains of shattered windows. A heavy boot had kicked in the front door and another bottle smashed upstairs. The gunfire lasted forever, his body jerked just recalling the thuds, it lasted so long that he wasn't sure when the pain took him away from this world and into the darkness. Now that he was faintly awake, and knew how many had betrayed and beaten him, he wished for the comfort of the darkness to return.

"We have a live one." The firefighter called in a paramedic who was not far behind.

"Can we treat him here?" The paramedic asked unsure of how bad the fire might be.

"No we have a cellar ignition as well, he's got to go." The fireman helped lift Peter off the floor careful to keep his neck propped up and they raced him out the front entrance. A waft of warm air and thickening smoke followed them out into the yard.

A large heavy chair in the dining room suddenly fell through the floor allowing flames from the cellar to pour upward into the living room.

"We have an escalation. Get everyone out, right now!" The lead fireman commanded an evacuation of all emergency responders as the hoses started to blast high-pressure water through the open windows.

Peter caught one last look at his father's house as they put him on the gurney. It had been decimated. A person could play connect the dots across its second floor while waiting for the porch roof to collapse. The house was groaning from the fire that tortured it. He knew that he'd never walk inside his home again. So be it, his father had made it a den of sin, a nest from which all his young nightmares came to life. It was a place where Aubrey had committed the ultimate crime when he kidnapped and raped that little girl. "Kaitlin," Peter tried to smile as the flames spread through the first floor frame. If there was one proud moment in his entire life, it the moment he called the police and turned his father in. It was the moment he saved that little girl. "Let it burn," he whispered but no one heard him.

Peter was wheeled into the confined space of the ambulance and as the doors folded in so did his last shred of misdirected ambition. It had all been a mistake. Paul was probably dead, his Mom was still in the hospital, his father was deservingly in jail and now the family home was burning down. As his eyes glossed over into an unforgiving gray he only hoped he'd never have to open them again.

CHAPTER 80

▼

"We've got a block on them but our lead won't last." Psycho propped himself against the steel reinforced back doors watching the flashing lights of the police car who saw them leave Aubrey's house. Zombie managed to stay ahead of the cop by shutting off his lights and turning sharply through the east side grid as the HAWKS clung to the interior of the speeding van.

"You've been this way before?" John yelled up to him afraid that they might get lost or become trapped on a dead end road. His previous enthusiasm was fading. It was fun to imagine that they might be pursued by the cops in a dramatic chase but he never believed they would have to do it. Today's third dose of reality was more than he could handle, luckily Zombie was supremely confident.

"I can drive Brockton in my sleep." He had ceased to smile because of his intense concentration. It was no easy task to out pace a turbo charged cruiser. It was to his benefit that this part of town was so old and complicated. No driver would ever dare speed up so fast as to let the turbo kick in lest he miss a side street that a slower car could more easily swerve down. Unfortunately the police are required to memorize every road in the city as a part of the qualification test. This rote memorization gave them an advantage over most criminals but Zombie was not just any criminal.

Fully aware that he wasn't going to outrun the supercharged cruisers the only way he could escape was to stay out of a direct line of sight. He had to keep them guessing as to what direction he was going.

He leaned to the right as they bore up a steep hill and then darted left cutting off an old lady in a station wagon. She slammed on her brakes forcing the cop to slow down and drive around her. It was a classic move and earned him about ten seconds but little more.

"That was close." Damian's grip on a door panel was almost enough to cut off the circulation in his fingers. Unlike the other HAWKS who had no prior offenses, it was Damian who had the most to lose. His eyes stayed locked on the flashing lights that gave away the position of the police car each time they swung a corner or bounced out of a pothole.

The opposite side of that same hill sent them soaring down through the old Lithuanian village, a crossroad full of bars and burnt out factories. Zombie took a wide sweep down to the right and then another sharp turn. Dutch knew this part of Brockton as his Mom had taken him here as a child. There was a natural spring coming out of one of the rocks where they would fill up water bottles. Right now they were taking so many small corners that even he had no idea where they were. So long as Zombie had his mental map straight and could navigate at these speeds then they might actually pull this off.

"Ok, where do we go now?" Dutch asked just to make sure. "I don't see their lights."

The unlit black van sprinted like a fleeting shadow under the half-broken streets lights as it stressed every sharp brick court and lane. The driver was in a zone where all he saw through the periphery of his vision were mirror images off factory windows and the tightest inches of stone curbs that continued to miss the tires on either side.

Zombie looked for a street sign but kept his goal in mind and called back to Psycho. "Are they still following us?"

"They went straight I think." The tall, brooding industrial complexes reflected no colors, their parking areas crumpled and deserted; their floodlights dim and buzzing. "I'd say you did it, they missed a corner somewhere." Psycho was rightly impressed. In fact they all were. Zombie had committed himself to a chase, however brief, that was worthy of a clip in an action movie and everyone was thrilled to have been a part of it.

"Good, I mean wow!" Dutch returned to his question, "So where are we?"

"I don't know." Zombie took another turn and then another. "Give me a minute, I'll figure this out." He passed a row of neatly trimmed bushes hiding houses behind their leafy walls. On the right was a caged lot full of foreign cars. A light went off in Zombie's eyes. "Now I know where we are." He navigated by way of junkyard.

"Thank God," John had been sweating buckets and as he exhaled the others could smell his relief.

"John!" Damian coughed while holding his nose.

"Sorry." John mumbled as he blushed and hid his face.

"But where should we be going?" Zombie asked as he unbuckled his seat belt feeling that the danger had passed.

"Drop me off at home." John said passively but he didn't mean it, his car was at TC's house. He'd just have to wait.

"Back to Avon. We'll pass through Holbrook so we can stay out of sight and come into town on the back side by Southeastern construction."

"And then to Middleboro?" Zombie missed Lucy and wanted to brag to her about his great escape but Dutch settled them all back down to earth.

"No, we should all crash at TC's. We need to hide the van until daylight in case they are looking for us. Last year TC built a wall of branches that block his backyard, the van should fit in there?" He looked to his tall friend who had been calm and patient throughout the whole chase.

TC's mind was still dwelling on the catastrophe that had been Peter's house when he heard the question. "Yep, that's why I made it, to hide a car or van whatever."

In the back of the van Psycho nudged Damian and whispered underneath Dutch's hearing, "I found the journal, we'll talk at TC's."

Damian gave him a quizzical squint, "Journal?"

"I'll tell you later. It's important."

PARANOID
IMPERATIVE

CHAPTER 81

▼

"I can't believe he fell asleep. Too bad Becca couldn't see this, maybe she'd stop worrying about him." Psycho had an ungrateful pause in his statement. Damian caught it to take another meaning. Being wise in the ways of love and relationships, he heard just a hint of jealousy.

"Are you...?" Damian watched Dutch roll over and curl up in a ball under the blanket on TC's spare bed. After making sure that Dutch was definitely out for the night he finished his inquiry, "Psycho, are you seeing Becca?"

"Umm." His inability to immediately answer the question was a blatant giveaway.

TC sitting at the end of the other bed was playing Legend of Zelda and pretending that he was not listening. Damian knew otherwise.

"TC you're not going to tell him are you?"

"Hey keep me out of this." His eyes never left the screen. Link was his only consort.

Zombie shuffled next to the bed with a curious look, "What's going on?" He asked indifferent to the secrecy.

Damian and Psycho checked with each other but they owed their freedom to Zombie after he outran the police so he had to be deemed trustworthy. Besides, when it came to intra-team squabbles he didn't seem to care either way.

Psycho pulled the journal out of his coat. "I don't know if Dutch told you guys the whole story but he had made some big enemies at Blue Hills."

"He mentioned that. Said he got thrown out cause of a fight." Zombie shifted his seat to be a more active part of the conversation.

"I'm guessing he's ready to get back at them?" Damian asked as a man who had seen the faces of killers up close and recently saw that same cold desire in Dutch.

Psycho opened the journal and started studying the plans. "Yes he's ready," He continued, "Apparently everything we've been doing has been a build up, training for his big plan. He's trying to get us organized for one major assault on the high school. I'm talking about dead bodies. He's been working to figure out a way to murder the five offenders plus a dozen other students and that doesn't include any who might get in the way. All of his ideas are right here."

"Ok, I'm in." Zombie nodded waiting for the others to agree but they did not.

"No," Psycho jumped, "You don't get it. Dutch wants to sneak into our school and kill everyone, students, teachers, the guidance counselor...well, the guidance counselor is a dick..."

"Don't joke." Damian scolded him picking up the notebook so he could see a page more closely. Sketched across it in varying shades of ink was an electrical diagram with three colored wires, red, black and green. "Can you explain this part?"

"Well," Psycho took a deeper look, "Dutch had a year and a half in electrical shop so...he clearly intends to rewire something."

"No," Damian turned the page where a sketch of the school was laid out very neatly. It showed where the wire box was located and what it was supposed to do.

"He's trying to set the school on fire." John said suddenly peering down on them. He was not surprised at all. "Look at it, he wants to sabotage the circuit breaker so that it sets off a fire and these..." He pointed to ten rectangular boxes each marked with a red letter X. "These are where the shop kids practice, those wooden booths would go up like tinder especially if he sets those in place." He pointed to three cylindrical shapes that sat immediately above the boxes. "The flames would reach these gas cans hidden on top and BOOM! No one in that shop would be able to escape. The whole wing would catch fire before anyone knew what had happened."

Zombie's face showed no change in emotion. If Dutch wanted to firebomb the school he would be fine with that, especially if they deserved it. So what was the problem? "But you guy's don't want to do it?"

"No we don't, of course we don't," John sat on the end of TC's bed. Earlier he had snuck downstairs to wash his face off and change from military fatigues back into his civilian clothes and now he was putting on his shoes. "Tim, Becca and I are going to graduate from Blue Hills and I'd greatly appreciate it if it happens without any missing students."

"But," Zombie started but John was not listening to any more craziness.

"But nothing," The red in his eyes was not worth arguing against. "I have been going along with the HAWKS despite a mountain of moral misgivings and fears that they were always a step away from getting caught or killed but I stayed anyway. I stayed because they needed a buffer, a yellow light to slow them down, to keep them realistic." He was sure that one of the HAWKS would already have died by now if he had not been there to keep them from taking that one final step over a line from which they could never cross back. John trumped them all with his indignation, "Forget it, this is where we have to stand up to Dutch. I don't care what they did to him, if he gets into that school people who have nothing to do with his grudge will get hurt. Besides, this is not what we're about, it never has been. The HAWKS are about fighting injustice, not getting revenge. This is homicide and I'm not going to help him kill anyone."

No one spoke for thirty seconds. John had done his job, his words had stung them all and now it was time to go home. He had said his piece without waking Dutch and he wanted nothing more than to sleep in his own bed grateful for the fact that he survived the mission. "Don't argue with me on this, none of you. It's wrong and you all know it. We can't do it and we won't do it. And now, I'm leaving and don't try to stop me."

Damian and Psycho were amused by his insistence considering no one was telling him not to go.

"Have a good night buddy," TC said between clicks and blinks. He agreed with most of the rant but didn't like to pick sides, at least not publicly.

"Don't fall down the tree on your way out." Damian moved so John could step over the tangle of power cords on the floor and walk past Dutch's peaceful form to reach the window. "Oh John, one more thing."

"What?"

"Put the rifles back in your trunk."

"Why?" He asked even though he had planned to do it all along.

"We don't know what else he has planned." Psycho answered.

"Anyway," Damian waited for John to exit. "John's right, we do need to stop him." He watched Psycho agree without a shred of doubt. "It is your school, are you sure you don't have a grudge of any kind?"

"Are you kidding me? I played football with Joe, I met Rodger when I was a freshman we sat at the same lunch table for three years. Are these guys' assholes? Yes. Are they a bunch of druggies? Yes. Do they deserve to die in a massive explosion? Well, maybe but I'm not going to do it. I may not be the biggest fan of Blue

Hills but it's still my school. Like John said I still want to graduate so I'm not going to blow it up no matter how mad the General gets."

"Glad to hear you say that because he is going to get mad." Damian, ever the believer in loyalty, was cautiously elated. They had been letting Dutch play his own cards for a long time and there was always a fear that he would go too far. In part John wasn't the only one looking out for their best interests. Psycho and Damian never fully took Dutch's charge seriously so they too had stuck around to stop him when that day arrived.

"Are you with us on this Zombie?" Damian waited patiently for a reply but Zombie wasn't happy about letting anyone off the hook who deserved a beating or a good bombing. Unlike the core HAWKS, Zombie didn't have a sappy moral compass to hold him back but this was their team, their goals, their dreams however strange and he really had no say in it.

"I won't say anything." His eyes fell back upon the screen where TC had fallen into deep concentration.

"Do you want to break it to him?" Damian asked Psycho assuming that his practiced speech might be more convincing than Damian's somewhat dispassionate perspective. It wasn't his school he didn't have anything to lose so it had to come from someone who went there.

"No, Becca wants to do it."

"Why?"

"She says that she has evidence that will convince Dutch that those electrical shop guys are not worth killing."

"And you believe her?" Damian watched as Psycho's face filled with a rosy blush.

"Umm....yes."

"Ok, but for now we need to get rid of this." Damian picked up the notebook, opened to an offending page and began to rip.

CHAPTER 82

▼

Dutch awoke at ten in the morning feeling well rested. His eyes, known for being notoriously bloodshot, were clear, relaxed. The previous night's excitement left him with a mild buzz of positive energy and new sense that he had never felt before. The other HAWKS, except for Damian, were still sleeping, having stayed up most of the night talking about their grand adventure and what was to come next. Despite numerous attempts to change their minds, TC and Zombie refused to stand against Dutch but instead promised to stay out of it.

The drive intended to drop off Psycho was sidetracked by two very strange requests. First was that Damian, despite having not slept at all, wanted to go for the ride. He lived right there in Avon only a few blocks away but insisted on traveling to Dedham. Second, Psycho wanted to all of them to visit Becca in Norwood to tell her what had happened. Dutch got the faintest whiff of paranoia as Becca was waiting for them. Everyone kept an unusual silence when they reached the living room. No one wanted to speak first. Dutch could smell deceit in the air. He nearly exploded.

"What the hell is this all about?" While his words often had a ring of real hidden rage beneath them, he was having too good a day to hate anyone. He stood defiant in her living room even after having been asked by them all to sit. "NO, I want to know what this is all about. Right now!"

Becca, Damian and Psycho exchanged slight nods of agreement while Zombie stayed in the background perturbed at all the secrecy. She took Dutch by the hand, led him into her bedroom and locked the door.

"What's going on?" He continued to ask until Becca stopped him. She stood before him all alone having planned and practiced this conversation a hundred times. Before he could protest further she gripped the bottom of her sweater with both hands, pulled it up over her head and dropped it on the floor. Underneath was a black bra that drew his attention to her breasts but that was not what she was wanted to show him.

"What are you doing?" He moved to cover her with the closest fabric when her disrobing threw him off guard but before he could cover her, she held her arms up. His eyes left her breasts and traveled down to her wrists.

"It looks worse than it is." She said without caring about his response. Becca's slight forearms were covered with scars. She had tried to commit suicide at some time in the past but that was only the start. As he studied them more closely the lines of deeply colored tissue that stood out in jagged form went further up her arms. The light purple and pink had a logic to their connections, they were not merely scars but rather words or more specifically...

"Those are names." He had to twist his head almost upside down to read the older ones.

"Been wearing sweaters for the past four years.... I don't even think I own a T-shirt." Becca made fun of her self-mutilation and waited for the pertinent question to arise.

"Why did you do that?" He asked with remorse, inadvertently showing his concern for her well being. Had the men in white coats locked up the wrong HAWK? No sane person does this to themselves.

Becca rolled both arms over half a turn, palms facing up and pointed out two names in particular. "I used to party a lot. I used to get drunk and high with some boys back in freshman year." Her regret was palpable, enough to choke her up but not too much that she couldn't continue the story, this was too important not to be said. "When I slept with a guy I usually convinced myself that I was in love with him. Each time I found a new person, I thought that he was my prince charming, my one and only so I had to give myself completely. Each time I would devote myself prematurely and as a sign of my dedication I would...well...carve his name into my body. I wanted to prove to them and to myself that they would always be a part of my life, even if they left me."

"Why did you show me this?" He suddenly stiffened. "This doesn't change anything. I can't have you as a distraction on the team. Tim was right I can't..."

Her eyes closed as she asked, "Did you read the names?"

He stopped and studied her arms again, this time with careful attention to detail. They were all very common names for guys of their Generation but two in particular stood out. He couldn't believe that they were the same ones, but if they were...Dutch was afraid to ask.

She pointed to the two he was eyeing. "Here is Joe and here is Matt."

"From school?"

"Yes."

"You slept with them?" He was dazed but not angry nor was he completely surprised. His mind failed to grip a single emotion as a multitude of them performed dizzying loops from his heart to his head and back again.

"It was way before I knew you…I was stupid, I obsessed over everything…"

"But the HAWKS are anti-drug?" He mentioned a little confused by where she was going. How did it all connect? More importantly, how could she sleep with them? She hadn't even slept with him. The bad guys get laid and the good guy gets stiffed! How much more unjust could the fucking world be?

"I know the HAWKS are anti-drug. I know and that's why I wanted to join the team. I wanted to get away from that life, I wanted to better myself, I wanted…" Her eyes drifted up to Dutch's but he reflexively looked away.

Instead he faced the window that looked out at the backyard below. Why was she doing this? What was all of this supposed to accomplish? What was she appealing to? She could have shown him these at any time? Then it hit him. This was orchestrated by all three of them. This was an intervention of some type.

"I don't fucking believe it!" Dutch unlocked the door and swung it open, he stormed out into the living to face his so-called friends.

Becca chased him, still only partly clothed. "Dutch I don't love them anymore. They mean nothing to me, it was a phase of depression, I was suicidal like you were."

He stared down at the coffee table in disgust. His journal lay on it against the edge. They had stolen it. "You guys don't want me to get justice. That's what this is all about." He pointed at Becca and her scars. "I'm supposed to feel sorry for her or something?"

Damian, who was the least affected by seeing Becca partly nude, took offense, "It's not justice Dutch. Ok, they wronged you I get that. You took a beating, it sucks but shit happens. I've been wronged a hundred fucking times by my father but I'm not going to kill him."

"This isn't the same!"

"Bullshit it isn't!" Damian picked up the journal and shook it. "You lost a fight, someone got the better of you. Face it you're not Snake eyes, you're not Daredevil and we're not the A-team. We're fucking teenagers. In the real world people sometimes fall below their own expectations. Sometimes you lose! I had to learn that the hard way, why can't you? I understand that this reality hurts but denying it is not going to make the pain go away."

"Well then what is?"

"I don't know, use your pain for something else. Use it for stealth justice like we did last night. That wasn't about revenge; that was about bringing down the bad guys. We may have saved the lives of those cops and the SSP took a major blow and Peter might very well be dead. Face it Dutch you don't have many enemies left."

"I most certainly do."

Psycho had been silent through the conversation so Dutch turned to him for back up. Was his right hand man still on his side? Had the whole team turned against him? Was Damian making his move to take over the HAWKS? Then again, maybe it was only his tactics they were rebelling against? Maybe he could negotiate a new plan?

"What if we don't blow up the shop?" Dutch was swallowing his pride. He was trying to find an act they could agree on. Maybe if he bargained them down to a position where less people were killed then maybe…

Psycho only shook his head. "No. We have to leave the school alone." It was official; he had no allies left.

"James, lets talk in my bedroom. Please?" Becca took his hand and walked him out of sight closing the door behind her. He was so shocked that he merely followed without a sound. His head spun in confusion, doubt, and uncertainty.

"He's pissed at us." Damian sat back on the couch and dropped the journal in a small trashcan.

"She's not done yet, give her a chance." Psycho crossed his fingers. He didn't want the team to break up over this but Dutch had an explosive temper and so far it wasn't going very well.

Becca cornered Dutch against the closed door. Part of him wanted to move away but a more receptive part kept him in place. She stood only inches from his chest; he could feel her breath when she spoke.

"James, you accepted me for who I am. I know it sounds silly, you've had real friends all your life and they will do anything for you so…I guess what I'm saying is, I was never able to get anyone to like me unless I was tipsy or easy. When I met Matt & Joe I was young and stupid and naïve. No one ever gave me a chance to be something other than a one-night stand, a free ride, no one but you. You treated me with respect, as an equal."

Dutch leaned against the door behind him and made a real effort to look into her eyes as she confided in him.

"Psycho told me how dangerous the initiation really was but you let me do it anyway. Thank you."

He thought she would be mad about that but...

"I owe you so much and even if we don't have a relationship, I still want you to know what you mean to me."

He wanted to speak, to say something bold or macho or sensitive but words failed him.

"James, listen...Joe and Matt are bad seeds. They have been jaded by life just like you. Joe's father owns a huge construction company; he's cheating on his mother and the only thing he ever talks to his son about is football. The game is the only way he knows to keep his father's attention. He'll do anything to be a great player that's where the steroids come in."

Dutch blinked twice noting that he understood and oddly enough he did feel a little bit of sympathy but not enough to quell his desire for revenge. Who knew Joe had a weakness, he always acted so strong.

"Besides he's got nothing over you. Joe, for all his juiced up muscles and ego, has the smallest penis I've ever seen. Bet that makes you feel a little better?"

Dutch snickered in spite of himself. It took such a stupid thing to boost his confidence but it seemed to work, a little.

"No really, he's going to have to live with that tiny thing the rest of his life. It's no wonder he has to act like a bully."

Dutch let out a giggle but cleared his throat and tried to return to his emotionless stance. "I suppose..." He knew where she was going with this, "I suppose Matt's Dad was a hockey fan?"

"No, the opposite actually. Matt loved hockey and was a rabid fan but his Dad hated it. At one of Matt's games his Dad got in a fight with another parent and...um...he suffered a couple really bad blows to the head and..."

"Is he dead?"

Becca's eyes returned to Dutch's. She didn't want to be overwhelmed with emotion at this moment. If her tears got out of control she may lose track of her task, which was to change Dutch's mind not to empathize with old boyfriends.

Dutch reasoned it out loud, "So he's afraid of losing a fight and ending up like his Dad."

"He's terrified of the same fate." She added.

"I can see why."

"Just consider this, maybe they are not quite as bad as you envision them. Maybe they are acting out of weakness instead of strength. Besides you did get kicked out of school and so it's likely that you'll never see them again...for the rest of your life. It's over...they are long gone...you'll never have to deal with them."

He was taking that into consideration and it all made sense but there was one aspect of this night that he just couldn't fathom, the mutiny of his friends. They had all taken an oath, they had all committed to the Malevolent Philosophy so even if they didn't agree with his orders, they could not pull this kind of shit! They had used Becca to secretly plan this meeting. They had tore up the loyalty that underlies a disciplined fighting team. They stole his journal! Even if he was wrong, they had no right to disobey him. That's what being the General is all about.

"How long have you guys been planning this?"

"No, no, there is no plan, I swear. They must have been talking to each other about this, not to me and then Psycho and I were talking…"

"You guys talk a lot. Is he telling you team secrets?"

"No, I promise." But the promise sounded insincere and struck off yet another epiphany. "He's a sweet guy and we're good friends but…"

"A sweet guy? Are you in love with Psycho?"

"I, no, not exactly…I mean we…"

"We?" He could see the guilt written all over her face. That was the last straw. Dutch spun around and opened the door. "Damian, I'm leaving and I'm taking the guns with me!"

"You can't, I told John to take them."

"You what? Well then, give me my journal!"

"Sure, here." He plucked it out of the trash and flung it to Dutch who immediately felt its extra light weight.

"What did you do?" he opened it up to see that all of the pertinent pages had been torn out."

Damian saw the rage growing in his face. "I'm sorry Dutch but we can't let you do it."

"Well Fine!" He lashed out, "Thanks for destroying my team! Fuck you all!" He roared, red faced and out of control before fleeing out to the staircase with Zombie close behind.

Damian let him leave. He slumped on the couch exhausted and turned to Tim, "What should we do?"

"Nothing we can do. He probably thinks you're trying to steal the team. Probably thinks I stole Becca. Well, we were getting a little ahead of ourselves. The HAWKS couldn't last forever. It just sucks that it had to end like this."

CHAPTER 83

▼

"Is he gone?"

Degan Malone stopped in the doorway to Peter's hospital room and looked back down the hall to see that the tall, lanky form of TC had already disappeared around the corner.

"Yes, who was that?" He pulled a chair up to the side of the bed.

"An old friend." Peter was lying on his side. The bandages across his back and neck made him unable to lay flat. Apparently the bullet had pierced two of his back muscles and chipped a vertebra in his spine. The nails from the bat had cut several trapezious muscles making it nearly impossible to move his head without sever discomfort but these were minor concerns. The worst problem was the amount of smoke he had inhaled while unconscious inside the burning house. Aubrey's cellar was full of plastics and rubber that caught fire producing noxious products of combustion, volatile gases and possibly even cyanide. Since seventy-five percent of fire related deaths are caused by pulmonary injuries the doctors were keeping Peter as long as it takes to make sure there were no other complications. Thus far the prognosis did not look good.

"You probably know about…"

"Tyrone," Peter was very weak, his eyes mere slits against the bright hospital florescence. He took his time to pronounce each word, gasping a short breath between them from the oxygen mask that lay by his mouth. "He was my friend and you shot him."

"I'm so sorry. I thought he was Rafael. I thought I had your description down pat, he looked so much like him and he was trying to escape…"

Peter closed his eyes. He had been resisting the urge to cry ever since they brought him in. His mother was one wing over; still in stable condition but not yet able to leave. Paul, on the other hand, was gone for good. After getting wrapped up, bandaged and sent home he called the hospital to tell Peter that his parents were shipping him off to Florida to stay with his uncle. He didn't know if he'd ever be back, he confessed that he didn't want to do this anymore. They had a good run but the Shotgun Crew was through. Peter didn't need anymore bad news but it just kept coming.

"I'm sorry, I really am. They took my badge and my gun, after this I can't be a cop anywhere. I guess it's over."

"Over?" The slits returned.

"Yes, didn't you hear? Rafael is dead, Geoffrey is dead, and apparently he was the other leader. They identified him by the colors he was wearing. At the Drive-in they arrested fourteen gang members and the ones with the same colors confirmed that Geo was their boss. SWAT thinks they might have the whole top tier of the Spring Street gang behind bars. It was a huge victory."

Peter nodded that he understood. He knew that Geo wasn't the real leader but he didn't have the strength or desire to explain.

"Listen, like I said I'm really sorry about your friend Tyrone. Is there anything I can do? You helped me so much when you told me about Schmel, where and when to find him. You knew he had a gun on him but it's not your fault that it wasn't loaded. Then you gave me Rafael and now he's dead. I just feel so shitty that all of this happened to you...if there's anything I can do."

Peter motioned for him to move closer, "It's not over."

"No? What do you mean?"

Peter raised his eyes very slightly, "There's one more."

"One more what? Another gang? Who is it?"

His eyes opened a little wider, "He did this...to me."

"Was it another gang?"

"Yes."

"Who..."

"HAWKS..." Peter coughed and a spasm of chest pains made him lose control of his breathing. He grabbed the mask and held it tight to his face.

Degan knew what he had to do. He made a solemn promise to his late wife that he would end organized crime in the city of Brockton. It was the Spring Street Posse who killed her and they were never able to identify her murderer because they all dressed the same. Fighting these gangs was becoming his life work and it occurred to him now that this war, his war, was not yet over.

"Ok Pete, tell me, who leads this gang?" Degan had always believed in cutting the head off the snake. Assassinate the charismatic leader and the group falls apart. So far it hadn't worked exactly as he planned but deep down he was sure these criminals were getting weaker. Then again, he had no way of measuring the results. From his intimate perspective it almost appeared that the crimes were getting worse as the gangs broke into smaller groups but maybe this time it would make a difference.

"Who is he?"

Peter took a deep inhale of oxygen, moved aside the mask and concentrated on pronouncing the name with clarity.

"James...Ballum...they call him...Dutch."

"Dutch," Degan repeated it, "I've got it. Don't worry, this time I'll get the right guy. I don't care what I have to do to find him. You have my promise that James 'Dutch' Ballum will pay for what he did."

Peter closed his eyes again this time with the calm serenity that someone else will end this for him. Peter had never directly killed anyone, he was sure that he could but it wasn't the same as having Degan Malone, a street tested killer, a marksman and a former Brockton police officer do the job once and for all. So many people had tried to chase down the escape artist before but this time he employed a professional with local connections and a proven track record. Degan will not hesitate to shoot. Dutch's luck had to run out sometime.

Outside the open door, standing quiet as a reed in a swamp, TC listened to the whole conversation. "Not if I can help it." He whispered. Stepping backwards he took two long, gentle strides and disappeared around the corner.

CHAPTER 84

▼

"When D-Rod got arrested they found a whole closet full of weapons. Then he told them were he got everything." Becca nearly jumped out of the car as they reached the parking lot across from Mideon. None of this was new; she was recapping the events that Psycho had been ignoring in the media. Becca continued, "So he tries to frame Lazio saying that he was a partner. This is so he can blame the whole thing on the HAWKS but Lazio denied knowing anything and since he's in a crazy house they believed him."

"Go figure." Psycho was surprised that Lazio would still stand up for them, even from his padded cell.

"Right but it didn't work because Lazio was already in the nut house so..." They both crossed Guild Street towards the opening next to the warehouse.

"Good I'm glad they nailed him but the HAWKS have fallen apart so who cares?" Psycho had been depressed for weeks since Dutch left for Middleboro. He felt like he was responsible for breaking up the team so no amount of retro success was going to cheer him up. In fact, that made it worse. With the remainder of the SSP in hiding, the big news was that Peter had died in the hospital. The inevitable conviction of D-Rod was hardly noteworthy except for the reality that there was no one left for the HAWKS to fight. The well had dried up.

"It has everything to do with..."

"Why did you stop?" He bumped into her only to see a fence of yellow caution tape wrapped around the inner concrete pillar inside the first cave of Mideon. The police had checked it after all, or at least tried to.

"They locked up Lazio partly because he believed in horror stories that were told to scare him away from that hole. D-Rod claimed that it was a weapons cellar stored and maintained by the Boston mafia." She pulled aside the tape until it ripped out of her way. "I'm sort of surprised that Dutch knew about it." Becca had continued to collect and analyze the news stories and recently put some important clues together. Even though the police didn't find any actual cellar she couldn't help but think that there had to be a detail they missed. A detail only she knew about.

Psycho was at his wits end, "Why do you want to explore it?" He reluctantly followed his eager girlfriend past the tape and into the shady concrete caves.

"Lazio must have tried to get into Mideon. In all that time he must have gotten curious and wandered down there." Becca ducked under a low doorway and jumped to the center block that was surrounded by water. "But he failed, just like the cops." Her hands reached out to the wall almost forgetting that the hole itself was merely a shadow inside a crevasse. "But I think I know why."

"Why what?" Psycho caught up to her and they both stood on the block staring at that great and mysterious crack in the world. They half expected it to have been blocked by the police but here it was, still wide open.

"Dutch was right," She whispered in admiration.

"Right about what?"

Psycho bit his lip. He was so sick of hearing how great Dutch is. He wanted to tell her that Dutch had lots of hints and instincts that didn't come true. He wanted to say that Dutch had nothing to do with saving that little girl from Aubrey's house but...she would never believe him. Psycho was at a loss. No matter how hard he tried, Becca, his own girlfriend was always going to be obsessed with Dutch. He wondered if that was the real source of his depression. Psycho was happy that the gang wars ended the way they did, with one winner and several losers but it didn't feel like it was over. He couldn't get over the nagging sensation that some crucial part of this war was yet to be won.

"Dutch said that the police wouldn't find a way in." Her voice echoed as she leaned into the musky hole.

"But he already went down there, it's a dead end."

Becca looked up through the holes in the old train tracks above them. "Do you think that the building was made by the same people who created this tunnel?"

Psycho looked up at the building and his eyes followed the concrete lines that connected to the base of Mideon's framework. Being a student of structural wood he knew what a foundation looked like and could tell that this monolith of a warehouse was clearly built as one huge project. "Yeah, it's connected, it's the same foundation. Why?"

"Good, then I might know how to get in." She grabbed his hand and dragged him in into the tunnel behind her.

Half walking, half sliding into the dark they made their way deep under the tracks, down into the darkness until they reached a solid brick wall. Becca pulled out a pen light at the bottom. "Here hold this."

Psycho used the light to check the edges of the wall in front of him. The bricks were solid, firm. The wall didn't budge when he pushed against it. Picking away at the filler between them he saw that there was yet another row of bricks behind this one. "It's a real dead end."

"I don't think so." Came a hollow whisper.

"Becca?" He spun the light behind him to the right. Becca was leaning her back against the wall and pushing with her legs. An entire section of the wall, moving smoothly on wheels rolled outwards behind her back.

"Squeeze in." She prompted.

"You got it." He slipped inside and pulled her free from the door as it sprung back into place.

Psycho took a second to study the old rusty spring coils that connected to the back of it. It was a brilliant contraption that appeared to have been fixed in the last few years. Inside the door was a simple bolt lock to keep people out but the real genius of the trap door was its invisibility as a part of the wall.

"No wonder they couldn't find it." He mused.

"Um, Tim?" Becca tugged at his shirt.

"What?" He turned with the light to see where they were. Both of them paused in awe of the sight before them.

"I don't fucking believe it."

Sprawled out deep into the earth was a narrow cavern built of concrete and brick. On either side were old gas lamps hanging from the walls spaced every ten feet. Far above them bolted to the ceiling were more recently placed electric lights. The lights were out but there had to be a switch.

"I got it." Becca pulled a cord above them that lit the entire expanse with dirty yellow incandescent bulbs.

In the center of the room was a single set of train tracks that were well used. On either side were walkways with carefully set rows of empty pallets. They sat on the dusty floor as if waiting for the next shipment to roll in. Becca and Psycho were standing at the end of the line.

"It's an underground train station." She stepped closer to study the tracks, "These are new rails, they're so clean."

"But they can't run trains down here. Maybe trucks, something smaller that makes less noise."

Becca stood up and bumped into Psycho with her hip, "Is this what I think it is? I mean, D-Rod was arrested with tons of weapons and he said he got them down here so…"

Psycho finished the thought. "So he had been stealing from La Cosa Nostra who was shipping the guns out of Boston on an underground rail system."

"Did they build this?"

"No," Psycho saw that the tunnel was lined with old bricks, not the more durable cinderblocks used more often for building today. Plus, the tunnel itself had a circular ceiling instead of a more modern rectangular one. "No, I'll bet anything that this was an old abandoned sewer system. They taught us all about it in structural wood. Boston was the first city in America to have running water but they needed a place for it to go, so there are huge brick tunnels everywhere underneath the city. Most of them brought the refuse out to the sea. I'll bet that's what this was."

"So where would it lead?"

Psycho shrugged, "If they're shipping weapons down here then it would have to lead to a dock in Boston Harbor."

"This is so huge." Becca gleamed with excitement and Psycho started to feel it too. They had made a historic discovery that was bound to cripple the mafia and wind up on the nightly news. Working together the two of them had uncovered an incredible secret, a criminal infrastructure. Psycho was so proud. This was really going to strengthen their relationship. There was only one thing left to do so they could get credit for this find.

"We've go to…"

"I know!" She blurted over him. "We've got to tell Dutch right away!"

CHAPTER 85

▼

"This isn't easy for me either." Vinny squirmed in an orange plastic chair that they provided for people who were visiting the prisoners. He half expected some guard or cop to recognize him and try to drag him away in handcuffs. Vinny had a long list of arrests but he wasn't sure if there were any current warrants out for him. He was rightly paranoid but his nephew Gary, on the other side of the glass, was more rightly pissed off.

"I'm not going to..." He had to watch his words. They weren't sure if this conversation was being monitored. "...I won't visit my friend for that reason."

When Gary stared through the plexi-glass at his uncle it was like looking into a mirror that told the future. They appeared almost exactly the same except that Vinny was thirty pounds heavier, especially around the waist and his face bore the lines of recent unbearable stress.

"Gary I don't have a choice here, these are my orders."

"But Joey is your friend, you must be able to talk him out of this."

"He's not my friend anymore, he's my boss."

"Why is he making you do this Vin? He must have tons of people..."

"Shhh." Vinny wiped perspiration from his forehead. Out of the corner of his eye he watched two guards walk out the door at the end of the room but he swore they were looking at him the whole time. When he was sure they were gone he answered the question. "Look Gary, I screwed up. I told Joey, I promised him that I'd find James myself and take care of all this. For two months I visited house after house in Avon trying to find where he was hiding. I grabbed Peter, who nearly shit his pants, but he didn't know anything."

Gary cracked a smile.

"I roughed up that blonde kid Damian but he wouldn't tell me shit."

The smile went away.

"Hell, I even visited the Ballum's house one night but his bedroom was empty. I couldn't find him and that's why I need you."

"Why?" Gary egged him on. "Why is it such a big deal that you find him? What, because he had a little suburban gang? Is that it? He's not a threat to…"

"Shhhh!"

"Vinny, Dutch doesn't sell illicit narcotics or military paraphernalia, he doesn't sell anything that would constitute competition."

"Damn, you been reading the dictionary?"

"I got bored."

"Well here's what I know. Joey said that the Boston…um, that we have *special friends* in several different towns who are called from time to time for various jobs. These guys are usually below the radar. They're former teamsters who got laid off and such. These guys perform important functions for…us."

"So?"

"So James and the rest of you guys got one of our *special friends* arrested. You and your little werewolf hunt blew his cover."

Gary's mind twisted in reverse as he tried to recall who they got arrested?

"You mean the wolf man? Randolph? The guy who killed eight people and fed them to his mutant dog? He was a…*special friend?*"

"Yes."

"Oh." He leaned back in his chair letting the plastic bend to his form. "Sorry."

"Sorry doesn't!" Vinny's voice got too loud for the room. He hushed himself and returned to a controlled whisper. "Sorry doesn't cut it. Maybe if James had stopped with Mr. Randolph this might not be such a big deal. At that point they only wanted me to talk to him, to straighten him out but now…"

"Now what?"

"He got another one arrested."

"He did?" Gary was impressed. Dutch was really making waves out there. It's a shame he had to miss all the action.

"Yes and now both of these fuckers are hinting that they might testify against Joey and blow the fuckin system wide open."

Gary leaned up to the glass, "So you think James is onto you."

Vinny returned a quizzical look of his own, "Is he smart enough for that?"

Gary nodded and came to a stunning realization. If he didn't talk to Dutch before the mafia found him, then his friend, hell all of his friends from the HAWKS Foundation were probably going to get killed. Gary pinched the bridge of his nose and them mumbled reluctantly. "Even if I agreed to find him, look where I am."

"We can make arrangements."

"You're kidding me."

He was dead serious. The Boston mafia had connections everywhere in the city but especially in the police force and prison system. The truth is that prisoners escape all the time from Massachusetts' jails. The ones who get caught probably planned it on their own but the ones who simply vanish do so because they had some help.

"You can get me out?"

Vinny nodded.

"Would I have to…?"

"Don't say it, the answer is yes. We'd give you the tools and whatever leads we have but the rest is up to you. It just has to be clean, no witnesses."

Gary exhaled; he was too young to be sitting in jail for so long. He had already been in two cell fights and he managed to settle them before the guards found out but it is only a matter of time before someone picks him for a scape-goat.

"Gary," Vinny gestured for him to move closer to the glass. "This isn't really a question, I mean, you don't get to choose not to do this."

"Why not?"

"They can get to you on the inside and…" Vinny swallowed and looked away before gathering himself, "They could blame all of this on me."

"But Joey is your friend, you guys have known each other forever."

"It doesn't matter, there's no loyalty in this business. Joey will pull the trigger himself and have someone wipe my blood off his shoes."

Gary leaned away from the window. He had always admired his uncle Vinny. He was so resourceful, so capable of making his way in the world or at least that's what he thought before this day. Now he saw his uncle for who he really is, a subordinate coward. He was a social plumber who unclogged sewers full of money and drugs that ran through the worst parts of this city every day. Worst of all he had dragged Gary down with him. It was Vinny who taught Gary how to break into the freight trains, that's why he did it and that's how he ended up face to face with a Boston cop on the blackest of nights. Vinny was the reason Gary was in jail and now he put him a position where he would either have to kill his own friend or be stabbed to death one night in his sleep. This was what his life had become, an inheritance of criminal tendencies, a downward spiral that would land him back in jail over and over again. He was trapped, what choice did he have but to go along with it? Maybe, just maybe he could find a way to warn Dutch without having to kill him. It was worth a try.

"Gary? I need you on this."

He lifted his freckled face, his features stoic, making his attitude impossible to read.

"Just get me out of here."

"Are you gonna do it?"

Gary's eyes spoke of an intractable resolve, "Don't worry, I know a thing or two about loyalty."

CHAPTER 86

▼

"You're not here to shoot anyone are you?" Jodie had traversed the grassy hill faster than Dutch thought she would. She was dressed in a short black skirt that seemed more suitable for late night streetwalking than for a formal burial.

He eased out from behind a large oak that overlooked the graveyard. "I'm unarmed. I was just looking, wondering really."

Down below a very small gathering of Peter Truelson's distant family members somberly talked to each other about how horrible their family was. They badmouthed Lelaine and Aubrey as if they were the very spawn of Satan for how they lived their lives. They even nipped condescending tones about Peter as he was being lowered into the ground. "He got what he deserved." "It was bound to happen eventually." "He was a bad seed, there's no saving some people."

Two people stood apart from the crowd, Ben and Jodi. Ben hadn't spoken about his older brother's death for days. They didn't know if he was in shock or if he was mourning in his own way. Jodi had been Peter's friend since they were little kids attending Butler elementary together. She was rightly angered by his family's derision and since Ben wouldn't talk, she started to look at the trees and that's when she noticed Dutch walking amongst them.

"What were you wondering about?" She lingered closer and fiddled with a pull string on his camouflage jacket.

"Peter and I have been rivals since middle school."

"I know. I saw the fight." She winked.

"But in all this time, during all of the confrontations we've had, all the arguments and backstabbing, I just…"

"What? Do you regret it all now that he's dead? It's a little late for that."

"No, it's not regret, it's just that I never knew, I mean, I never found out why he hated me so much."

Jodi snickered. "You never thought to ask him?"

"I guess not."

"It's not that big a mystery."

"What do you mean?" He lightly knocked her hand away from his coat.

Jodi took a step back feeling rejected, "He was pissed at you for leaving him. Don't you remember that night at the Knights of Columbus building downtown? Remember, it was you and me, Gary, Peter, Eric and TC?"

Dutch struggled with the memory, he had in fact been dreaming about it for months but there were parts he couldn't remember. So far as he could recall nothing major happened that night. They all went into the old brick building near the pizza shop and explored it when a couple older high school kids showed up and started trouble. Gary helped Dutch escape from the building and then...

"TC told me the older kids chased them around in the dark but eventually they escaped the building too. What's the big deal?"

"James, you really must start reading the newspaper. You missed so much of the story."

"But TC didn't lie."

"No, that might have been what happened to him but Eric and Peter were trapped on the fourth floor. Those high school seniors tied them up and did awful things to them."

"Like what?"

"Well, after they beat them, they set fire to bingo balls and threw them at them. They were tied to an old piano with clothesline rope and had to hang by their wrists while these assholes chucked shards of bricks at them. But that wasn't enough; they laid all the broken wood at their feet and then set it on fire, like human sacrifices. The fire burnt its way into holes in the floor beneath the piano. When they couldn't put it out the seniors got scared and ran off leaving Eric and Peter to die there."

"How did they get out?" Dutch honestly never heard about any of this. Gary had helped him escape and then they kept their distance and their quiet about the whole affair.

Somehow Jodie knew all of the details. "Peter managed to get his arms free and untied them both. Eric was hurt worse by the beating, he had several broken ribs, so Peter helped him down four flights of stairs and out of the burning building."

Dutch leaned back against the tree, his eyes watched the proceedings down on the grassy hill as people began to leave. He couldn't believe what he was hearing.

"So Peter save his life. He rescued Eric. He was a hero." The words hurt just to speak them.

"Yes."

He looked back to Jodi, "Hey don't you have a brother named Eric?"

"Thanks to Peter I do."

Dutch felt his heart sink. "But I thought Eric moved away?"

"Yes, after that incident and the following court case my Mom didn't want him in Avon anymore. He lives with my Dad in Quincy."

"Peter blamed me for leaving him." Dutch realized, it wasn't a question; it was a statement of shame.

"My Mom blamed you, Eric blamed you and yes, Peter blamed you."

"But...I didn't know. Why me?"

"You were the brave one James. You are a natural leader. We did whatever you said. We all followed you into the building that night. We followed you up one flight after another. I was so scared of bats and monsters and heights but you kept me encouraged. One more floor, you said. We all trusted you. We assumed that you would know what to do if things went wrong or if someone got hurt but when the high school kids showed up...you ran away. The rest of us freaked so we ran away too but Peter and Eric didn't make it."

Dutch covered his face with his hands. "I never thought any of this would make sense. I just assumed..."

"Yes you did. You assumed a lot. You expected the worst from Peter and so you got it. It's a shame you guys never talked and sorted this out. Now it can never happen. You blew it James." She turned and walked down the hill.

Dutch felt the tears welling up in his eyes. How could he have been so wrong and for so many years? In some ways he really had been the bad guy all along. Dutch felt a deep mourning sink into his chest as he crossed back into the trees.

When Jodi reached the gravesite a man elegantly dressed in a black jacket approached her.

"Excuse me miss?"

Jodi's saunter returned as this fine looking man with dark hair and a fit physique stood very close by.

"Yes, what can I do for you?"

"That man atop the hill," He was watching them a minute ago but already the camouflaged figure had vanished. "Who was he?"

"Oh that was James. He's an old friend of Peter's."

"James? What's his last name?"

She pondered why he was asking but decided to keep her polite posture, "Ballum, that was James Ballum."

"Thanks," The man moved past her walking quickly up the hill. On the other side he heard a vehicle engine start up. He started to move faster now as the vehicle was driving away. Finally in a last desperate sprint he made it to the top of the hill.

Off in the distance, beyond tall tombstones and a rusty gate Degan Malone watched as a huge black van reached the main street and tore away towards Brockton.

"James Ballum. Now I know that you're for real." He said aloud.

Jodi suddenly appeared behind the man, she had run after him curious as to why he wanted to see James so bad. "Did you miss him?"

"Yeah, but I'll find him. Do you know where he lives?" He turned back to her instantly revitalizing a wanton mystique with his eyes. She could be an easy ticket into James's life. He might as well be nice.

"No, no one really knows where he lives."

"Oh," He dropped the act and walked past her heading down the hill.

Jodi thought she had blown it again; another fine looking man was going to walk out of her life without so much as a goodbye. She had to stop him.

"But..." She said in high voice so he'd be sure to hear. "I do know where his sister lives."

"Really?" He stopped and held out his arm. "Would you be so kind as to tell me?"

"Maybe." She took his arm. "Maybe I'll be so kind as to show you myself."

He smiled with victory in his manner, "I would like that very much."

About the Author

Alex Hutchinson is an award winning poet and novelist. As a former gang member he tells the terrifying stories that affected his life at a young age. *Almost Columbine* is the third book in his stunning HAWKS Foundation series.

978-0-595-41939-5
0-595-41939-9